Alexis Marie grew up in the suburbs of Georgia with her mom. She is married, has one sister, and can be found either under a heated blanket with her laptop and dog at her side or out in the garden pleading with her plants to stay alive in the Southern heat.

SIGHT UNSEEN

ALEXIS MARIE

PIATKUS

PIATKUS

First published in the US in 2026 by 47North,
An imprint of Amazon Publishing
Published in Great Britain in 2026 by Piatkus

1 3 5 7 9 10 8 6 4 2

Copyright © 2026 by Alexis Marie

The moral right of the author has been asserted.

*All characters and events in this publication, other than those
clearly in the public domain, are fictitious and any resemblance
to real persons, living or dead, is purely coincidental.*

All rights reserved.
No part of this publication may be reproduced, stored in a retrieval system, or
transmitted in any form or by any means, without the prior permission in writing of
the publisher, nor be otherwise circulated in any form of binding or cover other than
that in which it is published and without a similar condition including this condition
being imposed on the subsequent purchaser.

A CIP catalogue record for this book
is available from the British Library.

Trade paperback ISBN 978-0-349-44738-4
Paperback ISBN 978-0-349-44736-0

Printed and bound in Great Britain by Clays Ltd, Elcograf S.p.A.

Papers used by Piatkus are from well-managed forests
and other responsible sources.

Piatkus	The authorised representative
An imprint of	in the EEA is
Little, Brown Book Group	Hachette Ireland
Carmelite House	8 Castlecourt Centre, Dublin 15, D15
50 Victoria Embankment	XTP3, Ireland
London EC4Y 0DZ	(email: info@hbgi.ie)

An Hachette UK Company
www.hachette.co.uk

www.littlebrown.co.uk

Nothing. Something. Everything.

SIGHT UNSEEN

Prologue

On nights when nature defies its own rules, magic is most potent. The perfect time to find what she needs.

Armed with a worn leather foraging bag and a sharpening knife, Veda walks the old forest's twisted paths, ready for whatever lies in wait. Ducking under low-hanging branches, she dodges bushes and trees, stepping over fallen boughs with the ease of years spent foraging. Veda doesn't stop until echoes of her destination graze her awareness. After one final cut through thick foliage, the sound of the river's current spills through. Veda emerges, exposed to the sky. The blue moon remains veiled behind clouds, casting an ethereal glow.

Beneath riverbank rocks, luminescent moss flourishes. Using her knife, Veda digs out only what she needs and places it into a small black pouch. Foraging is a twofold pursuit: It keeps the school's supply closet full of otherwise expensive ingredients and satisfies Veda's joy for the hunt.

She retrieves a lantern from her bag and whispers, *"Lux."*

The Cosmos demand payment for every spell cast, and Mages' currency is physical pain and suffering—a price many pay willingly. But Veda is lucky. The eye-shaped sapphire amulet around her neck glows, absorbing the cost as the lantern floats ahead, illuminating the path.

What has been lurking in the darkness turns her bones to ice.

Bloodred spider lilies aren't native to Washington state, nor are they in season, yet they are in full bloom as far as she can see. Relief floods her veins when the flowers don't catch fire, but it does little to ease her fear. She tries to outwalk the prickly unease, heading downstream across slippery rocks, but anxiety clings to her like a vise.

A sudden storm of stirring winds and rumbling thunder charges the air like static fire. Veda searches for a path, a way home; the ticking seconds echo the rhythm of her heart. The sky opens, and rain turns dirt to mud, unearthing the sediments of her past. Taking root, fear blooms into petals of panic, driving Veda to run. Thin branches sting her face, but she doesn't stop until the downpour suddenly eases. Moonlight finds her between the thinning raindrops, pushing away the darkness and revealing not only the path home but the flowers that followed her. Bloodred, and too close for comfort.

Trouble.

One

Veda rips from the root as many spider lilies as she can carry and throws them into her makeshift firepit. Drenched from rain and dirty from weeding, she watches the crackling flames turn to ash. Sunbeams filter through the forest, painting the trees with a smoky golden glow. The hushed moment lulls her fears into dormancy until they reignite with the realization that fire purifies; it doesn't always destroy.

She extinguishes the last of the embers in favor of a trip back to her cabin for a hot shower, from which Veda emerges in a cloud of steam a short time later. She grabs a towel, noticing the welts on her brown skin from the trek through the forest. After gathering her thick copper-brown hair into a bun, she carefully spreads her arms in front of the mirror.

The Sanguis Curse slumbers in her blood. Fatal if not for the bewitching magic that keeps it sidelined, the curse feeds on her energy, growing stronger. For the past six years, purple bruises have deepened into angry clusters of raised skin. Black veins have branched like fractals, curving around her shoulder, inching toward her throat. Every avenue for a cure has ended in failure, meaning that, one day, the Sanguis Curse will consume her. But her curser's blood fills a cyst on her ribs, a reminder of a mistake that damns the culprit to die with Veda . . . if they don't kill her first.

Wincing, Veda rubs salve on what she can reach. Magic activates at first touch, cooling her skin and easing the pain. It's a temporary fix that helps her get through each day. She hides her mortality beneath jeans and long sleeves to avoid the looks and questions, then swallows a pain elixir, another for nutrients, and makes oatmeal to combat the impending nausea.

She's halfway finished eating when the blue gemstone sitting in a glass jar on the table pulses twice before glowing bright. Rendered obsolete by modern technology, lapis stone messages were once the only method of instant communication when secrecy was paramount. Ominous uncertainty knots her stomach. Veda picks it up. A shock of magic races up her arm as a familiar voice projects from the stone:

"Come quickly."

It goes inert.

"Shit."

Veda grabs a jacket and sets off.

Dense, tall trees create a canopy overhead, casting shadows across Veda's path.

A breeze rustles the trees as chirping birds dart to and fro. Lined with ivy and fern, the uneven trail is a worn path of her own creation. The scent of rich, damp earth is calming, the atmospheric fog and steady drizzle, peaceful. Without a spider lily sighting, the walk is a perfect distraction.

Veda emerges into the pasture behind Weston Academy. She's not fifty yards from the tree line when the first chicken scuttles past her feet. More follow, scattering across the field, pecking at the ground in noisy pursuit of critters. Their liberator, Peter Weston, waits by the gate, his fair skin flushed from time spent under the morning sun.

Peter is an intentional man. That he's straying from routine puts Veda on edge—a tension he tries to ease with a crooked smile. With green eyes, tousled blond hair, and soft yet strong features, the tall, slim Seer is handsome in all the ways that count, and none that soothe her nerves.

"Who died?" Veda asks cautiously.

"No one." His smile falters. "Oh shit. I only used the stone message because I thought you were already in the greenhouse without your phone. Sorry I scared you."

"It's fine." Veda wants to relax, but the anchored unease in her bones won't allow it.

Gaze sharpening, he gently tilts her chin to the side. "What happened to your face?"

"I didn't want to waste the blue moon, so I went foraging." She winces. "There were *hundreds* of spider lilies along the path about half a mile north of the cottage. I got spooked, it started raining, and I ran into a tree branch or five."

"Tomorrow is the last day of March, but spider lilies bloom in late summer," Peter muses thoughtfully. "It's too much of a coincidence to ignore."

"I know. I figured I'd talk to Gabriel after he drops off August."

"You do that, and I'll ask a forestry technician I know to guide them out there."

"Okay." Veda takes off her heavy satchel and slings it over his shoulder. The weight doesn't faze him. "My bag's still wet. I wanted to collect more, but what I did gather is safe and sound, ready to make anything the school needs."

Peter nudges her. "They could use a lesson from the best brewer I know."

"Ms. Everly is a good brewing master," Veda says, dismissing him with a wave as they walk toward the school. Weston Academy is a single-story brick-and-stone building with high ceilings and dozens of windows. It sits on a small butte, with steps shaped from the hillside and a large wraparound deck where students linger. Peter pauses at the top of the steps and squeezes Veda's shoulder. The chill of his spell tingles her skin before she can stop him. Soreness vanishes like it was never there.

While the price for magic isn't always equal or fair for Mages or those without amulets to absorb the cost of their spells, Seers like Peter are a minority who can use magic without physical consequences. *How* remains a mystery, though theories point to a specific gene cluster activated when Sight—the precognitive ability to glimpse the past, present, or future—manifests. Seers cannot brew potions or imbue magic into anything except amulets, and they're highly sensitive to magical neutralizing agents, but they don't suffer chills from casting light spells, broken bones from hexes, or organ failure from curses. Sight isn't a choice. It comes with a lifetime of discrimination, stereotyping, and unchecked harassment by some of the Mage majority that sees them as dangerous abominations.

"You could get in trouble for that," Veda mutters. "Then Khadijah is going to be mad as hell when enforcers kick down your door to arrest you for a casting violation . . . *again*."

Peter smiles at the mention of his wife. "They'd probably take her in, too, for mouthing off."

Veda shakes her head, amused. "True."

"Besides, that healing spell was weak enough for a Mage to cast without major injury, which makes it legal. As long as Seers don't display overt magical superiority, we're safe."

"I know. It doesn't stop me from worrying."

Calling Peter a friend doesn't quite match the true nature of the bond they forged years ago, when he sat beside her at orientation during freshman year at Crestwood University. It was the first year the campus integrated Mages and Seers, and tensions were high. He spoke first, cautious but polite, and their conversation turned genuine the moment Veda argued that integration should have happened *years* earlier. Born in that moment, their friendship grew during intellectual debates and bittersweet nostalgic ramblings about her childhood, and rooted deep enough to endure after Peter returned to Proventia to take over Weston

Academy from his retiring mother, while Veda moved to Philadelphia for medical school. He is the closest thing to a sibling she's had.

"Are you okay?" Peter asks.

Veda doesn't trust easily, a conditioned reflex after losing so much. Even though she's never doubted Peter, the answer is complicated. Best to keep her feelings buried and stick to the script.

"I'm fine."

Peter's timing either protects or prepares Veda—the hardest part is recognizing the difference. Outside his office, with a hand hovering over the knob, he becomes unusually cryptic. "This isn't an emergency in the traditional sense."

Before she can ask what the hell that means, Peter pushes open the door and gestures for her to enter. More suspicious than wary, she stays close to the wall. Peter's office is small and well lit, with neutral walls, oak floors, sparse furniture, and an antique ceramic tea set that serves as an icebreaker for parent meetings.

Standing in front of his wall of bookshelves is an older, petite woman who emanates an air so superior, Veda regrets not rinsing the mud off her boots before entering the room. The woman wears long deep-purple pants and a matching knee-length embroidered *kameez* with gold earrings and jewelry, and her makeup is as perfect as her silky black hair—streaked with gray at the temples and pulled back with a vintage gold hair clip adorned with a colorful array of tiny amulets. Freckles dot her brown skin, and crow's-feet indent the corners of round brown eyes. Both speak to her age and only heighten the powerful presence she exudes.

The woman's pensive focus is fixed on a target. Veda follows her gaze to a child no older than six occupying the chair in front of Peter's desk. Despite dangling feet, the boy reminds Veda of a micro-adult. With deep-tan skin, freckles, bright-hazel eyes, and dark-brown hair gelled and parted severely to one side, he carries a cautious, curious tension while maintaining a level of stillness children his age rarely possess. He's dressed in the standard school uniform—a white button-down, fitted black pants, and leather dress shoes—and his black knitted bow tie stands out as much as the standard blazer neatly draped over the back of his seat in an oddly tidy act.

"Apologies for keeping you both waiting. Veda, this is my godson, Antaris Fowler." Peter's introduction holds an uncertainty that earns him a quizzical glance from the child. "Today is his first day of school."

Unsure how to greet Antaris, Veda settles for an awkward "Welcome to Weston."

Antaris scrutinizes her in a silence that borders on painful until Peter gestures to the woman. "This is his grandmother, Simran."

Simran assesses Veda with equal interest before politely nodding. "Pleasure."

It doesn't sound like it.

"You as well," Veda replies with a practiced, put-on pleasantness.

"Please, do take a seat, Miss Thorne." Simran's British accent is gratingly posh yet smooth in a way that naturally develops after years in America. "I imagine you are curious about why you are here."

Veda is, but instead asks, "How did you know my last name?"

"I know many things."

"Subtlety won't get you anywhere with me." Veda smiles, saccharine sweet.

Peter's cough sounds like a chuckle. Every eye turns to him. "Just had something in my throat."

Veda folds her arms, still waiting for her question to be answered. A tight expression crosses Simran's face. "If you must know, I inquired about you, Miss Thorne. Peter tells me you spent a year studying Eastern brewing in my hometown, Bangalore, India. You were born in Maine, turned thirty eleven days ago, and do not possess Sight. Your mother was a tenured professor of theoretical Earth magic, and your father was an expert stonemaker. They Vanished when you were sixteen, during the Great Vanishing. To your credit, you did not let this tragedy stop you and went to college on scholarship, graduating with high honors in magiology and Earth medicine. You studied to be a doctor at Riverty University, where you again graduated with high honors, but quit during your internship. Pity."

Keeping quiet in the face of a woman who will talk more when given a stage is harder than Veda realized, but she's motivated by irritation at Simran's flippant attitude toward her tragedy, her life.

"That is all I was able to gather. You see, Miss Thorne, I like to know everything about those I invite into my personal space. I want to surround my grandson with the right *kind* of people, if you understand what I mean."

Veda's politeness dies. "Clearly."

Mages and Seers live, work, and are educated mostly separately because of the normalization of prejudice. Demeaning incidents, slurs, biases, and the desire to remain independent of each other are common occurrences. Casual cruelty. Mages' actions are dismissed as harmless yet cause tremendous damage. The most extreme bigots use rhetoric involving extermination, like "breeding out the gene," and express a desire to bring back a time when Seers were controlled by injecting them with magic-blocking serum and forcing them into compliant servitude. Where on the scale Simran lies, Veda can't tell. Her willingness to enroll Antaris in the only integrated school in Proventia is promising, considering there are other institutions that fit her taste. More importantly, Veda can't help but wonder what the hell Peter is thinking by allowing a proud bigot to set *foot* on the property.

With over three hundred students from years one to twelve, half of whom are Seers, security has always been tight due to threats from various hate groups. Since its opening, and more so in the years since Peter took over, the academy has been vandalized, Seer students attacked walking to and from campus, and law enforcement has made it clear they watch the school closely—not to protect anyone but to arrest any

Seer who steps out of line. Allowing a bigot free access to the faculty and student body is dangerous.

"I would not have requested this meeting had I not thought you were worthy." At Veda's visible tension, Simran continues. "Consider my approval a compliment, Miss Thorne."

Veda certainly does not.

Simran gestures to the chair once more, clearly used to getting her way. "Please sit. I insist."

"I prefer to stand."

"Very well."

From Veda's vantage point, observing Antaris and Simran comes naturally. Grandmother and grandson. Aside from the freckles, their features vastly differ. Simran's are delicate and fawn-like, a contrast to her strong presence, while Antaris's are rounder yet serious. The only resemblance Veda can find is that they both look *through* people, not at them.

She catches Antaris staring at her amulet.

"Is he Sensitive?" Veda asks.

Like oxygen, magic is omnipresent, but Sensitives are naturally able to feel or smell residual magic after a spell has been cast. Or when it has been imbued into objects like her necklace. Sensitivity is found only in Mages. Along with wealth, it's used to define social hierarchy, with wealthy Sensitives at the top.

"His father and grandfather are, but Antaris is not." Simran doesn't disguise her tinge of disappointment. "There will be no need for accommodations, if that is why you are asking."

It isn't, but Veda doesn't probe further. Despite working at a school, she finds teenagers and babies easier to manage than children old enough to talk yet young enough to lack the filter of common sense developed by experience. Veda glances at Peter, her patience slipping along with her manners. "Not to be rude, but why exactly am I here?"

"Simran wanted to discuss something with you."

The woman in question moves to stand at the end of the desk. "I take it Peter did not inform you about my visit."

"He didn't."

Simran assesses her further before nodding. "You will do as a tutor for my grandson."

Antaris looks more confused than Veda.

"Isn't he—" She refuses to keep talking about him like he isn't there, turning to the boy. "Aren't you in year one?"

"Yes, he is," Simran replies.

Irritation spikes, but Veda suppresses the unproductive emotion. "Typically, their curriculum—"

"Is not my concern. Tutor him for two hours a day following dismissal. I intend for him to be ready for testing to gain admittance into a respectable school."

From the corner of her eye, Veda catches Peter shifting his weight.

"Weston Academy is an excellent school," Veda says.

"It is. I can hardly tell it is an integrated school. The teenage Seers are well behaved and polite."

"They are no different than Mage teenagers." Veda glances at Peter, who pinches the bridge of his nose. "Are you aware *he* is a Seer?"

"Peter is not like the others."

It's not a compliment, responding is futile, but Veda can't leave well enough alone. "Why are his parents not here having this discussion?"

"My son is new to fatherhood, having only discovered his existence a mere two months ago. As a mother, I am better suited to guide Antaris's path."

Is he a commodity or a child?

Veda notices Antaris's pinched, wounded expression. "Have you had a tour of the grounds?"

This grabs his attention. His response is a quick shake of his head, but it's Peter's and Simran's surprise that leaves her puzzled. "Peter, will you show him around?"

He's already on his feet midway through her request, gesturing for Antaris to follow. The boy appears hesitant, but one stern look from his grandmother makes him comply. Once they're out the door, Veda excuses herself and follows. Antaris is already out of sight, Peter several steps behind.

She sharply whispers his name. Peter turns. "What?"

"Is she paying full tuition?"

"She is, and has made a sizable donation."

"Be that as it may, her being here is absolutely *insane*." When he offers no explanation, she glares. "What aren't you telling me?"

"I'll tell you more when you check your judgment at the door."

He's gone before she can argue. Seething, Veda returns to find Simran sitting in Peter's chair.

"Is there something wrong?" The tone implies she knows the answer. "*Or* did you need a moment to fuss at Peter for not preparing you for our intrusion?"

The room feels smaller, congested. Veda takes the seat Antaris left. "I was letting him know who was at the barn to help with the tour."

"Peter reminds me of myself," Simran says. "He moves in silence, not letting one string know how it fits with the others until they are all entwined."

That *is* Peter in a nutshell. Veda rests her hands on her lap. "What strings are we?"

"I do not know. My current concern is for my grandson. His mother recently passed on, as you probably know."

"No, I didn't." Nausea rises with the guilt of judging her absence.

"Antaris has been in the country for less than two weeks, and we have much to do to acclimate him."

"Where's he from?"

"London," Simran replies.

"That's not the moon. It shouldn't take much for him to—"

"Cosmos only knows what his Seer mother taught him before her death. Antaris was homeschooled and did not complete proper testing.

We had a comprehensive Sight panel done yesterday, and blessedly, he tested at a zero."

Stifling her growing anger is all Veda can do in the face of such bigotry. "Those tests are not accurate. Most Mages have the potential for Sight. How it manifests is a matter of genetics and chance."

"The chance, according to the test, is zero."

Veda smothers her original comment, amending it to something softer. "I'm struggling to see why it's so dire that I take him on."

"Antaris does not speak."

Once again, Veda silently apologizes for assuming he was being spoken over. "*Can* he speak?"

"He has not always been silent, according to his mother's stepfather, who helped raise him."

"Then he'll speak again, I suppose." Veda shrugs. "I'm not a child therapist."

"Be that as it may, from the moment you spoke, Antaris paid attention. You are the first adult outside of our family to gain his attention and response without prompting. I *need* him to speak again. No proper school will take him as he is now."

"I can't *make* him talk."

"Perhaps not." Simran's jaw is tight as she stands and crosses the room to the table to pick up her purse. After producing a collection of folded papers, she hands them to Veda. "This contract includes payment information, guidelines, and an ideal time frame. There is also a stipulation for time bonuses, should you get him speaking before August. All you need to do is sign."

It's not that simple.

When Simran realizes Veda isn't accepting the contract, she places it on the desk. "It appears you have already made a choice. Had you planned to accept my terms, this conversation would have gone differently."

"It would have."

Confirmation of Veda's decision deflates her. She sits back down, suddenly less rigid. "Are you going to tell me why you denied my request?"

"*No* is a complete sentence." Veda stands and dusts her jeans. "But since you're curious, I manage the grounds. Spring and summer are my busiest times of year. I won't have the time to tutor anyone."

Confusion flashes across Simran's face, but she remains composed. "I have been told you tutor Investigator Sallant's son."

The extent of Peter's association with Simran is a curious juxtaposition. Veda wants to jump to a hundred conclusions. Instead, she holds her judgment until they can talk. She owes him that much. "I don't tutor August, per se. He occasionally stays after school, plays in the dirt, chases the school's livestock. It's hardly educational. Peter should've known better. Wait, who is he to you? You've made it clear you don't associate with Seers."

"I do not, but his mother was my housekeeper before starting Weston Academy. Peter was my son's playmate until my son left for boarding school at twelve. From afar, I watched Peter grow into a respectable man. Sight notwithstanding."

"Ah, well, I hope you find what you're looking for." Veda extends her hand to shake, sighing when it's rejected. "My denial isn't personal."

Simran's facade collapses, and something honest rises. "I am asking for one session."

"It's best that you . . ."

Movement catches Veda's eye through the window. Antaris is at the top step of the deck, dubious in the face of Peter's welcoming smile and warm gestures. He turns, almost searching. Their eyes meet through the glass. Veda's list of excuses is long, but self-awareness lingers. In time, her curiosity will grow louder, resolute and insistent that this melancholic child needs help. *Her help.* Rationalizing that it's best she answer that call just this once, she looks back at Simran.

"Fine. One session."

Two

Hiram isn't impulsive.

He has never been the sort to make any major purchase without careful analysis and consideration of all consequences.

Until now.

The house is a five-bedroom blank slate of trendy renovated features: neutral colors, boring finishes, and an open concept on Lake Arnez. While stripped of character and identity, it's move-in ready, with more than enough space for two people. Hiram's steps echo on the oak floors as he examines the cleaners' work. It's leagues better than his sterile Los Angeles apartment and more spacious than the downtown hotel suite they're in now. Brick and wood, held together by nails and plaster, constructed into a dwelling. Not a home, but it's his job to make it one. Now he needs to figure out how.

Hiram is a loner who knows exactly how to get what he wants, but everything has changed. He's spent the last six weeks overthinking and overwhelmed as he navigates the silence of his traumatized son. He exists on a precipice. One miscalculation away from disaster. One wrong move from failing a child he doesn't know. Hiram needs to regain control, and the first step is accepting he might fail. He's still working on that. The second step? Establishing stability. Taking a hiatus from his law career, navigating reconciliation with the parents he abandoned at eighteen, and dropping his life in Los Angeles to buy a house in his hometown is a good enough start. He hopes. If not, it's too late to turn back.

As soon as he finishes his inspection, the home's built-in talisman alerts him of the moving crew's arrival. Time blurs as they unload boxes, set up beds, install appliances, and place furniture. Once they leave, he opens the windows for the breeze to dilute the smell of cleaning products and freshen the stale air. There are six hours before he needs to be at his parents' house to pick up his son, per their visitation agreement. It's enough time to set up the necessities and work up a sweat.

On the back porch, he cools down, noting that this is *another* blank that needs work, but the views of the cloudy skies and crystal-blue waters of Lake Arnez urge him to pause planning. Willows and cypress trees dot the sloping lawn until the grass transitions to the rocky shore. The wooden pier and shed look recently built, but the cobblestone path connecting them is old. The quiet here is a silence without a need for possibilities.

Peace is disrupted by a hazy orange glow encasing his property, alerting him to someone else's arrival. He isn't expecting visitors. Hiram leaves the back porch to check the peephole. An odd pair of men stand on the front stoop, looking around and muttering words Hiram can't hear. One is dressed like a lumberjack—short and burly, with pale skin, curly red hair, a beard, and far too much plaid. The other is a tall man with dark eyes and wavy black hair, dressed in jeans, a white shirt, and a suit jacket. When Hiram opens the door, they put on professional expressions and flash silver Federal Crime Division badges adorned with tiger's-eye amulets.

"Mr. Ellis? I'm Investigator Francisco Padillo, and this is Investigator Gabriel Sallant." The taller man's Northeastern accent is strong. "We're with the FCD. Do you have a moment to speak with us?"

Their badges glow gold at their touch, confirmation they are who they claim to be. Investigators are glorified federal enforcers who handle cold cases, ritual and serial crimes, and any cases involving Seer or interstate activity. They don't usually make house calls, which sparks Hiram's curiosity as to why they're here. With a family of more attorneys, business owners, and politicians than he can count, Hiram knows better than to let them in, but he's also aware of the shit he can start by not complying.

"What is this about?" He folds his arms with practiced ease.

Gabriel pulls out a stone no bigger than the palm of his hand. "This messenger stone was sent to me months ago. I thought it was a mistake until I received Grace Fowler's case file."

Although Hiram remains cool and composed, dread pools in the pit of his stomach. "Case file? She died fighting off a burglar."

"The burglary was a cover story. Our British counterparts conducted a two-month inquiry and concluded what we suspected."

"Which was?"

"Are you familiar with the Botanist serial-killer case?" Francisco asks, but when Hiram maintains his blank expression, he continues. "Well, I wouldn't expect you to be. Despite our efforts, it hasn't been widely covered because the victims are Seers."

"How many?"

"Ten—now eleven—over the last six years. We don't know the exact cause of death because the Botanist uses a powerful wasting curse to rapidly degrade their Imprint and, with it, any physical evidence." Every spell cast leaves behind residue, called Imprints. Like a fingerprint, a person's Imprint is unique and identifiable but fades after a few hours. "The amount of magic being used leads us to suspect the Botanist is either a Seer or a Mage with a powerful unregistered amulet."

"How do you know it's the same person if you don't have physical evidence or their Imprint?" Hiram asks.

"The victims' bodies are all in the same position, splayed out like a sacrifice," Francisco explains. "Also, according to Sensitives, the air at each scene smells like spoiled magic, indicative of a ritual gone wrong. Lastly, there are spider lilies in full bloom that burn when touched."

"Omnipotent magic," Gabriel adds.

Ritualistic magic is bad enough, but Omnipotent is magic that creates through sheer willpower. Just as likely to strip the ozone layer as it is to destabilize society, it's banned because it invites the type of instability that can manifest in unknown ways. Murders aren't uncommon, humans are the most dangerous predator, but a serial killer who disregards the fundamental magical laws keeping the world spinning on its axis is something else entirely.

The public's lack of interest signifies a recklessness he can't reconcile. It reminds Hiram that history doesn't repeat itself; it rephrases and rhymes. This has the makings of another Great Vanishing—the worst mass-casualty event in recent history. Hiram was in college when the first reports of inexplicable disappearances made the news. Dozens disappeared within the first week. Hundreds beyond that. It was declared a magical epidemic only when politicians, royalty, and the wealthiest, most influential figures began disappearing, too. Then one day, exactly a month after the first Vanishing, ten thousand people Vanished in broad daylight in various cities all over the world. Terror sent society into a free fall. Schools shut down, violence was rampant, rules ceased to matter, and the global economy crashed. When the source was apprehended, societal order returned, the incident swept under the rug. Rampant rumors about the source's identity left the world assuming they were a Seer—no one else could've sustained the physical cost of such magic—which led to a massive change in global laws. In America, hysteria worsened the oppression of Seers and their separation from Mages. The tragedy became a marker in history and yet another incident bigots point to as an explanation for their hatred.

"Grace was the only victim killed outside the country," Gabriel says carefully.

Hiram can tell when he's being studied. He doesn't like it. "And the others?"

"The first was a healer in Philadelphia. The next two were found in California. One in Upstate New York. Two down in Florida while they were on vacation. The rest were scattered across Colorado and Texas.

We don't have a pattern yet—timewise, temporal, or otherwise. No motivation. No profile. No fresh scene . . . until Grace, and even then, there wasn't an Imprint."

"The better question is: What *do* you know after investigating for six years?" Hiram asks.

"When we were assigned this case three years ago, it was just one murder. As we investigated, we came across more cases from all over the country with too many similarities to be coincidence. We have unclaimed rewards for information, and a cooperative witness that doesn't remember much. Now we have you."

"No, you don't. Trust me—you don't want me involved." Seers, aside from Peter Weston, his best friend, *hate* Hiram Ellis. "How did you get this address?"

"Grace led us here," Gabriel replies.

"Bullshit."

His annoyance simmers when Investigator Sallant whispers a spell over the messenger stone. *"Nuntius."*

Between the cracks of his fingers, the stone emits a hum, then flashes white. Gabriel opens his hands. The stone rises, spinning, until a distorted, familiar British accent he hasn't heard in seven years emerges. *"I am a dying star. I've Seen my end. I am not the last, but there is no fighting the end. The sun and moon spin out of orbit while Earth slumbers deep. Broken bonds form anew. You must compel the earth to live, the sun to shine, and the moon to show his face."*

The stone fades, landing in Gabriel's awaiting hand, the silence resounding.

"Do you know what she meant?"

"No," Hiram answers, still distracted after picking apart how time changed her voice. Paranoia and secrecy drive Seers to weave their visions in riddles to make interpretation harder and protect themselves from laws that prohibit them from speaking plainly. Hiram has a feeling they haven't shown the stone to anyone else, which means this conversation is unapproved and off the record. "What aren't you telling me?"

"A lot," Gabriel admits. "Grace also wrote a note that came with her stone, which was how we found this house and, ultimately, you. She said that we needed to find her old pin that conceals a true face. Do you know what she's talking about?"

"The only thing I can think of is her trickster pendant," Hiram says, noting the second glance the two men give each other. "Grace has the only one that's not hanging in a museum. Well, *had*. She lost it not long after I met her."

Francisco cocks his head. "Lost or stolen?"

Hiram shrugs. "She said she was out with friends and realized on her way home that it was gone."

"What does the pendant do?" Gabriel asks.

"It can change the appearance of the person who puts it on. I don't know what the trickster pendant truly looks like, because its appearance depends on who's wearing it. The pin looked like a cat when Grace wore it, but the one time I touched it, it turned into a wolf. It was a family heirloom, passed down from her grandmother. Odd that she told you to find something she lost years ago in New York City."

"Unless she knew something. Can we speak to her son about the night she was killed?" Francisco asks.

Hiram's expression hardens. "Absolutely not."

"Grace is the most solid lead yet. Her murder is an aberration. We need to figure out why the Botanist targeted her. Perhaps, with her son's statement, we can put the pieces together. If anyone else was there, where they went. *Anything* will help. There are a lot of families that need answers and want justice."

"I said no."

Gabriel and Francisco exchange glances before the former tags himself in. "As a father myself, I understand your concern. I know this is difficult, but her son was found at home, and there was evidence of a struggle. Why Grace left the house, we don't know, but she was found nearly a quarter mile away. Her son—"

"Her son is also *my* son," Hiram snaps. "He hasn't spoken since she was found, anyway, so you're wasting your time."

"There are other ways to interview him—"

"I'm more concerned with protecting him from the trauma you're asking him to revisit."

"If we could just—"

"No."

Hiram closes the door in their faces and returns to the pursuit of stability amid the chaos.

The Ellis name is complicated.

Hiram grew up sheltered and spoiled. As he caught glimpses of life beyond the carefully crafted confines of the Ellis way, he realized his identity was a python wrapped around his throat. The more he fought to unlearn the prejudiced lies taught as truths, the tighter his heritage constricted. College was Hiram's first gasp of freedom. He traveled to places where no one had heard of his family, made a name for himself without the unseemly association, and dated without caring whether they were acceptable matches. Each year, he distanced himself further from his old life—until two months ago, when learning of his son's existence sent him into a tailspin that ended with a phone call to his father and an invitation to come home and mend broken bridges. His confidence wavers now that he's back in Proventia, where the weight of his name is heavier.

He's in a children's boutique downtown when the owner, Nancy, says he looks familiar and asks for his name. Hiram considers lying, but truth wins out.

"Hiram Ellis."

Her face changes as she vehemently shakes his hand. "Ellis? Like *the* Ellis family?"

"Barrett Ellis is my father." *Unfortunately*, he doesn't add, despite the urge.

There are two types of people in Proventia: Mages who love his family, and Seers and sympathizers who don't. There are no in-betweens. Fortunately, Nancy is one of the former. It makes things easier, but also far more uncomfortable.

"Oh, you're *that* Hiram. Welcome back." She clasps her hands together. "The town's buzzing about your return."

To his credit, Hiram manages to mask his disdain. "I need clothes for a six-year-old boy."

"I'd be happy to help."

The more questions Hiram asks about the magical enhancements in the clothing, the more suggestions Nancy makes. The more clothing he picks out, the friendlier she becomes. Hiram is choosing between two bow ties when Nancy stands too close. He's been so focused, he hasn't realized he's made himself prey. She's figured out his status as a single father and joked that her beagle is the longest relationship she's ever had. Hiram smoothly puts space between them to inspect a pack of socks spelled to always find their mates. Judging by her surprise, this isn't the typical chat and number exchange Nancy expects. He understands why. With her tall, slim figure, blond hair, green eyes, fair skin, and freckles partially concealed by bronzer, she's attractive, decently witty, and clearly used to getting what she wants.

"We have other accessories you might be interested in. Bow ties are old-fashioned, but imbued animal pendants are in style. They can either protect your child from a spell being cast on them or act like an amulet and absorb the cost of a spell cast. Most on the market can absorb up to ten low-level spells, but these only do five. Child Mages don't pay for magic like teenagers and adults. What is your son's favorite animal?"

Hiram doesn't know, but he'll never admit it. "It changes every week."

"Oh, well, we have one that changes to their favorite each day, if you're interested."

The pendant is expensive, but Hiram agrees and follows Nancy to the counter while she totals everything up and removes the antitheft gemstones from the tags.

"Also . . . if you're interested in refamiliarizing yourself with Proventia, I'm available."

She's bold, Hiram will give her that. "I'll pay with cash."

Her smile fades. Hiram pays, grabs the four bags, and heads to the car. His next stop is Fallen Oak Apothecary for potions and elixirs to stock his medicine cabinets. Hiram is reaching for the doorknob when three enforcer patrol cars with lights on screech to a halt near his sedan. The talisman atop the door pulses and jingles when Hiram enters. Lavender and thyme are choked out by the scent of confrontation.

"Don't move!" A short, older woman points toward an aisle, shouting accusations of theft and illegal magic use. Hiram can't see the accused, but the older woman glances at him. "We're closed."

"The sign says otherwise."

The back door bursts open. "Enforcers! Slowly walk to the front!"

The standoff devolves into raised voices and shoes pounding on wood. Hiram sighs. They must have used the alley to access the back.

"Very well," a woman replies, bleeding defiance as she steps out of the aisle with a box and an enforcer at her back, his amulet badge aglow in warning. Hiram recognizes the tall, dark-skinned woman with white braids halfway down her back. Khadijah Desai.

"I picked up the box you dropped, and this is the thanks I get." She's calm to the point of boredom as she slowly puts it down at her feet and raises her hands. "I don't *need* to steal from you. The buffalo horns in the box are fake anyway."

"That's a lie, *Seer*." The clerk spits the word like it's acid. "You stole it, and you used magic on me to make me forget!"

A Seer using magic in public is an arrestable offense, but Khadijah remains unbothered, tilting her head at the enforcers. "Make you forget? Not only is that absurd, but that's not how Seer magic works. Do they teach you all *anything* other than stereotypes and misinformation? Don't answer that. A Sensitive can easily tell if I've cast anything. There's at least one here—I know your protocol."

As a Sensitive, Hiram knows a fresh spell can smell like anything, but there's always an undercurrent of ozone that he doesn't detect here. He clears his throat, alerting everyone to his presence. "Apologies for intruding, but do you have any proof of theft? Video? Anything on her person?"

The stream of questions flusters the clerk. Her justification for calling the enforcers fades into the background when Khadijah's gray-green eyes find him. They sharpen in recognition and narrow as if he's an invasive species she needs to eliminate. Hiram expects nothing less from his best friend's wife. Bad blood never does run clean.

"Sir," one of the enforcers says, "unless you're an advocate of this Seer, you should leave."

Hiram isn't, but doesn't have all day for them to figure out what he already knows for a fact. He pulls out his license and offers it to the closest enforcer.

"As a registered Sensitive, I can confirm there's no spell residue in the air. There are no cameras on the premises, because sound-emitting talismans, like the one above the door, interfere with the feed."

The clerk deflates as spell-happy enforcers look around with a new awareness.

One asks, "Ma'am, is that true?"

"Yes, but—"

"Now that we've established that *nothing* happened," Hiram interrupts with a cold glare, then smiles politely, "please release Mrs. Weston and move the patrol cars blocking me in."

"As I've told you before, it's *still* Desai." Khadijah doesn't spare him a glance when she leaves, but Hiram watches until she's safely out of sight.

Sight Unseen

The next morning, Hiram finds what he's looking for outside.

His son sits in the grass, hugging his knees while staring past the trees at the calm lake, lost in thought. Hiram grabs the bag on the table and joins him. Clearing his throat to announce his presence startles the boy, but before he can flee, Hiram joins him on the cold, dewy grass. His khakis will stain, but he doesn't care. They watch the clouds gather and roll over the water, which reflects the sky. A chill shrouds the air, heavy with unfamiliarity.

"Morning."

He doesn't expect a response.

Watching unabashed is something Hiram does often. Mostly in disbelief that he's a father responsible for not fucking his kid up, but sometimes, like now, Hiram watches to see if he can figure out which key will unlock the mystery of his son. So far, none have worked.

The first few weeks, Hiram remained calm and logical, but he's grown desperate. Being with a child who barely meets his eyes, can't stand his touch, and has nightmares that trigger magical reactions has left Hiram frustrated to the point of uncharacteristic self-pity. He's being beaten by a meticulous child who gels his own hair, is always dressed on time for school, and never lets anyone so much as touch the knitted bow tie he's worn since Hiram met him. He has plenty of different-colored bow ties, yet only wears black.

The color of mourning, but it's deeper than grief. Black was Grace's favorite color, an odd affinity for someone so colorful.

His son's hands are clasped tightly, as if the only comfort he can find is in himself. Instinct makes Hiram reach out, but his attempt is rebuffed when the boy shifts away. The reaction isn't new. Still, it stings more than he'll admit.

"Do you like it here?"

More silence. He's trying not to get used to it. Life with a kid is supposed to be a challenge, and grief complicates even the simplest matters. He wonders if he's doomed to fail.

His son dips his head in the smallest nod, eyes on the water.

His hope floats once more. "I do, too."

This earns him a slow, hesitant look. Hiram uses the moment to awkwardly offer a gift bag, watching the cautious boy pull out the gold animal pendant he purchased. In his hand, it changes from a bear to a dog to a horse before settling on a cat. Unbearable silence forces words out. "I had your name engraved on the back."

At this, the boy turns the pendant, a small finger tracing each letter as if a mystery lingers in the metal.

Antaris.

⁂

Time creates order within chaos. Constant and elusive, its passage is noticed most by those standing still long enough to witness the change. Hiram doesn't care about time's limitations, convinced it'll bend to compensate if he pushes hard enough. Like a strategist, he calculates the trajectory of each move. Armed with as many strengths as weaknesses, Hiram keeps his eyes on the parts that don't fit. The pieces he can't control.

One such piece is now at school. The other is Simran, his mother, waiting at his kitchen island with a newspaper. She dresses formally, even at home, but today wears a modest floral kurta. If she's trying to convince him she's changed, she's failing. That she let herself in like the house belongs to her proves that. He's disappointed but not surprised.

"I need to adjust the talisman to stop allowing in *every* immediate family member." Carefully schooling his features into impassivity, Hiram passes her on his way to the kitchen. Without pots and pans, ignoring her over a meal isn't an option.

"You will do no such thing." Simran has the gall to act like he's being unreasonable. "I thought we might talk. Over breakfast."

In an instant, Hiram remembers exactly who she is. How she operates. What she wants. "We have nothing to discuss outside our original agreement: You take Antaris to school and pick him up. But if you want, we can talk about how you've been overstepping."

Simran's jaw tenses. "I see Peter told you about the tutor."

"He's my best friend and Antaris's godfather. Of course he told me."

"Then I suppose there is nothing to discuss." She clasps her hands. "Give me a tour of the house, darling."

Simran has as many complaints as comments. According to her, the kitchen, living room, and great room are a good size, but the furniture is too casual. Hiram doesn't mention that he chose pieces Antaris took more than a passing glance at when they walked through the furniture store. From there, Simran laments the too-small owner's suite.

"It's only me."

The lack of whimsical decor in Antaris's room and bathroom.

"I hardly know Antaris, but *whimsical* isn't a word I'd use to describe him."

The halls that are too narrow and plain.

"Does it matter?"

There are no guest rooms, despite there being three spare bedrooms.

"We haven't had guests."

Hiram thinks the backyard will go uncriticized, but apparently the potential for the lake drying up is worth mentioning.

"There are a hundred and fifty rainy days a year."

Simran is tenacious when she wants something, a trait he's inherited. What she wants now is for Hiram to be within reach. To accomplish this, she'll sow seeds of doubt and leave him questioning his decisions. It's a wash, lather, rinse, repeat of a childhood Hiram spent torn between craving her hard-earned approval and wanting to tell her to fuck off . . . respectfully.

"I believe you were far too hasty purchasing this home." Simran returns to her seat in the kitchen. "You should have moved home for—"

"Reconciliation will fail if we're under the same roof."

Momentarily deterred, she reorients by laying out a breakfast prepared by her housekeeper. "I made sure to bring your favorites."

Hiram has always preferred eggs, toast, and coffee. The plate of sausages, ham, and French toast is a clear reminder of his mother's consistent inattention and disregard of what he wants. The reminder burns in all the ways he hates.

"Your uncle asked about Antaris." At his sharp look, she amends, "Cosmos, no. Not your uncle Phillip. He is too busy with his secret genetic case studies in Atlanta. I discourage your father from associating with him. I meant Robert."

The safer uncle, as far as Hiram is concerned. Robert's more focused on planting Ellises in as many political offices as possible than he will ever be on discovering Antaris's roots. "What did he ask?"

"General questions. He wanted to know about his mother, and I made an excuse. I also gave my spiel about his Sight test coming back zero, but I know they will grow curious as he gets older."

"I'll cross that bridge when I get there."

"Your carelessness will *not* be the reason I am shunned from a family I spent *years* in, clawing up the ranks. They finally see me as a pillar. A matriarch. Not an outsider who married into their family. Joining the firm will earn you respect. Your father has a seat on the board he would gladly give you. You can rise to a level where the family will not question you, and it will keep you here. It could even further your career into politics. You can run for mayor of Proventia."

"I'm not interested."

Simran makes a small, disbelieving noise. "Think of your son."

"I am." Every move he makes feels wrong, but her suggestions are worse.

"Are you?" As if sensing his rapidly souring mood, she pats his hand. "I am trying to help, but you remain obstinate."

He's not stubborn. He simply refuses to fall back into old habits, changing himself to fit her expectations.

"I want Antaris to be one less worry for you, which is why I found him a tutor. You had tutors and a proper education. He needs the same. I want him to be a respectable Ellis. I believe extra attention will benefit him until he is ready to go to Arcadia Academy. Besides, Miss Thorne is a Mage sympathetic to Seers. I figured you would approve."

Talking to his mother is the equivalent of running into a brick wall. Painful and futile. "I'm not sending him to boarding school."

"Why not? Antaris is a legacy." Simran frowns at Hiram's silence. "This brings up another topic of discussion. His surname. Fowler is—"

"His name."

Masterfully, she suppresses her irritation, but not fast enough. "Antaris should have had our name from the beginning. He is not related to the man whose name he carries."

"Blood doesn't make a family. John raised Grace after her father left and her mother died. She took his last name."

Unsurprisingly, Simran isn't moved. "I have completed the documentation to correct the error. All it requires is your signature."

"Absolutely not."

His mother's frown deepens. "He is *your* son."

"Does his last name change that?" Hiram doesn't wait for an answer. "Antaris has been taken away from everything he knows. The last thing he needs is to be suffocated by the new identity you're rushing to force on him."

"Not force. He needs structure. All children do. You may not understand why I am so insistent, but I want the best for him. We *must* set expectations."

Hiram's chuckle lacks humor. "Shame I never met yours."

Simran looks close to cracking, but returns to being the vision of poised composure. "I do not wish to argue with you when we are meant to reconcile."

"That will require compromise from everyone, not just me."

A quiet part of him still longs for a normal relationship with his parents, one that doesn't come with strings attached. But doubt clouds every interaction.

"We will finish discussing that later. For now, let us eat."

Hiram isn't hungry but forces a few bites. The silence has barely reached tolerable when his mother tsks at a page near the back. "Disaster after disaster. Nothing good. Apparently, Seers are in danger. They are *the* danger to society, but who am I to censor the press? For once, I wish to open the newspaper to a palatable story."

"Forgive the news for not tailoring itself to your specifications."

She raises a brow as she sips her tea. "You are snippy today."

"I'm not. If you want, I'll pre-read the news and highlight only the good parts." More than anything, Hiram wants to read the article himself to see if it mentions the Botanist.

A skeptical brow rises. "You are not sleeping because Antaris is still not sleeping through the night, is he? I told you that creating boundaries with the talisman I gave you would—"

"I'm not trapping him in his room like an animal."

"When did I say that? My endless mantra is that you must give Antaris *rules*."

"What would you have me do? Ignore him when he's having nightmares?"

"I would rather you did not reward his behavior." She laces her fingers together. "Raising a child is difficult, and it is okay to admit it. I would rather spend my time helping you than arguing. You and I have missed so much, and we have lost years with him due to his mother's alienation. We should not lose more."

"You know why she kept him away," Hiram replies.

When Hiram confessed to Grace that he was *that* kind of Ellis, she cut contact and disappeared. According to her stepfather, not long after Grace arrived back in London, she found out she was pregnant and kept it a secret. John never approved, always urged her to reach out and give Hiram a chance, but Hiram understood. He hadn't been free. The Ellis name and reputation had already smothered him long before he'd left. The last decade was a delusion of his own creation.

"We are not the monsters she believed us to be," Simran argues.

"Seers have centuries of proof to the contrary. We invented ways to subjugate them, poisons to sever their connection to magic, and imbued their weaknesses into things they needed. Yet we had the nerve to smile in their faces while presenting their oppression as gifts."

"The Great Vanishing—"

"Stop using that as an excuse to treat them as lesser."

"You were across the ocean at college. If you had been here, the experience would have changed you like it did me. That is the nature of consequence. You never return to the state of naivety, nor can you undo what you have seen. I will never trust anyone with the power to change the world and erase people from existence."

"I knew people who Vanished, but I'm not blaming an entire group for the actions of a single person. You can't rewrite history. Anti-Seer laws were already in place long before the Great Vanishing."

"This is futile." Simran checks her watch and stands. "I must go."

After she leaves, Hiram meticulously cleans every trace of their conversation, but it's not enough. It never is.

Too restless to stay home, Hiram goes for a walk. Not around the lake, but into the forest. It's midmorning, the sun is breaking through the trees, and the trail is congested. The farther he goes, the thinner the crowd becomes, until he sees only one or two people now and then.

Hiram hasn't been here in years, but the forest is not beholden to time. When the trees start to bow over the path, little more than fallen leaves and moss, he knows he's close. The first sounds of water trickle in, and a familiar western hemlock off the path is his cue to leave the comfort of the trail.

In daylight, directions are easier. Small carvings on trees guide his way as he walks for what feels like hours, sweating under the humid midday sun until he ducks beneath a low branch and comes face-to-face with the mouth of Nénuphar Cave.

It's not a secret, but it *is* sacred.

More than old, Nénuphar Cave is ancient. The tunnels and streams of a deep labyrinth branch far and wide. If there is an end, it remains a mystery. Hiram found the cave when he was ten, lost while hiking. He used to be a sickly kid, but that slowly changed after his first visit. The water, he realized, was not a cure but a boost to help him along the way.

The air inside is rich with raw, damp earth and something heady. Water drips rhythmically—the cave's pulse. Hiram's eyes are drawn to the stalactites above and stalagmites jutting from the earthen floor. Shadows from hanging lantern orbs dance across the deep cavern, swaying and looming, turning the cave into a mesmerizing display of light and dark.

At the edge of the water, Hiram strips down to his black swim shorts and steps in. The warm, waist-deep, luminescent waters are so clear, he can see the bottom. When he submerges, magic tingles his skin like electricity, and his first inhale after resurfacing soothes the tension in his shoulders. Careful of the darkness deeper in the cave, Hiram swims lazy laps. As he gently cuts through the water, thoughts cease. All the aches, anxieties, and worries that threaten to consume him . . . he lets them go. Releases them to the universe's embrace.

Floating on his back, he gazes at the amethyst walls and the limestone cavern ceiling. Eyes closed, he slips into a memory, another effect of the water. The visions are never the same.

With Peter surrounded like a shepherd among his flock, Hiram is bored, and the graduation party's saving grace is the liquor. He's on his second shot when he sees her. It's not the slit in her orange dress that makes her legs look longer or the voluminous hair under her graduation cap that catches his attention—it's the eye-shaped sapphire amulet around her neck.

The same one a Seer tattoo artist inked onto his skin last month. A vision made real.

Now, it watches. Torn between approaching and retreating, full of questions, Hiram lingers, observing the woman leaning against a table, drinking amber liquor straight from a bottle. She's talking animatedly to three men. Whatever the topic, she looks certain of victory. Without realizing, he drifts closer, now caught in her web.

"As Mages, you and I are more of a danger than any Seer," she says firmly. "Just like, as a man, you are more of a danger to me than—"

"That's not true," one argues.

"I'll tell you why you're wrong." She takes another swig from the bottle. "As long as men and Mages establish the standard for society, they bear responsibility for upholding a higher one. Mages don't, and men certainly don't. You're so blinded by your own privilege that you can't see the shackles ignorance has placed on you. Society would be much further along if Seers were allowed to be inventive and creative with magic. I—"

"Here you go, with all your dreamer shit," the second man mutters, rolling his eyes.

Hiram is transfixed.

"That dreamer shit is responsible for the amulet you wear around your neck," she argues firmly, touching her own with a sad fondness. "If a Seer hadn't figured out how to divert magical consequence from the human body to the stone, and learned to tie Imprints to an amulet, Mages would still be dying from physical damage due to long-term spell work."

They shift, uncomfortable. "We didn't mean—"

She hops off the table, excuses herself, and disappears into the crowd.

Awareness returns as the memory fades. Hiram floats until he hears footsteps on sand.

He rights himself in the water. Opens his eyes. Pauses. Blinks.

It's been a long time since Hiram last thought of that night, so when he sees her at the water's edge, he scrubs a hand over his face, wondering whether he's hallucinating. His foot scrapes against a rock under the water, and pain jolts through him. She's real.

Memory made flesh.

Same petite frame, brown skin, and deep-set brown eyes. Thinner than he remembers, cautious rather than carefree. There's a poise that's distinctively her, an awareness that's intriguing and screams perseverance, not preservation. She's wearing jeans, a gray Crestwood

University shirt, hiking boots, and the same amulet that drew him to her in the first place. Her hair, full and free as it was the first time Hiram saw her, is now longer, copper-brown instead of black, and halfway down her back, threatened by the cave's humidity. Hiram has never known her last name, but her first has been etched into his memory for a decade. *Veda*.

"Why is my amulet tattooed on you?" she asks, studying him with narrowed eyes.

"I . . . don't know."

He takes one sloshy step toward her, and she retreats in equal measure. She's gone before Hiram has a chance to follow.

Three

Clouds cloak the sky in gray gloom.

Veda is restless, nauseous with anxiety and questions after her visit to Nénuphar was altered by a wet, half-naked stranger bearing an exact replica of her amulet tattooed on his arm. She runs back to Weston, where Clinton Desai waits alone on a bench with a small radio on the table. It's turned down, but not off. There are two steaming cups of tea.

"You're late," Clinton's voice rumbles quietly.

"Am I?" Veda quips. "I was looking for Peter."

"I *Saw*."

A blind man with Sight. The irony isn't lost on Veda. Clinton is strong, not overly tall, and doesn't look a day over fifty, though he turned sixty late last year. Deep-brown skin. Black hair. Strands of white in his beard. The wrinkles at his eyes age him more than the scars he wears with pride like the decorated soldier he is. Dressed in a plum blazer, cream linen shirt, and gray slacks, he looks ready to teach one final lesson for the day.

"Peter left for his meeting with the school board just as I returned from speaking on Khadijah's behalf to the Oracle Council about what happened at the apothecary."

Seers answer to their state's Oracle Council, the governing body that addresses their community's problems and intervenes when they break the Mage Protection Laws. These laws forbid Seers from using magic on others, even accidentally or in self-defense. Those who intentionally break Seer Laws or defy the Code—which prohibits using visions to alter the future, meddle with time, or interfere with life and death—are punished. The Oracle Council strips them of Sight, leaving them as Unseen. To a Seer, that fate is worse than death.

"Will they punish her?" Veda asks.

"I do not understand their paranoia, their caginess." Clinton frowns. "There were no charges filed, yet I had to argue for leniency. It makes no sense."

"Did you argue as her uncle, head of the Oracle Council, or former congressman?"

"All of the above."

As the first Seer elected to Congress, Clinton is well known for standing firm in the face of outright hatred. Once retired from politics, he moved to Washington state, arguably one of the worst states for Seers' rights, returned to teaching, and has made headway fighting for Seers in his four years as head of the state's Oracle Council. There are still miles to go before progress takes hold.

"They believe missteps are a sign of trouble, but I disagree." Clinton angles his face to the breeze. "Drink your tea, Veda. You're rattled, more than usual. Tell me about Nénuphar."

Hiding the truth from a Seer is fruitless. "There was a man there. I don't—"

"Anyone in need of healing can find Nénuphar."

"I know, but his arm was covered in tattoos, and one looked *exactly* like my amulet, right down to the imperfections." She covers it with her hand. "It's one of a kind, my dad made it by hand. No one should have a replica."

"Unless you're linked through the Cosmos."

"I hope not."

Clinton chuckles. "Describe him."

"Well, he didn't look like he needed healing."

Tanned olive skin, a swimmer's build. Taller than Peter. Undeniably attractive. Dark hair, striking blue eyes, and a shadow of stubble darkening his jaw. Veda can't detail his tattoo sleeve, but she remembers his soaked hair clinging to his forehead. Funny how memories work.

"Some wounds live beneath the surface." Clinton brings his teacup to his lips and blows on the steam. "I can't read your mind, but I know you. I await the day your judgmental heuristics fail you."

"I'll be dead by then." Veda's dark humor neutralizes Clinton's amusement.

"Peter told me about the spider lilies. Not every omen means you harm. Sometimes they can be helpful warnings." Clinton turns off the radio and folds his mobility cane. "This fear you feel will change, in stages, and only when you reach beyond what you know."

Veda tenses. "Is that something you've Seen?"

"Yes and no."

It's dangerous and illegal to speak a clear truth, but Seers and their doublespeak grate her unlike anything else.

"You are worried about the Sanguis Curse awakening before you learn whose blood is in that cyst. I know there have been attempts to drain and extract the curse, but cursed blood does not spill like normal blood." He tilts his head, and a thoughtful *hmm* escapes. "I *do* wonder if anyone has considered that blood curses are man-made and parasitic in nature. They flee once the host stops benefiting them."

"You know Khadijah and Peter. They haven't left a stone unturned. I've been on every anticurse cocktail and potion known to man. They've attacked it with spells, cleansed my blood and energy, and used every connection to get a consult with the leading curse breaker only for them to tell me that all the research on my curse is privately owned and they don't share. Nothing works."

"Failure does not mean defeat." Clinton turns up the radio. More incoherent rage-baiting about protecting the masses from Seers. Veda cringes at the hate language.

"Why do you listen to this?" she asks.

"We are no longer cut off from magic, displaced and ripped from our families, but bigotry still thrives."

"Trust me, I know. Peter enrolled a bigot's grandson in school. The things she said, the way she dismissed Seers is—"

"Not uncommon."

"Doesn't it make you angry?"

"I won't give anyone the satisfaction of becoming the danger they think we are."

Fear brings out the worst in humanity.

"Your tea is cold," Clinton tells her.

"I prefer it cold and—"

"Bitter," he finishes, shaking his head slightly. "Not for taste but self-preservation."

"It's the best detection for poison."

"An outdated evolutionary warning." Clinton reaches for his cup and brings it to his lips. "The perfect poison is not strong or messy, it is quick and clean."

Veda listens to the low hum of bees in the nearby apiary and accepts the mint candy he offers.

"It's quiet," he says after a moment.

"You know as well as I do saying the q-word invites chaos."

He turns to her, his voice sharp as the wind. "I cannot say much, but *fissures bloom bloodred, and a trickster wears the face of a friend. Roots hold truths and lies. Take hold. There is one way out. What lies in the dark will come to light.*"

Veda's blood turns to ice. Clinton's visions are usually hints of feelings, vague until they draw closer to fruition. Although perplexing, this is the clearest riddle he's given so far. He relaxes in his seat, and they sit together, watching the ever-changing world in flux.

"There was another victim a couple of months ago," Veda says softly. "A woman in London. Gabriel said her body was found near her house, splayed open, blood everywhere, surrounded by spider lilies. Like the other victims."

"You still remember the first. You carry him when you should not."

But she must. His blood stains her hands, never to be washed clean. Even the healing waters can't drown the memories that torment her sleep. She remembers finding Healer Lawson, his body carved, arms spread, glowing spider lilies blooming from blood-soaked hospital floors, turning to ash at her touch. His attacker's rapidly shifting face, the moment they noticed her frozen in place. The surge of raw magic that fractured her memory. *They don't know what's coming*, Healer Lawson had gasped as the light left his eyes. Two days later, when his killer came for her at home, Veda understood. Healer Lawson's warning had been for her, too.

"Do you know why we meet like this, when you are most anxious?" Clinton asks.

"Typically, it's against my will."

He doesn't hide his amusement, but his expression softens. "I've never been able to ignore someone who is struggling to catch their breath."

Veda looks down at her hands, emotions forming an uncomfortable lump in her throat.

"I was a child when I lost my vision in a car accident. My Sight manifested as a result. It was a constant sensory overload that only eased when I had help learning to shut the world out and restore my strength. I learned that my answer wasn't solitude, it was family and community. That is what I hope I've taught you."

"I have a community: Peter, Khadijah, Gabriel, sometimes Francisco, and you."

"But you need more. Isn't it lonely with no one to tend to you?"

A childlike vulnerability emerges. Veda wants to hug herself for the comfort she pretends to never need. "Time isn't on my side."

"Time doesn't take sides," Clinton replies gently. "Don't waste energy chasing it. It's beyond your control. Use what you have wisely, and you will not walk through hell alone. Protect your strength. Open yourself to possibilities. What is meant to happen will."

Veda feels worse than she did when she sat down. "That doesn't make me feel better."

"It's not intended to." He pauses. "Let yourself stand still, but do not stop."

Veda shuts her eyes.

"What do you hear?" Clinton asks after a while.

"The bees. The breeze. The birds. The rustling trees. The incoming storm."

"I hear disorder."

Whether in her or in nature, he doesn't say.

Weston Academy's greenhouse is a marvelous mixture of magic and technology.

Designed to expand when needed and withstand anything short of a meteor strike, the greenhouse started as four glass panes bound by powerful incantations. Now two stories tall, it boasts a roof that shifts with the weather and the movement of the sun. Whimsical and cozy, it's cloaked in wisteria and ivy, blending seamlessly into the school's landscape. Inside, it's more impressive: a methodically organized maze of rich foliage, herbs, lush local and tropical trees, and rows of vegetables and flowers. Plants are potted, trellised, or hung from the ceilings and along the circular steps leading to the upper gardens and work areas. Everything bursts with color.

Veda's job is to monitor everything, plants and staff alike. The work is mundane, but she finds comfort in the routine, especially as her life spirals elsewhere. Midway through her morning tasks, she glances from the glass balcony and spots a disruption.

Everett Simpson is so nondescript, he seems faceless. A wiry beard elongates his face, and his sandy-brown hair fades gray at the temples. He looks like the sort who enjoys dry oats and has niche hobbies, like fly-fishing. A Seer and the school's new veterinarian, he replaced his predecessor last year. Veda has always been polite, but since the start of the year, something about him has unsettled her.

"Can I help you, Dr. Simpson?" she calls.

His head swivels in three directions before he spots her. "Oh, there you are, Veda."

The casual use of her name sharpens her suspicion.

"Is there something you need?" she asks.

Undeterred, he weaves through the winding paths to the spiral staircase. When Everett reaches her, Veda's arms are crossed. "I don't mean to be rude, but I don't let anyone up here without a bachelor's in magi-horticulture or a PhD in herbal biotechnology."

"I'm sorry, I didn't want to shout." Everett looks chastened. "I just—here."

He all but shoves a folded paper in her hands and quickly retreats. Confused, Veda starts to open it until a glance at the clock jolts her memory. She's late for her meeting with Antaris.

"Shit."

Veda sprints to the school. By the time she reaches Peter's office, she's breathless and ready to apologize, but stops short at the sight of Antaris pacing. His hand absently skims the spine of each book on the lower row once, then again. It's methodical. Five steps to the left, five to the right. Veda clears her throat, and he stops, startled, before his eyebrows knit in cautious observation. Every child has their own version of chaos. She's certain Antaris's is buried deep, but for now, he's unnervingly composed. It's been less than five minutes, and Veda is already at a loss, nervous that if she opens her mouth, the wrong thing will spill out, and she'll scare him off like a wild animal prone to run.

She takes the first step, just as hesitant. "Hi, Antaris."

Antaris keeps staring. It's uncomfortable. Veda usually relies on August's chatter to guide her, but this child offers no such cues.

"I see you like books," she tries.

He glances at the bookshelf, and just like that, Veda briefly loses his attention until hazel eyes slide back to her.

She clears her throat. "Do you want to pick out a book?"

He shakes his head.

Veda sits on the floor and watches him. No wrinkles are present on his clothes, his black knitted bow tie is perfectly straight, and his hair is as severely parted as it was when they first met. He's careful, first with his blazer, hanging on the chair, then with Peter's books, as if he understands actions have consequences. Curiosity grabs Veda and doesn't let go. What would he sound like laughing? Telling a story? Would he be animated? Does he get distracted and jump from subject to subject until he can't remember how the story began?

Why do I care? It's a question for which Veda has no answer.

Antaris catches her staring.

"Your grandmother wants me to tutor you. What do you think about that?"

His expression grows even more puzzled.

"You can shake your head no."

He doesn't.

"You can nod your head yes."

He doesn't do that, either.

"If you had five minutes to do anything, what would you do?"

Antaris looks as though he's never considered it.

She holds up her hand. "I mean it—*anything*."

It's a question Veda has asked before. *Mud pies* was August's answer, but Antaris is a much different child. He proves this by walking out of the room. Veda scrambles to follow, locking Peter's office before chasing the boy down the corridor. She finds him waiting by the academy's door to the grounds. Of all the things he could ask for . . . "You want to go outside?"

This earns Veda a hesitant nod.

"Okay." When she opens the door, Antaris pauses, casting a tentative gaze up at Veda for confirmation, which she gives by saying gently, "Five minutes starts now."

Antaris steps onto the deck with a panoramic view of the grounds. The sun shines above the trees; mountains frame clear blue skies. They can hear clucking chickens and the distant mooing of cows grazing in the pastures. It's beautiful, peaceful, but Veda isn't the only restless soul. Antaris closes his eyes, breath hitching. Hazel eyes fly open as he quickly scrubs at them, then tries to exhale slowly, mouth pursed—but it doesn't calm him.

Dread settles into Veda's bones as she bears witness to his struggles. Drowning doesn't always look like drowning. The ones in the most trouble don't kick, splash, or cry for help. Every shred of energy is used to stay afloat. Antaris has been treading water for Cosmos knows how long, and he's exhausted. She tosses the only lifeline she has. "Your grandmother wants me to tutor you in hopes that you'll talk, but I told her no."

There's no wonder in his eyes, only scrutiny.

"I'm . . . I . . ." Flustered, Veda fumbles over words. "I won't say no if *you* ask."

Antaris's breath catches.

"You don't have to speak. I won't push you. We can sit outside every day, rain or shine. We can color or read books, work through your workbook, or do nothing at all. It'll be your time. Sometimes, we all need a place in the day that's just ours. I'd like to give you that."

Antaris worries at his bottom lip, gaze drifting toward the trees and beyond. When he turns to her once more, Veda knows this is her last shot. She holds up a finger. "How about this? Touch my finger once for no, twice for yes."

The oar is cast, and Veda has done what she can. Antaris must do the rest, but she wonders if he's too deep in silence to grab the lifeline. Her own problems are louder than this silent child, yet empathy compels her to keep reaching into the harsh seas of his misery, hoping to pull him to safety.

"It's your choice," she says, finger still raised.

Hope takes many forms and wears many faces. Today, it's a boy timidly pressing a finger against hers. Once, then twice.

Unseasonably warm weather draws a large crowd to Proventia's outdoor farmers' market the first weekend of April. The atmosphere is surprisingly friendly and festive with Mages and Seers intermingling. They wander between vendors trying to outshine one another with an array of crafts, produce, meats, and art. A local cover band plays popular songs from two decades ago. Enforcers patrol while people sit on blankets, eating and talking, their dogs relaxing, playing, or nosing around the grass for dropped treats. An undercurrent of tension remains, a heightened awareness that Veda likens to the feel of magic. Often, it roars. Today it's a dull thrum.

Veda dislikes public places, but Weston Academy remains self-funded, and to keep the school functioning, without high tuition costs, they sell excess produce at events like this. Normally teachers volunteer to staff the booth, but today, Veda is alone. Between price questions and bulk-order requests, she watches the crowd, etching faces into memory, linking strangers through imagined connections.

The passing hours smooth Veda's serious edges and lower the volume of her ever-present anxiety. She's nearly sold out when her final customers approach.

Ruth and Everly Wells are an odd contrast in both appearance and temperament. Ruth, a Seer and member of the Oracle Council alongside Clinton, is tall and willowy with pale skin and gray hair. She always wears a wide-brimmed hat regardless of the weather, and today is no exception. Everly, on the other hand, isn't a Seer. She is as short as Veda and plump in a grandmotherly sort of way. Her skin is olive and her eyes are as brown as her hair. Despite their differences, they are sisters, but not by blood.

"Alone again, Veda?" Everly tsks. Since Veda's birthday, Everly has cut her long hair into a bob that suits her nicely. "I'm beginning to think you only come when no one else does."

Veda laughs awkwardly at the truth. "I don't mind. It's been a nice day."

While Everly overpays for the rest of the school's stock and refuses a discount, Ruth observes Veda like someone trying to decide whether food is too far past its expiration date to consume. Veda hates being scrutinized, but it's worse because it's Ruth. She doesn't have kids of her own and has spent years as something of a mother figure to anyone who needs one. Since Veda arrived in Proventia, Ruth invites her to holidays, and Everly brews the salve she puts on her back.

"What you think is loneliness is actually *hunger*."

Everly does a double take and gives her sister a small swat. "Don't scare the poor girl."

"It's fine," Veda says, bagging the produce in their reusable totes. "I've been accosted already with Clinton's visions."

That earns a sharp glance between the sisters. "When multiple Seers have visions about the same subject, it means there is something stirring in the Cosmos," Ruth says.

"Should I be worried?"

Ruth's smile is the nonanswer she expects.

Everly changes the subject. "How have you been? You haven't been around since your birthday dinner."

"Oh, you know me, I never sit still."

Ruth scrutinizes her. "You should come by for dinner, and don't say you're cooking, because we all know your idea of a meal is either frozen, packaged, or purchased."

It's true, but she mumbles something about eating at Peter's, places the last of their purchases into a bag, and immediately starts to clear her booth. Neither leaves. Worse, they start helping. As the women fold the checkered tablecloth, Veda pulls the empty bins from underneath the table, places three inside one, and stacks the lids. "How have *you* two been?"

"Pretty good," Ruth replies. "But birds keep shitting in my rain gauge."

Veda suppresses a laugh with her fist. "That's . . . unfortunate."

Everly snickers. "What are your plans for the rest of the day, Veda?"

"Home."

She shakes her head shamefully. "You should drive to Seattle or Olympia, get out of those jeans, take out that nose ring—"

"Or don't," Ruth chimes in. "The youths love that sort of look. Just put on something nice and show a little leg. Have some fun out on the town."

"Yes!" Everly grins. "Do it while your knees still work."

Veda rolls her eyes. She once had a healthy social life with friends and parties, flings, the occasional boyfriend. Nothing serious. Only fun. That was all she could commit to. But she's not that person anymore.

"I'm not looking for anything," Veda says.

Her words fall on deaf ears. "That's usually when you find your spouse."

"Sounds like a threat," Veda mutters.

Everly laughs while Ruth pats her hands. "Oh, honey, you're in for a rude awakening."

"I'll pray every day to the Cosmos that you're wrong."

Both women laugh raucously at her opposition. Everly pats Veda's shoulder. "As if you have any say in it. You're brilliant, Veda. Cynical and distant, but not to worry, someone will outlast your resistance. They'll wait patiently for you to open up and want everything they find." A soft, whimsical smile appears. "I can't wait for that to happen."

"*Still* feeling threatened right now."

Ruth snaps her fingers. "Now that I think about it, my nephew *Ian* is single, and he's a great young man."

Everly perks up. "I have someone better. What about Micah? Moab's grandson?"

They're off to the races on another round of Proventia's Most Eligible Bachelor. Veda has met their second contestant, Micah, a few times. He's perfectly pleasant and polite . . . if she were looking for a man pushing fifty.

"Now, Everly, stop trying to set Micah up with every woman in Proventia," Ruth fusses and turns to Veda. "If not Micah, I have the *perfect* catch for you, my dear. Dr. Simpson."

Paranoia makes Veda's fingers tingle.

"In fact, Everett asked about you earlier," Ruth adds with a conspiratorial waggle of her brows. At Veda's deepening frown, Ruth swats as if her distrust is a particularly annoying fly. "Don't look like that. His mom and I play bingo together. He's a good, stable man. You already work with him at Weston. He's a bit of a loner like you, and most importantly—"

"He's interested," Everly blurts out.

"Which is *such* good news. His mom was so worried. He hasn't been acting like himself since February, when he stopped dating . . . Sarah? Serena? Selena? All I know is she works for the FCD and she did a number on him. It's good he's back in the saddle."

"Congrats to him, but leave me out of it."

They cackle as if Veda has told a particularly funny joke.

"I'd set him up with Marlene"—Ruth sighs—"but she's sworn off dating to focus on her career."

"I still don't understand. I thought she and the Padillos' oldest son, Francisco, were interested in one another. Such a lovely man, but when I ask what happened, she doesn't want to talk about him. I fear I may never see grandchildren at this rate." Everly sighs with loving frustration.

Everly adopted Marlene at fifteen after Ruth rescued her and a group of teenage Seers from a boarding school that was a front for a quasi-legal experimental facility—not an uncommon fate for Seers abandoned after their Sight manifests. In fact, almost every Seer family in town has adopted at least one abandoned kid to protect them from ending up in the system. Ruth and Everly have a similar upbringing but spent the last four decades preventing kids from being taken advantage of, and even after the kids become adults, they never stop caring. It's evident with Marlene.

Veda awkwardly chuckles while agreeing. Marlene is more Khadijah's friend than Veda's, but she's listened to her talk plenty about not caring about the gender of her partner, only that she wants to marry and have a family of her own.

"Has she said anything to you and Khadijah?" Everly asks.

"I haven't seen her in at least a month."

Ruth frowns. "She must've meant Khadijah when she said she was spending time with friends."

As Veda nods along, her gaze falls on Dr. Simpson, who is watching from two tables over.

Ruth follows her line of sight. "Ah, there he is. What do you think?"

"I'm not interested."

"Beggars can't be choosy. You're losing time, dear."

Ruth's comment is less about Veda's age and more about the ticking bomb of her Sanguis Curse. Veda doesn't broadcast her affliction, but Ruth knows because Peter has involved the Oracle Council in his quest to heal her. Aside from Clinton, Ruth has been helpful in contacting old friends who work for the various Centers for Maledictum Research. The bureaucratic stonewall ended up being so high and dense that breaking through would've required an inconceivable amount of money or better connections. With hope for extraction dwindling, Ruth's comments have grown more pointed: Veda needs to live like she's dying, throw caution to the wind, and find someone to hold on to as long as she can. But that's not who Veda is. The malignant blood curse has only made her more determined to cling to her dignity until the bitter end. Each day is a new test Veda passes as often as she fails. On good days, she clings to routines that give her a reason to get dressed and leave her cottage. But when the weight of her curse bears down, her days turn dark, and the pain is heavily branded. Those days remind Veda why she doesn't make plans for a future she'll never see.

The air around them shifts, tinged with discomfort, until Ruth says, "If I'm not here when it's time for the summer bouquets, be a dear and set one aside for me."

"Okay," Veda replies. Ruth has said this for the last two years, yet she's always first in line for her bouquet of peach roses, pink ginger, and red cordyline mixed with masajeana leaves. Colorful and vibrant, like Ruth.

"Oh, and I'll see you at next month's town hall meeting."

Before Veda can decline, the sisters toddle off.

Veda glances at the nearby tables. A few trinkets catch her eye, but the less she owns, the less she has to think about. Everett approaching her is as inevitable as the awkward conversation that follows. Constantly wringing his hands as if to soothe himself, he's a skipping record, stammering through small talk as though either gives a damn about the weather or the size of today's crowd.

"Did you look at my note?" he asks, jamming his hands into his pockets.

"Sorry," she says, realizing she hasn't. Her meeting with Antaris made her forget all about it. Not that it matters, as Everett hands her another before rushing off. This time, she opens it. It looks like a half-finished phone number.

A blur of bright colors in the corner of her eye steals Veda's attention. Quickly, she identifies the child-size ball of energy barreling toward her with a colorful jersey and cleats as August Sallant.

"Miss Thorne! Miss Thorne! We won!"

"Congrats, August!" Veda doesn't have the heart to ask what sport, because he's wearing a blend of uniforms. To keep the hyperactive boy occupied, August plays everything his dad can reasonably sign him up for. How he has energy to play in the dirt after school she'll never know.

"I played today!" He holds up two fingers, flashing a smile that shows off burgeoning nubs of front teeth that are growing back. Then he launches into the story of how he won the game, but it starts with him getting up that morning and what he ate for breakfast. It'll be a minute, and the details will be convoluted and out of order. He retells parts of it in great detail and omits others entirely. "Then I scored two goals by myself!"

Goals narrows down the list of sports, but she gets her answer when Gabriel, his dad, approaches in a *Proud Hockey Dad* sweatshirt, looking every bit like someone whose last drop of energy was spent getting his son out of the house. He's barely brushed his red beard. Despite August's endless energy, Gabriel walks at a leisurely pace, carrying three reusable bags. He's always smiling and cheerful, greeting a couple of women as they pass by. They stare at him with interest when his back is turned.

". . . sparkling flowers *poofed*. It was so cool!"

Veda has no idea how they got to that point in his story, but she's happy for him. His dad, on the other hand, looks exhausted. "You okay, Gabriel?"

"Been busy on the case."

He and his partner, Francisco, inherited the Botanist case a few years ago, after it bounced around the department when no one wanted it. They were the first to link the murders, and they found Veda's home invasion by accident while searching keywords in the other Botanist files. She told them what she remembered, but spinning facial features and the smell of raw magic still make her queasy.

Eyeing her empty bins, Gabriel asks, "Need help carrying these?"

Veda considers declining, but the desire to get everything to the truck in one trip overrides her need for independence. After signing the table and chairs back in with the farmers' market coordinator, they gather everything and leave. August leads the way to the park's exit, making up nonsensical lyrics to a familiar song.

"Everything okay?" Gabriel asks.

She avoids his questioning gaze, watching August beam at a passing couple, who grin back, enamored. His joy is contagious, but she is immune.

"Are you sure about what you told me about the latest victim?"

"We are, but she's different than I originally thought."

"I'm scared to ask."

"She sent me a stone message before she died. I haven't reported it to my superiors, and I don't think I will."

Veda has trust issues for a long list of reasons, but Gabriel is as by the book as an investigator can be. His doubt is concerning. "Let me guess, you distrust your department as much as I do?"

"No . . . Well . . ." Gabriel shrugs. "My superiors have turned a blind eye to our investigation, so I don't want to introduce anything that might pique their interest."

"Sounds like you've got something."

"I might, I think." Gabriel looks around as if there's someone eavesdropping. "Do you know anything about trickster pendants?"

"Aside from the basics, I know they don't conceal cursed marks."

Fissures bloom bloodred, and a trickster wears the face of a friend.

Clinton's words can't be a coincidence. "You suspect the Botanist has one. Meaning . . ."

"The Botanist could look like anyone." Gabriel sounds excited, but all Veda feels is stony resolution. Distrusting everyone has never felt more justified. Still, validation tastes like bile. Memories yank her back to the night she was cursed. She shuts her eyes, head moving as if she's scanning the pages of a book, only they're her memories. Clouded from panic-induced adrenaline, fractured from flashes of pain, heavy from the pressure of a heart beating too fast. Veda turns inward to pull herself free, but instead sinks into the floodwaters of emotion. Absorbed in finality, she chokes on hopelessness, grasping for anything to drag her to safety.

This time, it's the pressure of Gabriel's hand on her jacket, concern in his eyes.

When she gasps, he asks, "Are you okay?"

"I'm fine." She waves him off. "I was just . . . Don't worry about it."

He doesn't listen to her. He never does. "Case aside, if you need to talk . . ."

"I'm good. Go on."

After a pause, he does. "I suspect the victim knew it was stolen and possibly the culprit, just like I think she knew what was coming and planned accordingly."

"She knew she was going to die?"

Gabriel shrugs. "I can't imagine knowing that kind of thing and continuing to live like nothing is happening. I—"

"Look, Dad!" August yells, pointing. "The poofies are still here! They're almost as tall as me!"

Veda looks past the gleeful boy. Her breath hitches. Spider lilies spring from the asphalt's cracks. Unlike in the forest, these glow with an eerie, unnatural hue, brightening by the second. A timer ticking down.

"Come here, August," Gabriel calmly instructs.

The boy's joy vanishes as he throws a worried glance at his dad. A small crowd is already gathering. More people join, whispering.

"It's okay. You're safe," Gabriel assures his son, eyes flicking to a man reaching toward the long stamens. "No one touch anything." His voice rises with authority. "Everyone, *back away*. This is Omnipotent magic. It's erratic and highly volatile."

The man nearly falls over himself stumbling back in alarm. August rushes to his dad's side. The last thing Veda hears before tuning out the world is Gabriel on the phone, calling for a team. It's not hot, barbed terror that rises in her chest but cold confirmation. This is a warning. The shift in the Cosmos.

Suddenly, Gabriel is in front of Veda. "I need to report this to my superiors, so you need to go. I can't keep you out of this if you're here when backup arrives."

"I want to stay—"

"Your name is part of a report that is easily pulled if anyone looks hard enough. You don't need to be here, and neither does August. Take him to Peter and Khadijah's. I'll meet you there and fill you in when I'm finished."

Veda wants to argue, but logic and one look at August simmer her fight. Before backup arrives to cast an Unbreakable Line around the spider lilies, she leaves.

Four

Hiram parks in front of his parents' house. He was raised here, but it's never been home.

White brick. Black trim and shutters. Modern yet classic fixtures. Award-winning landscaping. He knows the aesthetic continues inside: clinical and impersonal. Portraits of a perfect family hang alongside expensive abstract art. Hiram knows every inch of this house, has climbed every tree, overturned every rock, and remembers the weakest points in their security talisman.

He takes the stairs two at a time. The family talisman greets him with a green glow before the door creaks open. Hiram passes the grand foyer, entrance hall, and open-plan kitchen and living room, surprised Simran is nowhere to be seen. He ventures deeper, through the archway, passing the dining room and library.

"You're picking him up early today."

His father's voice startles him. Hiram's eyes scan three points before landing on the source in the adjacent sitting room. With broad shoulders, stern features, and the advantage of height, Barrett Ellis is the kind of man who makes everything around him look small. As a child, Hiram had hoped to surpass him, but fell three inches short. Despite his presence, Barrett is quiet by choice, not nature.

Hiram follows his gaze to Antaris behind the glass wall in the sunroom examining each potted plant intensely without touching.

"How long has he been at it?" Hiram asks.

"An hour," Barrett replies. "Your mother gave up trying to engage with him. I think it's his favorite room."

"What do you mean by *engage* with him?"

His father gives him a knowing look. "She talks to him at length, shows him Arcadia Academy pamphlets, and has now taken to giving him lessons on our family history."

Shit. "Where is she now?"

"In her dressing closet, decompressing and changing for dinner. Are you still going to Los Angeles to complete your move?"

"Yes, I fly out early in the morning and return the same evening. Everything's set up, I just need to sign the last of my leave-of-absence forms from the firm and the paperwork for the movers."

"Have you told Antaris?"

"No." Hiram isn't sure how to approach the conversation. "I'll be back before he notices I'm gone."

Barrett says nothing. The television is muted, gray silk curtains drawn, lights dimmed. Although retired, his father dresses like he's still the mayor: navy dress pants, white shirt, maroon tie, and leather shoes. His graying hair is slicked back, making his widow's peak more prominent, his pale skin starker. His reading glasses are on the table next to a sweating glass of lemon water, though he prefers brandy. His quiet rebellion includes resting his feet on the coffee table, one of the many things Hiram's mother has banned.

Barrett gestures over his shoulder. "You have a few things you need to take with you."

Hiram didn't notice the boxes and shopping bags filling the back corner. "I didn't order—"

"For your house." Barrett looks like he's swallowed salt water. "You mentioned needing kitchen and bathroom essentials. Charlotte was busy. I had time."

The significance slowly dawns on Hiram. His father pays for what he wants, money is no object, but he's never had the patience to shop around.

"Gift receipts are in the bags." His gesture is not up for discussion. "I asked the housekeeper what you might need to be comfortable. She suggested silverware, dishes, cups, pots and pans, kitchen utensils, and dish towels. She also mentioned bath towels, floor mats, and facecloths. I do not remember your color preferences, so I kept my purchases neutral."

"Thank you." It's the first time Hiram has said it in over a decade.

Barrett turns to him. "It is the only thing I can do. Fatherhood is . . . I cannot give advice on something I failed at."

Sitting with the part of himself that wants to reject the gifts and agree with his father is difficult, but Hiram waits until it's buried under apathy. As a child, he studied his father's cues obsessively, always watching from the outside in. The time for heart-to-hearts has long passed. He won't soothe Barrett's guilt with false platitudes. If Barrett believes he failed as a father, then he did. Years of evidence leave Hiram incapable of saying otherwise.

"I need to go."

His father raises his glass. "Brandy before you leave?"

It's an invitation Hiram has never received. He stiffly accepts. "Make it a double."

Unsurprisingly, the brandy is smooth.

"Your mother is desperate for you to spend more time here."

"I know."

The ensuing pause gives Hiram space to admit he's torn. Despite years of silence, they still came when he needed them. No questions asked. Sometimes, he feels he owes them more of himself than he is willing to give.

"Another?" His father taps the decanter.

"No." Hiram stands, dusts off his pants, and prepares to interrupt Antaris's exploration.

He's at the sunroom door when Barrett says, "Your son will be fine. Children are resilient."

From experience, Hiram knows they're not. Not always. He nods anyway.

On the table by the door, he spots an envelope with his name on it and picks it up. There's no sender information. Hiram holds it up, frowning. "Where did this come from?"

"It was on the front step. Charlotte brought it in."

Curious, Hiram opens the envelope and unfolds the letter. The penmanship is neat and straight, despite the lack of lines. He scans the page, confused. There are only two words:

BeeyardS rain.

Dinner is a failure.

Antaris picks at everything on his plate with a pointed frown, leaving most behind in favor of sitting in the center of the empty deck in pajamas and wild, curly hair, flipping through one of Hiram's old lawbooks. He must have hauled it from the living room bookcase without Hiram noticing. It's humid after the earlier rain. Dusk, but not dark enough for the deck lights to come on. Crickets chirp. Water laps against the shore of the lake. At first, Antaris doesn't hear Hiram approach, but soon his cursory glance becomes a stare.

"May I join you?"

A small shrug is the only reply before Antaris resumes flipping the pages.

"Do you want me to read it to you?"

Antaris quickly nods. It's not much, but he'll take it. Hiram sits, noting the way Antaris tenses when he gets too close. He shifts slightly, creating space. Only then does his son relax. Both encouraged and disheartened, Hiram pushes aside his feelings and tells the kid-friendly version of the last case he used this book to win.

For a time, Hiram has Antaris's undivided attention. He recounts the case of a Seer accused of kidnapping their own child, a claim made by their spouse's bigoted family. The case seemed unwinnable, with the family testifying that their Seer nature made them a danger to their child. But Hiram found an amended law in that book, allowing him to interview the child privately; that testimony ultimately changed the outcome.

In retrospect, it's a boring story full of legal jargon Antaris won't understand. Still, having his attention feels incredible until the story concludes. That's when the lights go out in Antaris's eyes. He retreats, staring blankly at the pages, while Hiram crashes from the high of a rare normal moment between them. He waits in the never-ending silence, but nothing changes. This is the end of the road for today.

Hiram showers, trying to ignore his mounting frustration. It *is* progress, he tells himself, but the chasm between them feels deeper than ever. He's hyperaware of how badly he wants to close the distance before it's too late. When he returns, changed and dried, Antaris still sits on the deck. Ready for their nightly ritual.

Antaris wanders every night. When anxious, they're out here for hours. When upset, he sobs while Hiram looks on, helpless, unable to soothe the root of his sadness. When withdrawn, he wraps himself in a blanket that covers everything except his eyes. Hiram has several theories about the source of his son's nocturnal wanderings, but none of them are comforting. The worst scream at him when Antaris starts looking. Under the deck. Around the bushes and trees. Behind the trash bins. Out over the water. *Searching*. It's as if he's trying to find what's missing. His mother.

Hiram knows the wandering is ending when Antaris slows enough for him to catch up. Each night, Hiram offers his hand. Each time, it's met with hesitation, never acceptance.

Back inside, Hiram checks his trip itinerary, folding it neatly. The earlier conversation with his dad lingers as he knocks on Antaris's bedroom door. Antaris is already in bed, squeezing a battered stuffed rabbit, cotton spilling out, one ear gone, a button eye barely holding on. He won't let anyone fix the unfortunate thing. Hiram stopped trying two weeks ago.

Tonight, he offers the folded piece of paper. Antaris looks confused, but Hiram nudges him to take it. "It's for you."

Antaris unfolds the note, blinking at the paper.

"While you're at school, I'll be away. I'm flying to Los Angeles to finish a few things. This is when I leave, and when I will return. You can keep track of me with this, and I'll know where you are because of a spell I cast on it."

To Hiram's shock, Antaris reacts. Face flushed, breathing ragged, he hyperventilates as the hands of the clock on his nightstand spin wildly—a warning of an imminent magical accident. Hiram hesitates twice, then rests his hand on the bed.

"I'm coming back."

He has to say it three times before Antaris lifts his head, still on the verge of tears.

"I promise."

Still, it's not enough. Antaris looks away, rocking and hugging his rabbit tighter, his eyes distant. The clock spins out of control, and Hiram finds himself just as lost. How does he even begin to approach the topic of his mother, who left and never returned?

"I know it's not much, but . . ."

Fumbling for a pen, Hiram scribbles a note. A written oath he vows to never break.

I'll always come back.

Hiram keeps his promise by making it home with hours to spare, but his head is spinning from the chaos of the day.

Finalizing the shipping of his belongings was far easier than handling the last signatures to officially begin his hiatus. He reached the airport with plenty of time, only to be bombarded with calls from his uncle Robert. Apparently, Simran told him Hiram was in town, and he wanted to discuss an opportunity at the family's firm. When Robert brought Antaris into it, advising that moving firms would benefit his kid the most, Hiram told his uncle he'd rather be disbarred. Now, back home, Hiram deletes his mother's voicemails on the way to the mailbox.

The only thing inside is a card. *Gabriel Sallant. Investigator.*

Hiram almost tears the card in half before the address catches his eye. Moments later, he's en route to the investigator's downtown office. He flashes his identification at security and shows the card to the building receptionist, who mumbles, "Fourth floor," and points to the elevator.

Avoiding eye contact in the elevator is easy. He steps out to find himself face-to-face with a door marked *Federal Crime Division*. He lets himself in.

Before he can ring the bell at the secretary's desk, a woman—presumably Seren Landry, according to the precariously placed golden nameplate on the desk—pops up from behind a mountain of folders. She looks no older than thirty-five, with fair skin, a sleek blond bob, and piercing green eyes. She's dressed in black tailored pants and a white shirt, a bird amulet brooch pinned to her jacket. Folders seem more capable of withstanding a breeze than she does.

"Hey there, how can I help ya?" Her Southern accent is unexpected this far northwest.

"I'm looking for Investigator Sallant. He left this in my mailbox." Hiram holds up the card.

"That sounds like Gabriel. He's awfully dedicated to his cases."

"Dedicated?" Hiram scoffs. "More like relentless."

"I doubt the victims or their families think that's a bad thing." Seren touches a lone lavender bloom rising from the serrated leaves beside her. "The dead can't seek justice, but the living can."

She has a point.

"Who are you and what case are you here about?"

"Hiram Ellis and the Botanist."

Seren nods slowly. "Ah yes. He and Francisco were working on that one long before I joined the team. Are you giving a statement? I can find a private room for you to wait in."

"That won't be necessary."

An awkward beat follows. "Oh my goodness, I never introduced myself. I'm—" She glances at her nameplate. "Well, you already know. I'll get Gabriel for ya. Have a seat anywhere."

Hiram nods and picks a chair, checking his watch. An hour and a half left until he needs to be home for Antaris. He doesn't wait long, surreptitiously glancing at Seren while she works. Gabriel emerges first, only a few inches taller than the secretary. He's still wearing a criminal amount of plaid, but Hiram is more interested in why the hell he put the card in his mailbox.

"How can I—"

"I already said questioning my son is off-limits." Hiram slaps the card onto the secretary's desk.

"The card wasn't for him, it was for you." Gabriel gestures to the door. "Wanna talk in my office?"

"No."

Gabriel grins and turns to Seren. "Can you bring him a bottle of water?"

"Sure thing, hun."

Once Seren disappears, Hiram reluctantly follows Gabriel back to a cluttered office shared with Francisco, per the twin nameplates. Francisco's half is tidy, decorated with framed photos and a bamboo plant. Gabriel's is chaotic. Childlike drawings plaster one wall, and a rock sits on his desk with the name *August* painted on it in four different colors. Catching Hiram's stare, Gabriel shrugs. "Kids, am I right?"

Hiram doesn't understand what the hell Gabriel is implying. "What do you want?"

"I did some digging to prepare for this conversation. Grace Fowler didn't list you as next of kin, but since hers didn't arrive, you were notified and given custody of your son. Correct?"

"Yes."

"Did she have any enemies?"

"No, but she had plenty of friends you should track down and interrogate." Hiram's reply is clipped with growing irritation. Light flickers, drawing his attention to the window. It's cloudy out, the air ripe for rain. Probably lightning.

"This isn't an interrogation. I wanted to talk more about the trickster pendant. I also want to discuss more of the case, but I can't divulge too much, since you're not Grace's immediate family."

"My son is." Hiram isn't fully settled into fatherhood, but he knows he'll have difficult conversations with Antaris about his mother's murder in the future. It'll be worse if he has to explain why he didn't help with the investigation into her death. "Is he in any danger?"

"He shouldn't be, but I don't know what he's seen, if anything."

"I won't—"

"I understand."

Hiram shifts uncomfortably. "What should I tell him?"

Gabriel's shoulders sag in the silence. "That his mother fought. She lured the Botanist away from her house, likely to protect him. Right now, that's all I know. We're working hard to give you both the rest of those answers."

A strange tightness presses in Hiram's chest.

"One more question," Gabriel adds. "Are you the sun or the moon?"

Before Hiram can answer, Seren knocks on the glass and brings a bottle of water for Hiram and a message for Gabriel. He reads it and rises. "Excuse me for a minute."

Seren stays behind, tucking her blond hair behind her ear. Hiram notices the discoloration.

"It's a birthmark," she volunteers. "Wherever I go, or however I do my hair, people stare. It's better to get it out in the open, I think." She glances over her shoulder. "Oh, someone just walked up to my desk. Excuse me. Gabriel should be back soon."

Hiram ignores the water and glances around. He shouldn't snoop, but with Gabriel gone, he has a little time to satisfy his curiosity. The files on Gabriel's desk are from the Botanist case, though they don't pertain to Grace's murder. Perplexingly, the top file details a home invasion six years ago with a sticky note that has keywords like *Omnipresent magic, curse detection,* and *witness to the first Botanist killing two days before.* The photos show a violent encounter. The place looks like a bomb went off.

Discrepancies jump out immediately. The assailant's point of entry is listed as the front door, and their exit is listed as the window, which makes sense, but the splintered wood of the front door doesn't look right. Pictures of the patio door on the ground-floor apartment show no damage. It doesn't make sense. Hiram flips the page to the victim's statement and nearly drops the file when he sees a picture of the victim.

Veda.

He memorizes every angle, bruise, and cut—down to her busted lip—and scours the file for more details. Not about the case but about *her.* All pertinent information appears to be redacted, including her last name. Hiram shuts the file and leaves before Gabriel returns.

As Hiram approaches the front entrance of Weston Academy from the parking lot, a teenager on a skateboard barrels past, slapping a hand on Hiram's chest as he flies by. Disoriented, Hiram stumbles back, but when he turns around to yell at the kid, he's gone.

A coin is stuck to his shirt. Hiram pulls it off and frowns at the Standing Liberty etched in gold. He drops it, and it jumps back into his hand. He hurls it into the grass, and it flies straight back into his palm.

Shit—it's spelled. Meant for him. Irritated, Hiram walks inside and manages to charm his way into Peter's office without an appointment, only to find his best friend expecting him.

"You Saw me coming, did you?"

Peter's smile is maddeningly familiar. "A few weeks ago. I told Simran she didn't need to pick him up today because I'm taking him to the used book fair after school. He doesn't have a tutoring session. I'll bring him home if you grab dinner after your errands. Khadijah has a lot of patients and won't be home until late. We'll watch the game."

Hiram's brow raises. "Errands?"

"You're picking out an office desk, right?" Peter hands him a card. "This place is downtown off Main Street. They do great work. I told them you were coming today."

Hiram frowns at the card. "I wasn't planning to get a desk yet."

"It'll be ready when you need it."

Hiram squints at his friend. "You're having multiple visions about me again, aren't you?"

Peter gives a tight smile. "It's annoying."

To Seers, multiple visions mean a shift in the Cosmos, but the shift isn't always overt. The last time this happened was around Peter's graduation, and Hiram can't think of anything major changing now.

Peter's eyes slide to his hand. "Are you going to tell me about the coin, or . . ."

"I'd give it to you, but it's liable to take out my eye."

"The Standing Liberty symbolizes a readiness for battle, and a desire for peace," Peter rattles off, then mutters, "Of course they'd give it to you when I'm going to be busy that night."

"What does that mean?"

"Your return to town has been noticed by everyone, especially Seers. That coin gets you into our monthly town hall meeting."

"Why would they invite me? I'm an Ellis, one of the only self-aware ones who can say that my family members are some of the worst anti-Seers in the country. That hasn't changed, and it's not going to. There isn't a Seer alive who should want me anywhere near them."

Peter waves. "Excuse you, I'm right here."

Hiram laughs. "You know what I mean. Everyone gives you shit for being my friend."

"It *is* a thankless job."

"Khadijah ready to forbid you from seeing me?"

"We've argued about you four times since you returned, and she's only called you a danger to me once."

"A record low," he says. "Although I agree with her sometimes. You teeter too close to the line. My mother might begrudgingly like you, but—"

"I'm careful." Peter gets up to make them peppermint tea. "Might need a lawyer down the road, if you're up to it."

Hiram doesn't think twice. "I'll start the process."

"Good. As for the coin, my advice is either figure out why you were invited or keep getting accosted with more enchanted coins."

"Fantastic." Hiram rolls his eyes.

"Aren't you curious?"

"No."

Peter makes a small, throaty noise. "Then you're accepting the status quo, but doing that only breeds complacency, which is a dangerous mentality given your proximity to your mother."

Hiram rolls his eyes. "I'm not curious because I don't have the bandwidth to give a damn about anything else."

"That, *and* you've always hated the pressure that comes with being challenged. You know what's right and what's wrong, and hate expending the energy you need to hold people accountable."

Peter isn't wrong, and Hiram can't stand it. Silence overtakes the room but doesn't last.

"Do you have any remedies for nightmares? I have back pain from sleeping on Antaris's floor."

Peter tilts his head. "There's a story here."

"It's been the only solution to keep his nightmares from spiraling out of control these past few nights."

"What does his therapist say?"

"I shouldn't expect improvement this soon."

This earns Hiram his first sidelong glance from Peter. "What do *you* think?"

"I'm not sure," Hiram admits.

"You're the most decisive person I know."

He isn't wrong. Sighing, Hiram lets the first thought escape unchecked. "I'd fire Dr. Kidane just to spite my mother for hiring him. Is that the right decision? I'm not sure, but I do know he's the highest-rated child therapist in the area."

"But is he the best?" Peter presses. "They don't allow Seers on those lists. I've mentioned Antaris to a few Seer therapists I know in the area. They're interested in his case, if you change your mind."

"You already know how my mother would react. I'm keeping the peace."

"How peaceful is it, really, if your decision is at your son's expense?"

Hiram winces. "Are you going to lecture me or tell me how he's doing in school?"

"He's struggling, but not academically." Peter's expression shifts. "You know, I've been meaning to apologize for how he ended up with a tutor."

"Don't worry about it. I trust you."

"I can vouch for her. She—"

"Oh, I've heard," Hiram says dismissively. "I'm giving my mother three strikes, and she's already used one by overstepping with this tutor. I left her once, I can do it again."

"Is that why your house looks like a staged listing?" Peter gives him a knowing look. "I don't think I've asked how you are in all of this."

No one has, but his feelings don't matter. "My focus is on Antaris."

"Grace meant something to you, too."

"A long time ago."

After meeting through mutual friends, Hiram can count on one hand how many conversations they had before sleeping together. Sporadically at first, then more often. After two years of casually dating long distance, he moved to New York City, hoping to build something lasting.

Obviously, it didn't.

A world without Grace is nothing new; she's been gone from his life longer than she was in it. Still, her death *was* a shock. There was no guide to help him navigate how he felt in the aftermath. Over the last few months, he's wondered if she would have ever told him about Antaris. But her stone message answered that. She'd planned to take his existence to her grave.

It hurt like hell to learn he hadn't earned the trust he'd given her so easily. But Hiram isn't angry. Just determined to prove her wrong.

"I'm fine. I'd rather hear your ideas about keeping my mother at bay."

Peter snorts. "No, you wouldn't. Because I'll tell you that keeping the peace is easier than preparing for war, yet sometimes, war is necessary to find peace."

"Smart-ass." Hiram lets the sage comment marinate.

"Come on, let's see if I can find anything to help with nightmares." Peter leads the way into the storage room full of potions, ingredients, and student creations organized on three and a half walls of floor-to-ceiling shelving, complete with a rolling ladder.

While Peter searches, Hiram whistles low, spotting a dark jar labeled *luminescent moss*. "Let me guess, you've arranged everything alphabetically, by state of matter, and purpose."

Peter's scowl tells Hiram everything he needs to know. He chuckles and returns the jar to its place.

"Surely you came to do more than vent and ask for a tonic you could have bought from an apothecary," Peter says, holding out a vial. "This was made by our brewing instructor. One drop a night works wonders on Mages."

In places like Proventia, there's always one person who knows more than most. Peter has made it his business to fill that role, even among upper-class Mages who dismiss Seers. Hiram decides to try his luck.

"What ever happened to your friend from college? What was her name again?" He snaps his fingers, pretending to think. "Veda, right? I saw her at your grad party and asked her name to look her up. You said she was dating someone . . ." Hiram trails off, rolling his hand as if trying to prompt Peter's memory.

One blond brow rises. "Veda? Well, yeah. I still talk to her, obviously. You know she's—"

"This FCD investigators asked me some questions about Grace's case. Apparently, Grace was a victim of a serial killer called—"

"The Botanist," Peter finishes. "Did Grace ever come to Proventia?"

"Not that I know of. Why? What does this have to do with Veda?"

"Tell me what happened at the FCD."

Hiram frowns. "Investigator Sallant keeps the Botanist files on his desk," he explains. "When he stepped out of the room, I happened to see one of them. I thought it would be Grace's file, since she's the latest victim, but it was a report from a home invasion six years ago. Veda's. Did you know about that?"

Peter blinks as if Hiram has done something horrible. "I did, but let's circle back to *happened to see*. You were breaking the law by looking at confidential investigation files on a serial killer that's been on the loose for six years."

"Details." Hiram waves him off. "Did you know that two days after she witnessed the first Botanist killing, the killer broke into her apartment and she fought them off?"

"It's more complicated than that, but that's her story, not mine." He pats Hiram's shoulder. "Soon enough, you'll know everything . . ."

It doesn't take Hiram long to choose the shape and finish of his desk. On the way back to his car, he's too preoccupied with deciding what to order for dinner to pay much attention. Head down, he walks without looking. The first two times he hears approaching footsteps, he glances up. The third, he doesn't. Disoriented, he stumbles.

A bike helmet hits the pavement. Apologies tumble out as he stoops to pick it up. "Pardon me, I wasn't paying—"

"Sorry."

Hiram blinks, needing a second to confirm what he instantly knows. Of course it's Veda.

Much like at Nénuphar, she looks strikingly different, but this time he's close enough to see her properly. Dark jeans, a plain red shirt, black leather jacket, and riding gloves. Unremarkable for the season, yet there's a coldness to her, a fierceness like grazing steel. He spies her necklace; the amulet's eye catches the light with a brief glint before fading. It's strange seeing it outside of ink, but his artist did it justice. Most amulets are made with diamonds or rubies, the hardest gemstones by magical standards, but hers is a sapphire. Seeing the imperfections up close makes it clear her amulet was crafted specifically for her.

Hiram knows he should walk away, but the urge to speak overrides common sense. "Do we know each other?"

He expects Veda to play along, as people do, but she surprises him. "I don't know, *do we?*"

No recognition. Understandable. Peter's party was years ago, and they were never introduced. What's more puzzling is that she doesn't seem to recognize him from the cave—at least, not his face. Veda takes her helmet from his hand, her cautious annoyance disarming. Equally dismaying is the stark contrast between who she once was and who she appears to be now.

Honesty is the best policy. "I was the man swimming in Nénuphar."

Veda tilts her head. "The one with my amulet tattooed on him."

"The tattoo artist drew their vision on me. No explanation. I didn't want to know."

She remains suspicious. "And Nénuphar?"

"I've known about it since I was ten. I only told one person, and you know him. Peter Weston."

She rolls her eyes. "Peter knows too many people."

"It's a pleasure to finally meet you, Veda," Hiram drawls, extending a hand politely.

She doesn't accept. Instead, she scans the area. For witnesses or help, Hiram isn't sure. She closes like a fist, and the chance for a surface-level conversation vanishes. "Who *are* you? How do you know me? Why are you following me?"

Hiram's reaction to her volley of questions sparks visible aggravation in Veda, which bleeds into his own frustration. "I'm not following you, but if I'd known you'd be so damn paranoid, I wouldn't have said your name."

She recoils like one would from an exposed flame. She barely reaches his shoulders, but the magic wafting from her amulet feels immense. He's never felt a regulated amulet this strong, which means it's like his onyx amulet ring: *illegal*. "What's *your* name?"

"Why?"

"Quid pro quo."

Hiram's irritation stalls, and he can't figure out why. "Hiram Ellis. Two *L*'s."

Veda's scowl softens into cold suspicion. There it is: a spark of the sharp woman he remembers.

"Ellis? Interesting." His name rolls off her tongue like a curse. It's not the first time he's heard it said that way, but something about *her* scrutiny unsettles him in a way he can't describe.

"Just like it's interesting that you're walking around freely when the person who tried to kill you is still out there," he retorts.

It's the wrong thing to say, and Hiram knows it. Proving him right, Veda's amulet flares, its sapphire eye glowing brighter, poised to cut him down with a single spell. It's unlike him to play with fire, but there's pretense blazing in her eyes. She isn't defensive, she's *frightened*. Fear distorts the world, twisting caution into perceived threat. Hiram keeps this in mind when Veda puts distance between them, then turns sharply on her boots. She doesn't run to her bike, but it's a close thing. Without sparing a thought for the consequences to his own safety, Hiram follows.

"They think the Botanist has a pendant that changes their appearance. Did you notice any of their features blurring? Were they wearing—"

"I don't remember *anything*."

Hiram doesn't believe her. "Where did they enter your apartment? Your file lists the door and the window, but the door looks blown outward, and your window was broken. Yet the patio door, the only undamaged entrance, was unlocked."

Veda whirls on him, fury and fear erupting in tandem. "Oh, so *you're* an investigator now? Tracking me down to interrogate me?"

Hiram searches her face, his expression even. This wasn't his plan, but each question births more. The most pressing of all rattles in his brain. "They say they have no leads. But they do. A survivor. *You*. There's a reason you're still alive."

Veda goes still for a moment, then hardens. "Stay *out* of my file and *away* from me, or else I'll—"

"If you were going to use magic on me, you would've already." He grips her handlebar, forcing her to look at him. "We're on the same side."

"I'll be the judge of that."

Hiram raises his hands. "I'll leave the questions to the investigators if you'll have a conversation with me. We have the same goal: catching the Botanist."

Before he can say another word, Veda shoves on her helmet, turns the key, and revs her bike. Her parting shot is a single raised middle finger.

Five

Since finding the spider lilies in the forest, everything that's happened adds up to too much of a coincidence for Veda to ignore. She sits down with Dr. Simpson's note, a pen, and a bowl of Ruth's clam chowder.

19114721919

It irritates Veda that she can't make sense of the riddle. Eleven digits. Not a phone number, but a message with too many combinations. She's on her third attempt at decoding, about to give up, when she flips it over and stares at the numbers on the back.

22541. BBEDA.

Veda stops.

Instead of reading the letters individually, she combines the first two.

The twenty-second letter of the alphabet is *V.*

Veda.

Now she's invested. She sits down at the table, making dozens of guesses, filling in letters until one finally forms a word she recognizes.

19-1-14-7-21-9-19

Sanguis.

Blind to everything except her destination, Veda runs out the door. Trees dwarf her on all sides, casting odd shadows in the setting sun. The air is charged with an electric expectancy. She stumbles, trying to catch her breath and ease the burn in her chest, but doesn't stop until she clears the tree line outside Weston Academy.

Sunset makes the world look peaceful, but Veda is not as she searches each barn and animal unit until she finds Dr. Simpson. He's kneeling, checking a sheep's hoof, but her arrival brings him to his full height. "What are you doing here?"

"I decoded your note," Veda replies, stone-faced and breathing heavily. "What the *hell* do you know about Sanguis?"

Everett tenses, then picks up his bag and leaves the sheep pen. Veda steps back, more so when he rubs his neck, choosing his words carefully. "I know the Sanguis Curse is in you."

"How?"

"Your marks. The potions Everly brews. She can't always find living sheep's horn powder, so she asks me. I . . ." He points to her, starts to say more, but shudders instead, fists curling at his sides. "Curses of the blood are difficult to cast, easy to contaminate, and difficult to cure. But nothing is impossible."

Hope sparks where resignation once reigned. Still skeptical, torn between listening and leaving, she stays rooted. "How do you know this?"

"*Mine* is incurable. It looks nothing like yours."

Veda recoils. "You're cursed?"

"Something like that," Everett replies cryptically. "There's no name for what was done to me. Not a curse, not a malediction, more like a cage. The closer I get to telling a certain truth, the further I descend into madness. Truth is both my liberator and captor."

Horrified, Veda wants to ask who did this to him, but she's sure he can't answer. "Can it be undone?"

"No." He winces, dropping his bag and clutching his side. "I can't say more."

"Does anyone else know?"

"You . . . and the person who cursed me." Everett dry heaves, covering his mouth, eyes flashing red before he closes them tight.

"Your eyes." Veda steps back. "Is that part of the curse?"

"Yes," he replies shakily. "I Saw their real face in a vision. I found them. They promised to turn themselves in, but I woke up cursed."

"You could run."

"That's what they wanted me to do, but I can't. I've Seen what's coming. I'll never be free until everyone knows the truth." He wipes his bleeding nose, bitterly murmuring, "Past. Present. Future. *Birth. Life. Death.* They don't care for natural order and disrespect the rules of Sight."

"I can't believe I'm saying this, but you should go to the FCD and—"

"No," Everett snaps. "The sheep is a wolf."

She has no idea what that means. "I don't trust many people, but Gabriel and Francisco can help you. I can call them now, and we can meet outside the department."

"Not yet. Tell them if you must, but I have a few last things to do."

Veda can't imagine what could be more important. She pulls out her phone, only for Everett to tense. "What is it?"

"The one who cursed you is trapped and does not yet know it. *You* are their answer and also their downfall." Everett drops to his knees, head hanging as blood drips onto his shirt. The shift in him is alarming. His shoulders stiffen, veins appear, sweat beads at his hairline. He pants and trembles violently.

"Are you—"

"I'm fine!" he explodes suddenly, head jerking, eyes burning red.

Veda backs away until she hits the wall.

"Sorry, sorry," Everett rasps. "I . . . You need to know. The trickster flies."

Dr. Simpson is gone by the time Gabriel and Francisco arrive.

"One second he was there, and the next, I was alone." Veda paces from one side of the barn to the other while Gabriel writes down everything she remembers from her conversation with Everett. Peter and

Khadijah, having just finished searching the grounds with Francisco, approach, shaking their heads.

"Gone," they say as one.

"I doubt he'll come in tomorrow," Peter adds, looking around once more. "I have his personnel stone in my office. The information is up to date."

The walk inside is quiet until Peter hands over the stone.

"Thank you," Francisco says. "If he turns up, call us, but don't approach him yourself."

Gabriel leans against the wall. "We need to talk about the Oracle Council. They're ignoring my inquiries."

"My uncle thinks they're hiding something," Khadijah says.

Gabriel scoffs. "Obviously."

"We've tried to speak with them plenty of times during other investigations—the attacks on Seers, the false arrests, even when we told them about the Botanist. But it's been crickets. I'm surprised Clinton wants to help."

"Can you blame them?" Khadijah asks. "Seers haven't had a reason to trust the FCD since its inception. The wounds run deep. Despite my uncle's efforts to bridge the gap, the Council prefers to handle things internally."

"You need to change their minds, especially now that we have clear signs of the Botanist being here. There wasn't a body with those spider lilies, but after what Dr. Simpson said, I'm convinced they were a warning. The Council needs to get on board, preferably before another member is killed."

This perks Veda up. "Every victim was on the Council?"

"The last few tried to scrub themselves from existence, but yes. All of them, except the one in London. She had no ties to Washington state."

"Then you should assume she had a tie to the Botanist."

Francisco sighs. "We're still combing through her friends. There are a lot, and I'm not finished. So far, they've agreed to help. Based on what Everett told you, I know you're going to decline, but I think you should consider protection."

"I'd sooner invite the Botanist to my house for dinner." Veda folds her arms. "I trust Gabriel mostly, you partly, and the FCD not at all."

"Partly?" Francisco sulks. "I thought we were better than that."

"You don't curse, and you're too calm," she replies. "Not cursing is inauthentic, and calm men are suspicious. Well, except Peter, who internalizes everything. I don't make the rules."

Peter doesn't dignify Veda with a response, while Khadijah snickers.

"I have dozens of young nieces, nephews, and cousins who repeat everything," Francisco argues. "Also, *someone* has to balance out Gabriel. He's either too patient with suspects or too friendly with witnesses."

A fair point.

Gabriel stands straighter. "How did *I* get dragged into this?"

They ignore him.

Francisco checks his watch. "We'll examine the personnel stone, get what we need, and go to Dr. Simpson's house tonight. If he doesn't answer, we'll talk to his neighbors and family. How long has he been working here?"

"A year," Peter replies.

"His mom plays bingo with Ruth, from the Oracle Council," Veda recalls.

The investigators exchange a look.

"Another link," Gabriel mutters. "We need to talk to him ourselves—quietly. He already doesn't trust us. He hasn't done anything wrong, so the last thing we need is this getting out and the commander sending the entire FCD after a Seer cursed to go mad if he tells a truth we don't yet know."

"And a lot of spell-happy investigators and bigots who'd love finding him," Francisco adds, then turns back to Veda. "Think about my offer."

"I won't."

Veda spends the next morning harvesting, the afternoon assembling orders for wholesale customers, and every spare minute in between completing payroll. She can't risk idleness; it's a one-way trip to anxiety. The Botanist's arrival means years of wondering what will happen to her are finally approaching a conclusion. Good or bad, at least it'll be over.

Before she knows it, the school day is ending, and it's time to find Antaris. He's in an empty classroom, staring at a piece of paper that looks like it's been folded and unfolded multiple times.

"Hi."

Antaris jolts, quickly shoving it into his pocket. Veda pretends not to notice. It's their fifth session, and she's learning more about him each day. He prefers the outdoors, always carries the same note, rarely eats his packed lunch, and usually finishes his workbook assignments before the school day ends.

He also likes choosing what they do. Today, he opts to sit on the steps and watch the chickens scuttle about in the pasture. It's hard to decipher his mood, so Veda watches for signs of distress.

"How was your day?" she asks.

He startles again, as if he's forgotten something. After rummaging through his pockets and the book bag between them, he finds the folded paper. Up close, Veda sees it's fraying, but he covets it nonetheless. Antaris catches her looking and puts it back in his pocket.

"It's not my business unless you want me to see." Veda offers her finger. "I have something I need to do. Want to help me?"

Antaris taps twice. *Yes.*

She leads the way to the kitchens. Antaris looks around in awe. She offers him a strawberry as a test and is surprised when he accepts. While he eats, Veda gets an idea.

"What else do you like?" she asks. "Will you show me?"

The hesitance Antaris always carries is present, but after a reassuring thumbs-up, he explores the kitchen, not touching anything, only pointing, eyes wide, glancing at Veda. He's asking for help.

As it turns out, Antaris likes a lot of food.

Veda finds a pen and paper to make a list, but from what she gathers, he enjoys fresh fruit, crunchy vegetables, and sandwiches with no crusts. Unsurprisingly, he has a sweet tooth, but is more curious about candy than familiar with it. She hides a smile when he makes faces at food that touches, even incidentally. He's not the only child who dislikes anything mashed or is picky about meat, but his squinty side-eyes make it hard to not laugh.

With each nod, Antaris's list grows alongside her spirits. It's strange how time with him has become a balm after long days. Stranger still is how quickly the lights dim in his eyes when his grandmother arrives. Veda hands the list to Simran, ready to share the success of the day, but Simran simply skims the paper, makes a dismissive noise, and pockets it. It might have been a *thank you*.

Veda watches them leave, frowning all the way to the greenhouse. The image of a stone-faced child glancing back at her once before climbing into the car plagues her until a voice cuts through the quiet.

"I thought you'd be out here."

Thoughts scatter in all directions. She whips her head to Peter. "You scared me."

"Sorry," he says, sheepish. "I saw Simran leave with Antaris and thought you'd come back here. After last night, I'd suggest taking the day off, because I can tell you didn't sleep, but you'll ignore me. Or cuss me out . . . again."

She considers both options but is too tired for either. "My thoughts are loud today."

Peter steps back as she stands up. "Come with me."

"The last time I followed you, I ended up with a mentee." Still, she dusts off her hands on her jeans and follows him into the pasture.

"Everything going okay with Antaris?"

"Each day I learn something new," Veda replies, rattling off what she's learned, including the food list and how he likes being read to. "He was the only one who actually sat and listened during story time."

"There's no doubting genetics." When she gives Peter a funny look, he adds, "His dad was that way, too, always had his nose in a book. He shipped his entire library separately when they moved here. I think he values it more than his clothes."

"Is he involved?"

"With Antaris? Yes. He has primary custody."

Veda frowns. "I've only seen Simran with him."

"They have an agreement. She does pickups and drop-offs. He's with Antaris the rest of the time. He'll appreciate that list."

"We went through so many options. I could tell whether he liked or hated something just by his expression. I'd say he's unfurling like a cat. Keeps watching me like one."

"Anxiety?"

"Definitely. He's in therapy, right?"

"Yeah, but that's a topic for another day."

Veda nods, eyes on the path ahead. "He draws sometimes."

Peter perks up. "What does he draw?"

"Doodles on his workbooks and scrap paper. I think one was a cat. Another might have been a flower. A tree and a boat. A house?"

Peter appears amused. "Noted."

The days are getting longer, but a cloudy gray sky hides the sun. Their decision to leave the school grounds is silent and easy. The forest, lush and green, grows increasingly narrow. Veda considers turning back, not for herself, but for Peter, who is dressed in nice pants and a gray shirt, his white tennis shoes unsuitable for walking in the forest.

"Tomorrow marks six years since Khadijah bound my curse."

Peter's apprehension resurrects every bit of tension Veda temporarily freed herself from in the greenhouse. "I should make a not-dead-yet cake, but that's morbid, even for me."

"Not if it's vanilla." His smile belies his otherwise somber demeanor. "They haven't found Everett," he continues. "I was thinking about your file and—"

"My file? The same one your *friend*, Mr. Ellis with two *L*'s, has seen," she cuts in, scoffing as she climbs over a felled tree.

Peter bursts out laughing, then sobers under her glare. "Oh, you're pissed. But in his defense, he's part of the investigation."

That *Hiram Ellis*, of all people, has anything to do with the Botanist case is beyond absurd. Since all the victims are Seers, it took years for even a single article to be published. The little public awareness they've gained hasn't produced any real leads.

"Who is he to you?" she asks.

Peter looks uncharacteristically surprised by the question. "My mom worked for his family. When she realized he was just a lonely, misguided kid, she brought me to play with him. I hated him when we first met, but over time, I saw he didn't have the charmed life I assumed. Prejudice is taught, not innate. We became friends, and he figured out his family—"

"Are *horrible* people," she interjects. "Beautiful story of friendship forming from the pits of hell, but you're a Seer and friends with an *Ellis*. That entire family is infesting the government, using their wealth to get elected into positions where they make life harder for you, my parents when they were alive, and everyone you care about. Why didn't you say anything about your link to them?"

"It's complicated."

"Does Khadijah know?"

"Yes, she knows. Hates it, we used to argue about it early on in our relationship, but it's been a nonissue until he returned. The Oracle Council knows, too." Peter glances away and sighs. "I get it. The Ellis family caused a lot of generational harm. They're the worst of everything you can imagine."

"An understatement. Your friend's grandfather argued for harsh laws and penalties against Seers. His father came up with automating the Registration and tied it to a Seer's Imprint. The Ellis firm defends corporations nationwide that prey on desperate Seers, working them under horrible conditions and draining their magic like fodder. The fact that anyone in that family even knows my name pisses me off more than anything."

"I apologized for that." Peter levels her with a look, then sighs. "My mom managed to stop Hiram's parents from sending him to Arcadia Academy until she quit to start Weston Academy when he was in year six. He left and barely returned."

"Am I supposed to empathize?"

"Wouldn't dream of it," he fires back, rolling his eyes. "*But* . . . it takes a lot to realize everything you were taught is hateful and wrong. It takes even more to actively rebel and separate yourself from it. Hiram did both, refusing to work for their law firm. He spent years away, and—"

"Now he's come home to Mommy and Daddy." Veda sits on a wide tree stump, completely unconvinced. "Tale as old as time."

"It's not what you think. *I* was the one who convinced him to tentatively accept their olive branch and move back. It was the quickest way to secure custody of his son. If Hiram had his way, he never would've returned. Proventia isn't a happy place for him. His father was absent at best. And his mother . . . well, you've met Simran, she's—"

"*What?*" Veda balks. "*Simran?* So Antaris is—"

"Hiram's son."

Veda's jaw falls open. "And you didn't tell me this earlier because . . ."

"I'd rather you didn't judge Antaris for a family he wasn't raised in."

"He's a *child*," she snaps. "Do you think that little of me?"

"No, I don't. But you've got tunnel vision. You judged *me* for knowing the Ellis family, and you've judged Hiram without knowing *him*."

"I know enough."

Peter looks unimpressed. "You're better than this."

"And so are you. Simran's only compliment about you was that you're *not like other Seers*. She sees you as a convenience, not a person, and worse, *you let her*. People like her don't change."

"Perhaps not, but I choose to hope, because giving up is not an option." Peter sits beside her, silent for a moment as the air between them settles. "I didn't let Simran treat me like anything, I just know how she is. Play her game, let her think she's winning, and she'll do what you want. That's how I got Antaris enrolled in Weston versus a different Mage-only school across town. I'd rather have him here, where I can keep an eye on him, and help Hiram sort through all this."

"But—"

"Antaris is my godson for a reason. If anything happens to Hiram, the *last* people he wants to raise his son are his parents. He filed guardianship papers the moment he arrived." Peter looks up as a bird flies overhead. "It's not my place to explain to you who Hiram is. That's for you to decide, though it sounds like you already have."

Veda snorts. "I sure have."

Peter shakes his head, faintly amused. "Trust me, he's not the enemy."

"He's not a friend, either."

Veda's cottage is her fortress. Magic shields it from the outside world. Here, behind her walls, there's no need to hide. The bricks keep her secrets, the mirrors see her pain. Living here is simultaneously comforting and suffocating.

After her talk with Peter, Veda returns to her fortress, sheds her jacket, peels off her shirt, careful of her cursed scars, and opens the window to let in a breeze to cool her inflamed skin. Too uncomfortable to apply salve herself, Veda throws on an oversized shirt and shuffles into the kitchen. Half-molding leftovers means she has only one option for dinner: noodles.

Her talisman activates, glowing a hazy orange. Someone is here, and she isn't expecting guests. Veda flips the porch light on and peers through the peephole, relaxing at the sight of white braids and a familiar face.

Veda opens the door. "I thought you were busy."

"Change of plans," Khadijah says. "Peter is having dinner with his best friend and godson tonight, Marlene blew me off again, so I thought I'd come check on you."

"Glad to know I'm your third option."

"What do you mean? I've saved the best for last." Khadijah removes her shoes and wanders into the kitchen. She looks fresh from meditation, dressed in sweatpants, a T-shirt, and wearing a serene expression, at least until she realizes what Veda is cooking. "Noodles? You're supposed to be eating a lot more than this. Your curse consumes energy, even in its dormant state with the block on it. You need to eat enough to keep your strength."

"These are nutrient-dense noodles. They have everything I need."

"And bland. How you survive on the bare minimum, I'll never understand."

"It's quick, and I don't need more than what I have."

Khadijah's expression turns somber. "I wish you knew how wrong you are."

The water boils. Time to add the noodles.

"Add a pack for me, too, and I'll boil an egg. What else do you have to throw in?"

Veda doesn't know why she asks—Khadijah does what she wants anyway. Twenty minutes later, they're sitting at the table in Veda's favorite room. The solarium is four glass panels long, four wide, with four overhead. It's cramped, large enough for a love seat and a small table, but the scenery is unmatched. Tonight, the fairy lights are on, casting a soft glow over their plates.

They eat mostly in silence. Veda won't admit it, but Khadijah's added frozen vegetables, eggs, and spices have elevated the meal.

"How are you?" Khadijah asks.

"Surprised you're here, but given the timing between my talk with Peter about his best friend and your arrival, I'm expecting a lecture."

"Eh, we don't agree about Hiram, so . . ." She shrugs.

"How are things with the clinic?" Veda asks.

Khadijah is a healer who runs a clinic funded by Seer community donations and a quarter of the profits from her bar, Olive. It's vital in a city where hospitals may employ Seers but won't treat them. Instead, sick or injured Seers are directed to Khadijah's clinic. Medical segregation is frowned upon in more liberal cities. Proventia *is* changing, albeit slowly, but many still cling to archaic beliefs: Seers have a higher pain tolerance, are immune to certain diseases, and overburden resources due to higher potion and elixir needs. None of this is true, but facts don't matter to bigots.

"We've made enough profit at Olive to order new beds and restock potions with ingredients you can't forage. The bar runs itself, so I've been focusing more on the clinic. Peter's still looking for a doctor to brew as many potions and elixirs in-house as possible, and he sells spare herbs from Weston. We got a grant from a pro-Seer group for new equipment. Might bring in another healer to handle emergencies so we're not making house calls all night."

Only Seers can be healers, and they do the heavy lifting in health care. With their infinite wells of magic, it's one of the few places they can use incantations and spells to cure as many ails as possible. Doctors, the Mage equivalent to healers, pull up the rear by handling smaller crises and brewing and administering all potions, draughts, and elixirs.

Before Veda became interested in medicine, she believed the relationship between healers and doctors was lopsided—Seers did all the work, and doctors got the glory. But in medical school, under the tutelage of some of the best doctors and healers in the country, she learned the truth: It was mostly symbiotic. Simply put, Seers heal from the inside out, while doctors heal from the outside in. There was mutual respect on both sides.

"Have you been going to Nénuphar?"

"I went yesterday," Veda replies. *Fortunately, there were no tattooed men swimming around this time,* she adds silently.

"Good. The healing waters won't cure your curse, but regular soaks will ease the symptoms." Khadijah gets up. "Let me look."

Veda sighs and takes off her shirt.

"You suck at putting on salve," Khadijah chastises as she retrieves the salve. Veda jolts from the cooling sensation, then relaxes as the earlier irritation fades.

"I can't reach everything."

"Then ask."

Stubbornness won't allow her. A brush of warmth is all Veda feels of Khadijah's diagnostic spell. "How is it looking?"

"Good enough. The curse is still dormant. The cyst hasn't gotten any larger." All good news, but Khadijah sighs, her expression tightening with guilt. "I wonder if the Botanist figured out the mistake they made when they cursed you and tracked you down, with the spider lilies at the park serving as a warning."

"Why warn me if they want to kill me?"

"Maybe what Everett said has some truth. You're an answer."

"To what question?"

"We need to figure that out." Khadijah helps Veda with her shirt. "I'm glad I was able to save you, but I wish it hadn't meant trapping Sanguis inside you. I haven't done what I promised and figured out a safe way to get it out."

"You and Peter have done everything you can. I appreciate it."

Khadijah gives her a meaningful look. "Don't negate your own participation. You figured out the blood in the cyst isn't yours and hypothesized that it belongs to the person who cursed you, the Botanist."

"Yeah, but we can't test it or find their name." Cursed blood never spills. It can't be extracted willingly or by force. Veda chuckles darkly at the irony of having the identity of a serial killer trapped inside her, but there's nothing she can do about it except wait for the dam to break and see who drowns with her.

"At least we know they have a matching mark, and now they're probably in town."

"That narrows it down. Like finding a weed in a pasture."

"Not really," Khadijah replies darkly. "I imagine they'll find you before you find them. They at least know who they're looking for."

"True." Veda sighs. "I'm just ready for this to be over."

They stare at one another until Khadijah softly asks, "Are you ready to die?"

The question is an open wound, another truth Veda refuses to face. She's exhausted. In the quiet, when she's most terrified and overwhelmed, she *is* ready. But when someone cares, even a little, she hesitates.

"I need to believe this curse has a purpose beyond killing me. If enough of their blood is cursed, they'll die with me when this block fades. I'm willing to make that sacrifice."

Khadijah looks away, visibly stricken. "We can keep trying to get it out safely."

"You have another idea we haven't already tried?"

"Not yet." She folds her arms. "You don't have to be a hero, Veda."

"Not trying to be. But we've tried everything. Exhausted all known research. Connections can't get us anywhere. There's nothing left except to cause as much damage on my way out as possible."

Khadijah hugs her in silent comfort. Veda almost says something self-deprecating to lighten the mood, but instead, she drops the act and holds on tighter, longer than she means to, before pulling away and blurting, "I need a drink."

All she has is a half-full bottle of wine. They sit out back, facing the dark forest, passing it between them in a companionable silence.

"You're allowed to be upset about what's happening," Khadijah says, finally breaking the silence. "You don't always have to keep your head high while you suffer in silence."

"I do," Veda replies softly. "If I stop, I'll drown. It's self-preservation."

"Self-preservation isn't always about holding on through every storm."

"That's all I know how to do."

Six

As the doleful cry of chaotic magic swirls about, doors rattle and floorboards creak. The scent of worms and driftwood permeates the air, intensifying as the walls weep tears that vanish before they touch the floor.

Antaris's nightmares are getting worse.

Hiram can do nothing but watch as his son, drenched through his clothes and shivering, tosses and turns. He won't let Hiram near. Each attempt to approach his son is blocked by a magical wall. Still, Hiram refuses to leave, standing guard, waiting for the barrier to vanish. Tonight, it takes only minutes. Antaris wakes up mid-gasp. The barrier pops like a bubble. The stench of magic fades, and for the first time in hours, silence settles. The urge to do something, anything, overpowers the advice he's been given: *Go at his pace. Be present. Give him space when he needs it.*

Hiram kneels beside the bed, grabs the fallen rabbit, and puts it gently in Antaris's arms. He hugs it tightly as Hiram places a tentative hand on his back.

"*Breathe.*"

Antaris's breaths race on.

There's more he wants to say: that he's okay, that he doesn't need to worry. Empty platitudes won't form, but truth does. "I can tell you're scared, and that's okay. I'll stay here, if you want."

He repeats it until Antaris loosens his death grip on the rabbit. Antaris lies back down, owl-wide eyes fixed on him. Hiram makes a quick decision.

"Just a second, okay?"

Antaris's expression morphs into alarm.

"I'm coming back."

Hiram moves quickly, first to the kitchen for a glass of water, then to his bedroom for a blanket and pillow. When he returns, Antaris is sitting up, holding the rabbit and a folded piece of paper. Hiram recognizes it immediately. *He still has the itinerary?* Confusion flickers into something warm as Hiram drops the pillow on the floor and spreads the blanket before sitting. Only then does Antaris lie back down on his side, blinking at Hiram.

"I told you I'll always come back."

It takes half an hour for the twitch in Antaris's lip to stop, and another hour for him to finally sleep. Only when his son's breathing deepens does Hiram lie down on the blanket beside the bed. He checks his phone and notices one missed call from John, Grace's stepfather. Needing someone to talk to, he returns the call. It's morning in London.

"Hiram?" John answers. "How are you?"

"Fine," Hiram replies stiffly, worn to the bone. "You?"

"Holding on."

They sit in broken silence with so much to say.

"And Antaris?" Soft and wary, there's sadness laced in John's question.

"School helps, but he has nightmares. I used to have them like this when I was his age. He had one tonight, but he's asleep now. I've been meaning to ask if he had them . . . before?"

"Not often, no. Is he . . ."

"Talking? No." Hiram hesitates to get the next question out even though he's dying to know. "What was he like?"

The ensuing silence is so unbearable, Hiram almost changes the subject, until John's ragged sigh cuts through the line, his exhausted exhale is soul deep. "Antaris was . . . shy with strangers, but overall happy, creative, and observant. He loved the bow ties Grace made him. Like her, he was curious. Smiled often, laughed more. She used to call him the sun because he brightened her world."

Hiram tenses.

Compel the sun to shine.

"I—I miss her every day." John's pain is palpable. "I can't believe she's gone, but I also can't shake the feeling that Grace knew she wouldn't see him grow up."

No combination of words can return what he lost. "Grace sent a stone message to the FCD three months before . . . She left clues for the investigators, and called herself a *dying star*. She said she had Seen her end."

Knowledge is a double-edged sword that cuts John deep. He bleeds the sound of pain slipping through the line. Hiram pulls the phone away, giving him a moment of peace to grieve the daughter he raised from childhood. When he presses the phone back to his ear, the line is still and silent.

"I'm sorry," Hiram murmurs.

"Nothing to apologize for. It's not your fault. I . . ." A pause. "They told me she was murdered, but since she was a victim of a serial killer in the States, they would be handling the case. Have you—"

"They've spoken to me. Twice. They wanted to speak to Antaris, too, but I wouldn't let them."

"Are you assisting with the investigation? I remember how you pulled strings here when—"

"My father did, but I doubt he cares. Not many people do."

"You do."

To an extent that it involves Grace, and that's because of Antaris.

Hiram stares at the blank wall. "I've done all I can. I've been compliant, answered their questions, but it's best if I let the authorities do their jobs. Mine is to take care of Antaris."

"You're right." John clears his throat. "Help him find his voice."

"Right now, I'd take his trust over his voice," Hiram admits quietly, scrubbing a hand over his face. "It's late. When he wakes up, I'll have him—"

"No, no. You don't have to." John pauses. "His silence . . . is hard."

Hiram, who doesn't even know what Antaris's voice sounds like, understands more than he'll ever admit. "You can write to him. I've started giving him notes each morning. He likes it."

"Yeah? Okay, I'll do that. Call me next month?"

"I will." They've agreed to keep the communication open, no matter how difficult it is.

When Hiram ends the call, he lies back down on the floor beside Antaris's bed. His indifference to the white walls and crown molding reshapes into distaste.

Sleep is impossible, but he tries.

Lunch on Saturday is yet another in a series of failures. Hiram's still cleaning up when Peter arrives, the talisman letting him in without hesitation. Antaris greets Peter with a squint, but he's mostly gotten used to his godfather's presence. And his gifts.

Today, Peter brings a watercolor activity book that excites Antaris more than anything he's received so far. Once the boy is settled and painting a picture of a cat—the animal matching his pendant—Peter joins Hiram at the table, where he's sipping coffee because it's too early for liquor.

"How did you know he likes painting?"

"Teachers and his tutor. Apparently, he's most focused during art class and story time."

"Maybe I should work on cracking his picky eating."

Peter's brow rises. "What do you mean? Didn't you get the list?"

Hiram frowns. "What list?"

"Of course she didn't give it to you."

"Explain."

"Antaris got a walk-through of the school kitchens. They made a list of everything he likes. It was given to Simran, but I guess she didn't pass it on to you."

"No, she didn't." Antaris barely touched the meat loaf and mashed potatoes he made last night, but he *did* catch him eating baby carrots and apple slices later. He didn't say anything at the time, just felt grateful his kid was eating. Meanwhile, there was a goddamn list.

Is he surprised? No.

His mother has always liked to control the narrative, twisting details so she comes out on top. She'd rather let Hiram spiral into failure, to swoop in like a hero with a solution she already had.

He excuses himself to call his mother, who doesn't answer. He tries twice more; the last call is declined after one ring. A strategic avoidance tactic. Irritated, he calls his father, who answers and tells him that his mother is playing games, but can't remember where she went. Hiram knows, though.

"Can you do me a favor?" he asks Peter. "Watch him while I step out?"

"Of course."

After telling Antaris that he will return, just like he wrote on his note, which earns him a cautious look, Hiram leaves.

Simran is a creature of habit, like Hiram. She loves board games, and has a short list of places she frequents. Hiram pulls up outside Zephyr, the members-only lounge his mother has frequented since his childhood. The sign outside confirms she's probably here. It's Mancala Day. Simran prefers *Pallankuli*, but this is the closest she's found in America. The entry fee is exorbitant for nonmembers, but Hiram pays with his Imprint and ignores the hostess asking where he'd like to sit. He's not staying.

Inside, the ambience is a strange mix of pretentious displays of wealth and the casualness of a bar. Music hums beneath the chatter of the city's elite. Some drink and laugh; others gamble over pachisi games with more money than most people earn in a month. He spots her instantly, surrounded by older women, a white porcelain teacup in her hand—masala chai, knowing her—smile wide and gleaming.

It falters when she sees him, then snaps back into place, too tight. "Hiram, love. What brings you here?"

The table turns to look. He flashes a polite, practiced smile. "Afternoon, ladies. I just wanted to borrow my mother. It won't be long."

"Take her," one woman says. "She's been beating us for the last hour."

"I cannot help that you are all sore losers," Simran preens.

They playfully mock her as she leads Hiram to a quiet corner. Her smile vanishes the moment they're alone. She's not happy with him. *Good*. It's mutual.

"How rude of you to barge into my game. What is it that you need?"

"The list."

"What list?"

Hiram stares at her. "The last thing I'd ever describe you as is stupid."

Simran's eyes harden, but she pulls a folded paper out of the pocket of her navy saree. Hiram scans it, folds it, then slips it into his jacket pocket.

"Where is Antaris?"

"At home painting with Peter."

"I have several friends with grandchildren his age. Th—"

"No," Hiram cuts her off. "You're not doing this today."

Simran's face shifts to confusion. "Surely you are not upset with me."

"Not upset. Disappointed. This is your second strike," Hiram warns with a tight smile, knowing they have an audience. "Enjoy your day, Mother."

He steps around her and walks out without looking back.

Fueled by frustration, he walks four blocks, happens upon a grocery store, skims the list long enough to pick out what he needs for dinner, and leaves calmer than he arrived.

That night, he makes pasta with three vegetables the list notes Antaris likes. When he eats two plates without prompting, for the first time in months, Hiram doesn't feel so lost.

The moving boxes from London and Los Angeles arrive on Monday morning.

While Antaris is at school, Hiram unpacks his son's old life. He organizes his closet, anchors pictures to the wall, and fills his empty shelves with books. He suspects Antaris would rather decide where his belongings go, a suspicion that's confirmed when he sees the boy's face as they open the first box after Antaris gets home from school.

He isn't prepared for the lessons packed into each box. The first reveals that Antaris likes to paint more than the doodles Peter told him about. The box is filled with art supplies, a small foldable easel, and several wrapped watercolor paintings. Antaris stares at them for so long, Hiram wonders if they'll finish unpacking at all today. Trees with a winding trail. A gray cat with green eyes. A vase of flowers. Storm clouds over trees. None of them look like they were painted by a child.

"Your mom painted these?" Hiram feels odd for asking.

Antaris's tension confirms it. Unsure what to say, Hiram watches as his son props each piece against the mirror on his dresser.

"We can get them framed and hang them up, if you'd like."

Antaris looks over his shoulder, hazel eyes wide and hopeful.

Hiram sees his next mission. "We . . . can go buy frames together."

Antaris looks at the art one last time, then nods. Hiram's tempted to go now, to capitalize on the momentum, but he doesn't want to push.

The second box reveals that his son shares Simran's love of games and puzzles. The building blocks inside are the same kind Hiram had as a child. He stacks them in the empty hall closet while Antaris watches with curious concern.

"You can open the closet whenever you want," Hiram assures him.

The boy relaxes, and they move on to the third box.

It's the heaviest, and confirms that his son's college-professor sense of style is normal. The box is full of clothes he can wear now, and knitted bow ties that Antaris organizes with unusual care. A few casual things Hiram folds and puts away, shirts with grass stains and jeans with paint splatter, but what he finds odd is the abundance of hooded coats, boots, gloves, and scarves. They're out of season, and all have tags. Why Grace bought winter clothes in March is as unsettling as realizing everything is a size too big—perfect for the upcoming winter.

Antaris is too short to hang his own clothes, so he watches as Hiram does it for him. The last box remains unopened when their pizza arrives. Antaris likes extra cheese. Hiram prefers meat lovers, but it's a small sacrifice to see his son practically inhale two slices. They finish eating in record time, and Hiram is surprised when Antaris brings his plate and cup to the sink.

"You don't ha—" Hiram stops when worry etches Antaris's brow. "You want to help?"

This is how he learns his son knows how to wash dishes, as well as a six-year-old can.

Hiram dries and wipes the counters. When he finishes, Antaris stands in the living room doorway in rain boots, shuffling, note in hand. Hiram doesn't understand what it means until he gets closer and Antaris hands it to him.

In only a couple of weeks, the itinerary Hiram gave him is now worn. He unfolds it and sees the issue: It's torn.

"You want me to fix it?"

Antaris nods.

The only tape Hiram has is for moving boxes, but he sits at the coffee table and does what he can while Antaris hovers. Three strips later, the paper is whole again. After handing it back to his son, who leaves in the direction of his room, Hiram's eyes fall on the table. Before he knows what he's doing, he's writing another note to replace the one that's torn. Just in case.

He's on his fifth balled-up paper when he notices Antaris again, now in a rain jacket that matches his boots, hood up, despite clear skies. Ready to wander, no doubt. Feeling like he's been caught doing something wrong, Hiram awkwardly folds the paper and offers it. The same reassurance on fresh paper. "I thought you might want a new one to keep?"

Hiram is prepared to blame himself for trying too hard, but Antaris accepts it with both hands.

Seven

Veda isn't late for her tutoring session with Antaris, but she will be if she doesn't leave the greenhouse now.

She finds Antaris alone in the cafeteria, tidy as usual in his uniform and bow tie. His book bag is on the seat beside him, lunch box on the table, jacket on the back of his chair. She observes until he lifts his head. That's her cue. Pushing open the door, she lets in a breeze with her entrance. It's been just over a month since Antaris came into her life, and each session reinforces the quiet rhythm they've found together. Veda isn't sure who's helping whom more.

"Hello there."

That gets his attention, until his eyes drop to her side. In her haste, Veda forgot to drop off the lavender sprigs meant for the school's stores. She sits beside him and places them on the table.

His eyes never leave.

"Do you like plants?"

He taps the table twice. *Yes*.

"These are just some stems that broke off, but there are plenty more ready to go in the ground." She's not one for interpreting his silence, but his open awe is easy to translate. "I can take you to the garden, and we can plant the rest together."

Antaris nearly jumps to his feet.

Veda cracks a slow smile, tucking the lavender away and leading him out of the cafeteria. Outside, he grows cautious and unsure, trailing behind. She glances encouragingly over her shoulder. "Come on."

He dashes back inside before she can stop him. Confused, Veda waits until he returns, umbrella in hand.

"Oh, it's going to rain later. I suppose we can't be too prepared." Before she can talk herself out of it, she offers her hand. He doesn't take it but walks beside her, close yet distant.

His eyes roam curiously over the animals. The trees. The sky. Watching him, Veda notices his bow tie is now crooked. She reaches to fix it, but panic plays across his face. "I'm sorry, I should have asked first. May I?"

He holds her gaze, then slowly nods. Veda carefully adjusts the bow tie while he bends his head down as best as he can to watch. It's twisted around the back, so she fixes it under his collar. He's slow to relax, careful to move.

"There you go," she murmurs. "Is this your favorite? It's the only one I've seen you wear." When he nods, Veda smiles. "Well, I like it, too. Whoever made it is talented."

The bottom of her heart drops when Antaris's eyes water. He turns away to hide his face, and his broken whimper tells Veda she's made a mistake and unearthed his pain.

The bow tie. His mother must have made it.

His shoulders shake with each ragged breath as he fights to keep inside what desperately wants out. Silence amplifies his grief, shaking her to the core as she watches him struggle, fighting it . . . until Veda whispers his name, reminding him that he's not alone. With red cheeks and wet eyes, he starts to back away but freezes when she calls him again. Lips quivering, he scrubs his tears away with clenched fists, and hides his face again.

"Can I help?" The urge to do *something*, to reach for him, give this hurting child the comfort he so desperately needs. But he shakes his head.

"Okay. We'll stay here until you're ready. Take as long as you need."

Antaris sinks to his knees, gazing at the sky. She's done the same countless times before, but when she joins him, she wonders if it's for the same reason.

"My parents are gone. Like your mom," Veda says gently. The heartbreak in his eyes steals her breath. "We spent every summer riding around the country in an old camper van because my parents loved road trips. I used to hate it, always complaining because I wanted to stay home. When I was sixteen, I was swimming in a lake we were parked by while they were grilling lunch. One moment they were there, the next . . . gone. Vanished. Like so many others."

When she feels a small hand on hers, Veda smiles sadly.

"I haven't stopped missing them, just like you haven't stopped missing your mom. Some days are easier. Some aren't. The worst is forgetting the little things, so when that happens, I look to the sky, because even though I can't see them, I know they're still with me—woven into the Cosmos. Your mom, too."

Antaris nods in teary understanding, eyes not leaving the sky. Veda doesn't realize her own eyes are wet until her vision blurs. The breeze dries their cheeks as the sun peeks out once the clouds roll on. It feels like hours pass before Antaris stands.

"Are you sure you're ready?"

He nods slowly, then points, as if asking her the same.

"I'm sure." Veda points toward their destination. "Let's go."

The garden swells with freshly planted life. Veda hangs his umbrella on the gate latch while Antaris wanders between rows of fruits, vegetables, and herbs.

Raised beds line four grassy aisles leading to the greenhouses. Flowering bushes border the fences that enclose the garden. Veda lingers near the entrance, watching as Antaris looks around with his hands behind his back. Careful. Respectful. But when he reaches the bed with an assortment of camas, red columbines, and common yarrow wildflowers that are in full bloom, Veda joins him.

Still worried about his outburst, she puts on a brave face. "Do you like them?"

He doesn't need to answer; his fascination is clear. It's as if he's trying to memorize the smallest details, examining them from every angle, but he doesn't touch. Veda follows his lead, naming the flowers for him. "Each one was planted to bring in bees to help with pollination."

Antaris turns, listening.

"Have you seen bees?"

His confirmation is still stilted, but she takes whatever she can get. Emboldened, she steers him to where her tools remain, but there's only one pair of gloves. Veda turns to find Antaris waiting for her next move.

It's one neither of them expects. She kneels before him, startling him back a step, and beckons him closer. "Gloves will protect your hands while we're planting. They're too big for you, but something is better than nothing."

The standoff doesn't last as long as she expects. Antaris takes one cautious step closer, then another, before finally holding out his hands.

"Next time, I'll have a pair that fits you."

Antaris's expression doesn't change, but with one oversized glove on, he points at her hand.

"Don't worry, my hands are rough. They can take it."

Apparently that isn't it. He steps closer, eyes on her arm, head tilted. She doesn't realize why until she notices the scars from her curse peeking out from under her sleeve. She quickly adjusts it. "It's from a while ago. An accident."

He frowns.

"I'm okay," she lies gently, slipping on the second glove for him. He won't be able to grip much, but he doesn't seem to mind. Veda leads him to a half-dug hole and drops to her knees in the dirt. Antaris stands beside her, watching intently. She picks up the hand shovel and digs into the soft earth. "Do you want to plant this one?"

He nods.

Veda gestures for him to kneel like her. He does, nearly stumbling. Embarrassed, he settles and looks to her, waiting. She almost asks if he's okay but decides against it. Loosening the soil, she pulls a lavender plant from its plastic pot and hands it over. "Right here."

Antaris works with care, gently filling the hole with the surrounding dirt. They move to the next spot, and Veda grabs another baby lavender plant, starting to dig a new hole.

"Sometimes, when I feel nervous or scared, when everything feels too heavy, I come here. Watching things grow and change makes me feel better. Stronger. Planting, watering, and harvesting remind me that, no matter what, everything will be fine."

Antaris listens, rapt.

"I'm out here more than I like to admit." She chuckles, shaking her head. "Cosmos, I'm unloading on a six-year-old."

But he doesn't seem to mind. He's quietly taking it all in.

"You understand how I feel, don't you?"

He taps the dirt twice.

"How about this? I'll show you everything my mom taught me about gardening, and this place can be your reminder, too. Would you like that?"

He nods.

She looks around. "First, a bountiful garden needs planning. Everything works in harmony with nature, even if we don't always see it."

There's more she could say, but emotions, too complicated to digest, make it hard. Abandoning the hand shovel, Veda digs into the earth. She usually wears gloves and can't remember the last time she felt the soil between her fingers. Then another hand joins hers.

Antaris has removed the gloves, choosing to feel the cool soil, too. She hands him another lavender plant, and together they nestle it in the ground, then move to the next. This time, Veda slows him down, letting him focus on his hands.

When they finish, Veda offers a dirt-covered finger. "Better?"

He taps it twice.

Soil is the foundation of everything. Where life starts and returns. As Antaris stands among their work, gazing in awe, Veda wonders whether this garden might be a place where *he* can begin anew.

Veda allows herself to miss her parents the next afternoon when she's alone.

Memories torment and soothe. Her mother taught her that despite the intrinsic fight for divergence, all things are connected. Evolved in nature's womb, magic is the foundation of everything.

How a person wields magic means nothing in the greater universe.

Her father showed her how to call on celestial bodies to extract magic in precise quantities to fuse with earth's creations: stones, gems, and metals. Never too much or too little. Never too fast or too slow. He often spoke of perspective and problem-solving, temperance and patience.

You don't always need an answer. Without wonder and mystery, magic dies.

But when the teaching ended, they'd sit under the stars and tell stories, reminding Veda that magic, like any element, is forged by cosmic events and phenomena. Falling meteors, solar flares, the births and deaths of stars. Energy. The days she remembers best are those filled with stories of lives lived before her: her parents' childhoods, their Sight. They would laugh, cry, and hold each other in those moments. It was then her parents stopped being giants in her world and became real.

Gardening with Antaris reopens the wound their absence left. She didn't lie when she said the pain hadn't changed. It follows her, lies beside her at night, and rises early with her to inspect the greenhouse. Some days it whispers. Today, it screams. Veda can't quiet it until she lets herself *remember*.

When she opens her eyes again, Khadijah is on her knees, facing east, glowing in the sun.

"How long have you been here?"

"A few minutes. I was giving you time with your parents." She looks over her shoulder at Veda. "Rough day?"

"Yeah."

"Ready to get out of here?"

"Where are we going?"

"Panoramic."

A microcosm of Seers, Panoramic lies in uptown Proventia, bustling and thriving with all the necessities of life found within its nine-block radius. It's the only place that's truly theirs. Inside, Seers relax, their guards down and smiles genuine. Still, to the chagrin of separatist-leaning Seers, everyone is allowed in. Some Mages treat it like a zoo, taking pictures of Seers going about their day. Others come to shop or pitch business deals. Even at Khadijah's side, Veda's early visits used to draw curious stares. But now, Seers wave as they walk into the Conclave, the largest event hall in Panorama, for the town hall meeting.

"I'm going with my uncle to update the Council on Everett after the meeting, and give them Gabriel's and Francisco's information if they want to talk. I'm prepared for an argument," Khadijah says. "Have you seen Marlene?"

They spot her only because she's in a floral pastel-blue dress with a blue-jay amulet hanging around her neck. Her hair is pulled back in a ponytail of tight coils so black they look blue. The look is pretty and accentuates her curves and fuller figure, but is not her usual style of monochrome with bold pops of color.

Khadijah folds her arms. "Well, well, well. Hello, stranger."

Marlene grins like a kid caught with their hand in the cookie jar and throws an arm around her friend. "Khadijah! I know, I know. Don't start yelling. I'm sorry I canceled our plans the other day, but I've been swamped at work. I'm gunnin' for a promotion, so I've been picking up extra shifts."

Veda isn't sure why she frowns, but the excuse is good enough for the equally career-minded Khadijah. "Don't work yourself too hard."

"I won't." Marlene turns and smiles. "Hey, Veda."

The seats next to them are open. Veda takes the aisle, Khadijah and Marlene sit beside her, Everly at the end. As she catches pieces of their conversation, Veda scans the nearly full meeting hall. She hopes Everett turns up, but sees only his mother, who looks stressed out.

"What happened there?" Khadijah asks, pointing at a bruise under Marlene's ear. "Want me to heal—"

"No, it's fine. I had a little work accident," she says with a roll of her eyes.

"Typical." Khadijah laughs. "Be careful."

The clock tower chimes seven times, and a hush falls. It's time for the meeting to start. Tonight, they are nearly at capacity, and when they do roll call, Veda learns some are from as far east as Spokane. There's a strange charge in the room; murmurs hum and people look around as if expecting someone famous to jump out. The doors open for the Oracle Council to enter.

The Council is made up of thirteen women and five men. Veda knows only five by name: Clinton, their leader; district representatives Moab, Ruth Wells, and Ani Johnson; and lastly, Lucinda Hampton, their deponent, an appointed member who oversees magical agreements. The rest of the Council perform a variety of duties. Most have been voted in over the last five years as old members retire or leave Proventia. Moab helps Clinton settle in his chair before taking his own seat. The rest follow suit.

The first order of business is the good news: new Seer-friendly businesses, proposals to local officials, Panoramic's street-repaving schedule, and a clothing drive for displaced Seer teenagers. Then come the cautions: areas to avoid due to rising attacks on Seers, and a reminder not to wander the streets alone at any time of day. Overall, it's a routine meeting until Clinton announces, "I have invited a guest tonight and given him a Standing Liberty coin."

Murmurs ripple through the room. This, it seems, is what they've been waiting for. Receiving a coin is an honor. It allows the recipient to formally introduce themselves. Veda received hers months after her arrival, and while she didn't like the spotlight, it helped her integrate.

"Remember, the lion's den is where you test yourself."

Clinton's ominous words bring silence. Veda joins everyone in searching for the guest. Slowly, a man in a baseball hat and sunglasses walks down the long aisle. At the podium, he removes both the hat and sunglasses.

Gasps and chatter erupt.

"What the fuck is *he* doing here?" Khadijah blurts.

The subject of all the commotion in the room glances at the crowd. Veda recognizes the sky-blue eyes of Hiram Ellis. A wise man might walk away from such ire. Hiram doesn't. Still, he looks like he'd rather be anywhere else.

The blurring insults and angry voices reach a fevered pitch.

Clinton raises his hand. *"Silence."*

A hush falls instantly. The spell would leave most Mages with migraines for days, but Clinton remains unbothered. Power, when freely used, never ceases to amaze Veda. He drops the spell effortlessly. The quiet holds.

"Before we continue," Clinton says, voice stern and commanding, blind eyes locked on Hiram, "please state your name for the record."

"Hiram Ellis." Smooth and posh, his voice now has an edge that wasn't there when Veda ran into him. He places the coin on the podium. "I was unaware this was a summons. I had no plans to speak, only observe."

"Observe for what purpose, Ellis?" Moab asks, turning to Clinton. "Bold of you to invite *him*."

"Change comes from strange places," Clinton replies.

"Whatever you're trying to prove, you'd have better success with someone who actually wants what you're offering." Hiram's bluntness should be unsettling, but it's refreshing. "I'm not here to make friends or change anything. I'm staying out of it."

"Be that as it may, you are here. And change is inevitable." Clinton straightens in his seat. "We have a common interest."

Khadijah frowns. Marlene leans forward, temporarily distracting Veda until Moab's voice grabs her attention. "What could we *possibly* have in common with him?"

Hiram shifts, placing his hands at his sides.

"Will you address the room, or shall I?" Clinton's question is a challenge. When Hiram stays silent, Clinton clears his throat. "Very well. This is about the Botanist. The person who has been killing members of our community for six years. Hiram is as much of a victim as any Seer who has lost loved ones to their violence. His so—"

"Leave him out of this," Hiram snaps. "I'm not the friend your community wants. That much is abundantly clear."

Given the consensus of the room, Veda can't disagree.

Hiram's detachment earns no sympathy, but Peter's advice lingers in Veda's mind: Be open to Hiram's intentions. She recalls Hiram's earlier words—*we have the same goal: catching the Botanist*. She dismissed him then. Now, with Clinton's invitation, she wonders how much of that is true.

"Your lack of respect is typical for someone like you," Moab spits.

"Would you prefer false courtesy?" Hiram's response inflames the room.

Lucinda and Ruth have been silent, but Lucinda straightens in her seat. "Clinton, unless you have Seen something the rest of us have not, how do you know you have not invited the killer into our safe space?"

Painfully human, Hiram recoils at the implication. A crack in his perfect armor. "So now I'm a serial killer?"

"I put nothing past you Ellises, especially when your uncle has been studying us like lab rats for decades."

"I don't know anything about that." He turns to Clinton. "I'm done."

"Are you?" is Clinton's cryptic reply. "I do not think we have even begun."

"He is." Moab looks ready to grind his teeth on quartz.

"Why would we want you here?" Ruth lashes out with a venom that surprises Veda. It's a far cry from the kind, sassy old woman who gives advice and makes sure Veda doesn't spend her birthdays wallowing.

"I never asked for your protection," Hiram replies.

"Of course not. You Ellises have spent generations spreading your hatred of us across the country. When your father retired and you left, we celebrated, thinking the cycle was over, but now you're back."

Veda flinches. So does Hiram.

"I left my family *years* ago. Why I've returned is of no concern to anyone in this room—"

"No concern?" Ruth cuts him off, seething. "Your family rose to power on the backs of Seers, betraying our trust, twisting laws to make it a crime for us to use magic and protect ourselves and our children. Your father is the worst of you, spreading hatred by creating the Registration. *Seers* built that mansion you live in. Did you know that? We've not only built a city that treats us worse than animals, but we are the foundation of a country with laws that allow people to treat us worse than animals, then punish us for not suffering the same consequences of magic. Your presence alone endangers us."

Only when she finishes does Veda finally exhale.

"The only thing I want is to be left alone. Your issues with my family are not mine." Hiram remains unflappable in the face of the generational rage thrown at him. "I'm not here to stand trial for sins I didn't commit, especially when I already know the verdict."

Clinton rests his hand on the table. "You are right."

"Perhaps he *should* stand trial," Lucinda says, ignoring Clinton's shake of the head. "It may not be fair, Clinton. Nothing is. You know this better than anyone, and yet you invited him here. You want us to accept him because he's been affected by the Botanist, just like us. But he's never spoken up for us. Why should we care about him?"

"Regardless of why I was invited, it's clear nothing productive was ever meant to happen here. You want someone to crucify, and you've decided it's me."

Moab chuckles darkly. "Sins of the bloodline—"

"Are *not* mine."

"But they are," Ani counters with quiet conviction. "We have suffered from allowing your ilk into our community, and we won't ever be fooled again."

"Thank you for coming," Clinton says sincerely, though it's clearly a dismissal.

In the storm of whispers and stares, Hiram leaves the podium, abandoning his hat and sunglasses. Veda catches a glimpse of his face but can't read his expression.

All eyes follow Hiram until Clinton slowly stands. "This was not a failure. Only a beginning."

As if his words are a spell, Hiram pauses. He doesn't turn to face the Council. Instead, he squares his shoulders, fists curling as though preparing for another round. "No. It's the end."

"Character is the consequence of a choice, Hiram." Clinton's voice softens. "Will you choose the path of ease and comfort, or the one less traveled? I look forward to seeing what you decide."

When the meeting adjourns, the hall, still buzzing from Hiram's appearance, empties for the banquet next door. It's a customary end to each meeting, a time for fellowship and connection. Khadijah is deep in conversation with a growing cluster of Council members, while Marlene chats with Lucinda. Without a reason to socialize, Veda returns to the now-empty meeting hall, frowning upon seeing the forgotten hat and glasses.

Watching Hiram get torn apart didn't bring her the satisfaction she'd expected. Her talk with Peter didn't change her opinions, yet something sits uneasily in the pit of her stomach, a weight no food or drink will soothe.

Everything they said was true. But was it right?

Veda picks up Hiram's belongings, intending to pass them to Peter. The side door opens, and the man himself cautiously walks inside, stopping short upon seeing her. His eyes slide to the entrance door as if expecting security to burst into the room.

"Respectfully, I'm not here to argue or do anything that makes that amulet of yours glow." Hiram approaches with the same caution she reserves for him. "Just grabbing my hat and glasses, then I'll be on my way."

Veda hands him both. "Weird that you got back in. That door is usually locked."

Hiram studies her, confused, as though he can't quite place something. "Okay, I'll lean fully into masochism and ask why you haven't gone on a paranoid rant accusing me of following you."

Veda rolls her eyes. "I talked to Peter. You're a lot of things but apparently not a stalker."

"A glowing endorsement," he drawls. "Now, if you don't mind, I'd like Peter's shitty idea of a disguise back so I can leave before someone accuses me of murder again."

Of course it was Peter's idea. Veda meant what she said: She has no interest in being Hiram's friend. Whatever his story, she doesn't care, but she no longer feels the same intensity.

Hiram puts on the hat and pockets the sunglasses. There's no reason to stay, yet Veda doesn't leave. Her gaze falls in every direction except his. The moment hangs like a pendulum at the tip of its arc until the door opens again.

Khadijah stands frozen at the end of the aisle, smile faltering. She walks briskly toward them on a mission. From the corner of her eye, Veda watches Hiram shift. A man resigned, ready for another confrontation.

"Ellis." Khadijah's arms fold.

"Desai," Hiram replies. "You're welcome, by the way. For the apothecary."

"Don't pretend like you did it out of the kindness of your heart."

Khadijah turns to Veda. "I'm going to a small room to talk to the Council. Walk to Olive and get us a table. I'll meet you there." The verbal skirmish concludes with Khadijah excusing herself.

"What was that all about?" Veda asks the only person left to give answers.

"Bad blood" is all Hiram says.

Veda sidesteps him and leaves out the side door, no goodbye needed. The city's lights dim the stars, clouds partially conceal the moon, but the spring air is crisp and clean. She hasn't made it far when she remembers to ask Everly to make her another tin of salve for her scars. Sighing, Veda turns on her heels just to see the door closing behind Hiram, who stops, awaiting her next move. It should be to head back inside, but there's a question smoldering that won't extinguish. "How do you know Clinton?"

"I don't," he says, irritated.

Veda isn't buying it. "He seems to know you."

"If he did, he'd know I hate all that cryptic Seer speak."

An amused huff slips past her lips. "Same."

They're under a streetlamp, light casting shadows in all directions. Hiram slides his hands into the pockets of his navy pants. He seems more open like this—vulnerable, even.

His expression is curious as it falls on her once more. "Why were *you* there?"

"Apparently to see you be raked over the coals."

He ignores her sarcasm. "Are you a Seer?"

"No, but they trust me."

"Why?" Hiram's question is low, private. He doesn't move when Veda takes a step back, ready to go to Olive for that much-needed drink. "Never mind. You won't tell me."

The truth is complicated. She doesn't owe him an explanation.

There's a gleam in his blue eyes, shadowed by a fleeting heaviness, a weight that sleep can't cure. "My ex was the Botanist's latest victim."

The fire inside her cools to a simmer. *Antaris's mother?* "The London case?"

Hiram nods. "Let me guess, Gabriel told you."

"Yeah." Quietly, Veda wrestles with two truths: sorrow for Antaris, and disbelief that someone like Hiram once dated a Seer.

"I stumbled onto yours while looking for more information on hers." Hiram moves closer, approaching like she's a bird he's trying not to frighten, not within reach but enough to eclipse the glow from the streetlamp. He stops when Veda steps back, contempt in his eyes. "You think I'm a killer, too?"

She stares at him blankly. "I'm not ruling anything out."

"You don't know *shit* about me."

"I'm not trying to," Veda snaps. "But Peter won't shut up about you. And my judgment is the result of your actions—like accosting me with questions about the worst night of my life. You have other priorities to focus on instead of me."

"My priorities are none of your business."

Unconsciously, Veda takes a step toward him, looking him up and down. His eyes follow her every move. "Peter's belief in you clashes with everything I've seen. I have my opinions, and you've done nothing to change them."

"My questions were abrupt, I apologize for that. As for anything you've seen tonight, I'm not in the business of kissing the ass of every person I meet simply because of my surname. I haven't done anything wrong."

"If you believe that, you're a damn fool." Veda tilts her head, eyes narrowed. "I'm not saying I agree with everything that was said, but you can't ignore the reasons no one wants you as their ally, whether you asked for it or not."

"I didn't," Hiram retorts firmly.

"You can't pretend their concerns don't exist. The past happened, and no, you weren't there, but you benefit from it now. The damage lingers. They can't be forced to move on, nor do you get to decide that you're forgiven—it's up to them. Your family—"

"I am *not* my family." There are signs of struggle where there was once arrogance. "I don't even know why Clinton invited me. Whatever he's Seen, I don't care, nor do I want any part of it. I just want to raise my kid in peace. It's what he deserves after all the shit he's been through."

"You *should* care. If only to be a better example for your son and a better friend."

His blue eyes search hers. For what, Veda isn't sure, but he must find what he's looking for because he leans just a hair closer. She doesn't back down. Peter's insistence and Hiram's contradictions push her to question things in ways she hasn't in a long time. If she strips away everything she's assumed, what's left is a blank slate.

"If you're not like your family, you don't have the luxury of being neutral," Veda says. "No one knows what you stand for, so they assume. And that makes you just as complicit as your family."

Hiram's jaw ticks. "I don't have to prove what I believe to anyone."

"No, you don't, and you lose nothing watching Seers be dehumanized," Veda says slowly. "Since it's not your reality, it's not your problem, isn't that right?"

"That's *not* what I said."

"You don't need to. Your silence says enough. Raise your son, no one can fault you, but don't act like you're better than your family because you're not a loud, proud bigot. Say something, say *anything*. Have an original thought. *Take a stand*."

Veda turns to leave, then stops. "Peter says you're a good man despite your family, but I've never known a good man who spectates."

Eight

Photographs, like memories, bridge the present and past. The album that beckons Hiram from bed just after five in the morning is not filled with *his* memories.

They're Grace's.

Hiram has never met the woman on the first page, but he's certain she's Grace's mother, because Antaris's hair curls like hers when it's wet, and Grace shared the glimmer in her eyes. The pendant on her shirt catches his attention: a jade frog with citrine eyes. He suspects it's the trickster pendant. Other photographs prove its lineage in Grace's family, a reminder that it won't pass to Antaris unless by miracle. Taking the album with him, Hiram boils water for tea and sits on the stool, flipping to the next page.

The first row of pictures makes him stop. Grace and a newborn Antaris. Exhausted wonder in one frame, joy in the next, her soft smile captured as he yawns. There are more pictures. Antaris sitting, standing, walking, running. She documented it all. Hiram keeps staring at the boy's smile, as contagious as it is unfamiliar. Intimate and warm, he tries to forge false memories—to be there, to hold him, to name him, to help. But they crumble like dry dough. He missed everything. A flicker of bitterness surfaces.

He shuts the album and reminds himself of the present. Antaris is still asleep, and Hiram has a few things to accomplish before that changes. He returns the photo album and starts with Antaris's book bag, which he didn't unpack last night.

The teacher's daily report details high scores, completed assignments, and satisfactory behavior. It also notes his struggles. His silence. His isolation. His reluctance to interact with his peers. Her last comment is new.

He's ready to make a friend.

The wheels in his mind turn as Hiram signs the note and slips it back into the book bag. He pulls out a few loose papers and finds paintings from art class. One looks like two trees, one with fruit, one bare. Another shows at least a dozen stick figures, all drawn with black paint, holding hands. Their hair is the only difference: two red, two gray, the rest brown and black.

Hiram stares until the kettle whistles, then sticks them to the refrigerator. That's where he always wanted to put his successes as a kid. It's fitting.

Antaris is a quarter of the way through breakfast when he notices. He drops his fork, eyes widening. Hiram doesn't know if he's upset or happy, so he says, "If you don't want them there, I won't do that again . . ." Antaris's expression begins to sour. "But if you do, it's fine. You can add whatever you want."

A tense silence passes with Hiram internally sweating from second-guessing everything . . .

Antaris runs from the table.

His mother's voice creeps in. *You are doing it wrong. You are making the wrong decisions. I have more experience and am the better choice.* Hiram knows it's a lie, but it's hard to ignore in the face of defeat.

Without hesitation, he would bend the world for Antaris. That's how much he loves him. Strange how fast it happened, how deeply he feels for a child he didn't know existed six months ago. Antaris is a choice Hiram made in an instant, one he doesn't regret, but sometimes, he mourns the simplicity of his old life, when he only had to care about himself.

Those two truths can coexist.

Antaris shyly peers around the corner. Hiram straightens, masking his spiral as his son shuffles in with a stack of papers. *His drawings.*

Maybe he had it wrong.

One by one, Antaris covers the refrigerator. Little oranges, trees, something that looks like a chicken. When he runs out of reachable space, Hiram plucks magnets from the side and helps him place the rest, adjusting each one until Antaris nods in approval.

Finished, Hiram stands beside Antaris, who peers at him, freckles standing out against the ruddiness of his cheeks. His brows furrow and relax until it clicks what his son is trying to communicate.

"It's perfect," Hiram says earnestly. "Thanks for letting me see them."

There's a ghost of a smile on his son's face. It lingers even as they sit by the pier, feet dangling over the edge. Wearing the brightest yellow raincoat despite there not being a cloud in the sky, Antaris is color in a muted world. The water is calm. It's easy to get lost in the stillness, but Hiram's mind is loud. He could block out Veda's accusatory voice, ignore her words, and live however he wants.

But what about Antaris?

Bigotry complicates his son's roots. As he grows older, those tangles will turn into knots. Out of sight, out of mind. That was one of Hiram's reasons for returning to Proventia. Simran loves optics too much to admit her grandson has a Seer mother, and Barrett barely talks to anyone. This allows Hiram to keep Antaris out of the public eye. It's a good plan, but not foolproof.

One day, Antaris will ask about his father's initial absence. One day, he'll see how the world is for people like his mother. Hiram will have answers; he is good at weaving the best ones, but now there's a growing weight of worry as he wonders if his reasons are good enough.

Unforecasted rain tempers his thoughts, but it does not extinguish them.

❀

Antaris likes herbal tea with breakfast.

The sample boxes have run out, leaving Hiram standing in the grocery store, overwhelmed by choices. He leans toward the pricier loose teas, but grabs two boxes of fruit blends Antaris seemed most eager about.

On his way back to the car, he spots a coffee shop and detours. The talisman flashes as he enters, but he hardly notices it as the strong scent of coffee pulls at his senses. It's crowded with limited seating and music humming beneath the chatter. Hiram orders a medium coffee and an apple Danish, then immediately regrets not getting both to go when he notices a familiar face at the first table.

Clinton Desai is alone, sipping what looks like tea, cane propped on the wall beside him. "Hello, Hiram Ellis. You are more than welcome to share my table."

The last thing he wants to do. "No, thank you. I'll find my own seat."

Unfortunately, by the time he collects his order, every table is either taken or occupied by people unwilling to share. Hiram sighs. When he takes a seat opposite Clinton, the blind man smiles. "Thank you for meeting me."

"I'm not meeting you." Hiram scowls. "In fact, after the spectacle that was the town hall meeting, I'd hoped to never see you again."

"It seems fate has other plans."

"No, I randomly decided to come here for coffee."

"Did you?" The old man doesn't let the question linger. "Perhaps my invitation to the town hall was not the best course of action. For that, I apologize."

"What do you want from me?"

"Everything I said at the meeting was true. I believe we could form an alliance. There are things beyond my reach I think you can help bring to light."

"I'm not the man you think I am."

"No, you're not, but you have the potential to be."

"So, what? You think I'll hunt down a serial killer?" Hiram almost laughs. "Not only is that ludicrous, it's insane. Why can't you use your Sight to find the Botanist?"

"Our magic may not be limited, but our Sight is. Our visions are impacted by free will. I have seen many iterations of you over the years, future flashes that change as you do. I do not know which version will unfold."

"I've already answered the investigators' questions."

"This isn't only about the Botanist. This is about your impact on the world. I invited you to the meeting so you would see the world beyond the fence you've been sitting on. People are more than objects in your line of sight. You want to be judged by your character, not your last name? Then look beyond what you know."

"I'm not here to form alliances. Living here isn't a permanent plan."

Clinton looks amused. He finishes his tea, then slides a card across the table. His name and phone number, printed and in braille. "For scheduling our next meeting. Please choose a quieter location. I concentrate better without external distractions."

"What are you—"

"Until next time, Hiram Ellis." Clinton reaches for his cane and slowly stands. "You will run forever. No place will be safe until you turn to face what's chasing you."

It's too quiet.

Hiram stops cutting the crust off the sandwich he's making and goes to find his son. Antaris has opened the final box. Books cover the floor and bed, but he's fixated on something in his hand. It's a picture of Antaris and Grace in front of a birthday cake, a number-six candle lit. His birthday was New Year's Eve, just a month before Grace died. In the photo, she doesn't look like time has touched her: smooth, light-brown skin, curly hair, hazel-green eyes, and a bright smile. Antaris is a perfect combination of their mixed heritage.

For a year after Grace broke things off and disappeared without a trace, questions clouded Hiram's world. Eventually, self-reflection gave him clarity. He doesn't consider letting her go to be a mistake. He would never chase someone running from him. He accepts the blame now, realizing he overestimated how far he'd distanced himself from his family and trusted too easily that it would be enough. Antaris places the picture on his nightstand.

Hiram sits on the bed beside him, jiggling one knee. "Do you . . ."

Antaris shakes his head.

"If you ever have questions about your mom, or want to hear stories about her, I'll tell you."

Until then, Hiram leaves to give him space.

The next ten minutes are heavy with silence until Antaris emerges carrying a stack of books. His expression is blank, his eyes wet. Hiram wants to help, but Antaris simply places the books on the table and returns to his bedroom. The top title catches his eye. *The Hidden Powers of Rituals and Oddities*. Likely one of Grace's mixed in with others. She specialized in obscure magic and rituals, and spent most of her career helping the Unseen readjust to their new normal of having to monitor their magic like a Mage.

As soon as Hiram puts it on a shelf, Antaris returns, struggling with another armful of books. Then a third. Hiram doesn't understand until Antaris peers up at the first bookcase.

Ah, there's no space.

Hiram adjusts his arrangement on one shelf, then two. It's still not enough.

"I think we need another bookshelf." He rubs the back of his neck. "Want to get out of the house?"

Fresh air does Antaris wonders. Sadness lingers—Hiram doubts it will ever fully leave—but at least he's no longer hiding like in those first few weeks. It's Saturday, and the stores are crowded with families.

Antaris sticks close, frowning at misbehaving kids. Hiram has to stifle his amusement more than once.

The bookshelves they choose won't fit in his car, so Hiram arranges for delivery. Normally they eat lunch at home, but the weather is warm, and the sun is bright. Hamburgers at Lewie's Diner sound better.

Some people recognize Hiram; more look puzzled or intrigued by Antaris's presence. The waitress is charmed by the silent, well-behaved boy. Hiram barely notices anyone else. He's watching his son's mood improve, especially when the elderly waitress offers him a free scoop of ice cream and a wink.

Hiram catches Antaris watching him, and he raises both hands. "It's all yours."

Only then does his son eat.

Later, as they drive home, Hiram checks the rearview mirror. Antaris is watching the world rush past, hair flopping in the wind.

"How about one more stop?"

Antaris nods.

It's just before two o'clock, and the library is packed with children and families. Unbeknownst to Hiram, it's story time. One hopeful glance from Antaris, and Hiram knows he's about to spend twenty minutes on the floor. He stays for the first story, glancing repeatedly at his enraptured son. When the second story begins, Antaris wants to stay, so Hiram tells him he'll go look for a book. While the story unfolds, Hiram roams the aisles in search of something to catch his attention.

What he finds is the last thing he expects to see. After years of being nothing more than a footnote in a surreal night, now Veda is everywhere.

Despite the crowd, she stands alone in the amulet section, seemingly undecided about which book to choose. Torn between irritation and curiosity, Hiram considers ignoring her but calls his own bluff. He's always been a glutton for punishment.

"We've got to stop meeting like this," he declares.

Veda closes her eyes and exhales before looking at him, unimpressed. "To what do I owe this latest displeasure?"

"I saw you and thought it would be more polite to speak than threaten magical violence."

"But not nearly as fun."

Hiram smirks. "I see you've acquired a sense of humor."

"Funny how you mistake sarcasm for humor. You can't catch a hint."

"Speaking of hints, call your advocate off. I'm sick of his cryptic word salad."

Veda looks confused, then her eyes widen slightly. "Wait. *Clinton?*"

"Who else?"

She laughs. "He's got a knack for popping up in places, but I didn't set him on you. Cosmos only knows what he's Seen."

Hiram frowns. "So it wasn't you—"

"Now *why* would I do that?"

"His topics of conversation were similar to yours."

"Clinton was the only person in that room who wanted you as an ally. I said my piece and had no plans to see you again." She gives him a glowering once-over. "Yet here we are. You're stubborn, and clearly that overwhelms what little common sense you have."

"Stubborn?" He chuckles dryly. "Sounds about right." Hiram steps close enough to see the title of the book in her hand: *Theory of Curses*. When she plucks a thick volume on amulet and talisman creation, he sizes it up. "Why would a Mage be interested in amulet creation?"

"It takes an inordinate amount of magic to create a single amulet or talisman, which is why Seers can make them with ease. It's also why they're regulated. Can't allow the masses free rein to subvert the consequences of magic use."

"Would be a shit show," he agrees.

"What people fail to realize is that anyone can create them. Infusing the magic is as tedious as destroying it—and just as dangerous—but it's far from impossible." Veda glances at Hiram. "It takes time and requires patience. I suspect you're not familiar with either."

"Believe it or not, I'm a patient man," he says in a low, private tone as he takes the book from her. Her smugness fades into something unreadable as he opens the first page, flips to the second, then closes it. Veda reaches for it, but he pulls it back. "Aht-aht, I might consider checking this out. You've convinced me."

"You're so full of—" Veda's focus shifts to something behind him.

Hiram turns to find Antaris with five books and a hopeful gleam that turns into excitement when he sees Veda.

Her reaction to his son isn't what he expects.

She *smiles*. The world must be ending. "Hi there."

To his further confusion, Antaris walks right past him like he's invisible.

"Oh my, you've picked out *a lot* of books," Veda says warmly.

Antaris glances back at Hiram, proud.

"Is this your . . ."

"Father?" Hiram smirks at her waning smile. "Why, yes, I am."

She doesn't seem surprised.

His smirk fades, eyes sliding from her to Antaris, who's blinking like a baby owl. "How do you know my son?"

"Are you *that* uninvolved as to not know who his tutor is?"

"My mother handles that, but she referred to . . . you, I suppose, as *Miss Thorne*."

She rolls her eyes. "Ah yes, your mother knows my last name and everything about me. She's a"—her eyes slide to Antaris, ready with a wide, fake smile—"*delight*."

"And during our previous encounters, you didn't think to mention that you're tutoring my son?"

"Not my job to tell you what you should already know."

The look he gives her could melt steel. "You don't know a *thing* about—"

A passing librarian shushes them.

Veda pastes on a smile and snatches the book from Hiram, rougher than necessary. When she looks at Antaris, her expression softens. "I'll see you on Monday, okay?"

Looking puzzled, Antaris nods slowly.

They watch her go. Hiram's brain is spinning with questions only Peter can answer, still trying to figure out what the hell just happened. But first, Antaris is back at his side, silently holding out the books, clearly seeking permission to check them out.

Hiram's pretty sure the limit is five books. "Whatever you want."

They get in line behind Veda, who uses her Imprint to check out her selections. She's nearly out the door when she turns around, bag in hand, hand on hip. Hiram hasn't checked out a book in years and fumbles through the process. The instructions are confusing. He's slow, times out the machine twice, and the line behind them grows. Antaris starts shuffling anxiously. Veda sighs and slides in between him and the machine.

"Not at *all* surprised you've never been to a public library." She taps through the prompts and scans her finger. The receipt prints. She hands it to him, grumbling, "You better return them on time."

Words dry in his mouth when he realizes how close she is.

Close enough to see the browns in her eyes settle on him. Close enough to see her swallow. A flyaway curl beckons, but Hiram isn't crazy enough to tuck it behind her ear.

The person behind them clears their throat.

Antaris walks between them as they exit. Veda's motorcycle is parked in the opposite direction of their car. Antaris peers up at Veda and waves bashfully, earning him another smile that dies when Veda notices Hiram once more.

She walks away without a word. Hiram thinks that's the end of it until Antaris hands him the books and bolts after her. Confused and intrigued, Hiram watches as his son catches up.

At first, Veda is startled. Then she places her books on the seat of her bike and kneels before him.

Hiram can't stop staring.

At her. At *them*.

Antaris is usually hard to read, but not now. He hangs on her every word in a way Hiram has never seen with anyone else. *How has Veda earned this kind of trust so quickly?* And, in turn, he wonders the same about her. There's warmth in her eyes where Hiram has only seen coldness. What does she know about his son that he doesn't?

When Veda lifts a finger while speaking, it looks like reassurance. About what? Hiram's stomach churns. Antaris gently taps her finger twice. As his son walks back, Veda's dark eyes catch him across the lot, silently warning him to stay away.

Hiram responds with a small smile, quietly rejecting her unspoken demand.

It's too late.

She holds the key to understanding his son.

Nine

Antaris isn't in his usual place.

After searching the school, growing frantic, Veda finds him kneeling on the balcony. He's staring out at the cluster of swaying trees near the garden, face pressed between the two railings he grips tightly. She doesn't know what he's looking at, but it's a lonely sight. Veda steps beside him, trying to see what's captured his attention, but there's nothing obvious. Antaris sits back on his heels, visibly distressed.

"What's wrong?"

He opens his mouth, and Veda's heart stops. It doesn't resume its regular rhythm until he closes his eyes, defeated, clutching the little cat pendant he wears.

"You want to talk, but you can't," she concludes.

His pitiful nod stirs the hopelessness she felt early on.

"What's holding you back?"

He looks around before rushing to the exterior wall, touching it, then looking up. Veda doesn't understand. When he returns, she simply offers her hand. "Show me what you're looking at."

Trust is his hesitant fingers, squirming uncertainty, solidifying into a firm grip. Rain begins to fall as they walk toward the garden. He's shaking, and Veda's concern crests until he stops and stares at her, insistent. A soft mewling cry pierces the wind. She looks to her left and right before hearing it again.

"Is that . . . ?"

She follows the sound as it grows louder, closer, until they spot the source. A tiny, wet kitten is huddled at the base of a bush, crying in distress.

"How did you hear this?"

Before she can move or warn him to be careful—kids aren't always safe around frightened animals—Antaris is on his knees in the wet grass, curling a finger in front of the kitten's nose. It sniffs, allowing Antaris to gently wrap it in his school jacket. He focuses on the kitten, and the only sounds are raindrops and his soft shushing, as if soothing a fussy baby. Veda is transfixed by his compassion, watching the way the kitten settles, its distress waning. Antaris looks nervous, like he's done something wrong.

"You're doing great," she reassures him, and he relaxes. "The kitten is lost. Its mother might be nearby. We shouldn't take it."

Antaris shakes his head vigorously, not to be reasoned with. The rain falls harder. A clap of lightning comes before the thunder rolls. Veda, unwilling to get drenched, starts looking for the kitten's mother. She doesn't get far—she finds the cat already dead. It hasn't been long.

What a cruel fate disguised as an act of nature.

She covers the body with dirt and leaves, making a mental note to ask a farmhand to bury it properly, deep enough not to attract larger wildlife. When she returns, Antaris is still waiting, shirt soaked. She doesn't have the heart to vocalize a truth he seems to know.

"Let's take the kitten inside."

Solemn and careful, he leads the way to the school. Inside, Veda examines the mewling kitten. It looks about a month old. Maybe male. Antaris helps bathe off the fleas and holds it while Veda scours the kitchen for a bottle and some goat's milk. It'll do for now. She guides Antaris as he bottle-feeds the kitten, now swaddled in a small towel. Without Dr. Simpson, there's no veterinarian on-site. She'll leave that to Peter.

"Have you had a cat before?"

Antaris shakes his head. His eyes hold a mix of fascination and concern. He comforts the kitten the only way he knows: holding it, keeping it warm, making sure it's not alone. Not abandoned.

A war brews within her. Part of her hopes that a boy this kind won't be tainted by a family so terrible. Another part reminds her there's no scale to measure a person, nothing to prove who they'll become. Veda knows the sort of people the Ellises are.

Losing a parent can destroy someone's goodness, but Antaris's remains intact, brightening the world in spite of the lingering darkness. The desire to ensure he thrives beyond her potential demise wrestles with Veda's illogical desire to walk every step with him. Smothering every warring emotion doesn't happen fast enough to escape the notice of the most observant child she's ever met.

"I'm fine." He doesn't seem to believe her, but there's something familiar in his expression. Bitter amusement prickles in her chest. "I think I see the resemblance between you and your dad."

Antaris perks up. His interest is loud and clear.

"You want to know about your dad?"

He gravitates closer, eager. Veda isn't sure what to say. Hiram Ellis is infuriating at best, mystifying at worst. She wants Hiram to be the problem, but perspective humanizes him in a way she doesn't care for.

Fortunately, this isn't about Hiram. It's about Antaris. Veda scrambles to remember every positive detail about an infuriating man she's interacted with only three times.

"He likes to read . . ." She trails off, chuckling when Antaris points to himself. "Yeah, like you. He also likes to swim." This makes his mouth purse in thoughtful consternation. "He might like art, too, but I'll be honest, I've only just met him. Your godfather, Peter, knows him best." She slowly removes the bottle from the now-sleeping kitten, murmuring, "I think we'll both have to figure him out."

Veda barges into Peter's office after Simran leaves with Antaris, his brows rising at the bundle in her arms.

"What's that?"

"You didn't *See* this coming?" Veda sarcastically remarks.

There is no hint of amusement on Peter's face. "You know how Sight works and still make this terrible joke."

"Couldn't help myself." Veda transfers the sleeping kitten into Peter's arms despite his protest. "Long story short, this is a kitten Antaris found. No idea how he heard meowing from the balcony, but . . ."

Peter blinks like he's stared at the sun too long. "Why are you giving it to me?"

"Because our vet is missing in action, and yesterday, you asked me to drop off Lucinda's produce order today after Antaris leaves. So, congratulations, you're cat sitting."

"Khadijah is going to kill me if I bring home another stray."

Veda squints. "What do you mean *another*?"

"I found eggs abandoned in the park a few weeks ago. I thought they were ducks, which I've been wanting to add to our flock, but they hatched a couple of days ago. Turns out they're chickens. None of the chickens will take them, so they're living in my spare bathroom for now. I didn't realize how loud they'd be. Khadijah keeps calling them *chicken nuggets*. They're named after sauces."

Veda bursts out laughing as Peter grabs a wicker basket and gently deposits the kitten inside, blanket and all.

"How was your visit to the library?"

"Oddly specific question." Veda glares. "You're not quite at Clinton's level of cryptic yet."

"Cosmos, no. The date on the check-out slip was in a vision. This past weekend?"

"Yeah. I ran into Hiram and Antaris at the library." She taps her foot, hands on her hips. "He had no idea I was Antaris's tutor. How is that possible?"

Peter scratches behind the kitten's ear until it purrs, placing the basket on his desk. "I assumed he knew. Apparently, I was mistaken."

"You were also mistaken thinking my opinion of him would change. Fine, he's not a bigot, but that doesn't mean I want to be his friend."

He gestures, giving her the floor. "You sound like you need to get it off your chest, so I'm listening."

Thrown slightly, she charges on. "I could talk about how arrogant he is, how he's dripping in inherited wealth, how he has more audacity than I can stand in a single person. But honestly, my biggest gripe is his absence. He doesn't bring Antaris to school *or* pick him up. The teachers haven't seen him. Hell, *I* didn't even meet him when I was hired. I know he's your best friend, but letting Simran call the shots is a mistake. A *massive* one. Antaris doesn't even like her. He's always stiff and makes himself small around her. I wouldn't let someone like that near my kid, relative or not."

"It's complicated."

"You're making excuses for him."

"Yes, I am, but he'll reconcile this soon enough."

"You've Seen that?"

Peter half shrugs.

"My second point of contention is that he looked at my file from the night I was attacked—*illegally*—then tried to have a *gotcha* moment about wrong information. Yeah, he apologized, but I'm still upset. He threw one of the worst nights of my life in my face, then had the gall to look shocked when I reacted."

"I will agree he was wrong for his approach—"

"Antaris wants to know him," she barrels on. "And after talking to him after the verbal abuse he took at the town hall, I do, too—if only to figure out why a Seer tattooed *my amulet* on his arm."

Peter leans back in his chair, calm as ever. "Why does it matter?"

Veda opens her mouth twice and fails to answer.

"Look," Peter says, "I understand why you're defensive and paranoid. I even understand why he aggravates the hell out of you. But have you even thought about his question?"

Leave it to Peter to douse her fire. "No, I didn't."

"I know your memory from that night is spotty at best before you ran, but don't focus on the whole night. Try to remember pieces. When did you get home? What did you eat? What time of day was it? Were you alone, or was your roommate there?"

Veda closes her eyes. She remembers the sounds, the smells, their voice. Being *exhausted* as she fought for her life. Running. Knowing she couldn't stop or she'd die. The Sanguis Curse catching her, the cursed blood melting into her skin, liquefying, something *wrong* beneath her flesh. She tries to recall earlier memories, but they turn to sand, slipping through her fingers.

She opens her eyes, defeated, and grabs the keys to the school's truck.

"Let me know what they say about the cat," she mutters. "I'm dropping Lucinda's order off like I promised, then going home. I'll bring the truck back in the morning."

She doesn't wait for a reply.

Veda stews during the drive to East Proventia. She turns into one of the many subdivisions that have multiplied around the city. After passing a community pool and two stop signs, she parks in front of a pale-yellow house with green shutters and a matching front door.

Beyond her Oracle Council role, she doesn't know Lucinda well. The drop should be quick, but this assumption unravels the moment she reaches the door. Lucinda's talisman is rusted, and the gemstone, normally shining, is now opaque.

Something is wrong.

Only a handful of spells can alter a talisman; the spell must match the strength of the magic used to create it. It's a dangerous guessing game for Mages, even those with amulets. Upon further examination, Veda realizes it's not damaged. It's sleeping.

Her interest is piqued.

One rap on the door creaks it open slightly. It's eerily quiet.

Like a mausoleum. Veda shudders, stomach churning. The wrongness is why she dials the number Peter gave her for Lucinda.

The phone rings from inside the house. Once, twice, then cuts off mid-ring. No voicemail. Veda knows better than to call enforcers to a Seer's home. It never ends well. Instead, she calls Gabriel. He answers on the second ring.

"I'm at Lucinda Hampton's house at five-six-three Shelling Port Drive. Her talisman is opaque, the door's slightly open, and the phone disconnected mid-ring. How close are you?"

After a pause, he replies, "Ten minutes out."

Veda waits on the porch, growing anxious. Birds stop chirping. The breeze holds its breath. Time stills. It's so quiet, she can hear her wristwatch ticking . . .

And footsteps on the floorboards inside.

The door creaks open a fraction more. Then more.

Shattered glass and fractured wood float in suspended animation. Black scorch marks streak the walls. Gray ash coats the furniture. Blood soaks the carpet. Music plays from a destroyed record player, its needle still spinning on the vinyl.

"Come in, Veda."

Dread coils around her throat. Eyes darting, searching for the source, she sees no one . . . until she does.

The figure lives in her nightmares: a grotesque blur of shifting features, surrounded by red spider lilies that have sprouted from the carpet and lead to the open doorway. *It's them.* Veda steps back, ready to run, but a black flash strikes Lucinda's talisman. The door explodes, windows shattering with it. Blinding magic engulfs her, burning hot. The blast throws the impostor and Veda in opposite directions. Veda lands on her side in the grass, eyes burning, head pounding from bouncing off the ground. Glass and wood rain down.

Pain blurs her vision. Blood fills her mouth.

Another wave slams into her, tossing her through magic's torrential current. Her scream is a silent shout in the chaotic haze of power, noise, and light. She shields her aching head until someone grabs her arms and drags her away. Her ears still ring, but Veda makes out the vague figure standing over her, their muffled voice asking if she's okay.

She coughs violently.

Clearer now, they say, "You're safe, you're safe." Then they swear and run away.

She's unsure how much time passes, but eventually Gabriel's voice cuts through the smoke, frantically shouting her name. "Shit, are you okay?"

"I—I think," she stammers, though her body protests when he helps her sit. Francisco is with him, on the phone with dispatch, requesting medics and backup. The house—walls, roof, even the grass—has been scorched black by magic.

Gabriel and Francisco stay until investigators swarm the yard and the paramedics arrive to usher Veda to an ambulance. She's forced to swallow vile-tasting tonics, injected with potions that dull pain and emotion. The burns on her hands throb while they wrap them in healing gauze.

"They won't heal instantly," the paramedic says. "Magical injuries can't be healed with magic, but it can speed it up."

"How long?"

"Re-bandage daily, or at least every other day."

"Okay."

A grim-faced Gabriel joins Veda in the ambulance while the medic pulls glass from her arm using a minor spell, her standard-issue medic amulet glowing green. Suddenly, she gasps. The blood hovers on the edge of Veda's cut but doesn't spill. "What the—"

"Sanguis Curse," Veda says casually, earning a wide-eyed look. "Antiseptic salve and a bandage will do to keep it out of sight. My blood is here to stay, and it's not all mine . . . it's a *long* story."

"You—you shouldn't be able to walk around—"

"It's dormant." *For now.*

The medic's eyes somehow bulge further.

Gabriel pinches the bridge of his nose. "I'll take over. Go report."

The medic looks ready to argue but nods and leaves. Gabriel finishes the bandaging, his thoughts elsewhere.

"Was Lucinda home?" Veda asks.

"Yes," he reluctantly replies. "We found her in bed. Marlene is doing a scene analysis, but preliminary findings suggest she had been dead for hours when you arrived. The explosion was her talisman self-destructing to expel intruders. Do you remember what happened?"

She recounts everything, from the talisman's state to the door opening and the distorted figure whispering her name. "It was the Botanist. Same scrambled facial features, the music, everything floating, the spider lilies. Someone else was there, too. After the talisman woke, they pulled me from the magical tidal wave, asked if I was okay, then ran. I didn't see their face."

Before Gabriel can respond, Marlene lumbers toward them, wearing a baggy white bodysuit that resembles a marshmallow. She's subdued and wincing, gait uneven.

"Are you okay?" Gabriel asks.

"Yeah, I tripped getting into the house and fell on my ass."

"Almost did the same myself. Be careful."

"I will." She sighs heavily, turning to Veda. "Shit day, huh?"

"That's putting it lightly."

"Glad you're not seriously injured."

"Could have been worse," Gabriel says grimly. "Did you finish the scene analysis?"

"We can't confirm what spell killed Lucinda because of the wasting curse degrading the Imprints, just like all the other killings. There were spider lilies all over her living room and under her bed."

Confirmation makes Veda sick.

"Call your aunt Ruth," Gabriel tells Marlene. "The Council will come for Lucinda's body to give her a proper burial."

Veda taps her foot, biting her lip. "Actually, don't call Ruth yet."

Gabriel looks up from applying the last patch over her cut. "Why not?"

"You need to answer that question, gather evidence, and then approach them with all the facts. Otherwise it's pointless." She rolls her sore shoulders. "Were there *any* Imprints?"

"One," Marlene replies slowly. "A Seer's. Dr. Everett Simpson."

"Do you think he came to save you?" Gabriel's question confirms that they're thinking the same thing.

"What do you mean?" Marlene's sharp gaze mirrors Gabriel's.

"He warned me to be careful of who I trust. That tricksters fly."

Marlene sucks in a breath. "What else did he say?"

Veda jiggles her foot, restless. "A lot, but also a little. How did he know I'd be here?"

"He's watching you," Gabriel says grimly. "Francisco was right. You need protection."

"I'm not letting enforcers into my cottage. It's cloaked. I'm safe there."

"And when you're not there?"

Veda doesn't know. "I'll figure it out."

Once they leave to finish their investigation, Veda calls Khadijah to pick her up. Her thoughts spiral in every direction. Everything is connected—but *how*?

Ten

Antaris left with Simran in a strangely good mood, clutching his tea thermos in both hands like a prized possession, so distracted he forgot his lunch on the counter. Hiram grabs it on his way out.

Ten minutes later, he parks in the visitor's lot. School hasn't started yet. Early arrivals are out back, surrounded by tables and chairs under a banner that says *Appreciation Day*. Hiram spots his son quickly, tracking him as he makes a beeline for Veda. She's handing out fruit, sunglasses shielding her eyes from the bright sky. She greets Antaris with a pear. He shyly offers his thermos in return.

From her lack of surprise, it's not the first time. The urge to linger and observe is strong, but Hiram leaves to deliver the lunch box to Antaris's classroom. He finds the third-, fifth-, and ninth-year classrooms before giving up and walking to Peter's office instead.

Every surface is cluttered with folders and books. It would be alarming if Peter weren't so immaculate, even while working. Rather than knock, Hiram leans on the doorframe. "*Miss Thorne*, is it?"

Peter stops writing and sighs, lifting his head to the ceiling. "I spent the night bottle-feeding a kitten your son heard mewling from the balcony, and there are chickens in my bathroom. I'm too tired for this." He pinches the bridge of his nose, runs a hand through his hair, and shoots Hiram a sharp glance. "When I wanted to apologize for helping Simran find him a tutor, you said you'd heard. So I assumed you knew about her."

"Oh."

"Are you upset?" Peter asks. "You were interested in her once."

"Operative tense being past," he says darkly. "When she didn't know I existed, and I was an Ellis. Since she's connected the dots, she's lashed out at me every chance she gets. We've had three conversations, and at no point did I know whether they would end in peace or violence."

Peter glances at what he's holding. "Lunch box?"

"Couldn't find his classroom."

"Ah." Peter gives him a look. "You know, first impressions set the tone."

"She told you?"

"Of course she did," he replies, reasonable as ever. A faint smirk follows. "I'm surprised she didn't push you into traffic."

"She considered it," Hiram grumbles, recalling the threatening glow of her amulet's eye.

Hostility and flattery are nothing new, but Veda's ire grates him. She isn't committed to her disdain. Dissecting every shade of Veda's gray is impossible. He should avoid her presence outside of what she means to Antaris, but too much of him wants to peel back each of her layers and disprove her accusations. Just because he can. Just because he wants the approval of someone he hardly knows. Which is baffling.

"Veda is paranoid for good reason, and just as judgmental," Peter tells him. "She's already ranted about you once or twice. But I *do* have a question. She said you mentioned something incorrect in her file."

"It's a discrepancy," Hiram amends. "Didn't she look at it?"

Peter sighs and looks away. "No one enjoys reliving their darkest days, especially when all they remember are the worst parts."

When put that way, Hiram understands. "There's more to it, though, right?"

"There always is," Peter says, checking his watch. "Shit. I've got a parent memo to send out about a staff member being a person of interest in the Botanist murders."

"What?" Hiram's icy response makes Peter flinch. "You should have led with that."

"You were keen on ranting about Veda." At Hiram's *go on* look, Peter runs a hand through his blond hair. "Our staff vet, Dr. Simpson, might be involved—possibly against his will. The investigators are looking for him. All I know is another murder happened yesterday. An Oracle Council member named Lucinda Hampton."

"I remember the name." And what she practically yelled at him. "What happened?"

Peter shares what he knows while working on his memo. "Oh, one more thing. If you see Veda, don't engage. Antaris has been the first thing to make her smile today."

Hiram snorts. "You're better off hoping we don't cross paths."

"True." Peter shakes his head. "She can't stand you, but she needs all the help she can get."

Hiram raises a brow. "With what?"

"The list is too long to go through right now." Peter sips his water. "Let me finish this. We'll talk later. I'll have Antaris's lunch box delivered to his classroom."

"Thanks." Hiram mulls over what he's learned as he leaves. Near the entrance, he spots Veda holding his son's thermos. Her puzzled, pleased smile vanishes into an arched brow.

"Not today" is all she says before turning and walking off.

Hiram lets her go, but is surprised when he finds her around the corner leaning against the bench by the fountain. Heeding Peter's advice, he continues walking, stopping only when she says, "You *never* come here."

"I was dropping off Antaris's lunch box."

"In Peter's office?"

"I didn't know where his classroom was."

Veda scoffs. "Unbelievable."

Irritation sparks at her comment, but it dies when he sees the bruises on her collar, the scrape on her chin. Her hands are bandaged and trembling. She's stiff, and the exhaustion in her eyes is unmistakable.

"What happened?" Veda's dagger glare makes him concede, hands raised. "Fine. None of my business."

"Glad you figured that out." She sounds hollow, not hostile, fatigue thick in her voice. When Veda catches him staring, she thrusts the thermos into his hands and walks away. He doesn't have a good grip and nearly drops the thermos, juggling and securing it, but not before having to use his hand to catch himself from falling into the fountain. It's only as he grumbles about his soaked clothes that he realizes his onyx amulet ring must have slid off in the shuffle and is now at the bottom of the fountain.

"Fuck it." He fishes out the ring and slides it back on.

Ready to leave, Hiram turns to find Gabriel with a wide-eyed miniature version of himself that's missing a front tooth.

"How long have you been standing there?" Hiram asks.

"I'm clumsy, too!" the boy announces proudly.

"August," Gabriel says gently, "remember what I said about filtering our words?"

The boy pauses, then shakes his head. "Nope."

Gabriel closes his eyes briefly, clearly trying not to laugh. "I'll remind you later. Now, say hi to Mr. Ellis."

August beams, his smile impossibly bright. "Hi!"

Hiram's awkward wave makes Gabriel smile. "This is my son, August. He's in year two."

Children weren't in Hiram's plan, but the more he meets, the more he realizes they are tiny, complicated humans with sticky hands and ever-fluctuating dispositions. One size doesn't fit all. Their multifaceted capabilities are on display in August, who fist-bumps when Hiram offers his hand to shake formally. Gabriel flushes red from holding back laughter, but his kid's grin is so wide, Hiram can see every tooth, and weirdly, this feels . . . *normal*.

There's a heaviness to Antaris that reminds Hiram of someone holding their breath, bracing for the world to crash on top of them. August couldn't be more different, a bright, chatty bundle of energy.

The shift is jarring enough for Hiram to wonder what might happen if Antaris felt comfortable enough to trust. To let his guard down. To believe Hiram is there for him.

"Mr. Ellis, do you have a kid who goes here?" August practically bounces with excitement.

"I do. My son, Antaris. He's in year one."

"Can he be my first friend? I don't have any." The light in August's eyes dims briefly, then reignites. "But I'll be a *good* one. I know it. I'll be the bestest friend *ever*."

Hiram and Gabriel exchange a look, one he oddly recognizes. They are parents of kids who don't quite fit the typical mold. The opportunity for judgment is there, especially given August's lack of filter, but Hiram doesn't use it. August is hyperactive with barely combed hair and a stain from breakfast, but not bad.

I think he's ready for a friend.

Hiram looks between them. Nothing beats failure but not trying. "We can arrange that."

August cheers while relief blooms into a smile on Gabriel's face. "Can you wait for a second while I check him in?"

"Yeah."

Gabriel leads August inside, and less than five minutes later, he returns alone, face set. "Look, if you don't want your kid to play with mine, say so now. I can distract him, and he'll forget."

Hiram frowns. "Why would I do that?"

"August gets too excited, which overwhelms the other kids, then he gets scared they won't like him. He shuts down, and it becomes a self-fulfilling prophecy."

"Antaris stopped talking after his mother was murdered. If he had friends in London, he's now a continent away."

Gabriel nods. "The socializing bar is in hell for us, isn't it?"

"Lower."

They laugh.

"Let's schedule a playdate and see what happens," Gabriel suggests.

"That might be good."

"Oh, and I noticed you talking to Veda. We might want to invite her as a buffer. She watches August sometimes. She's always been able to wrangle him."

"My mother hired her as Antaris's tutor," Hiram says. "Didn't know you two were friends."

"Occupational and situational friends. Veda seems cold and tough, but she's dealing with a lot of shit. More since yesterday."

"Peter mentioned something but wasn't specific. Care to enlighten me?"

Gabriel looks around, making sure no one is in earshot, then lowers his voice. "That's actually what I wanted to talk to you about. Do you have time to talk in private?"

Private means a small breakfast shop down the road called the Leaning Cactus.

The staff and patrons know Gabriel by name. They confirm his order of medium-well steak and eggs with cheese and clear his table on sight. In contrast, Hiram's presence draws whispers, stares, and disdainful glares. He can only imagine the rumors. He wonders how they'll have a private conversation amid the chaos, but when they sit, the noise dulls to a hum.

Gabriel opens his hand to reveal a vibrating crystal. The only sound is the friction between the crystal and the air, heightened by magic. No one outside the blocking stone's radius will hear them, and vice versa.

"I didn't know Washington legalized these for public use," Hiram remarks.

Gabriel pockets the stone. "They haven't, but no one will know unless you tell them."

When the waitress arrives with coffee, Hiram orders something simple: eggs and toast. While pouring himself a cup and adding creamer, he watches Gabriel drown his in sugar.

"Why a private conversation?"

"You looked in Veda's file the day you were in my office."

"I did," Hiram says, unfazed.

"That's illegal."

"I know."

"I could have you brought in."

"Okay."

"Veda gave me an earful about it."

"Of course she did."

"Right." Gabriel chuckles. "Then I'll cut to the chase. I shouldn't tell you this, but there was another murder in the Botanist case yesterday. Lucinda Hampton."

"One of the Oracle Council members?"

"How did you know that?"

"Peter mentioned something." Hiram recalls the town hall meeting to an enrapt Gabriel. Lucinda's face remains a blur. "I bet they're up in arms, probably accusing me of being the killer."

"Actually, it's been crickets."

It's his turn to listen in silence as Gabriel shares details about the latest murder. A twinge of guilt surfaces when he thinks back to his earlier interaction with Veda.

"That's not all," Gabriel adds. "I'm taking a shot in the dark here. She got a note with a series of numbers from the school vet, Dr. Simpson. Have you gotten anything like that?"

"Not numbers, but I did get a note that said, *BeeyardS rain*."

"What?" Gabriel looks as confused as Hiram feels. "Do you have it?"

"No, it's at home. I figured it was a mistake . . ." He shrugs.

"I'll need to see it, maybe test the handwriting."

"Okay."

Gabriel pulls a photo from his jacket and slides it across the table. "Do you recognize him?"

Hiram glances at the ordinary man with a sandy beard and matching hair. "No."

"That's Dr. Simpson." Gabriel lowers his voice. "I don't know where he fits in yet, but I assume it's somewhere. If you see him, don't call the enforcers. Call me."

Hiram nods. "Is he dangerous?"

"I'm not sure. He's been cursed to devolve into madness the more he tries to tell the truth—at least, that's what he told Veda." He straightens the salt and pepper shakers. "Did you ever receive Antaris's boxes from London?"

"I did."

"Let me guess, I need a search warrant?"

Hiram considers it. "After we're finished here, you can look. There's a book that's obviously Grace's called *The Hidden Powers of Rituals and Oddities*. She put it in his box to be found, I'll assume."

"Given her pattern, yeah, it's a good assumption."

"I'll let you see it if I can ask you a question."

"Okay."

"Veda—" Hiram watches Gabriel drain the rest of his coffee in two burning gulps, wincing. "Is she *that* difficult of a topic?"

"You've met her."

Fair point. "Has she always been . . ."

"Paranoid? Defensive? That's the only Veda I've ever known. She has her reasons."

"The home invasion?" Gabriel's silence is confirmation. Hiram taps his finger on the table. "Did she ever mention how they got in, with the windows and patio door locked?"

"The front door was in pieces," Gabriel says.

"In the wrong direction."

"I know, but Veda barely remembers that night. Looking at the file makes her zone out, like she's reliving it."

Hiram feels worse about accosting her. "I didn't get a good look in your office, but if you check, I bet there's an engaged lock in the rubble. Then ask how the hell someone entered a locked home with an active talisman—"

"That was untouched. Francisco thinks they broke into her house to kill her because of what she witnessed."

"How did you end up on the Botanist case?" Hiram presses.

"Punishment. We were pushy about a case involving an illegal program of experiments on Seers. We broke up the operation and all but forced the prosecutor to take the case. Everyone involved ended up walking, but we pissed off so many people that they assigned us to a case they thought we'd never solve. We spent six months staring at a dead end until I searched the national database for cases with the same elements, which is how I found the earlier victims . . . *and* Veda's home invasion. I thought it was a mistake, but after combing through scene photos, magical tests, and the interview with Sabine Dreary, her roommate, who wasn't home that night, I realized that her home invasion was a lead."

"How so?"

"Because it was an anomaly. Until Grace's murder," Gabriel replies. "Anyway, I learned Veda was in Proventia, and she's been helping with the case since I contacted her, but pushing her for more details is difficult because it's easy to see she went through hell." Empathy softens his voice. "That changes a person."

Francisco meets them at Hiram's home.

After a brief search, Hiram hands Gabriel *The Hidden Powers of Rituals and Oddities*, a photo album, and the *BeeyardS rain* note, raising a brow when Gabriel passes the first to Francisco and keeps the other two.

"He's better with oddities," Gabriel explains. "And I never forget a face. We're both not bad at puzzles."

Whatever works.

Hiram makes himself scarce, though he stays within earshot, unpacking the final boxes in his bedroom. Last on the list of priorities, it's something he's been putting off—anything to avoid the clean lines and white walls. Cold. Quiet. Devoid of character. Identity. He could make changes, but practicality nags about resale value and neutral tones. Too much personality, and it won't sell. But will he want to sell?

They could live anywhere, in any country; Hiram has the means to make the sky their limit. But after a little over a month here, he's not sure. Uprooting Antaris means separating him from Veda, and that feels wrong.

Unfortunately, he knows the truth. She's right . . . *and* wrong. He could try to make up for lost time by spoiling Antaris, buying his love, but Hiram knows from experience that love unearned means nothing.

"You should go with a neutral color."

Hiram doesn't jolt, but it's close. Gabriel's steps are lighter than expected.

"Cream or gray," he adds. "It'll pair well with the dark wood."

"Thanks, I guess." Hiram closes the bedroom door. "Find everything you need?"

"About that . . ." Gabriel gestures for him to follow, leading the way to the living room, where Francisco waits, closed book in hand. "Ask him what you asked me."

Francisco looks at Hiram. "As an Ellis, how connected are you?"

"No."

"We'd pay a consulting fee," he bargains.

"Does it *look* like I need money?" Hiram replies flatly.

Gabriel looks at the vaulted ceilings and crown molding. "Fair point."

"Grace used a scrambling hex on several pages." Francisco opens the book and holds it out. "If we don't break it, we'll lose whatever she was trying to hide. The department gave us the bare minimum in resources, but *you* might know someone who can help."

Hiram looks at the pages. Broken words and letters float and shift, quickening the longer he stares. Random letters glow in different colors.

It gives him a headache. He looks between the investigators and sighs. "I'll help. On one condition."

"What's the condition?" Gabriel asks.

"That you don't need my help again for *anything* in the foreseeable future."

Eleven

Veda has a shadow named Antaris.

He walks ahead, trails behind, veers off course, but never strays far from her side while roaming the greenhouse. Content without purpose, he explores every corner, touching nothing, and marveling at everything. Veda follows leisurely, happy to bask in the peace of watching him. The gloves she brought for him are bright yellow, and when he tries them on, they reach his elbows. The addition of goggles earns her a perplexed look.

"Follow me."

Veda leads him to the berries, pointing to the ripening blueberry bushes. "Look for the dark-blue ones. They'll fall into your hand easily."

Antaris follows instructions well, but the first berry he picks is his last. Initially confused, Veda kneels beside him, ready to help, until she sees him cradling the blueberry in both hands.

"My mom used to tell me to thank the earth when I picked my first fruit. You don't have to speak to say *thank you*. Just close your eyes and say the words in your head." She demonstrates, and when she opens her eyes, Antaris is doing the same. When he finishes, before she can tell him to rinse it, he eats it, brightening at the sweetness.

"Good?" He nods. Veda smiles and draws an X on the side of the terra-cotta pot holding the bush. "The X is a mark of protection. It's superstitious, but my mom swore by it."

He draws an X, not on the pot but on the back of her hand.

"You think I need protection?"

His expression sobers, then he leans against her. Not a hug, just a moment of shared space.

"Come on, let's pick some fruit for you to take home."

He picks two of everything: grapes, blackberries, strawberries, tangerines, and lemons. Veda adds more to the basket to wash later in the kitchen. By the time they finish, the basket is half full. She doesn't think twice about carrying it, but is amused when Antaris keeps hold of the handle. He's helping. They're nearly out when he stops at the last in a row of young olive trees, looking up. Everything in the greenhouse teems with life, but this tree has no leaves.

"It was sick not long ago. Normally, we'd uproot it, save our energy for the stronger ones, but I think it can be saved. It just needs extra care." Veda puts down the basket and brings him closer, pointing at tiny buds. "Even if you can't see it, there's life in there. As long as the tree keeps fighting, I won't give up on it."

Just as she will never give up on him.

"Do you know about olive trees?"

Antaris shakes his head.

"They mean peace." Veda touches the branch again. "It may be sick, but disease or drought will never kill it. I could cut it down, even burn it, and still it would heal and grow back."

Antaris traces an X at the base of the tree. Even indestructible things need care and hope.

When their time is nearly up, Veda sends Antaris to water the flowers along the edge of the fence. She sneaks glances as he stops at each plant, stoops to its level, and traces shapes on a petal before watering it. After, they sit on the bottom step of the school. Veda peels a tangerine and offers him a slice. "You deserve it."

Instead of eating, Antaris offers it back to her, eyes insistent.

"I deserve it?"

He nods. They split the slice in compromise. Antaris puts on his school jacket and book bag. She expects him to retreat before Simran's arrival, as usual, but today, he's distracted by a note in his hand. Consternation makes him look older than six.

"I can read that for you."

Antaris looks up. She expects him to tuck it away, keep it hidden and protected. Instead, he offers it with slow hesitation. Veda unfolds it with the same care he gives everything, and they look at it together. The penmanship is legible enough to know it's not meant for her eyes. Only his. She considers giving it back, but Antaris is watching her, waiting, hopeful that she can help him learn about the father he wants to know.

"It says . . ." She's struck by his father's written words of devotion. *"You're the best choice I've ever made."*

Veda rides to the bridge over Dalneau River to clear her mind. She parks her bike and leans on the railing. It's grounding, watching the water pass under the bridge and emerge on the other side. The river ebbs in some spots, flowing in others, painting the surface with tide pools and currents more stunning than any brushstrokes could capture on canvas.

Her phone rings, breaking the silence. She digs it out of her pocket and answers.

"Where are you?" Khadijah's voice is low and frantic.

"At the river."

"Alone?"

"Yeah . . ."

Khadijah's relief is audible. "Okay. I called Gabriel, and he's on the way here. Moab was attacked leaving the bank in Panoramic."

"Is he . . ."

"He escaped. All I got out of him was that someone intervened so he could get away. He ran to my clinic, and I pulled him in. He lost consciousness from whatever curse he was hit with, but he's stable now."

"His family . . . ?"

"Jordan is at school in Montana. I called Forestry for Tawa, but he's on shift in the Cascades and can't get here for another few hours. Once Moab was stable, I started looking for witnesses and clearing the area so no one disturbs the spider lilies."

"I'm on the way." Veda hangs up before Khadijah can protest.

The ride to Panoramic is twenty-five minutes with traffic. Veda makes it in twelve, rolling through yellow lights and weaving past slow vehicles. The only available motorcycle spot is occupied by a double-parked, sleek black sedan adorned with the thin paneling typical of cars powered by magic and gasoline. She considers taking the caps off their tires out of spite, but decides she doesn't have time for pettiness. At least, not today. Irritated, she parks in a no-parking zone at the end of the block and walks to the Conclave.

Spider lilies have followed Moab from the bank to the clinic, sprouting from pavement cracks. Bloodred blossoms shimmer in the sun, their dangerous hue catching her eye as glowing specks float upward. Khadijah emerges from the clinic next door, still in scrubs, looking ready to scold Veda. She stops short when something else catches her eye.

Gabriel has arrived, and he isn't alone.

Hiram is with him, ignoring the glares and stares of nearby bystanders. He wears black like it defines him. The color of power, elegance, and authority. Fitting. Unreadable blue eyes land on her; the quick set of his jaw means he knows an argument is coming.

He's right, but the first jab doesn't come from Veda. It comes from Khadijah.

"Why did you bring him here?"

Hiram barely reacts, but Gabriel flinches at her tone. "Hiram's been helping with the investigation. This concerns him as much as it does Veda and the Oracle Council."

"How?" she fires back.

"Not that I have to explain my presence to you," Hiram interjects coolly, "but my son's mother was a victim."

Khadijah falls silent and excuses herself to check on Moab.

"Let me know when he wakes up," Gabriel requests.

She salutes on her way inside.

Gabriel rubs the back of his neck and perks up as someone approaches. Veda follows his gaze to Francisco and Marlene. The former towers over the latter, carrying a large black bag. His face is guarded, tighter, far from the poised, relaxed man Veda knows. Marlene is tense, too. Her blue-black hair is pulled back into a thick bun at the top of her head. Despite the ridiculous-looking puffy jumpsuit, half unzipped to reveal a pastel-blue shirt and her blue-jay pendant, she wears professionalism to blanket her features. Veda notices the slight, skeptical twitch of Marlene's brow when she spots Hiram, but after giving everyone a friendly wave, she offers him one gloved hand.

"I'm Scene Analyst Marlene Wells," she offers in greeting. "I don't believe we've met."

"Hiram Ellis." He shakes her hand.

"You made it here quickly," Gabriel comments. "Francisco was leaving to pick you up from the office."

"I was nearby," Marlene replies, then smiles at Veda. "How are you feeling after what happened at Lucinda's?"

"A little sore but mostly better."

"Good."

Francisco sets the bag down, and Marlene immediately gets to work, retrieving masks for each Mage to protect them from the magical blowback Seers are immune to. She crosses the promenade to take photos of the spider lilies from multiple angles. When the flowers don't burn after the shifting breeze causes them to touch her jumpsuit, a relieved exhale escapes along with a nervous smile. "Close one, yeah?"

Marlene mock-wipes her brow and pulls out her hawk's-eye stone.

"So, in theory, what does this test do?" Veda asks.

"It shows what happened and lists the identities of everyone whose Imprint remains," Francisco explains.

"Even the Botanist?"

"If they're a Seer, the results appear instantly, thanks to the Registration being imprinted in each hawk's-eye stone."

Hiram frowns. "A test that could identify the Botanist. Why haven't you used it before?"

"Imprints fade quickly. Three hours, max. Every victim before, we've arrived long after their attacks, and we're only able to determine the type of magic used. At Lucinda's, Veda was there, but Lucinda had been dead for several hours before her arrival, and it doesn't appear as if the Botanist used magic after casting a wasting curse to scrub the scene clean. But with Moab, we're within the window of his attack, and with nothing cast to clean their Imprint, residuals should be still present. We should get a match."

Gabriel nudges his partner. "She still won't talk to you?"

"No," Francisco mutters. "I keep trying to figure out what happened, but she shuts me down. I don't know, it's been three months, and she seems . . . different."

"She doesn't seem all that different to me."

"That's because you don't pay attention—never mind . . ." Francisco runs a hand through his hair. "She usually hates birds and pastels, and likes it when I carry her bag. It's heavy, used to bruise her leg because she's not allowed to use anything beyond basic magic in public. But I had to take it from her because she was about to cast a weightless charm without even thinking what would happen if anyone saw. That's mid-level magic and illegal for Seers to do in public."

"You're just feeling the wrath of a woman who's changed her mind . . . and her style. My ex-wife changed her hair, clothes, and career. Now she's shooting a documentary on the effects of the Great Vanishing on Lewes, South Carolina, for the upcoming anniversary." Gabriel pats Francisco's shoulder. "Look, it sucks. But take it from someone who fought his divorce tooth and nail: You can't fight their choice."

Francisco's frustration smooths into concentration, but Veda sees the storm still brewing behind the easygoing man's dark eyes.

She watches Marlene and shrugs. "Maybe she's stressed. She's been pushing hard for a promotion. Barely hangs out with Khadijah."

Gabriel's brow raises. "Anything above scene analyst is management, and there are no Seers in management. Unless she's trying to be the first. I guess if anyone can do it, it's her."

Veda purses her lips, deep in thought as Marlene finishes setting up. She puts on her mask in odd anticipation, having never seen a scene analyzed in person, only depictions on procedural television shows.

A hand on her shoulder makes Veda jolt and whirl around. It's Hiram.

"You're too close," he murmurs, blue eyes sharp.

How ironic. That's exactly how she feels about him.

"You need to be outside the ten-foot radius or your Imprint could tamper with the test."

As if confirming, Gabriel waves them over. "Come on, you two. She's starting."

Veda shrugs Hiram's hand off and walks to Gabriel's side, aware that she's being watched.

Marlene holds the hawk's-eye above her head. *"Etreal."*

The veins in her arms glow as the space around her darkens, warping. Light bursts from her fingertips. Wind whirls in a tight vortex despite the still air outside the circle. The sound of a cracking whip startles Veda. Magic. Energy. A pulse ripples through the bubble where Marlene stands, her head tilted toward the spinning stone, her veins alight.

While Marlene's suit sways, her head cover holds. The stone rises higher, spinning faster. Random flashes of light illuminate in spots around the Conclave. Footsteps materialize, highlighting the paths of those who passed through. Shapes and symbols form like clouds in the air. Two sets of footsteps face each other. Nothing happens—then one attacks. Blue and red flares: hexes and curses. The other remains white. The attacker's color shifts from blue to an eerie golden yellow, a haze spreading outward, settling where spider lilies now bloom. A third figure appears from behind, glowing blue. The attacker turns white, inert, and the victim's steps move away. It confirms Moab's telling. The second clash is less clear. Both sets flare with color, then flee in opposite directions.

Suddenly, everything within the circle is drawn toward the hawk's-eye as if pulled by a black hole. It spins and glows, absorbing every trace of what happened. Marlene takes her eyes off it long enough to retrieve a small pouch from her bag with a curl of her finger. At her command, the stone lowers slowly into the pouch. When she seals it, the air clears. Veda removes her mask, reeling from what she's witnessed. The cleanup process is quick and efficient. By the time Veda regains her bearings, Marlene is ready to leave, but she's taking a few more pictures of the spider lilies.

"What did the gold mean?" Veda asks.

"Each color matches a spell type. Gold is Omnipresent magic." Gabriel sounds tired. "We already knew the spider lilies were Omnipresent, and possibly Everett's curse, too. If the same person's behind both . . . Well, that's worrying. It's cropped up for the second time in a month. Our commander will likely call in Washington, DC. The Oracle Council will be forced to cooperate, or risk disbandment."

"How long will that take?" Hiram's question surprises Veda, as does how intensely he appears to be listening.

"Four to six weeks. It will take time for the call to be made, answered, and for the staffing to be arranged."

"Then we better figure it out ourselves," Veda says. "The Council—"

"I'm still trying to gather info on all the members and anything special that transpired during their years of service," Gabriel cuts in. "Everett's still out there, and all you remember about the Botanist is their blurred face."

Hiram folds his arms. "So it's safe to assume this was the Botanist? Not an impostor?"

"It's never safe to assume anything, but it's likely."

"And the person who saved Moab?"

Francisco steps back, looking over his shoulder at the spider lilies. "Has to be Everett, based on what he said to Veda. Marlene, how long will it be before the analysis is ready?"

Veda turns, not realizing Marlene is standing behind her until she replies, "I'll put a rush on it."

Francisco's gaze hardens. "With the Registration embedded in each stone, you don't need to put a rush on anything to give a preliminary report on whether Seers are involved."

"I know that." Marlene's tone raises everyone's eyebrows. "Apologies for assuming you'd want a comprehensive report."

"In February, you told me that a comprehensive report is worthless if the stone is compromised at some point during processing."

"I did . . . fine." She pulls out the stone and casts a spell. Smoky symbols rise, one after another. Green. Orange. Red. The stone glows, spinning first clockwise, then counter. A white symbol emerges. The pieces separate and reform into a name.

Everett Simpson.

"He's the one who intervened?" Veda asks.

"Yeah," Gabriel replies. The stone keeps spinning and flipping before another symbol emerges, splitting and shifting into the second name. *Moab.* The victim.

"Now, the Botanist," Francisco murmurs, impatiently tapping his foot as the stone spins longer than before. Just when Veda thinks it'll fade, confirming their aggressor isn't a Seer, it flashes. The glow intensifies, flaring as if about to burst into flames. Then it splits to reform into the name they've all been dreading or hoping to see. What appears causes a silence to fall like a shroud, a purring, meditative stillness, before Veda blurts out:

"The name is locked?"

Veda's past is like a hot stove. She knows damn well it's going to burn, but she touches it anyway. She has to.

Home alone. Music in the air. Wine numbs her pain. The streetlight outside remains lit when the apartment suddenly goes dark. Startled, Veda sets down her glass. The upbeat melody doesn't falter, but she does.

"Veda?"

Memories and reality intertwine, weaving a messy tapestry that leaves Veda momentarily incapable of distinguishing the two. She's on a street corner. She's okay. She's also not alone.

Hiram is stone-faced in front of her, yet his eyes brim with a kind of concern she can't handle. "Are you okay? You look—"

"I'm fine." Veda studies the ground. "I'm leaving."

The sun barely crests the nearby trees. Cars and bikes pass. People mill about, wandering in and out of restaurants in Panoramic, enjoying the start to a pleasant evening. Some shoot concerned looks at Veda, which she pointedly ignores. Others glare at Hiram instead.

"Did you hear what I said?" Hiram asks, reaching, but she steps back.

"What?"

"Marlene left. Francisco is calling Commander Bishop about the blocked Imprint, and Gabriel is inside with Khadijah and Moab. I was about to leave when I saw you still standing here dazed." His gaze darts around before settling back on her. "Look, it's normal to feel off, especially if you're not used to witnessing magical testing. My first time was in law school—it's a requirement. I was cocky and didn't wear a mask. Big mistake. I was sick for days."

"I said I'm fine."

Exhaustion hits Veda like a freight train, leaving her weary. Hiram's skepticism is loud; she lacks the energy to argue. Instead, she gestures in the direction of her bike. His offer to accompany her is silent, but his presence is not. The breeze brings her back to complete awareness, leaving Veda regretful of leaving her jacket at home. Her strength doesn't return until Hiram stops at a food truck, buys two bottles of water, and steps in her path, ignoring her protests until she accepts.

When he's no longer looking, she ravenously gulps it down as if she's emerging from a desert.

Hiram's eyes are still elsewhere when he asks, "Better?"

Veda coughs. "Fuck off."

By the time they reach her bike, she's back to herself. The helmet is still on the seat, and the double-parked car is still there. No ticket. What a shame. She should have taken the tire caps when she had the chance.

"Ah, you're next to me."

Veda rolls her eyes. Of course it's his car. Hiram scans the area like he'll find the Botanist hidden behind a tree or blending into the crowd.

"You shouldn't be out in the open. Not with Dr. Simpson and the Botanist around."

"Dr. Simpson isn't a danger. He may be going mad, but he wanted to warn me, to protect me, and it looks like he helped Moab escape. As for the Botanist, I'd ask how you know they're a danger to me, but your answer is going to piss me off, so I won't bother."

"I put the pieces together that I was given." At her dirty look, he amends, "Fine, the pieces I took without permission. I'm an attorney, so I'm nosy and I know how to keep a secret. It doesn't matter how I know. What matters is, you've come face-to-face with the Botanist three times. Of course you're in danger."

"You're not wrong."

He tilts his head. "It looks like we've gone over a hundred words without arguing. A record."

Veda rolls her eyes. "Good to know. I'll go back to being a pain in the ass."

"Glad you're acknowledging it, at least to me." A car slows down, eager for their spots. Hiram waves them off. "Don't act like you're not hot and cold. Last time I saw you, I nearly fell into a fountain trying to apologize, but now you're willingly speaking to me."

"Blame it on how I'm feeling."

"Right. After that . . . staring episode you just had. You're fine, of course."

Something about his voice, an odd mix of sardonic and warm, unsettles her. Fist tight against her side, warm and irritated, she hates feeling nervous like this. Hiram is an abstraction Veda shouldn't notice, much less acknowledge. "I'll be back to normal next time."

"Next time?" Hiram's brow waggles suggestively, earning him an unimpressed look that makes him raise both hands in surrender. "Then I should use this rare opportunity to ask why Antaris is now drawing X's on the plants in the yard before you're back to being angry at my existence."

Veda ignores the tinge of embarrassment. Last time they spoke, Veda was one day out from being blown off the porch, up all night with insomnia, and in a terrible mood. Unfortunately, she can't call him unreasonable. "He's protecting the plants."

"Oh," Hiram mutters, surprised by her direct response. "Let's see if we can extend this streak of cooperation. Have a good evening."

"You were right," Veda says, albeit reluctantly. "We do need to talk, if only to admit I don't trust your involvement in this. Antaris's mother sends a message to Gabriel that leads him to you. Then you to me. My amulet is on your arm. You illegally search my file and—"

"It doesn't make sense," he interrupts. "Every window was locked. How did they get in?"

"It was like someone dropped a bomb on the apartment. I keep trying, but the first thing I recall is running. I don't even remember how I got out. Sometimes, I get flashes—my staring episode was me remembering—but it never lasts. I never see the full picture." Admitting this makes Veda itch to throw on her helmet and flee to the safety of home, but more truths spill before she can leave. "The Botanist cursed me that night. Sanguis Curse."

Hiram goes still. "That curse is—how are you still alive?"

"Blood curses have to be cast perfectly or they fuck everything up. After I got out, they cursed the blood in the apartment and sent it to find me, but their blood was mixed in, too. My blood treated it like a foreign invader, creating a cyst on my side, trapping it there. I barely made it to Proventia, to Peter. He arranged for Seers along the bus route to use healing spells to keep me going at each stop, and when I made it, Khadijah forced the curse into dormancy."

"That doesn't sound legal."

"It's not."

"How long will it sleep?"

"No one knows because I've passed the point where an ordinary curse would wake." Veda looks away. "Peter and Khadijah have done everything to get it out safely, but I'm on borrowed time. They haven't given up, but—"

"You have." He tsks. "That's a damn shame."

Anger sparks from the pity wafting from him. "Don't act like you care."

"As long as you don't pretend you're not terrified." Hiram studies her closely, something unreadable in his eyes. "Maybe it's fear that makes you so different from how I remember you."

She stiffens. "What are you talking about? W—"

"I saw you at Peter's graduation party. Arguing with three idiots. You never backed down."

Veda can't react because he's too close. The topic is too personal.

"Where's your fight, Veda?"

The bitter urge to run from his pointed, painful question makes her head swim. "I know what I'm up against. The odds aren't in my favor. This curse has been growing inside me, and now with the Botanist knowing where I am—" She shakes her head, trying to control her mounting anxiety.

"You're one blocked Imprint from having a name. Gabriel and Francisco finally have a direction and pieces to put together. It may be a clusterfuck, but it's not over."

"I wish that were true. What I know is that the Botanist's blood is trapped in me. It's as cursed as mine. The moment it's free, I can use the same incantation to have their blood find them like it found me. They will suffer as I have and die as I will. The Botanist won't kill anyone else."

"Or you could extract the curse."

Frustration crawls up her spine. "I *told* you. We've tried. Eight times, to be exact."

Hiram cards his fingers through his hair. "Peter said you needed all the help you could get. Now I understand why."

Veda rolls her eyes. "His optimism remains delusional."

A dark, determined look overtakes Hiram's expression. "Then let me try the ninth time. What do you have to lose?"

Veda stares, stunned. "You're an attorney. Not a healer, doctor, or medic. What could you possibly do for me?"

"I'm an Ellis, and while that's everything you hate, the name comes with the privilege of connections. I can throw a wider net for your curse."

"We've looked up everything that's been published."

"Then I'll start with what hasn't." In the face of her skepticism, he lifts his hands. "All legal and aboveboard, of course."

"Why would you help me?"

Hiram shrugs. "My son is attached to you. I'd rather he not lose anyone else."

It's one thing to have these errant thoughts when she's alone, and another to hear it said out loud by someone who will have to pick up the pieces when she's gone. Not a thought anymore but tangible with the power to shape reality.

"More than that," he adds quietly, "you can pretend all you want, but we both know you're not ready to die."

Hiram's smirk grows the longer she doesn't rebut.

"That's what I thought." He extends his hand. "Be prepared to be sick of me."

She smacks it away. "I already am."

"It's mutual." He's unfazed, smug yet serious. Weirdly charming. "You'll live. I'll see to it."

"Sounds like you're about to overpromise and under-deliver on—"

"I have a high success rate of making good on promises."

Veda snatches her helmet and puts it on. "Well, aren't *you* a smug asshole?"

"I am." He leans in, determined eyes set on her. The corners of his lips twitch. "I'm also more than that. You'll see."

Twelve

Promises made, now Hiram has to deliver.

He gathers patience before making calls to several of his father's contacts. No one answers, but he doesn't think much of it until his phone rings.

Barrett skips the greeting. "The last time you called this many of my friends, it was for rushed paperwork, genetic and Imprint testing, and a custody hearing for Antaris. Anything I should know?"

"No," Hiram replies, tapping his finger. "I need information."

There is a pause. "You could have called me."

"I doubt you'd want to be involved."

"Try me."

"I need access. Peter mentioned trying and failing to obtain research on the Sanguis Curse: unpublished articles, unsanctioned extraction attempts, survival rates, everything hidden under the bureaucratic rugs. I called Uncle Phillip because he's the silent partner of a curse research institute in Atlanta, and likely the reason that research is guarded."

Phillip is a well-connected figure in magical research—a fanatic believer of Mage supremacy, a mad scientist, and a raging bigot all wrapped up in one terrifying human being. He believes magic is the answer to the "Seer problem." Eugenics. Scientific dogmatism. Sterilization in families with high Seer birth rates. All of it. Odd views for someone with a dozen illegitimate children he refuses to claim.

"How do you know this?" Barrett murmurs.

"It wasn't hard. There are Seer-interest groups tracking bigots with too much money and influence. They make sure they're boycotting the right places." From what Hiram's gathered, these groups monitor the entire family, but Barrett and his brothers get special attention.

"Smart." Barrett offers the rare compliment, but Hiram doesn't trust it. "I'll handle my brother."

"Why?"

"He's become paranoid. Calling after years of silence will only fuel his fire."

"I get it," Hiram says.

"Besides, I don't need to talk to him to get what you need. He uses his house in Medina as overflow for whatever he does. I have access, and he has an extensive organization system. This shouldn't take long."

It sounds too good to be true. "If you do this, what do you want?"

"Nothing."

Hiram isn't convinced, but won't look a gift horse in the mouth. "Fine. Can you also point me to someone who can reverse a scrambling hex? Unofficially, of course. It's for an investigation."

"I did not realize you'd started consulting," Barrett replies, as casually as if he were commenting on the weather. "Commander Bishop only mentioned you visiting the FCD."

"Your informant is correct." Of course his father is watching him. "Like I said, it's unofficial. A favor of sorts, but keep that to yourself. Or do I need your permission—"

"I was checking up on you, Hiram. Your mother is concerned with how secretive you have been. You only provide the bare minimum, so we look for other ways to connect with you. How are we to fix things when you hardly visit and never call?"

"Not as fun when the tables turn, is it?"

Barrett sidesteps the topic. "What sort of case is it?"

"One you disagree with morally. It involves Seers. A murder case."

"The Botanist killings."

Hiram frowns. "How do you know about it?"

"I make it my business to know about cases that could lead to another mass Vanishing." Barrett falls silent. "You should not get involved in these things. It is dangerous, and you have Antaris to think about."

"Too late," Hiram says flatly. "What do you know?"

"The monsters we create are an extension of us, our fears and desires. We fit them with our entitlement and tell them they deserve what they have not earned. But in the end, nature has a way of balancing wrong into right, if not immediately, then eventually."

Hiram doesn't like how this sounds. "What aren't you telling me?"

"A lot, but I will bring you what you need to know." His father pauses. "As for the scrambling hex, they are nearly impossible to undo—you must have a grasp of the language as well as talent. I would normally suggest your cousin Francis, but no. Ask former Congressman Desai. I have never seen anyone decode like he can."

Hiram is surprised. "How do you know him?"

"When he was elected to Congress, I was in my third term. Your grandfather was finishing his last in the Senate. There was a firestorm when he first arrived; some refused to be in the same room with Desai, let alone serve on the same committee. They had to translate everything into braille. Someone always sent his official correspondences with a scrambling hex, thinking it would stop him, but he was always on time, prepared. Your grandfather could not stand it . . . or him, for that matter."

Not a single insult. If anything, his father sounds impressed. "What about you?"

"What about me?"

"Did you participate?"

"No."

"But you did nothing to stop it."

"No."

"I see." Apathetic avoidance is the pitfall of a peacekeeper. Discomfort leaves Hiram feeling uneasy. "I'll ask Clinton for assistance."

"You're welcome," Barrett says. "Allow me to be delusional enough to believe you were going to thank me."

Hiram will. Just once. "Thank you."

"Is there anything else?" his father asks.

No. Yet the question burns, leaving Hiram choking on smoke. "Did you ever want to stand up for him?"

Barrett exhales. "The past is complicated. I did what I needed to get where I wanted to—"

"That wasn't my question."

His father is silent for so long that Hiram hunts for ways, short of just hanging up, to end it.

"Yes, I did," Barrett finally confesses.

"Then why didn't you?"

"It wasn't my fight."

The words rattle in Hiram's bones.

Hazel eyes peer out from behind the armchair. Antaris picks up a children's dictionary, flips through it while sitting, sets it on the table, and scoots to the end of the sofa.

Hiram sneaks glances during each part of his approach, hiding his amusement as a head of damp curls pops up at the edge of the kitchen island.

"Would you like to help?"

The answer is a decisive, enthusiastic nod and something odd: Antaris taps the table twice.

Hiram looks around the kitchen before finding a step stool that brings Antaris to a height fit to see everything.

"Your list has pasta and cheese," he says, bending slightly to show him. He and Antaris are close but not quite touching. "I thought I'd make Alfredo with grilled chicken on the side."

Antaris's excitement dims. After cycling through reasons, Hiram thinks he's found the answer.

"Did your mom make this for you?"

Antaris nods slowly.

"Ah, yeah. It was her favorite."

Hiram feels strange saying it out loud. Antaris knows more about Grace than Hiram knows about him.

"I can make something else if you . . ." Antaris shakes his head. "Okay."

Still a little blue, Antaris touches the bag of pasta, fingers lingering on the crinkled plastic.

"I usually like to make it from scratch," Hiram admits. "I enjoy making something out of nothing, but if we want to eat before midnight"—he gestures to the clock—"this'll do."

He sets the water to boil, tossing in a generous pinch of salt. At Antaris's inquiring look, he explains, "It helps it boil faster."

Cooking has always been a solitary task for Hiram, quiet and focused. A time to challenge himself with balancing tastes and textures. He never had much time before, always working, but now, creating three meals a day for a picky eater has become more satisfying.

Strange how easily his life has changed. How quickly he's adapted to Antaris's presence. How naturally the words spill when his hands are busy.

"I was about your age when I learned to make eggs," he says, measuring flour for the roux. "I burned them each time, but I never gave up."

Antaris watches closely while Hiram makes the roux, seeming surprised when Hiram offers him the whisk.

"It's mostly done, but it's important to keep stirring while I add the ingredients."

Antaris accepts the task with care, stirring slowly. He freezes at Hiram's suggestions and relaxes with each hushed word of praise. They cook like this, with anecdotes from the parts of Hiram's childhood that have nothing to do with his parents. Antaris gradually unfurls. When the sauce is ready, Hiram offers him the first taste. They move on to the chicken. Hiram demonstrates how to clean and slice the chicken breast; Antaris watches, fascinated.

"Now we season it. How many can you recognize?"

Antaris points to the salt and pepper. Hiram nods and lets him sprinkle both on the chicken. More here, less there. It goes offtrack when Antaris starts pointing to random spices on the rack: dill, cinnamon, star anise.

"That's not how it works," Hiram explains. "We season to make food taste better." He lets Antaris taste each one, hiding a smile when his son grimaces after the first two and outright refuses the third. "None of them taste good in this type of dish, so we try others until we find what works. Luckily for you, I already know."

He picks out garlic and a few others from the rack, showing Antaris how to sprinkle them evenly. After the chicken has cooked and the pasta boiled, they sit at the table with their plates. Hiram's anxiety spikes when Antaris stares at his meal, unmoving.

"Does it look good?"

Antaris bobs his head.

"Does it look like your mom's?"

A second nod, this one slower.

"I can make it whenever you want. Just . . ." Hiram trails off, searching for something memorable. "Just bring me the pasta if you ever want to make it."

Light returns to Antaris's eyes.

"You should—"

Antaris picks up his fork and starts eating.

"Next time, I'll show you how to cook something else like . . ." Hiram trails off again, taking in his son's pleased expression at the prospect of next time. "Actually, anytime you want to help, you can. There's so much I want to show you."

Six days later, five boxes appear on Hiram's doorstep with a note attached in his father's slanted scrawl. He trashes it after a cursory glance. Unfortunately, the information isn't imbued into stones. The boxes are packed with manila folders stuffed with papers. He checks each one, skimming for keywords.

He glances at his watch, then cracks his knuckles, eyes on his target. He has time. A moderate weightless charm should do.

"Sine pondere."

The onyx amulet on his ring flashes purple. The boxes lift, bobbing off each other like listless balloons. He guides them into an empty room and leaves for his next destination. The drive to the FCD is longer than usual thanks to morning traffic. After checking in and ignoring the suspicious look from the old Seer at the security desk, he goes up to the fourth floor.

Hiram is unprepared for the chaos.

Investigators and enforcers crowd the lobby, talking with varying degrees of panic. An acrid scent drenches the room. From fragments of conversation, he picks up: *Breach. Stone. Investigation. Compromised. Oracle Council.*

In the middle, Hiram spots Seren juggling two conversations while also on the phone. Impressive. Her brow rises when she notices him. She holds up a finger, finishes her call, then waves him over. The closer he gets, the more flustered she looks. The door opens with a curl of her fingers as more investigators stream in, carrying bags of broken stones, ready to report the damage. Seren casts a levitating charm on a particularly heavy stone, the spell not quite enough to activate her bird amulet. Hiram wonders if she's hurt with how flushed her cheeks are, only a shade lighter than her birthmark.

Not that she notices. "Hey, we're dealin' with a minor crisis. Why don't you come back in a few hours—"

Gabriel emerges from the sea of officers.

"Oh! I was just telling Mr. Ellis to come back later."

"Please call me Hiram," he quickly interjects. She nods.

"It's okay," Gabriel tells Seren. "I can take it from here."

She nods. "Nice seein' ya again."

Gabriel leads the way to the office he shares with Francisco, though he's not there when they enter. Once the glass door closes behind them, Gabriel exhales.

"What's all that?"

"A real shit show. Stone data breach. Fifty hawk's-eye stones full of evidence from an array of crimes were broken either magically or physically. Most already have Seers in custody, but without the evidence, they'll be released, which is why they're blaming the Oracle Council."

"That's a stretch." Hiram scoffs. "Spells can't be cast from a great distance, and no one from the Council would willingly set foot in here."

"Clinton has. He bails out Seers who get entangled with enforcers. If it's not Khadijah he's bailed out, she usually drives him. Aside from that, no Seers come within a mile of this place." Gabriel frowns. "But no one wanted to hear logic."

"Are any of your cases missing?" Hiram asks.

"The Conclave testing Marlene did and two others from the Botanist investigation. Not the worst of it, but some major cases were part of the breach." He pauses, eyes widening. "We must've found something."

"If that's the case, then you need to consider the possibility of a mole."

"You sound like Veda," Gabriel says. "That's why she won't come here."

Hiram recalls her haunted expression the other night, still fresh in his mind. "Paranoia isn't paranoia if there's even a bit of truth, no matter how small."

"Francisco is trying to explain to our commander why our analysis requests were with the ones that were destroyed, because they weren't signed off on." Gabriel grabs his half-empty bottle of water and pours it into a lavender plant on the windowsill. Wincing, he adds, "Don't tell Seren I did that. She hates when I use stale water."

Hiram is no magibiology expert, but he doubts stale water is fatal to plants.

"If Veda is right, let's talk outside."

At the end of the hallway are the stairs. Gabriel uses his Imprint to open the back door to the parking lot. They walk to Hiram's car, where he presses his thumb to the door; the film obscuring the interior vanishes.

"Any leads on someone to unscramble Grace's book?"

"My father is certain Clinton's capable. He also sent me boxes of research." At Gabriel's puzzled look, Hiram adds, "It's a long story. I left them at my house for now, and good thing. Did you find anything about the blocked Imprint?"

"Commander Bishop called us into his office and told us not to keep digging into it."

"That's not suspicious at all."

"Right?" Gabriel rolls his eyes. "So I went on an expedition on why someone would have their Imprint blocked from the record. Whatever they did, it's top secret, likely horrific, and important people want to keep their identity a secret."

"Murder?"

"Worse."

"What's worse than murder?"

"Plenty. Child marriages. Human exploitation and experimentation. Vanishings. Eugenics. Slavery. Corruption."

Hiram glances up to see Seren at the back door, waving frantically. "Looks like you're being summoned."

Gabriel holds a finger up to Seren. "We'll find the Botanist."

"You're confident."

"Of course I am." Gabriel smiles. "Their Imprint may be blocked, but we know one thing—if they're in Proventia, they're hiding in plain sight."

Hiram opens the first box, barely managing to pull out a file before his talisman hums. Someone is here. Irritated, he covers the box and leaves the empty room, closing the door behind him. By the time he rounds the corner, his parents are already inside, permission granted by the talisman.

"Once again, I'd prefer you call before walking into my house."

"I did call. You did not answer," his mother replies, removing her shawl and handing it to his father. Her silk saree, the color of turmeric, gives her a warm, inviting look, but there are cracks beneath her facade. She's upset. Probably with him. "I would like for us to talk."

Definitely him.

He could easily avoid the impending conversation, but decides not to give her more ammunition to make his day worse. They convene in the great room. His mother sits on the sofa, while his father stands by the window, glancing out. The clink of Hiram's glass on the kitchen island is the bell that starts the match.

"Are you not going to offer us tea?"

Hiram sighs. "Would either of you like tea?"

Barrett declines, but Simran accepts—peppermint, steeped five minutes, no honey or lemon, one cube of sugar. Hiram delivers exactly what she wants, then sits in the armchair and braces for the next phase of this ambush. From years of experience, he knows how this will go. They'll circle each other with metaphorical fists raised to protect their faces, take a few practice jabs until one gets brave enough to take the first swing. Hiram never strikes first. For him, verbal sparring is about strategy, not force. He needs to figure out the source of her discontent and get out unscathed.

Simran sets down her tea and clears her throat. "We were in the area and decided to stop by for a talk while Antaris is at school."

"A talk about what?"

"Your father went to Medina. After some prodding, he admitted it was for you. Boxes that you requested." Her tone is one he's familiar with. She's being gentle for information-gathering purposes.

"Yes."

"I have also heard troubling news that you have been seen around town with investigators, particularly the pair that handles Seer crimes. I do not think it is wise to involve yourself with Seers, let alone help with their cases. You should be focused on Antaris. Is it true? Are you assisting them?"

He expects her to wield his son like a weapon. She's been doing it from the start. Yet it still cuts. "Yes, I am. If you must know, Antaris's mother was murdered by the suspect in one of their cases."

Simran looks between him and Barrett, then back. "That is all the more reason not to involve yourself."

"He'll need answers."

"He needs his father. And you need to leave this matter to the professionals. Perhaps it is time that you return to your career."

It takes most of his restraint not to snap. Hiram looks to his father to say something, but he remains silent. "What kind of man would I be if I stood by and did nothing?"

"If Seers are indeed being murdered, maybe it is punishment for the power they wield," she says.

"The irony of anyone in our family saying that isn't lost on me."

Simran gives Barrett a concerned look. "Dear, you look tense."

"It's nothing," he mutters. "We should go. Let him find the answers he needs."

But his mother doesn't budge. "Since we are here, and you refuse to listen to us or make yourself available, I would like to discuss another topic we have been unable to speak with you about."

Hiram crosses his arms as his mother pulls out a paper. "Go on."

"We want to file this request to become Antaris's legal guardians should anything happen to you. I know that you appointed Peter godfather, and as much as I like him, he is unfit to care for Antaris in your absence."

Volcanic rage is ready to spew molten emotions, but on the surface, Hiram is calm. Rage is anger not caught in time, and he's not eighteen anymore. A dull, humorless chuckle escapes. Simran's expression shifts to alarmed.

"Do what you want. You're going to anyway."

"Hiram—"

"I've walked into your web once again. I should've stayed away, but I was overwhelmed after finding out about Antaris and needed help, a home, and my family's support. Did I believe you would change? No. But I thought I could tolerate it. I was wrong."

"What does that mean?"

"I came here with the plan to leave the moment I got Antaris to a version of okay where I could get away from you both again."

For the first time, his father's expression shifts from blank to something wounded.

His mother's eyes flash with fury. "I cannot believe you are planning to leave."

"I don't know why you're surprised. I left once. Why not again?" His words land like a blow. Simran flinches. "You pushed your ambitions so far down my throat that I suffocated on your expectations. I did everything you wanted, at my own expense, and was ignored the rest of the time. It'll be a cold day in hell before I let you control me through my son."

"That is not what I said."

"It's what you meant," Hiram snaps. "I have your letters begging me to come back, promising that you'd fix what you broke. But now I'm here, and it's clear you don't give a fuck about me."

Simran rises, tucking the paper back in her bag. "That is not true. You know what my life was before I met your father. I push, I demand. I was hard on you to make you strong, not because I do not care. Everything I have ever done, all I have *ever* wanted, is the best for you."

"And still you look me in the face and tell me what I've already set in place is not to your liking. You overstep. You want more and more from me—well, that's not true, you just want control. You've earned your third strike. If you file that, I'll see you both in court."

Barrett tries to placate him. "Hiram—"

He turns on his father. "I almost forgot you were here. Good on you for joining the conversation. Fascinating that you've decided to vocalize a single original thought." Silence rings in Hiram's ears. Anger finally crests. He stares at his father, the weight of Veda's words echoing in his mind, her frustration with his silence. The truth of it makes him ill.

"I'm just like you," he admits in a whisper.

Barrett stiffens.

"But that's about to change," Hiram continues. "Because I'm finished." He turns to his mother. "Consider your access to me and my son revoked." Then he faces his father. "I don't want anything from *either* of you."

"Hiram," Simran tries. "Be reasonable—"

"This is me being reasonable," Hiram says, cold and final. *"Get out."*

Thirteen

Beneath a bright, cloudless sky, Antaris watches cows and sheep graze in the pasture behind the school while Veda marks his growing fascination with every little gasp and smile. Only when Peter arrives with a tiny guest does he finally tear his eyes away. The moment it's placed on the blanket, the kitten wobbles over to Antaris, who scoops it up with a grin.

"He seems to be gaining weight properly. We've been feeding him gruel," Peter says, kneeling beside Veda's outstretched legs. "The mom was probably feral, but I don't think any of the barn cats will take him in. I'll keep him until we figure something out."

Veda nods silently.

"What do you want to name him, Antaris?" Peter asks.

He goes still, looking to Veda for permission.

"You don't have to decide today," she assures. "When you're ready, you can name him whatever you like."

Antaris's slow, hesitant smile softens Peter's expression. The little boy brings the kitten to his face, tilting his head to study it. He nods, gets up, and carries the kitten a few feet away, gently placing it on the grass to let it explore. He watches closely, not letting it stray far.

"Khadijah and I take turns waking up to feed him, yet he merely tolerates us."

"Bitter much?"

"No, but clearly that's his cat." Peter shakes his head. "Poor Hiram."

Veda tears her gaze from the adorable sight. "Why?"

"He's allergic."

Antaris is on his hands and knees, gently encouraging the kitten to walk. He looks happy. Laughter bubbles in her chest at the thought of Hiram sneezing uncontrollably.

"Oh, and for you." Peter hands her the bag and stands. "I need to take the kitten back for a little while to go to a vet appointment," he says to Antaris. "But I'll bring him back soon, and maybe something else, too." Eventually he leaves with a promise to bring the kitten back tomorrow after class.

Antaris settles beside Veda to share carrots and celery. He angles his face toward the sun, looking more childlike than she's seen before.

"I have a gift for you," she says.

His eyes open, head tilting with curiosity. The expression shifts to confusion when he sees the contents.

"It's a lantern." The same as hers, it's made from brass with a rope handle. Veda whispers the activation spell, *"Voster."*

Antaris is enraptured as the lantern floats from her hand to him. She looks on as it hovers until he takes hold of the handle. Light appears inside. He gives her another confused look.

"That means the spell has been activated by your touch. The lantern will draw light from the sun, and it will always follow you." Veda offers him a warm smile. "I have one just like it. My dad gave it to me when I was little. He told me to carry it in the woods in case I got lost, and keep it in my room so it could catch all my bad dreams and sadness. He said when I've finally caught everything, when I no longer need the light, and I'm ready to let it go, I can release it into the sky."

Antaris frowns and tries to hand it back.

"Oh no, this is yours. I've got mine," Veda says. "I'm not ready to let it go just yet. I need the light a little longer."

Sadness clouds his hazel eyes. He doesn't need to tell her he understands why she holds on to hers. There's nothing like having her emotions cracked open by a silent child's gaze.

Veda nudges him. "There's something else in the bag for you."

Antaris sets the lantern between them. Veda moves it away as he pulls out the last item: a book on beginner's sign language.

"So we can talk with our hands." She wiggles hers. "Do you want to learn?"

He nods.

Veda has been practicing the letters since purchasing the book for this exact moment. She guides him through them, speaking the letters aloud as she adjusts his hands. Once they finish, they start again. This time, she spells a small word.

H and *I*.

Antaris mimics her, beaming when she moves his hands. *Hi.*

Communication in its purest form.

Antaris doesn't realize anything is amiss until Veda picks up a basket of tangerines and walks to the greenhouse, not the school.

When he tugs anxiously at her hand, she stops and kneels in front of him. "I have a surprise for you. Come on. I want you to meet my friend."

She expects to see Simran waiting to accompany Antaris on his playdate, but to her pleasant surprise, his grandmother is absent. Her replacement is only slightly more favorable, though she'd never admit it to anyone but herself. Dressed in all black, Hiram watches as they approach. Veda can't say she hasn't thought about him since their last interaction.

An excited giggle draws her attention. August is out of sight but approaching quickly, based on his volume and pounding footsteps. Antaris goes rigid, fidgeting with his knitted bow tie. Kneeling in front of him, Veda gently straightens it. "If it's too much, just stand by me or your dad, okay?"

She notices Hiram tense slightly until Antaris nods, slipping a hand into hers and squeezing tight. Veda sees Hiram's double take, but she's too busy calculating the chances of success versus failure to care. Knowing how August's anxiety functions, this match may not go well. Children are unpredictable. Still, she has hope.

August is a tornado of energy barreling past the row of flowers. Peter follows, sunglasses on, carrying muddy shoes and followed closely by Gabriel. Only then does she realize August is in socks. How that happened is anyone's guess.

Pleasantries are exchanged between the adults while the boys size each other up for the first time. Hiram moves to the other side of his son, sneaking glances at their joined hands. Antaris clings to Veda's leg while August grins, flushed red. Veda dissects their contrasts: Antaris is neat and reserved; August is messy and eager. Their similarities shine, too, both waiting for the other to make the first move.

August takes initiative. "Can I call you Ant?"

Peter and Gabriel suppress their amusement with coughs. Antaris's confusion smothers his father's intrigue. Veda rests her hand on his shoulder to unfreeze him. "It's a nickname."

He considers this like one would a business deal, then nods.

August's face lights, then immediately crumples. "I forgot I'm s'posed to say *hi* first."

"It's okay," Veda reassures. "You did great! Right, Antaris?"

He nods and shyly waves, signing the letters Veda just taught him. From the corner of her eye, she sees Hiram's shock.

August's smile returns. "Can you teach me to talk with my hands, too?"

Antaris peers up at Veda. She can't help thinking they're cute, both hanging on her response. "Sure, we'll try to work something out with your dad."

August steps closer. "My dad says you don't talk, but he says I talk enough for the both of us."

Gabriel palms his forehead. "That's not what I said."

Peter's shoulders shake with silent laughter.

August asks, "Can we go back with the chickens?"

Veda tilts her head, questioning, as Peter nods. "Of course." Then, to Veda, he adds, "I brought the baby chickens today. The cat is tired after getting shots."

"Yes, of course."

Only then does Antaris let her hand go and follow August, Peter and Gabriel trailing after. In her bones, she knows it's Hiram who slips quietly into step beside her. The natural way he raises her hackles should be studied. "Surprised to see you here."

"You'll be seeing me more often."

"I'll believe it when I see it."

His expression remains neutral, eyes fixed on the boys now inside the small enclosure, instantly swarmed by five chirping chicks. They look like they're in heaven. Antaris doesn't stay reserved for long. He cracks his first smile when he successfully picks up one, dimples on full display.

"That's Honey Mustard," Peter tells them.

Hiram balks while Gabriel cackles, joined by Veda. "What kind of name . . ."

"Khadijah," Peter says.

The boys pick up each chick to present to Peter for their names. When Antaris strokes Barbecue's head with fascination, she glances around the greenery surrounding them. As it turns out, she didn't need to do much facilitating at all.

"I'll be right back. Going to pick a few strawberries and lettuce for the chicks." She's not far when footsteps follow. She stops by the tomatoes, picking the ripest one. "I don't need any help."

"I know," Hiram replies, but stays anyway. "I just wanted to let you know that my father secured research and had five boxes of it delivered to my house. I haven't had time to go through them yet, but if you want to look together, we can. I don't know where you live, and I know you won't come to my place. The downtown library has private study rooms we could use."

It's a surprisingly reasonable offer. "Okay."

"Since you're in a nonconfrontational and honest mood today . . . Peter mentioned losing sleep because of chickens and a kitten—"

"Your son's, yes. Peter's waiting for you to figure it out, make peace, buy allergy elixir, and assume custody."

Hiram cracks a smile. Veda rolls her eyes, but a matching smile sneaks onto her face.

"I think I just might do that," he says, mostly to himself.

She can't tell if he's joking or—

"It'll be worth it, seeing him this happy."

She doesn't know what to say, so she walks on. Hiram remains at her side, his purposeful stride slowing to match hers, hands behind his back like Antaris. They never leave the beaten path. When their eyes meet, she realizes the watcher has become the watched.

"I got him a lantern. It's with his book bag, along with a sign language book."

A quiet intensity lingers in his gaze. "Why?"

"Aside from the fact that it floats on its own and stores sunlight, it captures the energy from bad dreams."

"How did you know he was having nightmares?"

"I would be surprised if he wasn't."

"Peter gave him an elixir to help that didn't work."

"Hopefully this might." They reach the strawberry beds. Veda stoops to comb through the leaves, finding two plump fruits.

"And the book?"

Veda winces slightly. "I was planning to talk to Simran, but I think he needs some way to communicate until he's ready to speak. We learned some basics today. Maybe—"

"I wish I'd thought of it myself."

Veda can admit she's usually the aggressor in their sparring matches, yet praise isn't what she expects. It's disarming. "It'll be good for him. Peter is going to ask his teacher if she can fit it into the lesson plan to teach his class so the kids can communicate with him. It's not much, but if we work on it during our sessions and you incorporate it at home, he—"

"Thank you. For what you've done with him. He seems comfortable with you."

She flounders under his appreciation, looking at everything except him. "Antaris is a great kid. Kind. Compassionate. Earnest. He reads your notes, wants to know you. He's loud, even in his silence." Veda continues to actively ignore the look on his face, muttering, "Need to grab some lettuce."

When raised garden beds full of herbs divide them, Veda stops focusing on her shoes and looks at Hiram. Black clashes with color and light. She would sooner lie than admit it aloud, but against the lush backdrop of the greenhouse, Hiram is hard to ignore. His height and the lean lines of his build. Tailored clothes. Dark hair, parted like his son's. Deliberate, defiant blue eyes. The beginnings of a five-o'clock shadow replacing smooth skin. Today, Hiram bears ink stains on his fingers, a few creases in his shirt, and the faint impression of glasses on the bridge of his nose. Unfortunately, the imperfections make him human. Natural. Handsome.

"I happen to know when I'm being studied." Hiram's back is to her as he examines the flowering cucumber vines. "Ever since Nénuphar, you've taken every opportunity to assess me. Even when I irritate you." He turns to face her. "Have you found what you're looking for?"

"Your audacity." Her sarcasm is weak.

His smirk confirms he knows it, too. *Damn him.*

"We never agreed on a date."

"Excu—oh, you mean the library."

"What did you think I meant?"

Veda ignores the amusement in his voice. "Anyway, maybe next Friday. I'm not working." She walks on, but their paths converge again near the olive trees.

Hiram peers up. "It looks dead."

"It's an olive tree, it'll recover."

She shows him the buds forming on the blackened branches. They're growing faster than she expects. There'll be leaves soon. Veda kneels and draws an X in the dirt. Hiram watches.

They return to the group with the treats for the chicks, and everyone's attention shifts to them. Veda lays the strawberry, tomato, and lettuce leaf down. The chicks descend on the offering as the boys hurry over.

"My dad said to ask you to go to pizza, Mr. Hiram," August announces.

"It's Mr. Ellis."

"Okay, Mr. Hiram."

He closes his eyes and pinches between his eyes.

"My dad does that when someone is being a pain in the—"

"August," Gabriel interrupts. Peter is behind him, silently wheezing. "Remember your question?"

"Oh yeah! Can we?"

Hiram looks understandably puzzled but crouches in front of Antaris. "Do you want to have pizza with August tonight?"

Antaris shifts closer, glances around, then taps the back of his hand twice. Hiram frowns, and he repeats the gesture, more insistently. Veda sees when he finally understands.

"That means yes, right?" Hiram confirms.

The corners of Antaris's lips curve.

Peter invites Veda over for an impromptu dinner the following night. It's suspiciously well planned.

He makes the sauce for Mughlai chicken while she skims the inventory of ingredients in his stores, sipping wine on the table and enjoying the kitten sleeping in her lap. Veda isn't one to complain about a free meal, and Peter's a decent cook. There's a purpose behind every action, even dinner, but the silence is companionable enough for her to relax. Fractionally.

Khadijah joins them later, fresh from an emergency call. She steals a few bites from Peter's plate, claims she's going to change, but crashes on the couch. Her snoring becomes the background to their conversation.

"Hiram told me that you agreed to research with him."

Veda grimaces. "Yeah, and I'll eat crow if he ends up being right."

Peter chuckles suspiciously.

She narrows her eyes. "Are you Clinton in disguise?"

He puts his fork down, dabbing his mouth with a napkin. "Just someone who noticed two people being civil, even sitting next to each other at the pizza place. Color me shocked."

"A temporary ceasefire."

Peter's knowing look is irritating. "You're the only one at war."

"Spare me."

"Only if you listen."

"You don't have to plead Hiram's case."

"I'm not, I'm defending my friend because it's warranted. This conversation is overdue." Peter finishes his wine in one gulp. "He's not perfect, but neither are you."

"I know that. Hiram is . . ." The unfinished sentence dissipates without a fitting end.

"He's a lot of things," Peter says. "Not all of them are congruent, but I think that's what frustrates you most. You want him to be everything you've decided he is. Maybe he is some of those things, but not all."

Veda feels warm from the spices and wine.

"It's normal to be frustrated by what you don't understand. Or maybe you're curious."

"You're making a lot of assumptions," she deadpans.

"Am I? You've been on autopilot for years. Existing like you're terminal and your days are almost up. Now you're waking up and paying attention. I think you want to live more than you've prepared to die. Antaris has muddied things. So has Hiram."

Veda laughs.

"Laugh all you want, but you're attached. And it's mutual. There is no way you can keep separating Antaris from Hiram. His son is part of him. It's tenuous, but their bond will grow. So will yours—to both. You won't be able to help it."

Veda jiggles her knee, fingers trailing between the kitten's ears. "Then stop shoving Hiram in my damn face."

Peter frowns. "I haven't."

"Oh? So you had nothing to do with Hiram offering to help me get rid of this curse?" She tilts her head. "From what he told me, you said I needed all the help I could get."

"I did, but I didn't say it expecting him to—"

"Get his hand on classified research with a snap of his fingers? Why didn't you ask him before?"

"Honestly? He was never an option because he refused to get involved." Peter raises an eyebrow. "But now he is, and I'm intrigued."

Veda scoffs. "I'm leaving."

A smirk tugs at his mouth. "Hiram does nothing without reason or a plan, but I have a feeling he might not have either when it comes to you."

Fourteen

June passes as time often does—slow and surreal. Yet in a blink, the last week of the month arrives.

Before Hiram can settle into a routine, free from Simran, it's almost time for the three-week school break that marks the end of the quarter. He doesn't have a plan for how they'll spend it, but he has time to figure it out, and he's looking forward to sleeping in.

A soft meow from the living room reminds him that won't be happening. He peers over at the still unnamed kitten, confined to its toy-filled play area, and sighs before chugging a foul-tasting elixir to keep from sneezing on everything.

Up early, he's reading research papers on the Sanguis Curse on his newly delivered office desk, highlighting bits for Veda to review when they finally meet. It will be their third attempt at scheduling after each of them canceled, Veda after the school was overwhelmed with orders, and Hiram when he spent hours waiting to be sworn into the Washington State Bar Association. He's just finished highlighting when there's movement from his son's room. Hiram leaves everything as is, grabs the note he wrote last night, and places it on the table where Antaris usually sits. He starts breakfast, eggs, toast, and chopped fruit, and by the time Antaris emerges, dressed and hauling his book bag to the door, everything is ready.

Normally, Hiram would shower, but today he makes a plate for himself and joins Antaris at the table. At first, Antaris focuses on the note. Then he notices Hiram is staying, and his eyes go wide.

Breakfast fluctuates between staring and eating. If Antaris is happy, sad, confused, or anxious about his presence, he can't tell, because all his son gives him are owl blinks. Bits of eggs fail to make it from Antaris's fork to his mouth, landing on the napkin tucked into his shirt or back on his plate. The second time it happens, Hiram realizes he needs to break the silence.

"We should finish up."

It doesn't make Antaris eat any faster, but it's a start. Hiram shifts in his seat, and Antaris freezes; he understands the issue now.

"I'm not working today. I wanted to have breakfast together."

Only then does Antaris eat in earnest.

Breakfast settles into something between normal and strange. When they finish, Antaris pockets the note and takes his plate to the sink. He begins searching for the stool he uses each night to help wash up, but Hiram shakes his head. "I'll do it later."

Before Antaris can scoop up the kitten for a goodbye cuddle, Hiram waves him over. Antaris pauses, curiously tilting his head.

"I'm . . ." The words die in Hiram's throat. He tries again, turning in his seat. He hesitates, just once, then asks, "Can I show you a word?"

Slowly, Antaris nods.

Hiram moves his hand to the side of his chin, then brings it forward with his thumb up, signing as he says, *"Tomorrow?"*

It's not perfect, but they practice after dinner each night. Letters. Basic signs. Last night, Hiram taught him the signs for each ingredient they used. Emboldened by the progress, Hiram stays up after Antaris goes to bed, poring over the book Veda gave him well into the night. He doesn't know if this will work until Antaris signs the word for himself. They sign it again, together. Sheer determination has carried Hiram to this point, where he finally asks for something simple yet monumental to him. Inconsequential to anyone else.

"Tomorrow," Hiram says and signs again. "I'd like to start eating breakfast with you. I think—"

Antaris doesn't let him finish. He makes a fist and signs one word. *Yes.*

Then he's off to play with the kitten.

Hiram's smile lingers while he makes tea for Antaris. After pulling the thermos from the dishwasher, he nearly jumps out of his skin when he finds his son standing there, holding both the kitten and another thermos. For Veda. That's right, they've been having tea before school.

"What tea do you want to make her?" Hiram asks.

Antaris looks down at the kitten in his arms, thinking.

He chooses mint.

※

The walls of the downtown library are high, arched into a painted ceiling. A grand staircase leads to the upper level, but the sight of endless floor-to-ceiling bookshelves and tall ladders brings Hiram to a halt. The scent of magic is heavy, comforting. Books float from shelf to shelf until they find their way home.

Hiram is early for an appointment he scheduled reluctantly, but first . . .

"Mr. Ellis, the Authorized Book Room is available for the requested hour," says a meek librarian behind him. "Thank you for your family's patronage."

The Ellis family has funded the library's rare-book acquisition, restoration efforts, and translations for decades. Hiram never has to join the monthslong wait list for access, only walk in, ask for what he needs, and watch them scramble to oblige.

"The talisman will reactivate in an hour," she adds.

The lights are dim until he enters the Authorized Book Room, and only then do they brighten. It's spacious, lined with more floor-to-ceiling bookcases centered around a table with four chairs. The books are old but impeccably cared for. Hiram puts on his reading glasses, hoping to find history.

The book describes how Sanguis consumes from the inside, shows pictures of the ravaged bodies of its victims, and outlines the brief but excruciating agony it causes. There are survivors, and their cases are inconsistent. The clearest note in the entire book is: *The longer Sanguis resides in the body, the harder it is to extricate.* Hiram removes his glasses and pinches the bridge of his nose. Veda's life is being held together by sheer cosmic luck and Khadijah's determination.

There's a smudge on the bottom of the page that turns into words when Hiram puts his glasses back on.

Death will lead it out.

Hiram frowns. "What kind of direction is that?"

Flipping the page, he finds an entirely different spell.

"Sight Unseen . . ." he reads aloud.

The words act as an activation spell, breaking the letters apart and sending them flying around the pages, bouncing off the edges of the paper. Hiram sits back and checks his watch. The timing couldn't be more perfect. He can ask Clinton to unscramble both hexes, but first, he has questions for the librarian. It may have nothing to do with Sanguis, but this scrambling hex is too specific to be a coincidence. When he calls the librarian back in to notify her about the hex, she's flustered, terrified of getting into trouble. The book, she tells him, is irreplaceable, the only one of its kind in the country.

"Is there a record of everyone who has been in this room?" Hiram asks.

"There is," she replies shakily.

"May I see it?"

She leaves and returns with a book almost as thick as the tomes kept in the room, and just as dusty. "It automatically registers the Imprints of whomever walks into the room, staff excluded."

There aren't many entries for this room. Aside from his name, there are five others. *Nadir Christianson, Sybil Brice. Ariadne Byers, Nicholas Dobbs. Deanna Gibbs.* Hiram scans the names again, returning to one.

Ariadne Byers.

The name isn't one he knows, but he faintly remembers it being whispered a few times when no one thought he was listening. He can't remember when or by whom, but he checks the date of entry. Fifteen years ago. Asking the librarian, who barely looks thirty, if she remembers one name is a waste of time. "May I borrow this book?"

She looks like he's asked to set it on fire. "I'm sorry, but you can't. This book—"

"Is useless unless you break the hex." He shows her the page, the letters ungrouping and regrouping in nonsensical words. "You'll need to report this and explain why no one noticed the spell. They'll run audits on your process, notify the owners of the rare books, and *I* know what will happen if they find discrepancies or if the owners want the books moved."

Judging from the librarian's ashen face, she knows, too.

"How about this: Allow me to leave with this book, and I will fix this without taking it out of the building. You can't tell anyone it's fixed, and if anyone comes into this room after I leave, you'll have to notify me."

She looks stricken but relents. "Okay, Mr. Ellis."

"Thank you." He pulls out his wallet and offers her his card.

Hiram leaves the room soon after she retreats. With ten minutes left before his meeting and armed with an extra book, he walks to the last room in the row—only to find it occupied.

By Clinton.

He's dressed like he's on his way to give a lecture at the closest college: tweed sports coat and khakis, walking cane in hand, glasses covering his eyes.

"Punctual as always, Mr. Ellis."

"I'm fifteen minutes early."

"To be early is to be on time."

Hiram leans heavily on tenacity to propel himself forward. Dialing Clinton's number was difficult, but talking to him long enough to schedule today's meeting was an exercise in endurance. He closes the door and sits at the table across from the blind man. The talisman hanging next to the door flashes blue, and the glass instantly frosts. For privacy. Hiram places the tome from the Authorized Book Room on the table with Grace's book on oddities. "These have scrambling hexes on them. I was told that you were skilled at undoing hexes."

"Ah, how *is* your father?"

"Alive," Hiram replies. "And not the subject of today's meeting."

How Clinton's expression is probing without looking at him is a mystery, but finally he touches the cover of the first book, then the second. "Very well. In the spirit of alliance, I will assist."

"We don't have an alliance."

"What do you think this is?" Clinton smiles.

"A favor."

He flexes his hands over the books but stops. "The talisman will neutralize my Imprints, so there will be no record of my spell work, but while this room permits the use of magic, the laws do not. All I ask for in return is your discretion about what you witness."

"Okay."

Clinton removes his glasses. "As a Sensitive, you might want to mute your senses."

"I'll be fine."

Hiram is wrong. Very wrong.

A single spell floods the room. Power pours into the space until the air thrums. Ozone and petrichor smother Hiram's senses, leaving the hair on his arms standing, stomach roiling, and eyes burning. Clinton's lips move, but Hiram can't hear, deafened by a pressure he's never gotten used to. Clinton's eyes flash silver as both books tremble and smoke. Just when he thinks they will catch fire, everything stops.

"There. It should be fixed."

Hiram accepts the books and flips one open to the page that was scrambled. All the letters are back where they belong. The librarian will be relieved. When he opens Grace's book to the page that was scrambled, he pauses, looking back and forth between them.

The scrambled words are on the same topic.

"What do you know about Sight Unseen?"

"It's a ritual that steals Sight from one person, but at a terrible cost. If it is cast on a Seer, it will render them Unseen. If cast on a Mage . . . it depends. When performed on the wrong person, it tricks the caster into believing it worked, but there are signs, warnings they do not sense, because they are blinded by their stolen Sight and power," Clinton explains.

"What type of signs?"

"Disturbances in the Cosmos. Unnatural events."

Hiram frowns. "What about flowers that grow out of concrete?"

"I see where you are going with this," Clinton replies slowly. "It is plausible."

"Spider lilies are thought to be a warning used to foreshadow an upcoming death. It doesn't get clearer than that."

"The only other thing I know is that the ritual is akin to a drug. The more it's done, the weaker the high is and the shorter it lasts. They will always chase the first one, and the incessant use of raw magic will run them into the ground. Fortunately, there is no known record of it ever being cast correctly, likely due to the misinterpretation of the ritual."

Hiram isn't so sure about that. "Someone scrambled that specific page of Grace's book about Sight Unseen, as well as the book here. There's no telling when the hexes were done, but as random as it seems, they might be linked."

"Stranger things have happened," Clinton says.

"Is the name Ariadne Byers familiar to you? I saw it in a log, and I vaguely recognized it, but can't recall why."

Clinton's expression softens. "From many years ago. I will look into it."

"Thank you."

"You are curious about something that is beyond you." A flash of intrigue streaks across his features. "The Cosmos are, *indeed*, shifting."

"No, they're not."

His denial makes Clinton smile. "I was wondering what was changing the trajectory of events, and believed it to be the movements happening beyond my limits. Now, I realize it's *you* beginning to show your face."

Hiram tenses. "Where did you hear that?"

"Khadijah had a vision recently of you hearing this."

"Yeah, I did. In April."

"Ah." Clinton can't disguise his intrigue. "It's rare for her to have visions about the past. This is fascinating. The future is, indeed, changing."

"No, it isn't." Hiram collects the books and stands. "Thanks for this, but consider it the last favor I ask of you."

"Oh, how wrong you are. You will see."

Clinton's smile is the last thing Hiram sees when he walks out. The frost reforms on the glass, closing the chapter on a strange encounter. After delivering the book to the librarian, who nearly sobs in relief, Hiram sends a message to Gabriel with pictures of the text from both books. He's walking out when he spies Clinton nearing the door, his hand on another librarian's arm. Waiting for him to leave is an option, but why should he? As he passes the pair, Clinton's comment stops Hiram mid-step.

"There he is, my ride."

"Actually—"

"Oh! Mr. Ellis. Perfect. I was just escorting him out now that his allotted time was complete." The librarian is already pulling away. "Next time, please use our Seer log to record your entrance."

"Must have slipped my mind." Clinton adds a frail quality to his voice Hiram knows is fake. The act falls the moment the librarian is out of earshot. "I'll give you directions."

"I didn't offer."

"Would you leave a blind man to fend for himself?"

Hiram doubts there are many who pose a danger to Clinton.

With a sigh, he places Clinton's hand on his arm and leads him out. Hiram doesn't realize they've walked into a situation until it's too late. Three enforcers surround a familiar little old woman wearing an oversized sun hat despite the cloudy skies. She doesn't look strong enough to harm anything, but they have her in neutralizing cuffs tight enough to leave marks. It's excessive when their perpetrator is already on her knees, defiantly glaring while the enforcers yell different things all at once. Their amulets give off a threatening glow while they demand answers.

It's none of Hiram's business. He plans to lead Clinton to his car, but when one of them calls the woman *Seer scum* and Clinton tenses, Hiram stops.

"As I said—"

Clinton turns sharply. "Ruth? What's going on?"

Of course he knows her.

Ruth whips to them, relief playing in her eyes. "Clinton, they—" Then she notices Hiram. "Well, shit." The cuffs burn red, making the old woman wince. "Take these off, I'm complying and these aren't necessary!"

"You haven't confessed to anything."

"Why would I? I've done nothing wrong."

Clinton lets go to approach in an attempt to defuse, but Hiram knows it's not going to end well for either of them. So he moves. It's too late. He doesn't hear the spell but sees the white bolt strike Ruth in the chest, causing her to tremble and grit her teeth in obvious distress while the enforcers continue yelling.

"I would advise that you stop," Clinton says coolly.

"You can get arrested, too," a different enforcer threatens.

Hiram intervenes. "What exactly happened here?"

The three enforcers look at him before one says, "We received multiple complaints about a suspicious Seer lurking in shops up and down the street, breaking into cars, and doing magic. This Seer matched the description and put up a fight, so we used neutralizing cuffs."

Hiram doesn't smell a thing except the copper coming off the officers. "*She* used magic?"

"No, I didn't," Ruth argues. "You can check for my Imprint!"

"Shut up," one of the enforcers says through gritted teeth, his amulet flaring.

"I refuse." Ruth squares her shoulders. "You all have nothing better to do than harass old ladies."

"You injured one of the patrol members," the tallest enforcer points out as the shortest one steps back to take a quick call.

"No, your piss-poor attempt to restrain me is what hurt him."

"Backup is on its way," the third enforcer says after hanging up their phone, frowning when he notices Clinton, then his walking stick. "Who are you?"

"Clinton Desai," he replies calmly. "Head of the Oracle Council, and Ruth is a member. Call your superiors. We can discuss this in private."

"No."

While they argue, and hopefully before the situation devolves further, Hiram gathers argument points. Two cameras on either side. No hint of magic lingering. The unnatural bruises on Ruth's arms and neck. The officers' badge numbers.

He doesn't finish in time. They're detaining her. Two haul Ruth to her feet while the third casts a silencing hex on her. Clinton is about to step forward when Hiram holds him back, then pushes past him, getting in the enforcers' way.

"Sir, get out of the way and let us do our job."

"Now *why* would I do that?" Hiram asks calmly. "That Seer is my client."

"If she's your client, why didn't she say that?"

"Doesn't matter."

"Mr.—"

"Ellis." Hiram cuts him off. "Hiram Ellis."

The light switches on. "The former mayor's son?"

Another example of when ends justify means. Or so he hopes.

"Yes." Hiram produces his identification. "I'm also Sensitive, and know the only magic wafting off anyone here is coming from you three. Cameras don't lie. You let Ruth go, or you—"

"If you're her attorney, you know how this works. You're not going to win this."

"We'll see."

They push past him and drag her away.

"I need to make a call," Clinton grumbles.

"No, you don't. Let's go."

It's a race, but Hiram marches into the shop as the enforcers pull away, pleasantly asking the clerk for footage of the last hour. It takes a few empty legal threats, but he gets what he needs. With Clinton in the passenger seat of his car, Hiram speeds to the FCD headquarters downtown, illegally parking and quickly finding the Seer holding cells.

The enforcers standing around sneer at Clinton. "Here to get another one of yours?"

"No, actually, *I* am." Hiram looks at Clinton, then helps him into a chair. "Wait here."

"I certainly will, ally." Clinton smiles.

"Shut up."

Walking away from the laughing old man, Hiram considers calling Gabriel for backup, but decides against it in favor of bypassing pleasantries, ignoring the uncooperative secretary, and opening three empty doors to find who he's looking for.

Enforcers crowd around a pissed-off and shackled Ruth. With a flick of his wrist, Hiram clears the path between him and the old woman, his ring's amulet flaring before dimming. Shocked enforcers peel themselves off the walls.

"Trust me," Hiram tells her. *"Hire me."*

"I would *never*—"

"Fine, then I'll leave you here alone until a Seer advocate arrives. It'll be hours, maybe days, before they allow them back here."

Ruth looks around at the enforcers, who are getting up, angrier than ever, and then Hiram feels her hand on his arm. "Don't disappoint me, Ellis."

It's dark when Hiram emerges from Holding with a freed Ruth in tow.

"Those assholes still have my hat," she grumbles.

"We'll get it back tomorrow."

Expecting to find Clinton gone, Hiram is surprised when he's still there. And not alone. Khadijah sits beside him, but for the first time, she's glaring with more suspicion than hate. Hiram scrubs a hand over his face, too tired for another fight after hours of arguing with enforcers on behalf of a person who didn't trust that he'd get her out without charges filed until the moment the signed release papers were in her hand.

"Thank you," Ruth says earnestly. "I can't believe you didn't fail me."

Hiram ignores the slight. "I'd be a terrible attorney if I were intimidated by a room full of people who share the same brain cell."

Ruth chuckles. "How much do I owe you?"

"I don't want your money." He glances over to find Ruth peering up at him, mouth tight. "What?"

"Clinton thinks you are the answer to bridging the gap, that you'll do great things for our community. It's why he invited you to the town hall. I called bullshit, and while I meant what I said, now I wonder . . ."

"Feel free to maintain your prior opinions about me."

"Then I owe you a favor."

Hiram doubts he'll collect. "Deal."

Clinton turns to the sound of their voices. "Ah, excellent work, Mr. Ellis. That only took six hours."

Hiram makes a face, but Clinton can't even see his expression. "You're joking, right?"

Khadijah rolls her eyes. "My uncle's sense of humor is baroque, at best. What he means is he's gracious."

"That I am."

Hiram is ready to go. "Whatever, it's—" His phone starts buzzing repeatedly. He glances at the screen and his heart crashes. Message after message from Peter. They begin shortly after four o'clock and become increasingly urgent as time passes. He fires a message back saying he's on the way.

He's late.

Without bothering to excuse himself, Hiram runs to his car, breaking several traffic laws as he races across town to Weston Academy. He calls Peter back five times, but there's no answer. It's nearly seven, and the school is dark except for a single light next to the front door. Hiram leaves the car running and knocks on the door, then pounds on it when there's no immediate answer.

Veda pushes the door open. In his hazy panic, he doesn't notice how furious she looks.

"You're late." Her voice is arctic. Unsettling. Her eyes are red like she's been crying.

"I was—"

"Save it. I don't want to hear your excuses." A dry laugh escapes and she shakes her head. "I can't believe I nearly fell for your good-father, I'll-be-here-more-often act. Utter bullshit."

"Where is he?"

"Asleep. But not before having a panic attack because the only parent he has left *forgot* him."

Hiram is stunned into silence, his guilt louder than Veda's fury. "It was an accident."

"An accident is mixing up salt and sugar. This was irresponsible."

"Irresponsible?" Hiram scoffs. Furious with himself, he can't help but lash out. "The *only* thing irresponsible is the fact that you're still around children despite having a serial killer after you."

"The only thing irresponsible?" Veda recoils as if slapped. "Seriously? When your mother is *right there*? Yes, that makes *perfect* sense."

"You care a lot about a child that isn't yours." It's another comment that's been lying low in his subconscious. It's out now. He can't take it back, even if he wants to, even if he hates the way her expression changes.

"You think I *want* to care about him when I don't know the minute this curse will wake up?" Veda scrubs her face. "You think I want that for him? To be someone else who leaves him? No. I'd rather fight the Botanist myself if it guarantees he won't be forgotten by another person. I know he's not mine. I am *completely* aware of this. The *only* reason I'm even here is because I saw a little boy who was hurting and grieving. You don't know what it's like to lose someone you love in an instant. I've been *exactly* where he is. Lost. Grieving. *Drowning*. And I *refused* to leave him to struggle alone."

Her words are raw and honest, and he can't face them without feeling like a complete asshole. "Congratulations, you're a decent person. I'm glad you don't treat him like you do me."

"He's *not* like you or your family."

"He's my son," Hiram snaps. "I didn't raise him, but he's a reflection of me, whether you like it or not."

Veda scoffs, but her demeanor cracks.

"I was late because—"

"I don't care," she fires back, hot tears running down her cheeks. "I'm so fucking *disappointed* in you. I thought—you know what, fuck it, I'm done."

She pushes past him, but instinctively he throws a hand out, stopping her. "Look—"

"Move." Veda looks ready to break him in half.

"Let me explain."

"No." They're nearly face-to-face; insolence and anger bleed from her. "You need to do better. No excuses. No bullshit. Antaris is kind and brilliant. He's so compassionate. You need to protect that. Protect *him*.

She—" Veda swallows thickly. "She'll suffocate the good out of him if you don't. He'll resent you, or worse, he'll *become* you."

Hiram flinches. As angry as he is, he can't ignore the pain of her words. "You don't know fuck all of what I have or have not done. You don't even know me, much less—fuck it, now *I'm* done talking. You're fired."

"You didn't hire me." Veda touches her forehead, and tears fill her eyes. "I would have already quit after spending the entire evening consoling him, assuring him that you haven't left him, that you were coming back, that you weren't dead somewhere. But you're stuck with me because, as long as I'm alive, I'm not abandoning him. You weren't here when he started wondering, worrying, when he started sobbing uncontrollably. I did the hard part, now it's your turn."

"Where is he?" Hiram asks tightly.

"In Peter's office." Veda pushes past him, storming off toward the dark parking lot. He watches her sit on the edge of the fountain and bury her face in her hands.

Hiram doesn't spare her another look. His mind is a cacophony of misfiring emotions. Peter's office doesn't make him feel any more settled. It's a mess of uneaten food and looks like a tornado went through it. The man himself looks haggard, straightening books and picking up papers.

Relief blooms at the sight of Hiram. "What happened to you? Veda—"

"Screamed at me and stormed off. I was downtown involving myself in Seer shit I shouldn't have bothered with had I known all this would have happened." Hiram's eyes land on Antaris. He's curled up on the couch, blanket clutched to his chest, face puffy from crying, distress radiating from him even in his sleep.

"I tried to call you—"

"My phone didn't turn back on until I left the building."

"I almost called Simran, but that would have made matters worse."

Peter's words fade to the background as Hiram kneels beside his son, flinching at his touch even in his sleep. Veda was right.

"I fucked up."

Fifteen

Veda wants to sleep, but a parade of colors dances behind her shut eyes.

Eventually, she gives up and ventures outside, where the air carries a chill uncommon for this time of year. Trees rustle in the soft breeze. She has the urge to both walk away and plant roots. But deep down, she knows the issue of her uncertainty stems from something her pride hasn't allowed her to acknowledge. Old habits don't die—they hibernate until the next relevant moment.

In the wake of her righteous indignation, the truth whispers that she's done something wrong. Veda sits with her guilt as daybreak's brilliant rays bleed streaks of color through the forest. It's Saturday, so there's no time to wallow.

Inside, the shower burns her cursed scars; the salve doesn't soothe as well as usual. After dressing, she sighs at her hair. Too tired to bother with it, she brushes it back into a bun, puts on her shoes, and makes the walk to Weston Academy.

The grounds are empty, save a few employees scattered about to tend to the animals. Veda takes refuge in the greenhouse, counting the buds on the bare cherry tree and pruning what she can reach. Being interrupted is normal, but the person who intrudes is not who she expects.

Khadijah is dressed for a day out in a black romper and flip-flops, gold jewelry, her white braids pulled back into a ponytail. "Peter told me about what happened last night. Do you want to talk about it?"

"No. I said a lot. Some of it I meant, some I didn't." Veda's close to erupting from her own frustration. "I don't know. I felt helpless. Even when Peter came, I couldn't help Antaris. I just held him until he fell asleep."

After gesturing for Veda to follow, Khadijah glares daggers until she complies. They leave the warm greenhouse and step into the sunlight. It's warm for the long-sleeved shirt and jeans Veda's wearing, but she'll survive.

They're halfway to the school when Khadijah says, "I saw Hiram when he realized how late he was."

Veda stops mid-step. "What?"

"Ruth got arrested on bullshit charges. Uncle Clinton called me to meet him at the FCD, and when I got there, he said she was in there with her attorney. I didn't know who it was until Hiram walked out with her. He got her released without charges being filed, and the enforcers even apologized, all thanks to an arrogant attorney who gathered enough evidence to prove her innocence." Khadijah sighs. "Trust me, I *hate* defending him, but he was late because he was helping right an injustice."

"He stopped spectating," Veda mutters to herself.

"What?"

"I told him good men didn't spectate, and the one time he didn't—" Veda wrings her hands, still shocked. "I thought I'd made a mistake before, but now . . . Now I *know* I did, and I'm not sure I can fix it."

Khadijah is about to speak when her phone rings. She takes the call while Veda paces. When she disconnects, she lays a sympathetic hand on her shoulder. "Come on, let's get out of here."

"To go where?"

"Does it matter?"

❦

A call from Clinton, asking Khadijah to stop by the FCD and pick up Ruth's belongings, determines their destination. They enter the building through different lines; Veda's cursory glance and amulet check by security are nothing compared to the intrusive security measures Khadijah endures. When the guard makes a derogatory comment, Veda steps forward, but Khadijah shakes her head. Veda gives the guard a nasty look before following her friend.

Veda decides to sit in the waiting area, feeling uncomfortable as is. She's torn between locking eyes with every person who passes and skimming through a year-old magazine when her phone rings.

"Are you busy right now?" Gabriel asks as soon as she picks up.

"I'm actually in the waiting area of the FCD, what's going on?"

"Seriously? I thought you never—"

"It's a long story," Veda says.

"We can talk about that later. For now, can you come up to the fourth floor? I'll meet you at the elevator. There are a few things I need to catch you up on."

"Khadijah is here with me. Can she come, too?"

"Sure thing. I'll call security and give them your names. Just register your Imprint."

It takes thirty minutes before Khadijah returns carrying a brown bag and wearing Ruth's hat, irritation etched on her face. Veda tells her about the detour as they walk to the security desk together. They give Khadijah a hard time with clearance to the fourth floor, but a second call from Gabriel makes it happen.

The elevator ride is quiet, tense, and Khadijah is understandably grouchy. Classical music filters from the speakers, bringing back memories that sour Veda's mood. She hasn't listened to this kind of music in years, but the melody lives in her head, a reminder from that night. Khadijah sneaks worried glances.

True to his word, Gabriel meets them outside the elevator. "Sorry about security," he says. "What brings you all here on a Saturday?"

"Khadijah came to pick up Ruth's belongings."

"Ah, yeah." Gabriel whistles low. "I heard about the hell Hiram raised yesterday. I got a call about it, but by the time I got here, he was already gone."

He leads the way to the investigators' office, mentioning he's putting in a few hours while August is bug-hunting with Francisco's little cousins. Artificial lights make the office look clinical. The silence sterilizes the atmosphere. There's a woman sitting at her desk, fiddling with the lavender plant while reading through papers. She looks up when the door shuts behind them. Petite with blond hair and innocuous eyes, her friendly smile feels familiar.

"Oh, sorry, Veda, Khadijah. Meet our overworked secretary, Seren Landry."

Veda gives her a cursory glance, still unable to recall where she's seen her before, but finds nothing odd except the flush that starts at her neck and disappears into her blond hair. Gabriel follows her line of sight and flashes a grin.

"Hey there. It's nice to finally meet ya, Khadijah."

"Do I know you?"

"It's hard to forget you." At her raised brow, Seren continues. "You've spent a lot of time in holdin'. Seems the enforcers have it out for ya, thanks to your uncle."

"You're not wrong."

Seren's eyes slide to Veda, and she tilts her head. "Veda, is it? You look familiar."

"I was just thinking the same thing."

"I've traveled a lot, basically since I quit medical school about seven years ago."

Everything slots into place. That Southern drawl is memorable. "Did you happen to go to the Redwood Institute of Mage Medicine at Riverty University?"

"Yeah, I did. *Oh!* Veda, as in Veda Thorne, right?"

Gabriel looks back and forth between them. "You know each other?"

"She was in my study group for licensing. We both were under . . ." Seren trails off, all the air exiting the room.

Veda knows why. Healer Oliver Lawson.

Seren is visibly uncomfortable. "Well, it was a mess. I left after what happened and . . . and you went missing."

Gabriel pauses. "Wait, Seren, you studied with Lawson? How did this never come up?"

Seren shrugs. "I guess I just never thought about it. It was another life. Once I dropped out, I didn't look back."

"Why did you drop out?" Veda asks, shocked. "You were passionate about precognition. You were easily the best in the group. I figured you had a future in the specialty."

"I was, but things changed." Manicured fingers fiddle with her blue-jay pendant. "The rumors about you were wild. What happened?"

"It's a long story."

"I've got time." She smiles sheepishly at Gabriel. "Well, I will after we finish up, if ya wanna catch up."

Veda considers it. "I've got some things to do. Maybe another time."

"Okay, well, you know where I work." She opens her hands, looking around the lobby. "Just drop by and give security my name. They'll send you up. If I'm not here, I'm out causin' problems," she jokes with a cheeky grin.

"I'll remember that," Veda says. "It's nice to see you again, Seren." And she means it. The odd clash of past and present isn't as horrific as she's imagined on and off over the years.

Gabriel rocks back on his heels. "Seren is doing audits of our cases after the latest breach, but I called you here to catch you up. Let's go back to my office."

"Where's Francisco?" Khadijah asks.

"Making a hundred elotes to bring to his brother's birthday party tomorrow, so with August out terrorizing nature, I'm working on a few things while Seren does these case audits."

"He never stops workin'." Seren rolls her eyes. "I tell him all the time to take a break. Leave things to me. Hardheaded as ever."

"I'm going to watch the game later. Don't worry, I won't burn myself out." Gabriel gestures to Veda and Khadijah. "Let's keep them—"

"Off the record? Sure thing." Seren smiles. "I'm going to head out soon. I'll see y'all around."

Gabriel leads the way to his office and offers Khadijah a seat at Francisco's empty desk. There are pictures strewn across his desk. They look like segments of text in various books. A stack of files and a notebook off to the side catch Veda's eye. Nonsensical words in all caps fill the top line, and four rows of words are crossed out right underneath. She's caught trying to read it upside down.

"Hiram got a letter last month, and we can't figure out what it is. I tried the same sequence as yours, but no luck."

"May I?" Veda asks.

Gabriel hands her the notebook. "Knock yourself out. In fact, take it with you, if you want, but that's not what I brought you here for."

He updates them on everything: Everett; the investigation into the Botanist's blocked Imprint; the hexed texts they asked Hiram to assist with unscrambling; what he's learned about a ritual called Sight Unseen; and the name Ariadne Byers, which neither of them recognizes.

"I'd look her up myself, but our access was temporarily restricted after the blocked-Imprint incident." Gabriel shrugs. "Our hands are tied right now. I'd hoped one of you might recognize something so we can move forward."

"Actually, there is something I've been thinking about. When Hiram looked at my file"—Veda grimaces—"he was hyperfixated on how the Botanist got into my apartment. I want to see the file to focus on what he's talking about. Maybe it'll jog my memory."

Gabriel doesn't hesitate, pulling one file from the stack on his desk. When he places it in front of her, Veda reads her statement line by line, the details, spells cast, and unredacted information. She hunts for familiarity . . . and finds none. Finally, Veda looks through the pictures, stopping at the photo Hiram must've looked at. The door was blown off, but it's strange seeing it in the light when that night was nothing but darkness. The scorched walls remind her of Lucinda's house. She shudders at the memory, trying to distract herself from thinking about it by grabbing the next folder.

It's too late to stop.

She's back at the hospital. Finding Healer Lawson on the ground, bleeding profusely. Veda flips to her statement and pauses, recoiling. "This isn't my statement—I mean, it is, but it's wrong. *Large man. Hispanic features. Deep voice.* None of this is . . . I didn't say that. It's not even true. They were . . ." Veda squeezes her eyes shut. "They weren't large. Their face was a kaleidoscope of changing features that never settled on one. Their voice was altered in a way I can't describe, and Healer Lawson actually spoke to me. He said they didn't know what was coming."

"Who spoke? And who are *they*?"

Veda flinches at the memory, rubbing her hands. She can see the blood. "It took too long for anyone to get there, just me and—and a *body* for almost an hour, and the first thing the investigator said to me was . . ." *You did what you could. Curses are unnatural for a reason. You can't save them all.* Veda opens her eyes, scrubbing a hand over her face. "None of that is in my statement. Who changed it?"

Gabriel stares at the file before his jaw sets, hand moving to hover over the page. He shuts his eyes and murmurs, *"Ostendo."*

The paper glows, hissing and screaming. Veda sits back hard, heart pounding, hands gripping the chair as the file tries to rip itself apart. "What in the hell are you—"

"Doing?" he shouts over the high-pitched scream as the file burns red hot, rising off the table. The edges smoke black, then white. "Oh, just something that will not only alert my superiors but might verge on illegal. Hypothetically speaking, do you think Hiram will represent me if I get arrested?"

Gabriel flashes a nervous smile as the file lands back on the table. Then he sobers, on alert. "The Imprints of the person who wrote up this file, submitted it, and reviewed it are concealed by law. The only people allowed to reveal their names are those with the rank of superior or higher. I'm just an investigator, so yeah, illegal."

"Why would you—"

"Because whoever altered your file worked for the FCD at the time this happened, and the only reason they would change your statement is—"

"To conceal the truth," Veda interrupts. "I thought if I looked, I could jog my memory, but all I remember is the power. I'm not Sensitive, but I swore I felt it. Wild. Out of control."

"Mages and the Unseen don't have access to that kind of magic, and Seers are taught control from the moment we present," Khadijah says. "I don't know—"

"It's working," Gabriel says.

They wait for one minute. Then two. Veda's vision blurs from staring so hard until Khadijah's hand grips her shoulder, grounding her. Finally, a golden signature appears on the corner of the page.

They all lean forward to read the name, but it's all too familiar.

"Blocked."

Gabriel is smiling.

Veda swears. "Why are you so happy? We still don't have a name."

"No, but we've been blocked too many times." Gabriel nearly vaults the table to get back into his seat. "They're all connected."

"What are you going to do?" Khadijah asks.

"Force my commander's hand for resources and stay out of jail."

"How exactly . . ."

Gabriel looks at Veda. "I think the Botanist and the person who wrote this are one and the same."

Sixteen

Antaris spends most of Saturday listless, barely eating or making eye contact with Hiram, yet keeping the nameless kitten and the lantern Veda gave him close. He is a shell of the boy whose trust Hiram almost had.

Sunday's tension is nearly nauseating. Hiram looks on while Antaris wanders during the day, a break in habit. Every attempt to talk ends with either avoidance or his son retreating, distrust radiating from him. By the evening, Antaris is looking at Grace's photo album and crying. Hiram is sick with worry by bedtime, when he looks in on Antaris, only to find him staring at the lantern. He's losing him.

Another day can't pass without action. So he plans. Talks to John. Spends most of the night writing note after note, but none feel right. By midnight, his attempts at excuses are balled up and scattered around the trash can. Hiram doesn't remember nodding off at the kitchen table, but wakes with a painful crick in his neck and . . .

Antaris is staring at him, eyes wide and searching, with one of his failed attempts at groveling in hand. Hiram ignores his pounding head and focuses on his son. There are things more enduring than promises, more important than pride, and for the first time in his life, Hiram stops agonizing over details that don't matter. The only thing that does is standing in front of him.

Hiram blurts out the first words that come to mind. "I'm sorry."

Antaris doesn't leave.

A lump forms in his throat as he conveys a remorse he struggles to express out loud. *"Please forgive me."*

Antaris's expression is more serious than it should be.

"I told you once that I would always come back, but Friday, I wasn't there and it hurt you." Hiram feels horrible all over again. It's obvious being late didn't hurt his son. It terrified him. "You didn't think I was coming back."

Antaris's eyes fill with tears as he nods, covering his face with his small hands.

"The last thing I want to do is leave you or hurt your feelings. I meant what I said, that I'll come back for you. I'll do my best to not break that promise again." Remembering how Antaris listened the last time he talked about a case, Hiram asks, "Can I tell you what happened that day?"

At his son's slow agreement, he wades through the murky topic as delicately as possible, telling a kid-friendly version of his day leading up to realizing how late it was. Hiram makes peppermint tea for Antaris while telling him about the library, his son's fascination waking up as he talks about the dusty books. He makes breakfast while describing Clinton's unscrambling magic. They eat while he chooses his words carefully when discussing Ruth and the trip to the FCD and how panicked he was after he realized he was late and how he rushed to the school. The longer he talks, the more enrapt Antaris becomes, angles to him, follows him, understands him. His tear streaks dry, and the tension he carries relaxes. As does Hiram.

They move to the dock. It's cool and muggy from last night's rain, the peaceful quiet makes the decision easy. He'll keep Antaris home from school in favor of watching the sun rise over the trees.

"When I was your age . . ." Hiram trails off when Antaris's head whips to him.

Veda's words haunt him: *He wants to know you.*

"I liked to create as a child. Still do. I start with an idea and a bunch of parts, build it, test it, refine it. That's probably why I cook and read as much as I do. I didn't get this from my father. He didn't teach me to read, to swim, or to ride a bike. I learned from tutors, boarding school, and my parents' staff—everyone except them. It's tradition; generations of Ellises were raised the same way, but I never wanted that for myself, and I don't want it for you. I want better."

Antaris shifts closer.

"I'd promise not to make another mistake, but that's not possible. It doesn't mean I don't care about you. It just means I'm not perfect. No one is, but I'll keep trying to do my best to be the father I always wanted."

He makes a small fist and rubs it in a circular motion over his chest. *Sorry.*

"I *am* sorry."

Antaris signs the word again with more intent. He means it . . . or perhaps, he's trying to communicate something he hasn't learned how to sign. Hiram raises his finger. "Do you forgive me?"

There is no hesitation in his response.

He taps twice.

Yes.

Tuesday is a new day.

Hiram walks Antaris to the school door, hand on his book bag, guiding him. For the first time, before they part, he kneels in front of his son. It's easier to talk to him like this. He points at the clock. "When the small hand gets to four, I will be here."

Antaris nods.

Hiram then offers his son the second thermos he's been holding. "This is for Miss Thorne. Can you give it to her?"

Antaris accepts the thermos, but is slow to leave, looking back twice and nearly bumping into another student. Hiram waits until he's inside, then waits a little longer. Finally, he allows relief to wash over him.

One down. One to go.

Hiram is debating whether now is the time to approach Veda when he hears his name, then sees Peter beckoning him into his office. Boxes of shirts litter every surface. Peter pulls out a small, checks the collar, then hands it to him. "It's for the end-of-term party Friday. The students are allowed to wear whatever they want, so long as it follows the dress code. The school day is basically a block party."

"Think I can make the bow tie work with this?"

"Good luck."

Hiram tosses the shirt over his shoulder and walks down the hall to the balcony. Students mill about, playing and talking and having breakfast before the first bell. He spots Antaris standing in front of the thriving herb garden, shyly offering the second thermos to Veda.

His son shines in her presence, and her smile breaks like dawn, transforming into something unforgivably alive. Critical but shortsighted, Veda took one look at Hiram and drilled straight to the heart of his painful truths. She's as right about him as she's wrong, and his urge to pick her apart in all the same ways remains. Not to critique but to understand.

"The bell is in five minutes," Peter says next to him. Hiram didn't know he was there. "You can go down there. Talk to her."

"I'll bet my entire trust fund that she doesn't want to talk to me. Double or nothing, she hates me."

"You'd lose." Peter laughs in the face of his disbelief. "Trust me, Veda is selective with her emotions and good at protecting herself from what she doesn't want to feel. Antaris is a blind spot for her, but so are you. She's decided how she sees you, and you're challenging her reality."

"I doubt that. You weren't there when she was cursing me out."

"No, but I heard it." Peter waves back at a group of students who yell their greetings. He leans on the safety railing. "My mom always says emotions masquerade as each other and blur the line between reality and belief. What you believe is anger may be fear or frustration. What looks like fear can be sadness or regret. The purpose of arguing with someone is to convince them to change their actions or beliefs. If

Veda truly hated you, she'd be apathetic. She wouldn't believe you were capable of change and wouldn't waste her energy confronting you, no matter how much she cares for Antaris."

Frowning, Hiram watches her taste the tea, approval given in her smile. "She said she was disappointed."

"Exactly my point." Peter nudges him in the shoulder. "Why *that* seems to bother you more than anything is a conversation for another day. For now, try talking to her again."

"This won't end badly at all," he mutters sarcastically.

Peter claps a hand on his shoulder. "How about you take the night off, clear your head, and get out of the house. I'll watch Antaris and the nameless cat. I need to set up the cat tower anyway. You haven't given yourself a break since you learned of his existence. You need a night to yourself."

"Is this negotiable?"

"No."

Hiram cards a hand through his hair, sighing. "Then I suppose it's a yes."

Later that day, Hiram finds liberation in declining seven of his mother's calls.

With his reinforced spine in place, he answers the eighth to prevent a ninth. "When I said I was done, it didn't mean I was done until you wanted something."

Hanging up before Simran can get a word in puts a pep in Hiram's step. When he wanders into the living room, Peter has put on music, and instead of easels, a small cauldron sits on the table, surrounded by goggles and gloves. Peter is in the kitchen with Antaris, who is standing on his step stool, eyeing the spaghetti with growing suspicion. Hiram glances at it and adds more onion powder, salt, pepper, and basil. Antaris approves enough to stop supervising and sit at the table. Hiram picks up a napkin and sets it next to his son, who neatly tucks it into his shirt.

"What are you planning to brew?"

"I figured I would walk him through a year-two giggle potion. I can't brew, but I do like watching."

Before he leaves, Hiram kneels next to Antaris's chair. "I'll be here when you wake up."

His son nods.

Peter recommended a lounge called Blossoms, apparently known for good drinks and live music on Tuesdays. The place is uptown, perched in the foothills beside the river that runs through the city. Picturesque on clear days, the view is stunning in the evening, draped in golden hues at this hour. He can see the nearby towns, forests, and the shapes of distant mountains. The place is crowded with a mix of professionals, tourists, and groups celebrating birthdays. It's an hour wait for a table because Hiram doesn't have a reservation and doesn't feel the need to throw his name around, so he settles in at the outdoor bar, listening to the band play as sunset transforms the skyline.

When the band takes a break, the trajectory of his evening changes. Veda is at the top of the stairs in a floral minidress and tights being led to a table by the hostess. To get to her destination, she has to pass him, which makes Hiram feel like he's justifying her paranoia.

He's surprised when, instead of a stalking accusation, he's met with a single raised brow as their eyes lock. Hiram approaches when she sits. The hostess shoots him a puzzled look and asks her, "I thought you were a party of one."

"I am," Veda replies coolly. "I'll let you know if I decide to change the reservation back."

With that, the hostess leaves.

Veda's glare is sharp when she reaches for the menu, opening it and covering her face. "You should be pissed off at me for not letting you speak before yelling at you the way I did."

She's too calm, like she's talking about the weather.

"Maybe, but I'm here for a quiet night, not an argument." Even as he sits, he's cautious, observant, but his focus scatters when he realizes the faint scent of jasmine is coming from her.

She tilts the menu down, giving him a long look. "As am I. Peter suggested this place and made my reservation. The fact that I need to apologize to you is secondary, and I can only do that with a stiff drink."

Peter. The puppet master. Hiram quietly cuts the strings they hadn't realized they were dangling from, but keeps his best friend's machinations to himself. A waiter arrives, pleasantly delivering the same greeting he's likely repeated a hundred times tonight. Veda asks a few questions before ordering the strongest cocktail on the menu. Hiram refreshes the drink he left the bar with.

She doesn't speak again until she's had her first wincing sip. "Perfect. Exactly what I needed."

"To apologize?"

"Yeah, Khadijah told me why you were late. Thanks for what you did for Ruth." Veda sighs. "I'm sorry I didn't let you speak, and that I took my personal issues and emotions out on you. I still meant some of what I said, but not the vast majority of it."

Hiram fights the urge to crack a smile. "You couldn't leave it at being sorry?"

"Of course not." She shields herself behind the menu again.

"In the spirit of reconciliation, I'll apologize for the part where I implied you were a danger to Antaris. I never meant that."

"How is he?" Veda asks carefully. "He seemed okay today, but it's not always easy to gauge what's on his mind."

Hiram tells her about the weekend, the corner of her mouth twitching when he recounts the successful apology and the day spent together. "What did you teach him today?"

"We practiced sign language," she replies. "He's picking up the basics so quickly. The days of the week, names of food."

"I read that book you gave him cover to cover, and have been practicing with him at home."

"That explains how he knew the sign for *cheese* before I did."

Hiram smiles, but can't help but notice the way she bites hers back. He polishes off his drink. "So, what else do you teach him during tutoring sessions?"

"Nothing much. We gardened and ate tangerines under the olive tree. It's popping leaves."

"I didn't know they grew that fast."

"They don't, but . . ." She shrugs. "Nature doesn't always follow the rules."

Their eyes meet. Veda looks away. Hiram doesn't.

"I won't intrude on your night any longer. I know we haven't been able to schedule that time to meet yet, but perhaps later this week?"

The easiest response comes quietly. "Okay."

Hiram pulls out his wallet and offers her a sleek card.

Veda accepts it. "Self-updating business cards? Fancy."

"Practical." Hiram stands up. "How about Friday?"

Veda studies him for a moment, then nods.

Hiram walks away, feeling oddly unsettled. He looks back once to see Veda staring at the card before pocketing it. She drains the rest of her drink. On his way out, he finds the waiter and stops him, pointing at Veda's back. "I want to pay for my drink and her entire bill."

"Yes, sir."

Hiram hands him more than enough money, the extra serving as a generous tip. He leaves for a nearby steak house, but not before giving clear instructions: "Make sure she gets the best service of her life."

Seventeen

Veda feels good. Thanks to the excellent drinks and food, both the day and her conversation with Hiram are hazy memories she can sort through tomorrow. Warm and pliant from the alcohol, Veda tries to pay, only to be told it has already been covered. With zero complaints, she heads toward the nearby river walk. She plans to wander into whatever shops draw her interest until she's sober enough to ride home.

She doesn't notice the shift.

How the steady flow of people slows to a trickle. How, even at her polite nod, people look through her as if she's invisible. How she can't hear the passing cars, the breeze, anything.

Something is wrong.

Plans abandoned, Veda starts back to her bike but stumbles on something she can't see and reaches out, only for her hand to rebound off nothing.

An invisible curtain. She sobers instantly. Magical layering is rare, complex magic that can't be done on a whim and is illegal in public places.

Veda walks faster, then cuts off the path, heading down a well-lit alley. But he emerges from the shadows.

In a few weeks, Everett's become haggard and barely recognizable, a pale shell of himself. His sandy-brown hair is oily, unkempt, and falling into hooded, luminescent red eyes. It's clear the man standing before her is not Dr. Simpson. He's lost to the curse.

"Veda." He sounds as rough as he looks, hoarse like he's been screaming for days. "You need my help."

"I think you're the one who needs help. Everyone has been looking for you."

"I'm no good to anyone locked away."

He steps forward, and Veda rocks back, looking over her shoulder. People are passing, none the wiser about what's happening. She pulls out her phone, careful to keep it at her side.

"The Botanist knows you're here. They've seen you." Truth makes a wounded noise escape him. "They know I talked to you. They know what you know. Veda, you need to see. To remember. It reminded you of home. Their faces lie . . ."

Veda doesn't move. "Who are they?"

His ticking time bomb explodes.

Smoky gray power rushes from him, tearing violently in every direction, burning like physical touch. There's something wrong about it. Fractured. It makes Veda nauseous. If this is what being Sensitive is like, she doesn't want it. The wind blows in an unnatural direction, wrapping around them. Mist rises from the grass. The concrete melts and bubbles. Her body feels heavy, veins filled with lead.

In the aftermath, his eyes are normal and clear yet filled with terror. He's having a moment of clarity when he whispers, *"Run."*

Veda doesn't need to be told twice. Stumbling, gripping her phone, she runs like the earth is threatening to drag her into the molten depths. The force with which she slams into the invisible curtain sends her sprawling. Her amulet flashes with her dismantling charm, ripping a hole through to the other side. Veda runs, but the lack of sound stuns her into turning around.

Everett is walking toward her, each step a glide. His eyes, bloodred once more, glow in the dusky light.

"Consisto."

The spell works as intended, stopping her in place. Its force drives Veda to her knees, her amulet glowing in a desperate bid to protect her. It won't be enough. She has to move. There's no spell to neutralize magic, but Veda tries something anyway, focusing everything on Everett. Her amulet glows brighter, the air shifting around her.

She screams for help the moment she's free.

Everett stumbles and drops to his knees, his veins glowing red.

Something dangerous wants out.

Heart hammering in her chest, Veda takes off. Knowing she isn't fast enough, she hides in the shadows between two closed shops. Each breath she takes is done with intention. To keep silent. To think. Trembling fingers dial Gabriel's number. She curses under her breath when it goes to voicemail. She tries Francisco. Then Peter. No one answers. Veda calls Gabriel again but keeps the message recording while she scans her surroundings for a landmark.

"Main and Second Avenue. Everett is here," she manages to whisper before ending the voicemail. With bated breath, she watches Everett stalk by.

Veda closes her eyes and counts, waiting long enough for him to be gone before deciding to make a move. It's now or never. Bolting from her hiding spot seems like a good idea until she's snatched off the ground, vision blurring even before she's shoved against the brick wall. Everett clamps a hand over her mouth, eyes darting.

"Shh, the Botanist will hear you. They told me . . ."

Veda hears nothing more.

A cold, sober clarity explodes behind her eyes. Beneath his hand, she shakily whispers, "You c-can't tell the truth."

Something changes. Everett's concern twists, morphing until it's almost amused, like a child caught in a lie.

"Oh, that's right." A giggle slips out. "He can't."

This is not Everett.

"It's you."

"In the flesh. Somewhat." Their expression turns sinister. "Still don't know who I am yet?"

Panic seizes Veda. The hand over her mouth clamps down harder, no longer trembling. Veda kicks, trying to knee the Botanist-as-Everett, clawing and clamoring at his clammy arms, desperate for freedom. But they are strong, radiating a power Veda has felt only once before: the last time she fought them. Her phone grows hot in her hand, bursting into flames, but she holds on, twisting and stretching, letting go only when the angle is right.

It lands in the grass. Fire roars to life, heat licking their feet as the blaze catches and spreads. It's enough of a distraction for her assailant to let go. Veda hits the ground with a gasp, coughing as her knees buckle.

Pain turns the world white. Smoke fills the air. Flames roar in the wrong direction. Her amulet pulses against her skin, drawing in what magic it can to shield her and keep her attacker at bay, but it's waning.

So is she.

"I underestimated you, Veda." Their voice has changed. No longer Everett's, it's a chilling blend of several. "You were supposed to die that night, but I'm glad you didn't, glad you've been holding that curse all these years."

Veda tries to push against the wave of magic, tries to crawl away, tries every spell she knows. It earns her nothing more than pain and a trickle of blood from her nose. Still, she drags herself forward, one knee after the other, crawling away from the fire and forcing herself to move with magic and might. Her amulet chars her skin, a reminder that she is no match against raw magic.

Impostor Everett grabs her ankle and pulls. The pressure intensifies until she can't breathe.

"One way or another, you're coming with me."

Veda claws the grass, twisting, blind with pain and terror. She kicks and screams until her boot connects with the pendant around their neck. Their features blur into a kaleidoscope, reforming into Veda's face.

Eyes squeezed shut, she kicks again. It lands hard. Everything dies when the impostor gasps like they've lost all their wind and then collapses.

Veda hauls herself upright. It's unsettling to see her own face grimacing in agony on the ground. Backing away, she nearly falls again when the bones in her ankle grind together. Every step is a battle. She nearly stumbles over the real Everett, slumped against the side of a building.

Drenched in sweat, he's rocking back and forth, and muttering, "I'm sorry. I'm sorry."

Veda can't stop. Summoning the last of her strength, she throws out a desperate cry for help. Her amulet sizzles, levitating from where it rests on her chest. A blinding bolt of light bursts from her fingertips. The streetlights explode with enough force to plunge the entire street into darkness. Someone notices the fire and yells, which creates instant, distracting chaos.

Veda's hobble turns into a hopping run. Down one alley, then another, she stumbles through the darkness. The crushing wave of magic presses in on all sides. The Botanist must be close. Veda doesn't know if she'll be able to fight again, yet adrenaline roars in her veins, her vision swimming in colors. Even at a distance, magic is volatile, dangerous, but the Botanist clearly doesn't care.

The spell hits. Then the world shifts. The path ahead lengthens, splitting and twisting as though she's looking through a fun house mirror. Reflections of herself mimic her movements. All but one. That one screams.

Raw magic slams into Veda, sending her sprawling. Before she can catch her breath, her clone is on top of her, hands closing around her throat once again, squeezing hard. Veda thrashes, kicking wildly, clawing at the hands around her throat, fighting to scream. But there's no air.

"Go to sleep," the clone croons. "We have experiments to do—"

A burst of light strikes her clone, tossing them backward. She hyperventilates on precious air, and her hand flies to cover her throat. She isn't prepared for the sudden touch of real Everett's hand, trembling as he frantically mutters, "They came to you at night. The music played on. The mark grows. Changes. It lives in you but is destined for her. For her!"

Veda's fingers tingle. Whatever unconscious magic he's using on her is incomplete. She clings to the tendrils of life, desperate to hold on.

Every ounce of magic her amulet has ever absorbed erupts from within the stone, detonating in a blinding wave of power. A final, sacrificial gift.

Deafened by its scream, paralyzed by the pressure, Veda watches her amulet's essence rise, mingling with the first sparks. Everett's hand is gone, his body hurled away in the explosion of color and warmth, magic and ozone. The pain fades as she *finally* draws in a full breath.

Light fractures into a thousand hues like the birth of a new star. Despair and gratitude rise in tandem, heavy in her chest.

Her head throbs. Her vision clouds.

Darkness swallows her whole.

"Don't move."

Veda gasps into consciousness. Coughing and flailing, she panics, sucking in as much air as her lungs will allow and sputtering. The tightness in her chest unwinds enough to carve out one desperate sound as she claws at the hands near her face until the world sharpens.

"Can you hear me?" they ask.

She knows the voice. She knows the face. Confusion halts her fight.

Hiram looks up, signaling to someone. "We're over here!"

What follows is a blur of Gabriel and Francisco and medics crowding around her. Questions fly, but Veda can't answer any. She jolts at every noise and touch, especially when they poke, prod, inject potions into her veins, and pour elixirs down her throat. They talk to each other, but Veda can't focus, too tired after crawling through hell.

Veda doesn't realize she's being moved until she's already off the ground. She screams.

"Give her a minute," Hiram snaps, then his focus is on her. "They're taking you to the hospital. You're hurt and your throat is . . ."

His words fade into a hum when a medic dabs at her eyes. Her head swims. Gently, someone touches her neck. She smells burning flesh and wonders if it's hers. Everything goes from too loud to too quiet. Air is lava in her lungs. Veda forces her head to the side. Gabriel is watching her, worried.

Hiram rides with her to the hospital, doesn't explain, nor does she ask. Under the harsh lights, subtle signs of his distress are easier to see. As are the burn marks on his knuckles, the cut on his forehead, his torn sleeve. Veda's injuries are deeper than pain, and his grimace once the doctors cut open her dress confirms this.

"You can wait outside, sir," someone says.

"I'm not leaving." He's firm, unmovable.

"At least let someone check out your injuries."

"No."

The healer blocks her sight of him, shining a light in her eyes. "I'm Healer Michaels. I'm going to put you to sleep while I heal you. Rest. *Somnum*."

The spell wraps its arms around her and drags her into the void.

The next time Veda opens her eyes, she's alone, but not for long.

Healer Michaels enters the room after a polite knock.

"I'm fine," she says automatically.

"You will be."

He walks her through everything. They found evidence of a nearly crushed windpipe, but not how she ended up healed. She knows, though she keeps that to herself. Veda touches her neck. The reason she's alive is gone. Healer Michaels explains that her burns are healed, ankle repaired, but her wrist needed to be set due to the number of broken bones. Her concussion must be monitored closely; he warns her that the bruises caused by magic will take days to heal.

"You need to have that Sanguis Curse checked out," Healer Michaels says. "I can see where the curse's scars have begun to retreat, which should not be happening. The bind is stable, and Sanguis doesn't typically retreat, it grows larger. Have you done anything differently? Has a Seer tried healing you?"

"No and no. I know the rules. Even if they could . . ."

"How long has it been in place?"

"Years," Veda replies, voice hoarse.

"Too long." The healer frowns and looks at the door as if someone is going to burst into the room. "I've seen your curse once before in a patient. Nasty creation. The worst of the worst. She was cursed by her sister in a fit of rage, and it didn't leave her body until she . . . died."

Well, that's comforting. The healer is about to say something else when a doctor knocks on the door. "We need you in room four for an arterial unblocking."

"Be there in a second." He lets his exhaustion show and apologizes. "Been here a long time?"

"I'm fifteen hours into a thirty-hour shift."

Veda winces.

"Yeah, rough." The healer steps back. "Excuse me. Duty calls."

He's gone before Veda can react.

Nothing has changed in the medical field. Healer Seers are still criminally overworked and underpaid. It's a shame.

Veda shifts in bed, frowning at her itchy gown, in desperate need of a shower and something to wipe her memory.

Hiram knocks on the door.

Before Veda can answer, magic allows him into her room like he belongs.

"How?" Veda croaks, her voice rough.

"Had to say you were my wife so they wouldn't kick me out. They tied my Imprint to your room."

Wife? She elects not to dignify that with a response. There are more pressing questions. "No, the alley. How?"

"How did I find you?" He sits in the chair next to her bed. "Gabriel got your message. Peter got your missed call. He called Gabriel, then me, because I was in the area. I saw the flare. It smelled like . . ." He clears his throat. "Doesn't matter. It led me to you."

"Everett?"

"Gone. You caused enough ruckus between the fire and your amulet's detonation that the news got involved. Apparently, Commander Bishop was on the way, and the FCD is conducting a manhunt, but he's hurt," Hiram says, flexing his fingers, curling them into a fist before wincing. "When I found you, the Botanist was getting up. They looked like you."

"I . . . yeah, I fought myself. I don't think I'm going to look in a mirror for a while."

He makes a small hum of understanding. "I hexed them, tried to restrain them, but they broke out, said my name, and told me that they would see me again."

"Shit," Veda says faintly. "Are you—were you injured?"

"A bit. I was checked out. It's just a consequence. My amulet only partially worked for a protection charm I cast on you. It's not meant to be used on someone unrelated to me." Hiram glances at her. "I'm not sure how it worked as much as it did."

Veda looks down at her splinted wrist. "I'm worried about Everett being out there, getting madder by the day. He needs to be found."

"You should rest."

Memories plunge her into fear's icy waters. "I don't think I can."

"I know, but—oh." He reaches into his pocket and pulls something out. Her amulet. It's cracked and burned, the chain rusted and blackened. "I found it and thought you might want it."

Hesitant fingers curl around the twisted stones that saved her life once, and sacrificed themselves for her now. Veda is so damn tired. But if she lets herself feel, even for a second, she'll drown. She forces herself to get past the night's horrors, only realizing she's forgotten gratitude when the words slip out.

"Thanking you is . . ." Veda tries to hold back the words.

Hiram's smirk spreads wider. "Is the last thing you want to do, I'm sure."

"It's the worst." It hurts to smile, but one twists her lips before she winces. Hiram reaches for a nearby compress and brings it to her sore cheek. When Veda takes over, their fingers incidentally brush. A flash of inviting warmth leaves her scrambling to reestablish the distance between them.

Hiram grows serious, his expression hardening into an unreadable mask. "You're welcome."

"If you get any nicer, I'll start insulting you to maintain our status quo."

"One *you* set."

Veda focuses on the growing numbness instead of his comment. It's easier.

Fortunately, Hiram's phone rings, and he excuses himself. The conversation doesn't last nearly long enough, and he returns with: "Gabriel said that Khadijah is on her way. She'll wait with you until you're discharged, take you home, and get your bike."

"Okay."

Hiram returns to his seat, blue eyes searching hers. "I can leave now, or I can wait until she gets here."

The first option would leave Veda alone, staring at sterile white walls and trying to hold herself together. It sounds miserable. But the second option is no easier. Whether now or later, she'll be alone with her thoughts soon enough.

"Wait." It's the hardest word Veda has ever uttered.

Hiram settles in his seat without hesitation. Adrenaline fades. Pain dulls into a cold hollowness as the past few hours hit Veda like a freight train, dismantling every painstaking measure of self-preservation she's managed to construct.

The dam doesn't crumble—it bursts.

Without permission, tears rise, pooling in her swollen eyes. They sting, burning hot trails down her battered face. She tries to stop them, scrubbing at each one with stubborn resolve, but the effort only brings a splitting headache. She can no longer keep up the charade of acting like she isn't scared. Like she didn't silently plead for her life despite believing that she was ready to lose it. Like on another day, in another way, the circumstances already beyond her control will have a different outcome.

Later, she'll rebuild the dam. Patch it. Reinforce it. But tonight, she lets her tears fall. Veda sobs with abandon, each breath raw and shuddering.

Hiram's hand covers hers, his grip warm and solid. A rescue from deep waters.

He's prickly like a rough rope. Quiet and steady. Her tether.

Eighteen

On the final day of school before the break, after watching the comical sight of Gabriel carrying August like a sack of potatoes—determined to keep him from ruining his clothes by jumping in puddles—Hiram lingers by the fountain, waiting with purpose.

Gabriel appears confused, but approaches nonetheless. "No more Everett sightings, and nothing on any sightings of the Botanist or, hell, anyone wearing Veda's face as a mask. We have alerts out for both," he says, unprompted. "We have preliminary results from the magical testing collected from Veda's attack and that blocked Imprint is there, mixed in with Veda's and Everett's Imprints. That's enough to confirm the Botanist for me. I took this to my superiors, and they've had *several* closed-door meetings about it. Veda—"

"How is she?" Hiram asks.

Gabriel's expression changes. "Still sore and shaken, but she went through some extra healing sessions with Khadijah and is on the mend."

Admittedly, Hiram is hungry for more details but can't be too greedy. This isn't enough, but it will suffice for now. It's hard to rest when Veda resides in his dreams: eerily still, not moving, not breathing, dying beneath an explosion of once-absorbed magic released in desperate sacrifice. He'll never unsee it or the tears she shed in the hospital, clutching the charred remains of the amulet that gave its life for her.

"She doesn't have a new phone yet," Gabriel adds. "But I'm dropping by Khadijah's to talk to her after her follow-up appointment."

"Ah." Hiram rubs the back of his neck. "Can you tell her that my invitation stands if she's up to it? Antaris would love to have her over."

Gabriel's brow rises sharply. "Antaris, huh?"

The comment earns Gabriel a glare.

"I'll let her know."

"Thanks."

It's after six when Hiram puts the finishing touches on the chicken biryani while Antaris plays on the floor with the kitten. He's about to tell Antaris to wash his hands when the talisman sends a sound echoing through the house. Antaris's head pops up, and they exchange a confused look before Hiram drops the kitchen towel and answers the door.

Veda stands on his front porch in jeans, a loose flannel shirt, and boots. Her hair is pulled back, highlighting the deep-purple bruise around her eye that splatters like paint down the side of her neck before disappearing under her collar.

"Hi."

"Hi," Veda says, pausing. "I, uh . . . brought a plant."

He realizes, as she offers it, that the plant is for him.

"Lavenders mean peace," Veda says, handing off the potted ceasefire. "I would have brought flowers, but potted plants are more sustainable, improve air quality, reduce stress, and—and I'm babbling. Please tell me to shut up."

"No." Hiram opens the door wider. "But you can come in."

"Khadijah thought I shouldn't ride, but I needed the fresh air. Sorry if I'm late."

"I didn't expect you to show. You're right on time."

It's instinct, Hiram thinks, how she immediately glares at him, though Veda's sharpness softens into amused disbelief. He looks back twice as Veda follows him deeper into the house to the great room.

Her eyes fall on Antaris, who is standing in the center, kitten in hand. Her smile grows wider than Hiram's ever seen. His son deposits the kitten in its play area, and rushes forward, stopping short when he notices the marks on her.

Veda kneels in front of him. "I got hurt, but I'm okay now, still a bit sore. Your dad helped me."

Antaris's eyes are twice their normal size as he swivels toward Hiram, who confirms with a nod. He places the lavender on the edge of the island, and like a moth to a flame, Antaris is drawn to it. "Veda gave this to us. What do we do?"

Hiram follows his son's lead, bringing his hand to his chin and moving it out. *Thank you.*

Veda's smile comes easily with Antaris. "You did that so well." To Hiram, her words are slower, guarded. "Because I wasn't able to see him this week, I was thinking—if it's okay with you—we can continue our sessions here or at the school during the break."

Antaris turns wide, hopeful eyes on Hiram.

He folds like a house of cards. "We can work something out."

"I suggested we practice brewing ahead of you starting year two, but Peter said the giggle potion didn't go well. Something about nearly starting a fire."

Hiram is confused. "He never said a word."

"To be fair, a lot happened that night," Veda says, then smooths down his blushing son's hair. "Accidents happen, okay? Only Seers can't brew, so you'll get it right next time."

Dinner is pleasant enough between a boy who doesn't talk and the adults who don't know what to say, but they figure it out. Afterward, Antaris leads her on a scattered tour of the house: first to Hiram's makeshift office, then to his closed bedroom door, and lastly to Antaris's bedroom.

Hiram lingers at the doorway while Antaris proceeds to show her every item he can get his hands on. The gifted lantern. His mother's photo album. Paintings and a few of his own drawings that didn't make it on the fridge. His collection of bow ties. His stuffed bunny that's losing more stuffing by the day. The tour concludes when Antaris puts on proper shoes for his nightly wandering.

Hiram explains once his son leads the way to the back door, "He wanders before bed."

"Why?" she asks, interest piqued.

"Looking for what he's missing, I've theorized."

"Have you ever asked?"

He hasn't. Every conversation with Antaris is a challenge he's only beginning to tackle. The kitten meows from the corner of the room, and Hiram retrieves him.

"Aren't you allergic?"

"I've been taking this terrible daily elixir." He frowns at the cat pawing at his finger. "The things I do for what my son cherishes."

"Maybe he's drawn to it because of the similarities." Veda reaches for the cat, and Hiram lets the wiggling creature go to her. She rubs behind the kitten's tiny ears. "They've both lost the world they once knew."

Hiram hangs back as she places the kitten in its play area once more, then they both follow Antaris outside.

Tonight's walk is different. Antaris slips a hand into Veda's and leads her to each spot, looking first, then inviting her to do the same. He seems to nearly speak up twice when he sees her wince, but Veda's encouraging nod subdues him. Hiram marvels at how at ease Antaris is with her here, how he always finds his way back to her side. There's trust, not hesitation. Belief instead of suspicion.

Hiram wants that. He's been working hard to earn it, patient and trusting that he'll get there. But tonight, the walk is less distressing because Hiram finds comfort knowing his son trusts someone. When Antaris finishes, they're all clearly tired.

"I'll start your bath," Hiram says to his son. While he's bathing, Hiram returns to the living room.

Veda is looking around, a curious frown on her face. "Still moving in?"

"Wasn't planning to stay long."

An understanding passes between them. "My walls at home are bare, too."

"Not done running?"

Veda shrugs.

"I think I want to paint," Hiram says casually.

"Put pictures on the walls. Something as pretentious as you are."

"How about a fur rug in the great room?"

"That'll work." Veda snaps her fingers. "Oh, and an herb garden on the back porch for Antaris. He'll like that."

"Fresh herbs for cooking would be nice. Unfortunately, my thumb is black."

"Your son's is quite green." Veda walks on, pushing her uninjured hand into her pocket. "You know what else would be nice? If your office had office-like things. For starters, a second chair."

"Bookshelves, too. I bought two more, but we're still running out of space."

"I saw that, yes." She nods. "Peter mentioned you read."

"Voraciously."

Something heavy rests between them, unspoken. The moment ends with her rolling her eyes and Hiram huffing a laugh.

"It appears my assumption that we could have a civil conversation was not premature. We've extended the streak too far to count."

She shrugs. "The night is still young."

Twenty minutes later, Antaris emerges from his room to get Hiram for bedtime, but today he shyly waits for Veda's agreement to join them. The lantern above his bed casts a low glow over the room. Once tucked in, he signs *tomorrow* to Veda, who looks taken aback.

"We'll see."

The answer satisfies him enough to settle into bed. Hiram excuses himself to grab Antaris's kitten and a glass of water for his bedside. When he returns, he lingers in the doorway, watching them practice signing, Veda struggling with one hand.

"Do you want to hear a story about your name?" Veda asks.

Antaris nods.

"It all starts with Orion, a hunter so great he vowed to kill every animal on the planet. But Mother Earth asked a giant scorpion to protect them. His name was Scorpio, and he fought Orion to the bitter end. He stung Orion, and as a reward for his bravery, Mother Earth placed Scorpio in the sky." She taps his nose, making him smile. "You are named after Scorpio's brightest star. Antares is the heart of the scorpion."

Hiram didn't know any of this. He barely pays attention to the sky, too preoccupied by what's happening on the ground.

Veda's expression grows serious as she pats down Antaris's drying curls. "You're the heart of the scorpion. You're brave and strong. You—oh."

Thanks to the kitten's meow, Hiram's been noticed. He places the water on the table while Veda looks away. *Good nights* are exchanged with hands and words before Hiram deposits the kitten in the new cat bed next to Antaris. He leaves the door cracked after Veda follows him back out.

"What do you drink?" Hiram asks.

It's the first question he's asked strictly to learn about her.

"Wine. White and sweet, if you have it."

A bottle of dessert wine should do. "It's not chilled."

"That's fine."

Hiram pours her a glass, then makes himself a brandy. They take the bottles and their glasses outside to the dock, sitting as dusk fades into darkness.

An incredulous chuckle breaks the silence. "I should be the last person you want in your house."

"As long as you're not accusing me of being a terrible parent, you're welcome to stay."

Veda cringes. "I deserve that."

"No, you don't." Hiram sips his drink. "I feel like a shit parent more often than not. I'm doing my best, and while you made some valid points, you don't know everything."

"Go on, then, and I'll reserve the right to call bullshit as I see it."

"You'll do it regardless."

Veda offers a half shrug.

"I'll spare you the tales about growing up. I'm sure Peter's told you enough."

"A bit, but he made it clear you left your parents."

"I secretly applied to a few universities abroad and ended up in England. Told my mother I was going on a graduation trip, then never came back. I had to get out before I became a version of myself that I hated to appease them. My father was always working, and when he was there, he wasn't. My mother . . . well, you've met her."

Veda snorts.

"I only called them because my father has a cousin in Parliament, and I needed help making everything for Antaris's custody move faster."

"Fancy."

"If that's what you want to call it." Hiram rolls his eyes. "My mother caught me at a weak moment, promising to mend things and help if I moved back, but it was Peter who ultimately finalized my decision. I figured if my parents had changed, I would stay long-term, but if they hadn't, I would stay long enough to get Antaris together and disappear for good."

"Have they changed?"

"I thought my father . . . but no."

"People rarely do unless something in their life prompts it."

"I'm not letting Antaris learn that lesson." Hiram looks up at the dusky sky. "I'd rather do this by myself, anyway. I've been alone for a long time now."

"You've got Peter."

"I kept my distance because he has a life, a wife who hates me on principle, not that I blame her. I know what it means for a Seer to be openly friendly with an Ellis. He'll lose credibility in his own community and make the target on his back even larger. I always tell him to be careful. He doesn't listen."

"No, he doesn't." Unease crosses Veda's features. "But being alone isn't all it's cracked up to be."

Intrigued, he asks, "Are you alone?"

"In all the ways that are glaringly obvious."

Hiram understands deep in his bones. "You're only as alone as you choose to be."

Veda hums and finishes her glass, pouring herself another. "My dad would say something like that."

"So you have parents . . ."

"Had," Veda replies, hollow. "Lost during the Great Vanishing. I was sixteen. It took months to get back home, and by then, people assumed I'd Vanished, too. Our house was gone, had new people living in it, and everything . . ." She trails off, staring at her hands before clearing her throat. "Anyway, I had to figure things out on my own until I was eighteen. The Seers in our community tried to take me in, but I refused. I parked our old camper in the woods and lived mostly off the land, like how we used to. I got a job, finished school, and went to college on a scholarship for minors orphaned by the Vanishing. I had to establish my existence because my parents lay low my entire life. My dad made amulets, and my mom's college covered for her. They were Seers."

Everything, from the wall around her to her intractable beliefs, makes sense.

"If my mother knew, I doubt she'd have allowed you within an inch of Antaris," Hiram says honestly.

"You know Seers were given a choice to add their names to the Registration. My parents came from families that kept their Sight a secret for generations. Before I was born, my dad had a vision that I wouldn't inherit their Sight. It's not uncommon. They moved to Maine and did their best to remain under the radar, to give me a normal life while keeping their status a closely guarded secret. Hate groups like to 'rescue' the Mage children of Seers. It never goes well for those kids."

Hiram shudders, vaguely familiar with the horror stories. "Where's the camper now?"

Veda barks out a dry laugh. "Long gone. Sold for my bus ticket to college."

"You're resilient."

"No, I'm not. I was traumatized. Being resilient isn't a trait; it's earned through the choices I was forced to make during the worst time of my life. I *had* to keep moving. I didn't know anything else. I'm not defined by the blows I've taken. Life moved on. So did I. For a few years, I thought I was safe. I thought it was over. But I'm back where I started, with my entire life in a bag. Only now, my amulet is dead. It was all I had left of my parents. My dad made it for my sixteenth birthday."

Hiram is speechless. The hurt in her voice is raw, even now. Especially now.

"But you kept it, right? After the hospital?"

"Yeah." Veda pulls it out of her shirt. "It's useless, but I can't part with it."

Hiram absently reaches for the blackened stone. It's inert, but he still feels it watching him . . . as is Veda, her expression inexplicable.

He pulls back. "I'm sorry."

"So am I. For unloading," Veda says quietly, covering the amulet and tucking it back into her shirt. "I don't talk about this much. Actually, I avoid it as much as I can."

"I don't mind listening," Hiram says. "I understand you better now."

Wary as ever, Veda watches, waiting for him to say more, but he lets the silence further melt the ice around them. He looks to the lake, the faintest breeze rippling the water. Crickets chirp as the last dregs of twilight darken into night.

Hiram sneaks glances at her until he catches her looking at him, too.

"I suppose we should make peace."

"If that's what you want," Hiram replies. "I was never fighting you."

"What happened to make you change?"

"Peter's mom, mostly. She's the best person I know. She talked when I was ready to listen, taught when I was ready to learn, explained when I was ready to understand. She taught me patience by waiting for my mistakes to teach me the right way. And the rest of what kept me dedicated to my family's ways and rhetoric was unhinged by logic."

"What do you mean?"

"It makes no sense that those with power at their fingertips, with the ability to see into the past and future, are somehow inferior. Bigotry has never stemmed from ignorance. It comes from knowledge. From fear."

"That's true." Veda's expression shifts. "So what now that you've cut them out? Do they finance anything?"

"No, I have more than enough. Between my own savings and an inheritance from my uncle Sebastian, who also left the family behind and married a Seer, I can live comfortably and still leave more than enough to Antaris." Hiram sighs. "The longer I'm here, the more I realize I can't go back to my job. I think it's more trouble than it's worth."

"Why?"

"It'll put me back in Los Angeles, too close to my purist extended family, who don't know Grace had Sight. The family used to make people who broke rank disappear or reform them. Now they make defectors' lives miserable. My uncle and his wife lived in virtual solitude for the rest of their lives once they stopped running."

"Is Antaris—"

"Safe? Yes. My mother keeps them busy."

"What's stopping her from exposing Grace as his mom now that you've cut her out?"

"The status she's worked hard to ascend to over the last thirty-five years." Hiram chuckles. "She won't risk taking herself down with me. My mother may have everything now, but she knows what it's like to have nothing."

"What about you?" Veda asks. "Do you have everything or nothing?"

"Neither. Both." Hiram watches the brandy as he swirls his glass. "I have everything for myself, but I'd give it up for him."

Veda falls silent, stealing glances at him now and then. Hiram's had enough alcohol to wonder what the heat in her eyes might mean, but not nearly enough to ask.

"You know"—she chuckles softly—"I didn't expect much tonight. I was coming to see Antaris and apologize to you again."

"And now?" Hiram asks, voice near a whisper.

"I'm figuring it out as I go."

Hiram tries his luck. "You could always come back to figure out, if you ever feel inclined."

"I'll think about it." The warmth in Veda cools as she searches his eyes. "Why did you help Ruth after what happened at the town hall? You didn't have to. You had every reason not to. Yet you did. Why?"

Hiram is surprised by the question. "I almost didn't, but I didn't feel like minding my business. Not heroic. Call it the bare minimum of human decency."

"You saw beyond yourself."

"I did," Hiram murmurs, leaning closer. "Now it's your turn to actually see *me*."

Nineteen

Antaris chooses green.

Not forest or sage, but mint, and remains steadfast, refusing all other options Hiram offers until he realizes decisiveness must be an inherited trait. That's why they have mint-green paint and supplies ready when Veda arrives. She hangs back while Hiram carefully takes everything off the walls and casts a charm for the brushes to start painting. His onyx ring flashes with each stroke.

Fascinated, Antaris sits cross-legged, elbows on his thighs, watching the brush move up and down the wall while the kitten plays with a toy. Hiram is the first to leave him to it, shaking his head with amusement.

Veda follows.

It's her third time over in the last week, her first visit where she isn't here for dinner, sign language lessons, or watching Antaris fail at a second brewing attempt. Today, she's here to study. Boxes of books are stacked everywhere, all opened, in Hiram's makeshift office, which now has two chairs and a new bookcase.

"Unpublished research we've needed to get to for a couple of weeks now," Hiram says, taking a seat and putting on his glasses. "Where do you want to start?"

"Actually, we need to start with *BeeyardS Rain*."

"Gabriel told you?"

"He let me take a crack at the anagram, and honestly, with everything that's happened, it slipped my mind until last night. I never figured out the code, but I remembered the name he mentioned, and it fit the anagram. Ariadne Byers. Gabriel said you vaguely knew the name. Clinton, too."

"Yeah," Hiram says.

"It's not looking like one of those coincidences, is it?"

"Not at all."

"I wonder what else Everett knows. The handwriting is the same as the note he gave me."

Hiram looks grim. "I have a feeling we won't find out in time."

"Then we should get started with something we *can* figure out. What have you found so far?"

"Not much, but I've sorted some." He points to one stack. "That's information on general curses, but I think you'd be more interested in this." He moves to the next. "Blood curses. How they're created, how they can survive while dormant, and several unconventional and dangerous ways they've been expelled from the body."

Veda skims the top file. "This is more of what I know. Only thing I need to know is whether there've been any successes using unconventional extraction methods."

"A few, but all of them have one thing in common. The blood in your veins must stop. *Death will lead it out.* I read that in a book."

"The healer at the hospital said he'd seen my curse before, in another patient. It didn't leave until she died. I think . . . Where are the reports of the tests that were run to extract the curse?"

Hiram flips through files, finds it, and hands it over. Veda reads it until words begin jumping out at her. *"Didn't leave until . . . death will lead it out . . ."* An idea strikes like lightning and rolls like thunder. She paces the width of the room twice, deep in thought. "Like a parasite."

"I wonder how long it takes to be expelled after death. We'll need to try something that mimics death. Poison?"

"I've never seen one that's both powerful enough while also slow-acting enough to do what we want it to do. Hmm . . . another option might be something that tricks the body into thinking it's dying."

"We can figure something out."

Veda glances at him, slow and reflective. He didn't misspeak. Wandering to the boxes lined against the wall, she asks, "What's in here?"

"From what I gathered, curse studies," Hiram replies, visibly uncomfortable. "My father said that everything I need to know is here, but I'm not sure how this applies."

"Sounds like some illegal shit."

"Probably. I'd turn it in to Gabriel for the hell of it, but they're spelled to burst into flames if they leave the custody of a blood relative." At her raised brow, he shrugs. "My uncle is bizarre, even for an Ellis. Paranoid, apparently. Likely for good reason."

"Are the subjects Seers?" Veda asks, already scanning for the answer herself.

"Not sure."

She doesn't get far before a more pressing question arises. "The subjects are all different, all Mages paid handsomely, but all the casters' names are redacted. Why?" Veda frowns. "Actually, better question, why didn't they redact their ages? One caster was *fifteen*!"

"Check the others," Hiram says.

He calls out dates and hands Veda the files to arrange chronologically. He starts from the beginning; she begins at the end. The more Veda reads, the more disturbed she becomes at the thought of teenagers casting serious curses under instruction. Soon, they've gone through an entire box of case studies.

"Says here that the curse studies were cut short because the school was shut down. There's an article listing Phillip Ellis as the lead science teacher . . . basically the person running these studies. I can't believe this was at *a school*." Revulsion is thick in her voice. "Shit, this reminds me of the horror stories Ruth used to tell me. Seers were sent to boarding schools after their parents gave up custody once their Sight manifested. Since the schools were unregulated, the Seers were used for free labor or experimenting on their magic, then the schools covered up the horrific details to publish their results."

Hiram doesn't respond, so Veda looks up. He's leaning against his desk, eyes glued to the document he's reading. His expression shifts. "This isn't about curses or experimenting on test subjects. This is about the fact that my uncle was a hypocrite."

"What do you mean?"

"He barely notes the types of curses and their results, but details everything about the curser, right down to their blood pressure and temperament. What they eat. What activities they do prior to each experimental curse. He even details what they do after."

Veda is deeply disturbed. "What was he trying to learn?"

"Take a look." Hiram flips back to the first page and shows her the file. She moves to his side to read.

Sight extraction—Sight Unseen.

"I've seen this ritual twice, scrambled in books," Hiram says. "Grace's book on oddities and one from the library. Both had scrambling hexes over what the ritual does, but Clinton told me as much as he knows about it."

As Hiram shares his conversation with Clinton, Veda's terror eclipses her anger. "Phillip Ellis is a bigot. Why would he want Sight?"

"It's a defense mechanism." Hiram angles his body toward hers, folder between them like a barrier. "It's easy to convince yourself that you don't want what you can't have, or that having what you want is wrong."

She mutters, "I thought you'd say *power*."

"Not everyone wants power. It is human nature to want to feel like we have some measure of control." Hiram crosses the room to the boxes, tilting his head curiously when something catches his eye. In the groove of the box is an envelope. He pulls it out, reads it, then shows her the word hastily scrawled: *Botanist*.

"What does he know?" Veda's voice is hushed.

"I need to find out." He opens the envelope and pulls out a picture. "I think we can assume one of these girls is our Botanist."

Veda looks at the photograph. There are five girls. Different races, heights, and sizes, linked by their hands. None are smiling, but they look like a unit, bonded by trauma and circumstance. Veda recognizes the one standing next to a brunette with blue eyes.

"I think I've figured out why Ruth has been refusing to help. They're protecting someone they care about. We need to talk to her *now*."

Hiram's already on the phone. "She owes me a favor. It's time to collect."

Ruth agrees to meet in a public place in half an hour.

With such a short window and Peter busy, Veda watches as Hiram grabs a small go bag for Antaris that looks like Italian leather and is worth more than her motorcycle. He packs it with snacks and books while Veda guides Antaris along without causing unnecessary anxiety. She's already getting into Hiram's car before she realizes what she's done, and he's starting it with his Imprint before she can argue.

The ride is quiet. Veda speaks only to announce upcoming turns and once to joke about the insufficient tint on the windows, since Antaris is squinting in the sunlight. Hiram removes his sunglasses and hands them to his stunned son. Veda steals a glance in the back seat at Antaris with his khakis, white shirt, and bow tie, nonchalantly gazing out the window with his father's oversized glasses perched on his face.

They arrive with ten minutes to spare. Sanctuary is a community center for troubled Seers located in Hope Park in the middle of Panoramic. With schools out and the weekend in full force, the nice weather has drawn people outside in droves. Live music. People grilling by the gazebos, and food vendors selling everything from ice cream to gyros. Walking through the crowd as a unit, even with his father's sunglasses on, Antaris looks overwhelmed, squeezing Veda's hand tightly. She steers him toward the community center.

The entrance is painted a similar shade of green to Antaris's bedroom; a pleasant calm separates the inside from the chaos outside. The grip on her hand loosens slightly. A teenager, Indica, with tanned olive skin that makes her blond hair seem even brighter is manning the front desk, her automatic smile turning genuine when she sees them.

"Hi and welcome! Ruth's waiting for you in room two." She points toward the closed double doors. "Go through there, past the kitchen, and down the second hall. Before you ask, what you're smelling is mint. Helps ground the littles. Some don't handle the transition well."

Indica's eyes drop to Antaris, head tilting slightly. "I think there's something in the main auditorium that'll interest you. Your fascination with the stars has only begun."

Veda's heart drops. She can practically feel Hiram's coils twist tight.

"Don't stress, little one," Indica says. "You'll speak again in time."

Antaris leans against Veda as they pass through the doors and down the first hallway.

"She obviously attends Clinton's School of Cryptic Shit," Hiram mutters.

Blessedly, Antaris doesn't seem to hear the comment. He steps behind them, looking around in awe. Veda covers her mouth so as not to laugh while passing the kitchens, where two rows of students are having cooking lessons taught by Ami, one of the Council members.

"Today, I'll teach you how to make sad pie . . ."

Hiram tries to watch, curious, but Veda clears her throat, which makes him move. "Sad pie?"

"Does baking not help when things aren't going your way? You're a great cook, but I bet if you're angry enough, you'll be spectacular," she says.

They spot an open door halfway down the second hallway. Ruth sticks her head out first, then steps out. She greets Veda with a warm hug and shakes Hiram's hand, which is jarringly friendly given the last interaction Veda witnessed. Then Ruth spots Antaris peering at her behind sunglasses.

"I'm afraid you won't need those to explore space."

Antaris perks up, giving them back to Hiram as Ruth opens her hand. The doors open wider so they can look inside. In the sea of children on blankets lining the floor, there is an empty space near the door. Ruth offers her hand to Antaris. "Would you like to hear the story about how the stars in the sky came to be?"

He looks from Veda to his father, then nods shyly.

"Good. You're in for a treat. That spot is yours."

After Hiram gives him two tangerines and a juice box, Antaris settles in an empty spot, looking around before lying down like every other child in the room.

"Will he be okay in here?" Hiram asks Ruth.

"Safe and sound," she replies, gesturing down the hall. "Khadijah usually does interactive storytelling as a way to help settle the more restless little ones, but today she's letting Marlene and the teenagers run the show."

Hiram looks at Veda, who scans the room and spots Khadijah, back turned as she talks to Marlene. Khadijah does a double take when she sees Veda with Hiram. Marlene peeks around her, a peculiar look flickering across her face before another volunteer stops her to chat.

Khadijah approaches, frowning at Hiram.

"What are you doing here?" she asks.

"We'll talk a little later," Veda answers. "Come by the cottage."

Khadijah squints at them before slowly replying, "Okay."

Veda ignores the question in her eyes and points at Antaris. "Can you stay with him?"

Khadijah's suspicion deepens. "In the four times I've met him, he only ever side-eyes me, but of course I will."

The third volunteer announces to the children that story time is about to begin. Khadijah sits, cross-legged, next to Antaris's blanket, which earns her the expected side-eye. A spell makes every light in the room draw into the bottle they're holding, plunging the space into darkness.

A collective gasp rings out. The children start giggling.

A burst of light projects across the ceiling as one of the teens begins a story about the formation of the Cosmos, magic, and how they came into being.

Ruth clears her throat, and Veda and Hiram follow her to an empty lounge overflowing with books and sofas. Ruth sits in an armchair next to a love seat Veda and Hiram have little choice but to share. From the snack-stuffed bag, Hiram produces the photo of the girls.

Ruth's expression freezes. "Where did you get this?"

"My uncle's house," Hiram replies.

"If I'd Seen this, I never would've offered that favor."

Veda recoils. "What's going on, Ruth? Marlene is in this photo, and the box holding it was labeled *Botanist*. Is she involved in this? Cosmos, is she the kill—"

Ruth looks at her like she's gone mad. "What? *No!* You're close, but wrong."

"What do you mean?"

Ruth turns the picture around, pointing at the girl *next* to Marlene. "We're protecting ourselves from *her*."

That isn't what Veda expects. Hiram, either, judging from the confusion on his face.

"Who is she?" Veda asks.

"Her name is Ariadne Byers."

They exchange looks. "What does she have to do with the Botanist?"

"She *is* the Botanist."

The words hit Veda like waves, one conflicting emotion after the next. Anger. Grief. Helplessness. Disbelief. Each strikes harder than the last. Ruth *knew*. She knew and stepped in like a quasi-parent, telling Veda to live while knowing exactly who haunts her. A hand grips her knee. Veda stares at the onyx ring, then turns. Concerned blue eyes study her, lips downturned.

It's too soon to be overwhelmed, practicality reminds her. *There's more to learn.*

"How long have you known?" Veda asks, voice stronger, focused.

"That's complicated."

"Tell me. Everything."

"Ariadne was at the same boarding school as Marlene. We took all the teenage Seers in. Ariadne was lonely, clung to any shred of kindness, and supposedly had a rough life prior to ending up at the school. She and Marlene were inseparable, so when Everly adopted Marlene, I adopted her. It took a while for her to open up, but when she did, Ariadne blossomed. She was smart as a whip and charming, fascinated by Omnipotent magic and creative expression. She had such *potential*." Ruth sounds like a proud parent. "But I forgot the cardinal rule."

"Which is?"

"The potential for anything is a thing itself." Ruth tenses. "Marlene started opening up about the curse studies they were involved in. She said Ariadne wanted to restart them, which terrified her so badly, she didn't want to be near her anymore. I asked more questions and learned something horrible. Seers can tear the world in two, but most of us can't curse anyone. It takes a certain kind of arrogance, detachment, and blatant disregard for others to cast curse after curse for years on end. Marlene said, and the others later corroborated, that Ariadne was the only one fascinated instead of repulsed by the experiments they were part of. I realized then that I didn't save Ariadne—I gave her the chance to field-test what she learned in that lab."

Veda feels nauseous, breathless, but the weight of Hiram's hand keeps her steady.

"I tried to help her. Therapy, distractions, everything. And for a while, it appeared to be working," Ruth gets up and goes to the window beside them, looking outside, arms folded around her small frame. All signs of the funny, no-nonsense Ruth who bought vegetables and told Veda to start living are absent. "I still can't believe she is this person. I now know she's good at pretending, saying the right things to the right people, and weaponizing her trauma."

"Ruth," Hiram says slowly. "What aren't you saying?"

She turns to them. "What do you know about the source of the Great Vanishing?"

Clarity makes Veda go rigid. *"No."*

"Yes." Ruth wraps her arms around herself. "Ariadne foresaw her own death. This isn't uncommon; sometimes our visions leave clues about what is to come, but we're not allowed to meddle, even if it means—"

"You die," Hiram finishes, toneless.

"But Ariadne didn't accept this. She changed minor details about her visions, and stopped them from taking place. Not once or twice. We estimate she did it at least ten times before she triggered the Vanishing event."

Disbelief transforms into anger. Veda can no longer sit still. "Is *this* what you're hiding?"

"Hiding? We were *forbidden* from talking about it. Veda, please—"

"Don't fucking—" She exhales harshly. "No." Veda looks out the window, fixating on a single spot to force herself to listen.

"When you meddle with the future, it creates ripples," Ruth explains. "Harmless if it's done once, maybe twice, but if it continues, the ripples spread. What was once barely a shift in the water becomes a tidal wave. That's why we're so harsh on Seers who meddle with time. It endangers the world. Every Seer knows this. Each state's Oracle Council banded together quickly to figure out who was doing this, and when we discovered it was her, we swooped in and she was arrested."

Veda closes her eyes, hoping to stop her head from pounding.

Hiram is the first to speak. "Clinton—"

"He wasn't on the Council at the time, so he wasn't bound by the same magic."

"Why keep this from him? *How?*" Veda asks, turning around. "You're endangering yourself. You're endangering *everyone*. She hurt thousands of people. My—" Her voice breaks. "My parents *Vanished* because of her, and you didn't have the *decency*—"

"I couldn't tell you, and Clinton knew far less than I did. He was on the outside looking in," Ruth says sadly. "Mages wanted the truth behind the Vanishings buried because they did not want the public to know the amount of damage one Seer can cause, nor did they want another Seer recreating a Vanishing event. We wanted to prevent an all-out war against Seers. Everyone who knew any shred of information was forced to take an oath. Lucinda was the deponent. She cast the magical agreement, and the penalties for breaking it were harsh—deadly for the Seers involved."

Hirman leaned forward. "Then how are you sharing this now?"

"The agreement broke upon her death. I didn't know she made that a caveat, but I had a vision of me speaking to you as I am now, which made me realize that I could."

"Was it guilt?" Veda hates the shake in her voice. "Did you care about me out of guilt? Because you knew . . ."

"No." Ruth is earnest, on the verge of tears. "I didn't need a reason to care about you, Veda. I just did. *I do.* You remind me of myself when I was younger. None of this changes anything."

"It changes *everything*," Veda snaps. "She doesn't deserve to be kept a secret. *Everybody* should know her name. And you've just been hiding her. *Protecting her!*"

"No! We *punished* her. Ariadne was sentenced to a life of being Unseen and forced to eat from the Tree of Knowledge. She begged and pleaded with us, groveled and promised she wouldn't meddle again, right up until Lucinda silenced her. Moab cut the fruit, and I forced her to bite down."

Veda feels too heavy to keep standing, numbly rejoining Hiram on the couch. His hand returns to her knee.

"She broke out of prison and vanished a few months later. We found signs of her activities: She stole a substantial amount of money from me, put Scrambling Hexes on multiple books, and took copies of the Oracle Council's personnel files. We looked for Ariadne for *years*. Put alerts out to law enforcement, the government. Everyone pretended like it never happened, so we kept searching without them, determined to find her. We looked in every place we could think of until the trail ran cold. Life went on . . . until Oliver. He was the same Council member who had found her during the Great Vanishing."

Veda puts her head in her hands. "Dr. Lawson . . ."

"He died without knowing—"

Veda looks up sharply, scrubbing a hand over her face, but there's no wiping away the memories. "He *knew* who killed him and why. I tried . . ."

"I know."

"What happened next?" Hiram asks.

"We kept begging the FCD to help us track her down, but they refused. Each victim was a Council member involved with capturing her after the Great Vanishing and carrying out her punishment. This is about revenge. It took four murders to attract a little media attention, enough to force them to put someone on the case. It went quiet after that, until Investigators Sallant and Padillo got involved."

"You never helped them," Hiram accuses. "You should have told them the truth."

"Why would we?" Ruth replies coldly. "We couldn't trust them to protect us then, and we can't now."

"And you all thought scattering was the best idea?"

"At the time, yes, but some of us banded together. There is safety in numbers, or so we believed after the next two were killed while in isolation. This is when we realized she was using the Registration to hunt us down. It tracks our every move. Even now, we are sitting ducks."

Veda's head pounds harder, but Hiram is relentless in his quest for knowledge. "And the spider lilies?"

"We found out about the spider lilies after Investigator Sallant started coming around, requesting meetings, telling us information. In January, spider lilies started appearing in the forest behind my house. Real ones. Not the ones she creates with Omnipotent magic."

Like the flowers Veda saw in the forest.

"Now I know they were a warning."

"What about Grace Fowler?" Hiram questions. "How is she involved in Ariadne's case?"

"She wasn't involved with Ariadne's punishment, but a member of the Oracle Council in New York was friends with Grace, and said she had an Unseen friend she met while working at her outreach program maybe nine years ago. Never said her name, but their description matches Ariadne. That's all I know."

Hiram sits back. "This doesn't make sense. Why kill Grace? Why plant real spider lilies? Why leave the spider lilies created by Omnipotent magic for Veda in the parking lot? Lucinda is murdered a few weeks later. Not long after, she attacks Moab, but he gets away. These gaps don't make sense if she's so methodical. How many original Council members are left?"

"Moab and I are the last."

"And she's after Veda," Hiram remarks, looking at her. "She has to have the trickster pendant. Nine years ago is about when Grace lost hers. I bet she took it. Grace trusted everyone, to an extent. Using the pendant is likely why, to Moab, she looked like his daughter. Everett figured her—"

"He told me he Saw her true face, and she cursed him to go insane if he tried to tell the truth." Veda's emotions are still twisted, but she tells Ruth about Everett's anagram, the attack, and what happened with her amulet. Ruth reaches to comfort her, but Veda avoids her touch. "You knew she was the one who cursed me this entire time."

Silence is confirmation. "I would have died the moment I so much as gave you a clue. I'm so sorry. For everything."

Veda understands so much was out of Ruth's hands, but still can't force down the bitter distrust and anger stuck in her throat.

"What about *Sight Unseen*?" Hiram asks. "We know my uncle wanted to use it to steal Sight. Is that even possible?"

"It is. We suspect Ariadne has been using it on everyone she attacks, stealing their Sight as they die, and covering the remnants of the ritual with a wasting curse." Ruth looks around urgently before leaning closer. "But there's one thing no one seems to have figured out yet: She's been doing it wrong."

Twenty

After Ruth's quiet exit, Veda stares out the window, hurrying to wipe her eyes when Hiram joins her.

"I'll tell Khadijah to take you home."

Her composure cracks with a whispered "Thank you."

It's the last thing they say to each other. Hiram points Khadijah in the direction of the room Veda is in, then collects Antaris from story time early. His disappointment at her premature departure fades fast when Veda offers him a tired smile and signs *tomorrow*. They spend the rest of the evening eating pizza and watching cartoons. Antaris doesn't make it through two episodes before falling asleep. After tucking him in, Hiram retires to his bedroom for a fitful night of sleep.

It's barely ten in the morning, but Hiram has been awake for hours. Rather than cook, he decides to treat Antaris by taking him to the Leaning Cactus for breakfast. The moment Antaris signs *bacon, please* to Hiram while ordering, Cathy, the waitress, fawns over him, showing him the signs for different menu items that they practice while she's putting their orders in. Antaris's meal is no charge because he reminds Cathy of her deaf granddaughter. Hiram leaves money on the table for her and lets Antaris write *thank you* on the back of the receipt in his uneven penmanship.

They don't have plans, but this changes when a familiar truck pulls onto the road, towing an even more familiar motorcycle. Veda is on the side of the road, phone to her ear. She does a double take when she sees him, hanging up with a roll of her eyes and approaching the passenger side as he slows to a stop beside her. Smiling at Antaris is routine, but the look she gives Hiram is less cold than usual. Progress.

"You missed Peter. He's dropping my bike off at the shop. It wouldn't crank. My Imprint reader isn't working."

"Why didn't you let him take you home?" Hiram asks. There's nothing around but trees lining the road.

"I *am* at home." When he and Antaris exchange dubious looks, she shakes her head. "My driveway is concealed from the road by illusionary magic to protect my cottage from prying eyes. It's about a mile into the forest."

Antaris squints at the forest line. He clearly wants to see where she lives, and Veda knows it. She surprises Hiram by getting into the passenger seat and closing the door. Eyes shut, she cups her hands and frowns in concentration until a blue orb materializes before her. Alarmed, Hiram puts the car in park, ready in case the consequences of magic hit her hard. "You don't have an amulet."

"It's already been paid for, years ago," Veda explains as the orb floats to Antaris. "It'll read and store your Imprint when you touch it and allow you to see beyond the illusion."

Antaris's trust in Veda shows in his lack of hesitation. He giggles at the sensation. Hiram's glad he's parked because the sound jolts him.

"Tickles?"

His son nods, a tinge of color in his cheeks.

Hiram's amusement fades when the orb floats to him. "Are you sure?" he asks Veda, understanding the depth of what she's offering.

"No, but I know you won't hurt me."

"I won't." He meets her eyes as he touches it. Warmth spreads through his fingertips, and the trees begin to fade, revealing a driveway behind her.

"*Reserare* is the incantation to open the path when I'm not around. Go on."

Hiram turns the car onto the narrow path.

Isolated is the first word that comes to mind. The forest is dense on both sides of the dirt road, growing thicker in parts, thinner in others. A few animals dash by the car, but none get too close. At last, the trees part to reveal her cottage.

"There's not much to see," she says as they climb out of the sedan.

Antaris slips his hand into Veda's, eager to see everything she shows him, from the talisman at the door to the solarium. He sees her lantern floating above her bed and sign language books spread all over the coffee table. While Antaris looks out the window at the forest behind her house with Hiram, Veda stands beside him.

"If I were lost and found this place, I wouldn't know it was yours," he says quietly.

"That's my intent," Veda replies honestly.

Antaris notices the herbs in the kitchen, pointing. They're leggy in parts, thin in others. Partially dead.

"Ah, yes. They were slightly neglected when I hurt my hand. You can have them, if you'd like. Your dad was going to start a little garden for you at home. Oregano, mint, dill, thyme, cilantro, rosemary. These are perfect."

Hiram appreciates the gift, but sours at Veda detaching herself from yet another thing. "You can share them with us," he suggests in a rush. "We'll provide the space and you can help us keep them alive." He waves his thumb. "Black thumb and all."

Veda studies him too long for it to be appropriate. "I think I've got an extra cedar raised bed that I built for the greenhouse and never used."

Antaris goes with her to find it, and not long after, it's in Hiram's trunk and they're all off to the greenhouse for spare dirt. It takes an hour for Veda to mix everything, explaining each part to an intrigued Antaris. Finally, they head back to his house and start working on the bed, the quacking ducks on the lake serving as background noise. Hiram leaves them to make pastitsio as a thank-you.

The windows are open. The sun is shining. He can see them outside as he cooks. Antaris is on his stool with gloves Veda snatched from the greenhouse, wielding a hand shovel. From the looks of it, they'll have room for more herbs in the bed. Having sage would be nice. Green onion and basil, too.

Having Veda here to plant it would be better.

As if hearing her name in his thoughts, she turns, catching his eye. A single brow raises. Hiram has to get out of his head, or he might do something to compromise this tenuous trust they've built. That would be terribly stupid.

Hiram swears to the empty kitchen as the water starts to boil.

Antaris falls asleep after dinner before he can wander. Hiram puts him to bed and returns to find Veda holding a glass of wine.

"Peter said he'd come by to take me home. My bike will be ready in two days."

He can't admit that he doesn't want her to leave, so he nods. "Thanks again for starting the herb garden."

"They'll do better here than in my kitchen. I only had them because they reminded me of home. My mom kept an herb garden. I've always loved the smell of fresh herbs. It's comforting."

The faint meowing of the cat makes Hiram sigh. "He acts like nobody ever feeds him."

"Do you not like animals?"

"Cats are fine, even though they make my face itch. I have a list of other animals I don't respect."

"Don't *respect*?" Veda bites back her smile. "Go on. Top three animals on that list and why."

"Orcas are bullies, mosquitoes are pests, and hippos are deceptive," Hiram rattles off without hesitation. Leaning closer, he adds, "And no, I won't explain."

She stares at him blankly, then laughs.

Hiram smiles at the sound. Veda's treatment has been less hate and more tolerance, leaving Hiram wondering how much he can continue to shift her wind.

Angling sideways to face her, he watches her laughter fade, her inscrutable countenance returning. Veda checks her watch, then reaches for the drink she already finished and grimaces. Hiram thinks she's going to wait by the door for Peter or check on the planted herbs, but she leans against the edge of the island and asks, "What do you do when he goes to bed?"

Hiram is slow to answer. "I mostly read. Either books or research. Why?"

"I'm making conversation, or else we're going to sit in silence until Peter gets here. So, do you have hobbies?"

"I don't have many hobbies, never had time for them, or quiet days or nights. Sometimes I finish tasks I've neglected, prepare for the next day, or clean. Or Peter comes over for beers."

"Do you ever stop moving?"

"No," Hiram says. "If I do, everything I balance will collapse."

Veda closes her eyes. "I feel like that sometimes. If I stop, the bind will fade, and this Sanguis Curse will consume me."

"Does it hurt?"

"When I neglect myself by not eating right to keep my energy up. It's worse when I skip swimming in Nénuphar."

"So . . . often."

Veda rolls her eyes. "You sound like Khadijah."

"Shocking that this is the one thing we agree on."

"Yeah, well, she gives a shit, while you—I'm not sure what you're doing, actually."

"I'm keeping my word." Because he wants to. And perhaps to prove he can.

"You don't have to." Veda's soft frown fades when she picks up the meowing kitten.

"I want to," Hiram replies.

"We don't always get what we want."

"No, but I am patient and willing to wait for what I want."

"Which is?"

"Everything or nothing. I won't settle for something in between or beg for scraps."

Out of habit, Hiram has been alone for years. Not lonely, there's a difference. He's okay with being alone, but sometimes, he wants more. Day by day, it's become increasingly obvious to him that the more he wants is *her*.

The walls around Veda could block out the sun, but she's lonelier than she realizes, and more vulnerable than she'll ever admit. Her fight-or-flight reaction looks like his, which is probably why Hiram can see the cracks in her facade. She can pretend and avoid reality, but at her core, he wonders if she wants what everyone wants—even him.

Genuine, human connection.

Hiram turns on the television for background noise and sits beside Veda on the sofa. She shoots him a sharp look but doesn't ask him to move. The kitten leans over, pawing at him. Veda scratches behind his ear, the motion halting when the evening news begins.

"Good evening. You're watching the Friday Night News. *I'm Finn Clark with breaking news. Reports of a serial killer are emerging from the FCD today. Known as the Botanist, with twelve victims, all from the Seer community, the killer now poses a danger to everyone. Please be on the lookout for . . ."*

A picture of Dr. Simpson flashes on screen. Veda swears, and Hiram shares the sentiment.

"Dr. Everett Simpson, a Seer who works as a veterinarian at Weston Academy, just outside of Proventia. He is a person of interest and potential

suspect in the case. Do not engage. He is considered dangerous. If you know anything, please contact the Investigator Department of the FCD."

No mention of Everett's curse.

"He's not a suspect," Veda says more to herself. "Fuck, this is going to put a target on every Seer's back. Parents at the school. *Students.*"

Hiram mutes the television. There's tension in the silence that has nothing to do with them.

Veda calls Peter, but he doesn't answer. "He's probably going to be late. Sorry for intruding."

"You're not. I can take you home if you'd like."

"I don't want to disturb Antaris."

"You can stay here. I'll sleep on the sofa and take you home in the morning."

The look she gives him is but a flicker. "Okay."

Hiram isn't sure when Veda falls asleep, probably while he's reading and she's petting the kitten. Hiram picks her up, carries her into his room, lays her on the bed, and removes her shoes without rousing her. She sleeps like the dead. Odd, for someone so paranoid. He keeps his room cool at night, so he covers her with a blanket, grabs a change of clothes, and heads to shower. After he's done, he checks on Antaris. The kitten has made his way back into the cat bed, and the lantern emits a soft glow. Once he looks in on Veda, who sleeps soundly, Hiram finds a blanket and a spare pillow, then settles on the couch with a book, too wired to sleep.

But there is a different feel in the air tonight. Quiet. Steady. Rain falls and thunder rolls. The house feels warm. Full. Alive. The earth's sigh lulls Hiram to sleep.

Twenty-One

Veda doesn't remember falling asleep. When she opens her eyes, dawn is approaching. Light paints the horizon outside, and the sky is empty, the stars tucked away in the wake of a new day. Still groggy, it takes her a minute to realize she's not in her bed, nor is she at home.

This shocks her awake.

The bedroom looks professionally designed, from the oak furniture to the monochrome accents. No plants. No unnecessary clutter. Neatly stacked books on the right nightstand catch her eye, classics, from the look of it, and a book on sign language.

A bedroom can reveal a lot about a person. But Hiram's confession that this isn't a home he intended to keep makes her wonder whether this is truly who he is or just who he pretends to be. Not that Veda has spent a single minute thinking about him beyond cataloging her disdain.

A small part of her calls out the lie.

Honesty makes Veda uncomfortable. It demands vulnerability, risks rejection, and disrupts her illusion of competence. Each time she talks to him, she can blame the ease with which truths spill out on something simple yet complex: She can no longer ignore the humanity of one man. Where does that leave her? Veda doesn't know, but she opens the door to find out.

Padding down the hall, she's careful not to disturb anything. There's a throw and a pillow neatly stacked on the couch, the only signs Hiram slept there. Now, though, he's in the kitchen with the phone to his ear, speaking quietly. Most of the time, when she sees him, long sleeves and pants conceal what's on full display this morning in the comfort of his home. He's dressed in gray sweats and a white T-shirt, and his tattoos remind her that he's more than the monochrome picture he presents. The replica of her amulet stands out. The irony of her only sentimental possession being inked on his skin isn't lost on her.

"Thanks, John, I'll let them know." He hangs up and turns. "You're awake."

"Yeah, but don't worry. I didn't hear much of your conversation."

"I was talking to Grace's stepfather," he explains. "Everything okay?"

"You could have left me where I fell asleep."

"On the sofa?" Hiram folds his arms.

"Yeah."

He gives her a look that needs no response, one brow lifted. She tries not to think about the fact that he carried her to his bed, took off her shoes, and tucked her in. She's a chronically light sleeper. She must have been exhausted, because she didn't wake once.

"Is Antaris still asleep?" she asks.

"He gets up in an hour. The nameless cat is in a food coma after meowing at me until I fed him." True to his word, the kitten is curled up in his little play area. Hiram is already in the process of making everyone else breakfast, too. The talisman's chime draws a confused look from him before he excuses himself to answer the door.

"What are you doing here?"

His icy greeting makes Veda creep down the hall to the foyer, where a furious Hiram is speaking to an older, taller man. "Did you miss the part where I told you to leave? Mother—"

"Doesn't know I'm here."

Veda knows more about Barrett Ellis than she cares to, but this is the first time she's seen him in person. Hiram has his eyes.

"Hiram . . ." Barrett sounds like someone who will burn a house down and claim not to understand why the owner is angry. "I'm here to talk about you."

"I wasn't aware that talking was your strong suit."

"It's not, but you were right. What you said weeks ago. I've turned a blind eye to so much, and I'm tired of keeping everyone's secrets. Did you look at the boxes? Did you see?"

If Hiram has any feelings about that comment, he doesn't let on. "I did."

"The picture—"

"That was *you*?" He recoils. "What do you know?"

"I've been trying to talk to you since you got involved—"

"A man who's made his career on speaking can't talk to his own son." Hiram chuckles bitterly. "The irony is astounding."

"I know—"

Veda's shoe squeaks on the wood, and both men turn to her. "Sorry, I was—"

"And *you are*?" Barrett asks, looking between them.

"Veda Thorne." She makes no move to shake his hand.

Barrett gestures between her and Hiram. "Are you two together?"

Veda is too stunned to properly react.

Hiram remains impassive. "What did you want to tell me about the picture?"

"We should talk inside."

They arrange themselves around the great room, waiting in silence until his father finally says, "I know more about the Botanist case than I've admitted. The Botanist is—"

"Ariadne Byers."

His father looks shocked. "You know?"

"Yes, we talked to a member of the Oracle Council. They told us everything," Veda replies, stomach twisting.

Barrett focuses on Hiram. "They told you? That must mean the oath—"

"Is broken," Hiram finishes.

His father looks relieved. "Then you understand why your grandfather suppressed the news."

Veda wasn't expecting that revelation. Her wide eyes slide to Hiram, only to find him frowning. "Why would he do that? Ariadne—"

"*Is your cousin.* She's Phillip's daughter. Not officially—he would never admit to fathering a Seer, but it was bound to come back to us the moment she started talking. The family would excommunicate him, cut him off. It wouldn't be a good look for the family."

A heaviness visibly settles on Hiram. It fills the room, tugging at Veda's emotions and bargaining with her empathy, but that doesn't stop her inner thought from slipping out, unfiltered: "Well, this is fucked up."

"I thought you figured it out?"

"Not the part about why you wanted me to stay out of it. Thanks for the evidence. It's shone a light on our fucked-up family," Hiram replies coldly. "Who's her mother?"

"One of Phillip's . . . I don't know what to call them, but he's fathered more children than I can count because of his obsession with having a Seer child. When he found out Ariadne manifested Sight, he challenged her mother for custody and won, then brought her to the boarding school with all the other Seers. He told her that he was her father and made her the star of his case studies. *She's* the one who's being chronicled in the records. When they caught her after she caused the Great Vanishing, Phillip didn't claim the girl as his own, and your grandfather spearheaded the cover-up. We all were part of the oath to keep it a secret. I covered all traces of her case studies and carried the truth in silence. My retirement wasn't an accident; it was a choice. I thought it was over until Phillip told me the truth in April, including—"

"The fact that she's the one whose Sight he wanted to steal?"

Barrett nods.

"And what am I supposed to do with that?"

"Whatever you want. Release it to the media. I no longer care. I've covered him for years and refuse to protect him anymore."

The talisman goes off again.

Veda jolts and Hiram swears, but bravado flees Barrett's face, leaving behind pure terror. This time, when Hiram answers the door, Veda is behind him, both of them relaxing at the sight of Khadijah, who doesn't at all look happy to be there. She peers around him at Veda, eyes narrowing curiously. They *will* talk later, Veda is sure of it, but to Hiram, her friend says, "Peter's with my uncle, and I'm here to babysit."

"*What?*"

Hiram's phone rings. He grits his teeth before answering. Whatever is said sobers him instantly. He steps aside to let Khadijah in. "Apparently, I *do* need a babysitter."

"What's going on?" Veda asks.

"We need to go," Hiram replies. "Good news: Everett was spotted near the school grounds. Bad news: Ariadne got to Moab."

Veda feels sick thinking about his family. They'll never be the same.

"You need to leave" is the first thing Hiram says to Barrett when they return to the great room.

The tension skyrockets as Khadijah comes around the corner and sees him. "What the—"

"I'm leaving." Barrett stands, but before he leaves, he looks back—not at Hiram, at Khadijah. "Tell your uncle I'm sorry I never spoke up for him."

Everyone is speechless when the door shuts behind Barrett.

Hiram starts the car and pulls out of the driveway. The ride is silent, tense, and uncomfortable. To Veda's surprise, he is the one who breaks it.

"I planned for a more relaxed morning. Sorry."

"You don't owe me an apology." Veda returns to looking out the window, thinking about what she witnessed before leaving: Hiram telling a sleepy Antaris that he's coming back. "Do you tell him that you'll always come back every time?"

"I do. It comforts him."

Veda understands.

"I'll admit I'm surprised at your reaction to meeting my father."

"I was practicing restraint," she deadpans.

"I'm shocked you know what that is," Hiram says, tense yet playful.

Veda rolls her eyes. "I also didn't think it would be appropriate to insult your dad without knowing if Antaris was awake and just staying in his room. The same went for you. I never talked bad about you in front of him. Even *I* have my limits."

"Thanks."

She glances at him. "Are you okay after what you just found out?"

"Were *you* okay after talking to Ruth?" he asks pointedly.

"Fair." Veda has been sitting with what she's learned and is far from being okay. Ruth has called her twice since they talked, and she can't answer. Everly sent a message she hasn't had the heart to read.

When they pull into the parking lot of Weston Academy, there are two cars parked outside. They get out, looking around, and something is . . . off. It's too quiet. Hiram looks ready to gag as he starts for the front doors. "The magic is acrid."

Veda grabs his arm and tugs him in a different direction. There's a barrier gate on the side that vanishes once they're inside. Spider lilies have sprouted everywhere. The way they shimmy oddly and glitch in the wind proves they aren't real, instead created by Omnipotent magic.

Veda stops, then takes a nervous step over the first.

"Follow me," Hiram says.

Less cautious but more observant, he walks ahead of Veda, careful to linger with each step. He glances over his shoulder twice. The first time, Veda is stubbornly making her own way through the grass. The second, she's following in his footsteps. Ahead, Marlene is setting up to analyze, and Gabriel and Francisco stand in the middle of the pasture, near Moab's body, which is covered with a white sheet.

"Where have you checked for Everett?" Veda asks.

"The greenhouse and stables," Francisco replies. "There were signs he spent some time living with the horses. We don't know when. We've requested backup to search the forest, but everything has been going to hell at the office. Our mole has opened a can of worms. So many are on desk duty for unethical activities that we now have an enforcer staffing problem."

"We also have a new problem," Hiram announces, stopping all conversation.

"Ariadne Byers is the source of the Great Vanishing, my curser, possibly a friend of Grace's, *and* the Botanist. She can take the form of anyone, and was a willing participant in the curse case studies Hiram's uncle ran. Oh, and she's Hiram's cousin." Veda turns to Hiram. "Does that cover it?"

"Yeah."

"Oh my Cosmos," Francisco mutters.

"What else do we know?" Gabriel asks.

"Well, nothing can conceal cursed marks. Not even trickster pendants." He taps his chin. "So you're looking for someone with a mark from accidentally cursing her own blood along with Veda's."

"Speaking of tricksters, Everett said that tricksters fly," Veda mentions. "Maybe he was being literal. The only birds I can think of as a trickster are a mockingbird—they mimic sounds in the environment—or the blue jay—they imitate hawk calls."

Marlene jogs over, her pendant swinging. "I'm all set up for the testing."

An incidental touch makes Veda's vision blur, Marlene's features twisting before they sharpen. She gasps so hard, she chokes.

"Are you okay?" Marlene asks, concerned.

Taking a harsh step back, Veda says, *"You're not Marlene."*

Silence crashes like a physical force.

Not-Marlene tilts her head, a bewildered look spreading across her features. "Of course I am."

"*No*, you're not." Veda lunges forward, yanking the pendant from Marlene's neck in one violent tug. The blue jay transforms into a fox as the sky darkens to gray, then black. Dark mist rises from the earth as Marlene's features bleed and condense, stretch and shrink, twist and contort. Her clothes hang looser, her hair grows longer, changing from black to brown, her limbs contracting. The rich brown of her skin fades to fair.

There's a tug, then a yank, before the pendant flies out of Veda's hand, and a slim, manicured fist curls around it. Marlene is gone. In her place stands the person they've been looking for all along.

Ariadne.

Brown eyes shift into a flat, icy blue. "Not exactly the reveal I had in mind, but this will *do*."

Ariadne's words are laced with unbridled power. It spreads like a virus, infecting everything in its wake. Hiram yanks Veda back with enough force to make her stumble, but she's not hit.

A black beam strikes Francisco in the stomach. Eyes wide, face twisting in pain, he clutches his chest and drops to his knees, blood pouring from wounds too fast to track.

"I've been wanting to do that for *months*. Let's get started."

The world is but a blaze of blinding light.

Twenty-Two

Pressure squeezes Hiram's skull tight as the scent of magic goes from acrid to ozone. With a pop, sound floods his awareness, his vision clearing. Hiram rushes to account for everyone. First he hears Francisco's harsh pants, then Gabriel's panicked shouts for backup a short distance away. Veda is . . .

Standing alone. *Frozen*, lost in a dream.

Ariadne is on her knees, momentarily staggered by her own spell. Her head jerks up. Hiram's running before he realizes it, snapping Veda out of her trance by wrapping his arms around her and yanking her behind a nearby tree, yelling the first protection spell he can think of. Ariadne's wild magic burns it up.

With the clap of her hands, magic showers the grass in ashes. She smiles at Hiram. "Hello, *cousin*."

Veda stretches to touch the base of the tree, whispering, *"Impetum."*

The leaves turn into blades and rain down on Ariadne. Veda crumples with a cry, paying the full price for her spell. Hiram reacts instinctively, summoning a cyclone that coils around his cousin, buying time as he pulls Veda to her feet. They need to get the hell away.

"Come on."

They run to Gabriel, who's bent over Francisco. There's blood on his face and hands from his efforts to stop the bleeding. Veda drops next to him. Francisco is breathing, only barely.

"Hiram, Veda, take over. I'll—"

"You'll what?" Hiram looks at Gabriel like he's lost his mind. "Fight her?"

The ground quakes as the tornado sparks and splits, no longer under Hiram's control. Ariadne emerges through it, bleeding from numerous cuts. Her face shifts from her own to a familiar blond. *Seren.*

"Hey, y'all."

"Shit," Gabriel breathes. "Not her, too."

"Yes, her, too," Ariadne mocks.

"This would be an *excellent* time to have unlimited magic," Hiram mutters.

Veda's obviously stunned, costing her an extra minute before she casts a spell that sends a familiar bolt of light into the sky. It strikes a tree, slicing it in half. Hiram holds his breath, thinking it'll fall just right, but Ariadne opens her hands.

A shock wave explodes, sending them all to their knees. The tree splinters into thousands of pieces that hang in suspended animation.

"That was cute." Ariadne's smile turns crazed. *"My turn."*

Hiram yanks Veda toward him as an ugly fireball flies past her head. He overcorrects, and she falls on top of him, her elbow jamming into his ribs. Another curse speeds over their heads. A third slams into the ground, blasting chunks of grass and dirt skyward. Hiram shields them in time, his amulet pulsing green as debris ricochets off the dome he's cast over all of them.

They're sitting ducks.

Hiram glances around for Gabriel, who is moving on the ground, clearly in pain. There's a gash on his head from debris, but he keeps muttering healing spells for Francisco. The dome extends over both, too.

"How long is this shield going to last?" Gabriel asks over Ariadne's attempt to rip it apart one spell at a time.

"Two minutes. Maybe three." Light explodes against the side of it. The shield shakes but holds. Hiram winces. "Or less."

"Shit. Everyone is at least ten minutes out." Gabriel panics when his partner goes still. "Francisco!"

Veda is a deer in headlights, but snaps herself out of it. "A—a cauterizing charm. *Kauter.* It'll hold as long as you need. Low stakes."

Gabriel nods, dazed, as he mutters the incantation. "It worked!"

Another flash of light crashes against the shield. Then a third.

Hiram scans the area, but he can't see Ariadne. He casts a spell to make it possible for Gabriel to pick up Francisco as if he's no heavier than a box of shirts, but his amulet doesn't absorb all the consequences of the spell. The rest is an electric shock that hurts like hell as it courses up his arms. It's worth it when Gabriel hoists Francisco up, ready to run with him the first moment it's safe.

"The greenhouse," Veda suggests. "It was built to withstand a storm."

And one is here.

"None of us can fight her alone," she says gravely, gesturing at the shield. "When that falls, she's going to obliterate us all."

Veda sounds like she's in a dream. Or a nightmare. The dome cracks, crashing around them. Trees are wrenched from the earth, floating into the sky.

Through the fog and smoke, Marlene appears with the trickster pendant back around her neck. Her features blur and reform again. She's back to Seren. Then Ariadne. Then Everett. Veda's face takes its place for a split second before they all blur together while burning white builds in her hand like a charge. Pure power. Hiram can't stop it. He braces himself, hands on Veda, his promises to Antaris fresh in his brain. He—

The light is extinguished by a bolt of darkness that strikes Ariadne in the chest.

Hiram turns in the direction of the curse.

Everett yells, *"Run!"*

The collision of magic is deafening.

Its thunderous clap shakes the ground, and the acrid sting of power burns Hiram's nose like sulfur. Running toward the greenhouse, he's right behind Veda when Gabriel speeds past them both with Francisco in his arms. Spider lilies explode into fire and ash beneath their shoes.

Once inside the greenhouse, they slam the doors shut. Hiram casts every locking spell he knows to keep Ariadne out, but it sounds like Everett is keeping her preoccupied outside. There's no time to look around. Gabriel lays Francisco on one of the empty tables. His skin is pale and streaked with blood, body trembling violently.

"Seven minutes away," he says grimly.

Veda all but stumbles over to Francisco, voice numb when she says, "He's going into shock."

Another loud bang from the battle outside makes her freeze. A tree sails over the roof. Wind pounds against the glass. Hiram bumps into Veda. She looks at him, terror in her eyes like he's never seen before.

"What does he need?" Hiram asks clearly.

"Pressure on his wound. And warmth," she says automatically. "There's a cloth in the cabinet by the door."

Gabriel rushes off. Veda, too, returning with a pair of scissors she uses to cut Francisco's shirt off. It's no wonder Gabriel was struggling to heal him. It's more than a cut. It looks as if she took a knife and carved a symbol—an Imprint—into his chest.

"I—I can't cast right now," Veda says.

"Tell me what to do." Hiram studies the wound. Parts of it still ooze blood until Veda directs him to cast the spell, his voice drowned out by the battle outside. Gabriel returns with the blanket. She covers Francisco with it and whispers the next spell for Hiram to repeat to warm the blanket. Slowly recovering from the consequences of using so much magic outside, she checks his pulse, closing her eyes, counting.

"How much longer?" Veda asks.

"Four minutes," Gabriel announces.

A flash of light turns everything white. Deafening silence follows.

The sky clears. The sun is out. The world has returned to normal. Only, when Gabriel opens the door to check, Hiram nearly vomits from the smell of darkness. The nausea is so bad, he can't escape it, even after Gabriel closes the door. He doesn't get a chance to recover before Gabriel bursts back in. "I need some help."

With Francisco stable and Gabriel looking faint, it falls to Hiram and Veda. His stomach rolls as he runs behind Veda—not toward Moab's body, but to another figure lying in the grass, writhing in pain.

Blood soaks the grass beneath Everett, and there's something sticking out of his stomach. A strangely shaped stone. Hiram doesn't need medical training to know there's nothing that can be done.

Everett knows it, too. "I . . ." he whispers, sputtering blood. "I'm finally . . . free." He's dying, but his mind is clear, sharp. Veda is still determined to help, but he whispers, "Stop."

Veda looks like she's about to be sick.

"She . . . she . . . cursed. My bones are stone."

Hiram can't imagine the pain his brain has blocked from him.

"I . . . that night. That wasn't—"

"I know." Veda rests her hand on his forehead gently. "I know that wasn't you. It was her."

"The Dalneau Bridge . . ." Everett says. "Rest of the truth . . . there. Did you . . ."

"We figured out what you've been trying to tell us. We won't let her get away with this."

Relief explodes on his face and tears roll down his cheeks. "I . . . I can rest?"

"Yes."

As if waiting for permission all along, the light in Everett's eyes extinguishes.

Twenty-Three

The world races, but Veda stands still.

Investigators swarm every inch of the school grounds and the surrounding forest. Scene analysts preserve what evidence they can. Medics rush Francisco to the hospital; even as they load him up, he's demanding they find Marlene. The real one.

Everyone who passes Veda asks if she's okay. She isn't.

A bottle of water appears in her line of sight. She's about to brush it off when she notices the onyx ring. Hiram has his own bottle and sits down beside her on the edge of the fountain. After he spits the first mouthful to clean out his mouth, they drink in silence, the quiet lasting only as long as their water.

"Gabriel?" she asks.

"Terrorizing everyone who isn't letting him leave. In addition to the media showing up, the FCD's higher-ups are here with questions. I'm trying to find out what they want to talk about that's more important than finding Ariadne or, better yet, the real Marlene and Seren."

"They probably want to talk about the wolves in their henhouse." Veda pauses. "I *do* have enough tact to not say that in front of him."

"Do you?"

It's oddly playful with the chaos surrounding them: People are running around, news reporters are setting up, and medics are only at bay because Veda bares her teeth. The combination forms a cacophony of incoherence. In that moment, they sit with the crushing realization that the Botanist has been steps ahead for months, maybe years. Changing Veda's statement sent them on a wild-goose chase, leaving Ariadne to work uninterrupted from the inside, and banking on the distrust of the Oracle Council as well as Veda's.

"I'm not heartless," Veda says, cutting her eyes at him. "They were fooled. Gabriel more than Francisco. They considered Marlene and Seren friends. This isn't an 'I told you I had a reason not to trust you all' moment."

Hiram hums in agreement.

Veda notices how pale and shaky he looks. "Still sick from the smell?"

"Yeah, but a medic gave me something to help." Hiram scrubs a hand over his face and winces. "What about you? Still shell-shocked?"

"I'm coming out of it."

"You did great out there," Hiram tells her. "Francisco wouldn't be alive if it weren't for you."

"You did the casting. I—" She's disarmed by the way he looks at her. "We wouldn't have made it without *you*. Who taught you how to fight?"

"I was a sick kid, and not everyone kissed my ass because I'm an Ellis." Before he can say more, blue eyes slide away, his body stiffening. "Part two of this shit show is about to begin."

Ruth has arrived in her van, blowing the horn like a battle cry Gabriel doesn't hesitate to answer. He breaks off mid-conversation and runs, escaping to the full van. The elderly woman peels out of the parking lot like she's being chased by enforcers. Hiram stands and extends a hand. "Shall we?"

❀

Their destination is a bungalow in a quiet neighborhood on the west side of Proventia. Before Hiram can turn off the car, news reports of a fire at the Federal Crime Division emit on the radio.

"She's insane," Veda says.

"Motivated," Hiram corrects. "I think I'm going to take Antaris out of town for a bit."

"Smart."

Dozens of cars and people are outside. Veda doesn't realize this is Marlene's house until an unfamiliar woman runs past them and announces, "They found her alive, thank the Cosmos! Everyone who can stay, please do. The home needs a restart."

Inside is tightly packed with people, but the crowd thins as they walk farther into the house. The first familiar face is a distraught Everly. "She's been here this entire time, and I knew *nothing*."

Veda's worry grows the closer they get to the back room. A hush falls, and as soon as she steps into the doorway, she understands why. The room looks and smells horrible. Marlene lies on filthy sheets, unrecognizable. Asleep or unconscious, Veda can't tell. Matted hair. Loose, sunken skin. There are pinpricks dotting her arms, cuff marks on her wrists. Gabriel is on his phone, shaken and furious. Ruth holds her niece's hand. Hiram grips Veda's shoulder.

"No hospital will take her, because she's a Seer." Gabriel is visibly shaken. "The closest Seer-friendly hospital is in Portland. The drive alone would kill her."

The weight of Hiram's hand on her shoulder disappears. "Excuse me for a second."

Veda glances back, watching him pull out his phone as he slips out the back door. She doesn't know where to start, but asks someone nearby for a warm, soapy towel. When it's brought, she kneels beside Marlene and gently dabs her forehead. The cloth comes back streaked with dirt and blood. Marlene groans at the touch. Veda keeps going, washing her neck and checking the needle marks on her arms. They look red and swollen, signs of infection, which is exceedingly rare in Seers.

"What was she given?"

"The Liquid Curse," Ruth replies. "There's a vial left in the kitchen."

Veda is struggling with seeing Ruth, but right now it's about Marlene. "Khadijah's clinic? Who's on duty?"

"They don't have anyone to spare, and Marlene needs more than the clinic can provide."

Veda pockets the vial. The Liquid Curse is illegal because it cuts someone off from magic. Likely given to subdue Marlene, and possibly injected to keep her too weak to fight back. Veda doesn't want to imagine her trauma, but given the length of time she's likely been dosed, it could take weeks or months for her to fully recover.

"I don't—"

Hiram reappears in the doorway. "Take her to Stillwater Medical. They'll take her."

Ruth frowns. "That's a—"

"Trust me," he says, earnest and firm. "Take her."

A long silence passes before Ruth whispers, "Okay."

Gabriel is the first to move. Veda warns against using magic around Marlene until her own restarts, but it doesn't take long before Marlene is packed into Ruth's van, Everly in the front seat, and Gabriel in the back. Veda expects everyone to clear out, but is reminded how deeply community centered Seers are. Knowing the FCD won't investigate, the crowd descends on Marlene's house, cleaning it from top to bottom, removing trash and furniture. When Hiram has to step out because of how overwhelming the magic becomes while they cleanse the air and talisman, Veda follows. A truck pulls up. The same woman who left earlier has returned with a new bed, mattress, and couch.

You could have this, too, a little voice reminds Veda. Distracting herself, she looks to Hiram, only to find him checking his phone; his satisfied smirk makes Veda suspicious.

"Gabriel messaged me. Stillwater took Marlene. Like I said."

"How did you do that?" The hospital is quasi-public, exclusive, and notoriously anti-Seer.

"I threw three things at the problem: my money, my name, and the threat of *unrelenting* litigation." Hiram shrugs. "Those always stick."

❀

Despite being so tired her bones ache, Veda doesn't fall asleep right away. It's after two in the afternoon when she and Hiram return to where their day began: his house.

After filling Khadijah in on where Marlene is being treated and making sure she doesn't want her to come with, Veda grabs spare clothes from her bag, showers in the guest bathroom, and eats a haphazard meal with Hiram and Antaris. She crashes on the couch under the weight of an excruciatingly long and stressful day, then wakes in the darkness, covered with a warm blanket, a spare pillow under her head. Her phone is on the coffee table with dozens of missed calls. It rings again before she can start checking messages.

Veda sobers. Skipping the greeting, she says, "Is Marlene . . ."

"I'm leaving the hospital now." Khadijah sounds numb. "How are you? Need me to pick you up?"

"I'm alive, apparently." Veda sits up and scratches her head, yawning. "And yeah. This sofa is more comfortable than mine, but I'd like to sleep in my own bed tonight."

"Fair enough. Give me a bit." A heavy pause passes. "How are you?"

Sad. Overwhelmed. Contemplative. Exhausted. Resigned. *Fucking terrified.* "Fine. You?"

"Same." Khadijah's silence is momentary. "I feel like a fucking idiot for not noticing that she wasn't who I thought she was. Gabriel filled me in."

"Ariadne knew Marlene well enough to fool a lot of people. She fooled me, too, with Seren. I bet she's not even a real person."

"*Actually*, Seren is her mother. Or at least, Ariadne used the trickster pendant to assume her identity. She was part of the Great Vanishing. Rules for obtaining identification were relaxed for Mages, so she was able to take advantage. Gabriel told me his superiors unblocked her Imprint, and they're learning everything about her past now. They used her picture and confirmed what Ruth said, that she was a friend of Grace Fowler's. A few of her old friends identified Ariadne from the picture Hiram sent. The timeline we have right now puts her meeting

Grace about six months after she disappeared. They thought she was on the run from abusive relatives or an ex. Grace 'lost' her trickster pendant a few years later."

Veda can't process the layers of information, and chooses another topic. "How's Marlene?"

"Awake. Traumatized. Angry. In a lot of pain. She can't feel her magic, and she's scared, even after we explained it wasn't going to be gone forever. I was fully prepared to cuss out everyone on her medical team, but the care she's getting is much better than I anticipated. Apparently that has to do with Hiram's threats." She pauses. "I have to thank him, don't I?"

"Perhaps."

"Damn it," Khadijah grumbles. "I'll text you when I'm outside."

Veda hangs up and closes her eyes, hanging her head back. This is when she hears a door open and close, Hiram emerging from the hallway. He's not his usual self. The one she's been learning more about the last few weeks. His beard is a little unkempt. He's wearing loose black sweats and a black shirt.

"Antaris asleep?"

"Yes." Hiram shuffles to the kitchen. "After you fell asleep, I explained what I could. He was stressed but okay. I think. We had dinner, and he wanted to sit in here with you, but fell asleep while listening to a book. The walls in his room are trees, so he's having a good dream."

"That's good," Veda replies. "I just found out a lot from Khadijah now."

As she recounts everything, Hiram collapses into the kitchen chair, looking worse for wear.

"Now we need to figure out why she cursed Everett."

"Yeah . . ." Veda trails off as his winces intensify to expressions of full-blown pain. "You're hurt."

"Is that worry I detect?" It's a glimmer of his usual attitude. "I've been sore. After rest and a pain elixir, I'll be fine."

Sore is a gross understatement. He's clammy, moving too carefully. "May I take a look?"

He raises a brow. "I thought you weren't able to cast after all that."

"It's been a little while. I'm not depleted anymore. Do you want my help or not?"

He doesn't budge. "Even if you can, I doubt body aches are your specialty."

"No, and I'm technically not a doctor, but I did attend medical school." Veda folds her arms and rises to her feet. "I still had to go through rotations in every specialty. I'm qualified enough, so take off your shirt."

"What?" Hiram blinks incredulously. "No date first? No drink?"

She rolls her eyes so hard, her head hurts. "Jokes about your modesty are significantly less funny when you could have permanent injuries."

Hiram slowly stands. Eyes on her, he pulls his shirt over his head and drops it on the floor, revealing tattoos mottled by deeply bruised skin. He is . . . well built. Lean. Muscular. Exactly as she remembers. Lowering his arms makes his breath hitch. No wonder he looks like shit. More bruises begin to form before her eyes, and there's a nasty gash on his side that looks more like a burn than a cut.

Her eyes skim his body, roaming across the definition of his muscled chest down to the waistband of his trousers—all before she gets a better look. Hiram slowly raises his hands, gripping the back of his neck and trying to steady his breathing, but it grows sharp each time her fingers brush his skin.

"Looks like a Contact Curse. It causes pain to the first person it contacts. You were likely hit while—" He shielded her from harm. Their eyes meet in silent acknowledgment. "You didn't have to do that."

"I know."

Uncomfortable under his watchful gaze, she keeps looking, frowning. "The pain would have started immediately. Odd that a medic didn't catch this."

"I didn't allow anyone to look."

Except her. She clears her throat. "You should have. You suffered this long when you didn't have to."

"Being a sick kid has given me a high pain tolerance."

"Understandable, but pain doesn't make you stronger; it tires you out, makes your body focus on the wrong thing enough for a minor curse like this to spread. Like it is now." Little red spots form on his chest and side. The more complex bruises darken from brown to black to a deep purple. "Soon, it'll be too much to contain."

"Any lasting effects?"

"Luckily it's low stakes to heal, but if it were higher, you'd need a healer, or at least a doctor with a working amulet." Veda's neck still feels bare without hers. "Do you have any potions?"

"None for pain."

Veda steps closer, trying to figure out where to start. She glances at his neck, watching his Adam's apple bob. She worries at her bottom lip. "I'll have to cure it myself. It's been a while since I've healed anything."

She's back in the empty hospital hall in Philadelphia, trying to save Dr. Lawson's life.

"Take your time." Gruff yet calm, Hiram's voice pulls her from her own head.

After pressing a hand to the bruise on his shoulder, she whispers the charm to stop the Contact Curse: *"Auxilium."*

Warm light flares beneath her open palm. She pays for magic with a shiver that chills her to the bone. The bruise doesn't fade, but given how Hiram's stiffness subsides and his face flushes right before her eyes, she can tell his pain is ebbing.

"Better?" she asks.

"Much."

Veda moves to the gash low on his side, healing it with ease. She works with clinical ease, knitting the skin back together with a spell that she pays for with a wave of momentary nausea. Once it passes, an errant thought escapes: It's the first time she's spared any attention to a body that isn't her own.

And the first time she's allowed herself to openly appreciate someone else's form.

No longer sallow from the Contact Curse, Hiram looks as good as he smells. Clean with a subtle woodsy scent. It's heady. She can admit he's handsome. She's thought as much, even during her active antagonism. But now she sees there's an allure about him. More than that, Veda understands why women look his way, why *she* looks his way.

For now, Veda lets her attention roam, combing every detail from the dusting of freckles on his shoulders to the intricate, albeit incomplete, sleeve of ink along his arm. She is only checking for bruises, of course. But her gaze lingers, drawn to the labyrinth of color and detailed art. The starry night sky with the rising sun and a waning moon on his shoulder. A compass and a handless watch entwined with flowers. Two trees, one skeletal, the other in full bloom. And then . . . the eye identical to the one on her amulet. She pauses, lifting her gaze to meet his. Hiram's expression gives nothing away. Her eyes drop again, still too curious. Wrapped around his wrist is a snake eating its own tail, while symbols fill in the spaces between each image. This is far from being a haphazard collection of impulsive decisions; it's a dedicated work of art. Every mark speaks of intention, of a calculated man. Even the clean stop at his wrist feels deliberate, designed to keep the inner workings of his life hidden from a world too eager to judge him. Just like she had.

"You don't seem like the tattoo type."

"I didn't know there was a type." Hiram gives her a look she can't interpret. "I never cared about what any of it meant until I recognized the eye on your amulet when I saw you in the cave."

"You scared me that day," Veda confesses.

"Do I scare you now?"

Increasingly so, but she doesn't take the bait. "The bruises should fade in a few days."

"I may swim in the healing waters and bring Antaris with me tomorrow. You should come, too."

Veda doesn't know what to make of the invitation, unable to shake the coiling that feels like *trouble*. "We'll see."

Hiram doesn't put on his shirt. Instead, he rolls his shoulders and stretches his arms out, every motion more fluid than the last. Beginning to relax, his head tilts slightly, eyes focused but hazy from the fading pain. Veda observes as he tests, works, and flexes the muscles of his shoulders until he catches her eye.

"I should get ready to go," she says quickly. "Khadijah is on her way."

"Have you eaten?"

Veda's stomach clenches at the thought of food.

"I made butter chicken," he adds.

"While in pain?"

Hiram nods and leads the way to the refrigerator, pulling out leftovers. "Life of a single parent. The show must go on."

Veda leans against the counter, watching him pack a plate for her to take. She ignores the energy in the air, the oddness growing into something tangible. She knows it's attraction. Logically, nothing deeper than the competence of a shirtless, bruised, and tattooed man packing up food he's cooked. A few minutes later, he places a container on the counter and studies her as if she's both the problem and the solution.

"It's ready."

Veda slips past him, but Hiram boxes her in with a hand on the counter, forcing her to turn toward him. Just like that, she's trapped, and he's far too close, challenging her with a look. Veda feels like forcing him away, with magic if she must. She'll pay the cost. "I healed you. It'd be a shame if I—"

"If you what?" Hiram asks, voice low, leaning a fraction closer. "I wanted to say thank you."

"You could have done that from across the room."

"I could have."

"And you thanked me with dinner."

"I did."

But when he doesn't move, Veda wonders if this is his intent. "What do you want?"

The smooth edge of the granite countertop digs into her lower back. Veda doesn't know why she shifts forward, but she does. Close enough to touch his arm, she has every intention of pushing it away. Sidestepping him. *Leaving*.

But warmth radiates from Hiram's skin. He's the kindling, the spark, *and* the flame.

"Do you know how you're looking at me?" His voice is but a whisper. "How you've *been* looking at me?"

Veda doesn't answer. She can't.

"I'm not impulsive." Hiram exhales, eyes falling to her lips. "I *am* a glutton for punishment."

"Let me guess . . . I'm the punishment."

"Yes." Hiram leans in with confidence, searching her eyes until he's a breath away. Hands cup her face, his lips ghost hers. "You're going to say no to me, aren't you?"

She means to. *Needs to*. But curiosity keeps her silent.

Hiram rests his forehead against hers, eyes fluttering shut. "Good."

A sharp inhale fills her lungs with air the moment he kisses her.

Veda hasn't done this in so long, yet falling into him feels natural. He's warm, and it's all too easy to kiss him, to touch his chest and catalog each sensation before she floats away. The pounding of her heart. The fluttering in her stomach that's far from nerves. It's human nature to seek connection through touch, to want more than the bare minimum—natural to take what she wants, what she *deserves*. Working Hiram's mouth open with hers, she feels his hands on her waist, his heart racing beneath her palms. He's a delicious push and pull, a sharp rise and a steep fall. The language of touch and sensation teases the coils of pleasure.

He lifts her up on the counter, parts her legs, pulls her closer. The permission Hiram seeks in touch is silent, but her answer is not. "I didn't say no."

"It's not that," he murmurs, blue eyes heavy on her. "Didn't think I'd get this far."

Neither did Veda, but her hands are already in his hair. "*This is nothing.*"

They're too far in to stop now. Hiram's hands slide to the small of her back, then lower. When Veda gasps and arches into him, he smirks. "Keep lying to yourself."

"Shut up."

Acquiescence comes with him tilting her chin and dragging her in for more. Aside from talking and arguing, breathing and sighing, kissing each other is what their mouths are made for.

Hiram seems determined to change her mind as kisses morph into something achingly deep and hungry. *It's good.* The feel of his hand on her hip, the other teasing the elastic on her waistband, anchoring her in place. *So good.* The way he nips at her bottom lip and pulls, none too gently. The perfect pressure of his tongue as it slips in unchecked, brushing against hers. *Too good.*

Freedom is exhilarating. Ignoring the future for the right now is addictive. Where Hiram will go and how far she'll allow him to take her is a mystery, but it's not one they'll solve tonight. Hiram's lips travel to her neck. The shock of him sucking on her pulse makes Veda moan, clench her thighs, and grip the back of his head like she needs a bit more to—

Hiram grunts and pulls away, wincing when her knees press against a bruise too hard.

"Shit, sorry," she blurts, her cheeks heating in embarrassment. She looks everywhere but at him, murmuring, "I didn't mean to—uh—I should go. Khadijah should be outside."

He nods after a beat, reluctantly stepping back.

Veda looks at the picture he makes. His hair is a mess, lips pink, and there's a high flush on his cheeks. Ignoring the tiny scratches on his chest where she unconsciously marked him, Veda hops off the countertop. Her legs are shaky, and her body feels far too warm. She wonders how disheveled she must look. Hiram's eyes are on her when she grabs the container of butter chicken and heads for the door.

His hand lands on her waist, stopping her. "Veda?"

"Yeah?" she replies awkwardly.

Contemplation blooms alongside the determination in his eyes. Hiram catches her chin and turns her head to meet his gaze. His thumb brushes over her lips. Instantly, her stomach is in knots. She nearly bites his finger in defense of her self-control.

"Our timing couldn't be worse."

That's not what she expects to hear.

"What?" Her voice is like a shared secret.

Hiram's fingers scrape against hers. Another spark of warmth searching for a way in. "You're free to fight this, to fight me. I know you will, but what I refuse to do is live in a delusion of your creation and pretend that *this* is nothing. Think about it. I'll wait."

One last kiss seals his promise.

Hiram opens the door as Khadijah pulls into his driveway.

The tingle of his lips on hers lingers all the way home.

Twenty-Four

Two hours later, Hiram wakes abruptly with one word on his breath.
"Shit."

Hiram knows a runner when he sees one. Veda is predictable, and Hiram has been paying attention to her tells. He knows when she's ruminating and wonders if kissing her was the right action at the wrong time.

By the time he's finished dressing, the decision is made. He keeps a packed bag under his bed—a habit from his first escape. He packed a similar bag for Antaris weeks ago. After grabbing snacks for the road, his phone, and his keys, he tosses both bags into the trunk of his car.

Waking Antaris is hard because he's sleeping so soundly, but Hiram manages it gently. "Let's go on that little trip I told you about earlier."

A blanket, his favorite bow tie, and a stuffed rabbit are all his son brings with him. Hiram turns on the automatic cat feeder until he can call Peter to cat sit. Antaris is already dozing again as Hiram pulls out of the driveway, activating the talisman as they leave. The drive slows as Hiram relies on memory to find the right spot. He misses it the first time, realizing he's gone too far when the river comes into view. But moonlight catches the path the second time.

"Reserare," Hiram murmurs, uncertain whether the driveway will open to him until it does, the trees peeling back like an invitation.

Floating light illuminates the path, guiding his car through the thick brush until he sees Veda's house. The outdoor lights glow dimly, and her bike is parked outside. Hiram checks on the still-sleeping Antaris before stepping out and approaching her front door. The talisman hums in welcome.

Inside, a light switches off. Hiram is about to write this entire night off as him coming to the wrong conclusion when the front door opens.

Veda steps out, bag slung over her shoulder. "What the *hell* are you doing here?"

"I had a feeling you might run."

"I wasn't running." The sharp tension in her doesn't ease.

"The bag says otherwise."

Irascible frustration sours her expression. "I couldn't sleep. So much is happening. If I leave . . ."

"It changes nothing."

"I'm in danger, which means you and Antaris are in danger because of—"

"You don't have a plan, and Ariadne probably expects you to be impulsive. She's been two steps ahead this entire time. If you're going to go somewhere, it needs to be a place she doesn't know or expect."

"With you?"

"Yes. Well, with us."

"Us?" She glances past him at the car. "Antaris is inside?"

"Sleeping," Hiram confirms. "We could get out of town and come back with a plan."

Veda studies him for a long moment before shaking her head. "What happened in your kitchen shouldn't have happened. It *can't* happen. Nothing changes the fact that I'm *cursed*, Hiram. There's a reason I don't let myself want. It's unattainable. I don't have a future. I've spent years living on the bare minimum because I know that it'll end in a second, and I can't get used to something that'll be ripped away. I tried to have hope. I tried to be positive. I left your house thinking—it doesn't matter, it put everything into perspective and made it clear that I need to go back to—"

"To what?" Hiram snaps. "Isolation in the greenhouse or your cottage or fortress, whatever you call it—and avoiding everyone who gives a damn about you?"

"Yes! Exactly that! Get used to me not being here, because I—" Veda falters, visibly struggling. Softer, she asks, "What happens when I die? Have you thought about that? Antaris is still grieving his mom, and losing me will send him spiraling backward. I know I started this by caring about him. He was drowning, I couldn't let him, but I should have backed away as soon as you got your shit together. I shouldn't have kept coming to your house, acting and pretending like everything is normal when it's not. He's a child. He can't take too many hits. It's better if I—"

"That isn't something you get to decide without our input after making yourself integral to us!"

Veda's eyes blow wide at his admission.

"Him," Hiram amends weakly, then throws it all out in the open between them. "Fuck it—*us*. Him. *Me*."

"Hiram . . ." There's disbelief in her whisper.

"Trust me, I've thought about running from you as much as I've thought about losing you. What will it do to Antaris? What will it do to me? I'm not willing to back away. I'm so fucking sick of running, of accepting things I want to change, of not arguing or fighting and just letting things happen. I meant what I said before. I'll show you who I am, but I'll do it by fighting for what I want. And that's *you*."

Veda is frozen. "What you want from me, I can't give."

"I know," Hiram replies, soft and tentative. "But you think about it sometimes."

When Veda says nothing, he takes a slow step toward her.

"You want to dream. To *want*. Am I wrong?"

Veda remains defiant, resolute, until the cracks split wider. "I was *fine* before Antaris. I was better before *you*. But now . . . I can see the people I'm going to miss, and hints of the life I won't get to live. And I . . ." She fights back tears. "I'm not fine. I'm fucking terrified, with too many regrets I keep pretending are sacrifices. I'm sick of fighting for every single day and having to hold the pieces of myself together when I'm falling apart."

"Then *rest*."

"I *can't*. I can't be weak. I'm supposed to—"

"No one asked you to be strong." Hiram takes another step. "Stop burdening yourself, you're not alone. You have people who will be here in a second to do whatever you need. Don't push us away."

Veda looks away. "I ca—"

"Just because you can handle everything alone doesn't mean you have to." He's close enough for his fingertips to skim her chin. "Share the weight, Veda. I'm strong enough to carry it."

"And if we can't figure this out?"

"Then we'll prepare."

She cracks more, a tear slipping down her cheek. A wet chuckle escapes. "You're going to regret this."

"I won't. *We* won't. Just don't shut us out. Trust me."

The air vibrates until her words cut through the silence like a knife. "You're asking for a lot."

"I know."

"I'm not worth the trouble."

"You are. *Trust me*."

Veda blinks back tears, scrubbing them away as they fall. "I don't know how."

Calm and controlled, despite the tremble of his own nerves, Hiram opens his hand. "Let me show you."

A six-hour drive takes them to the coast.

The journey is quiet, easy, with soft music playing in the background and two stops for bathroom breaks. It's the only time Veda lets go of his hand. When they arrive, it's dawn, and they have an hour and a half before their water flight. Antaris is awake and confused about their whereabouts, but too hungry to squint. They eat breakfast at a diner with a view of the channel. The more he eats, the more fascinated Antaris seems by everything.

Veda is subdued but asks, "Your family has an island."

"Technically, a few. My family has spent the last six generations collecting real estate like socks. However, we're going to a cabin on an island that I inherited from my uncle Sebastian. He built the place with his wife."

"So *you* have an island?"

"It's not entirely mine," Hiram says casually. "There are year-round residents, but most are seasonal. I haven't been there since I inherited the place."

After breakfast, while Antaris and Veda watch a nearby ferry dock, Hiram calls Peter to catch him up, but his friend's only response is: "What do you need?"

"A sitter for the nameless cat."

"I'll head over there in a few minutes. Cat carrier?"

"In the front closet."

"Okay." Peter pauses. "What else?"

"All your apothecary contacts and brewers in town. We're figuring things out."

"You're with the best brewer I know."

"She's taking a much-needed break."

Peter makes a small noise. "About time."

"Oh, and don't forget to water the herb garden, or it'll disappoint your godson."

"Consider it done. He's only just stopped squinting at us. I'd hate a regression," Peter laments. "Speaking of Antaris, when you get back, I'd like to have Khadijah give him a test. I have a few ideas that may help his socialization."

"Okay, that's fine."

"Good."

"What you need for Ariadne and the Sanguis Curse is in my office, if Gabriel and Francisco need to look," Hiram says. "There has to be more information about her in the files. They're enchanted. I'll figure that part out once I get what I need."

The pilot is ready when they arrive. Much like his last flight, Antaris looks like a baby owl just figuring out life while being strapped in. But this time, instead of sitting stiffly, Veda persuades him to look out the window after takeoff. At first, he shakes his head, covering his eyes, but then he peeks once. Then twice. It turns into a stare. Then he does something Hiram doesn't expect. Without looking, without knowing Hiram's already watching, Antaris taps his knee to get his attention.

"I see it."

Veda observes him intensely, then looks away. Hiram doesn't. Not even when Antaris falls asleep, leaning against Veda's arm. He only glances down when she gently shifts the sleeping boy so he's lying against Hiram instead.

"This isn't a cabin."

In Veda's defense, it's not. It's a two-story house with floor-to-ceiling windows overlooking the waterfront and a private seaplane dock. They're half a mile from the closest neighbors on either side, and behind the house is nothing but forests full of protected animals and plants.

Hiram's Imprint recognizes him, and the house flares to life. A cleaning talisman rids the house of dust. The lights flicker on. Doors unlock. Hiram registers Veda's and Antaris's Imprints to the house, then tells Antaris to pick a room. Only then does he realize, in his rush to depart, he left Antaris's lantern behind. Veda comes to the rescue, pulling hers out of her bag and offering it to him. Antaris accepts, but concern makes him frown.

"Don't worry about me," she insists. "I'll sleep fine tonight. Take it."

Antaris does, and Veda follows him to set it up.

Hiram's uncle was a man who masterfully played the Ellis game until Hiram's grandfather died. Then he quit the family firm, became a chef, and charted his own path, challenging prejudices within the family. His defiance culminated in marrying a Seer, a lovely woman named Talulah. Things were horrid for them until they left the country to travel the world teaching tolerance. They never had children. Hiram had been shocked to inherit everything in his uncle's will. He'd never met the man. There were a host of other Ellis family discards more deserving than he was. The only explanation came in a note that read: *My wife Saw who you will become.*

Hiram checks the pantry, finding it stocked with preserved foods, flour, and everything he needs to cook—all sealed by magic to withstand the elements. The refrigerator is blessedly clean. Still, there are other things they need.

"There's one store on the island," Hiram tells them once they're settled in.

"Shame you left your car on the mainland."

"I left it because I knew there was one here."

The vehicle, a rugged truck designed for all terrains, handles the wooded path easily as they make their way to the store. They pass the occasional resident on foot or in their own cars. At the store, curious looks follow them, but Hiram's identification and proof of residency turn those into friendly nods. The mention of his uncle sparks memories of a good man. Armed with everything they may need, they drive back to seclusion.

After dinner, Antaris naps, and Hiram finds Veda on the front porch gazing at the shimmering lake.

Hiram joins her on the bench she's sitting on, their thighs brushing.

She looks at him. "My head is a little clearer, so for now, I'll admit this might have been a good idea, but I think—"

"I know." Hiram does something foolish: He cups her jaw and brings his lips to hers, smothering her murmured words. "I know what you said, and I know what you're thinking, but I wanted to make myself clear. We'll get back to our problems when we go back. For now, we're in the present. Can you agree to that?"

Veda searches his eyes before biting her lip. "I can."

❀

Hiram isn't as in tune with nature as Veda or Antaris, but he appreciates its intrinsic value: food by farming and hunting, potions and elixirs from plants. Tonight, he appreciates it for providing the kind of irreplaceable peace he'll only find layered between the current, the breeze, and the blooms.

Antaris is the first to be swept away, sitting on the upper deck in the rocking chair with his battered rabbit on his chest, headphones, and a book charmed to read to him. While Veda naps beneath the open window of her bedroom, Hiram joins his son with a book of his own. Soon, he's so lost in the first non-research-related book he's read in months, exploring generational wars in a faraway galaxy, that he doesn't notice Antaris has moved onto the woven sofa with him, rabbit between them, eyes full of quiet curiosity.

"He wants to know what you're reading," Veda says from the screen door, a sleepy smirk on her lips, wavy hair wild and free.

Antaris confirms it by scooting closer, sitting on his knees.

Hiram shows the cover. "It's about an intergalactic war."

Veda sits on the other side of him. "Go on."

"It's a bit outside your age range, but it's one of my favorites. One day we'll read it together." Hiram notices that eagerness doesn't fade. "If you choose a book, I'll read it to you."

Antaris scurries off, returning with one Hiram has seen him read before. A tale of children playing pretend in an abandoned house. With every page, Antaris creeps closer until he's slipping under his father's arm, eyes fixed on him rather than the illustrations in the book. Hiram lays a careful hand on his shoulder, drawing his son even closer, snuggling into him. He stumbles over a sentence, skips two words, but refuses to move his hand. Veda takes over, turning the pages until Antaris's breathing deepens. Hiram's arm goes numb, but he doesn't move.

The next time he looks at Veda, she's studying Antaris so intensely, she jolts when she realizes she's being watched. The puzzle pieces of Grace's vision slot into place, creating the full picture.

"To find the truth, compel the earth to live, the sun to shine, and the moon to show his face," Hiram recites from memory. "It's Grace's vision, recorded for Gabriel, but I think she's talking to me. I've known for a while that Antaris is the sun, but now I know . . . you're the earth."

Morning and night. Oceans and mountains. War and peace. A study of extremes, she is life in an endless field of planets and stars.

"And I'm—"

"The moon," Veda whispers.

Untouchable to the lonely sun, locked in an orbital dance with Earth, held at arm's length by gravity.

Hiram looks to the rising moon. "I guess I need to show my face."

"You already have."

Twenty-Five

In solitude, they fit seamlessly.

Antaris presents Veda with morning tea to warm her spirits, while Hiram distracts her with companionship. This is a reprieve. Everything will return to normal when the bubble bursts. So, for now, she enjoys the haze. Walks in the forest are better with Antaris at her side, looking where she points, learning and experiencing nature through each of his senses. Where she goes, he follows. It's something she doesn't want to change, and she does her best to ignore every whisper that tells her it will.

Dry days are spent outdoors: sailing in the Sound, whale watching, exploring the beach, and enjoying the sun when it peeks through the clouds. Antaris didn't get his love for the outdoors from Hiram, who prefers any activity that doesn't involve mosquitoes or too much sun, but he shares his father's interest in working with his hands. They build together, not only sand castles and blanket forts, but memories. Wet days are quieter, spent watching movies, reading books, playing games in the house, and listening to music while Hiram experiments with baking. Veda enjoys the fruits of his labor while he takes a swim in the indoor saltwater pool on the lower level. Antaris isn't a fan of water. Hiram's gentle prodding has only moved him to stand on the top step. Nothing more.

It's peaceful here. The rest of the world is a distant memory. Nights are the biggest change, with stargazing, telling stories from memory, or roasting marshmallows until Antaris's bedtime, which Hiram won't relent on with school restarting next week. Hiram reads him a story before they tuck him in and linger as the lantern floats around the room.

Then she and Hiram are alone. They split dessert and dance around topics until they end up someplace quiet. He knows when Veda's silence shifts to stress and how to push back her encroaching anxiety. Even for a moment. Still fearful of what is to come, she can't deny the truth: She's tired, she needs the rest. The holes in her spirit are being repaired during these little moments of *more*. Veda doesn't wonder why she allows Hiram as close as he is. She knows, and plans to push it back into the recesses of her mind when they return. But for now, he's the reprieve from a harsh reality she never thought she needed: a safe distraction, a reminder of the happy, fearless person she once was.

At least, that's how she feels when he kisses her each night. Undemanding. Deceptively slow. Beneath the surface of him lies a blunt, unapologetic desire. She can see it's as cautious as he is. Hiram isn't pushing her, which sounds like the kind of bullshit men spew to charm their way into women's beds. But Veda has this festering urge to test the validity of his claims—for selfish reasons, of course.

One morning, Veda wakes up feeling relaxed yet stir-crazy and walks in on a comical scene. Flour is everywhere, on the counter, the floor, and Antaris himself, dusting his cheek, hands, and shirt. Hiram bears a small handprint on the leg of his jeans, and the front of his hair is streaked with white. It's sweet.

She holds herself in the present, smiling. "Should I ask?"

Antaris smiles bashfully.

"We had a little trouble," Hiram says, giving his son an encouraging look.

Veda joins them but doesn't offer help with the pancakes. She makes the tea and eggs, watching Hiram show Antaris how to perfectly flip a pancake. They eat in comfortable silence, Antaris proud of his oblong creations. He wanders away after helping with the dishes, clutching

Hiram's phone to wait for August's video call. It's how they've been keeping in touch during their separation.

Hiram lingers until Veda finishes wiping down the table and countertops before drawing her outside. Rain starts falling. He opens the doors to the deck, letting the sounds of the downpour and the scent of an incoming storm smother fragments of August's loud ramblings filtering from Antaris's open window.

"He meant it when he said he'd talk enough for the both of them," Hiram mutters.

Veda's laugh is cut off by Antaris's little giggle. "Chaos and order. They're good for each other."

He sighs. "Unfortunately, I agree."

Settling on the outdoor sofa, Veda doesn't make it to five before she feels his arm around her shoulder. "Peter called before you woke up. The fallout from Ariadne is massive. She did more than corrupt files and use the Registration to hunt down the Oracle Council." Hiram's expression turns grim. "She left the trickster pendant at the school with a note to Antaris, saying he was the rightful owner and his mom would have wanted him to have it."

Veda's blood chills at the murderer's message to her victim's child.

"She has no need for it anymore," he says. "She can't hide the pendant because everyone is looking for it, and she can't hide her cursed mark."

That heaviness returns. "I've fought her twice. You saw what she did at the school. I know she's coming for me, but I also know what's at stake if she succeeds."

"Who's to say she will?"

"You're an optimist."

"No, I'm a realist." Hiram turns to her. "There's a reason you've beaten her, and it has nothing to do with power. Ignore the fear, ignore what happened. What did she do both times?"

"She . . . hesitated. At least with me. I got lucky." Veda sighs. "Now that I know more, I understand being young and believing you have your entire life ahead of you only to find out you're going to die from a vision you had."

"Or from seeing something you shouldn't."

Hearing it from someone else hurts more. The scars on her back ache instinctively. "Yeah."

"I didn't mean—"

"No, you're right," Veda says softly, raising her head to stare out at the trees and water. "Realizing your life is a footnote in someone else's is hard."

"Would you do what she did?" Hiram asks. "Could you keep trying after seeing the consequences of your actions?"

"Would *you*?"

"I'm an attorney. My morals are situational," he replies, shrugging.

Veda rolls her eyes, huffing a laugh that fades as she turns the question over in her mind. "The desire to live can drown out any contemplation about the quality of the life you're fighting for and what that would look like. Am I capable? Sure. Would I? Never." She finishes her tea. "Being young doesn't justify her misguided punishment of those who held her accountable for her actions."

"No. But it does make her human."

"Capable of both great and terrible things."

The rain stops and the quiet deepens. Veda is so lost in thought, she doesn't realize Hiram has moved until she feels him at her back. She doesn't want to get used to this, but quickly melts into his embrace, stamping down jitters from his hand on her stomach. Much like every part of their relationship up to this point, it's an enigmatic contradiction that somehow feels . . . *right*.

"Peter is looking up every edible elixir and potion to try. Clinton has been securing magical-use permits, at my behest, to keep things aboveboard. Khadijah has been putting feelers out with other healers she knows. They've never had much information to go on until my uncle's case studies." Hiram massages her shoulders. "Amazing what can happen when everyone is on the same page."

Veda closes her eyes. "Sounding cocky there, Ellis with two *L*'s."

"Never letting me live that down?"

"Absolutely not."

Hiram rolls his eyes. "Come on, let's go swimming."

Together is silent.

A terrifying word, but she agrees.

Antaris graduates from the first step of the pool to the second, but is dubious about going any farther. Veda watches from the edge, skin still fully covered to avoid worried looks from Antaris. A book in hand, the sound of lapping water is soothing.

Hiram is as graceful in water as he is on land. She watches him dip beneath the surface in the center of the pool and swim to Antaris. He stands up in the shallow end, water rolling off his body. After wiping the excess water from his face, Hiram shakes his hair, making Antaris cover his own face to avoid the spray. Hiram sits next to where he stands on the step.

"I started swimming at your age," he says, drawing Antaris's attention. "I was always skinny and sick. I wasn't allowed to run or play sports, couldn't even go outside or anything. But I was allowed to swim, so I taught myself."

Antaris signs *scared* and points at his father.

"Was I scared?" Hiram asks, receiving a nod in confirmation. "Yeah. At first I was by myself, but I figured out how to float and tread water, then I read a few books and tested out kicking my feet while moving my arms."

Torn between impressed and sad at his lack of supervision, Veda asks, "You learned how to swim through books?"

"You don't know the half of it," Hiram replies candidly, his focus shifting back to his son. "May I show you?"

Antaris squints at him, hesitant, before giving a tentative nod.

He steps down cautiously, flinching at the chill of the water, and grabs Hiram, who doesn't let Antaris go. Veda watches as he shows Antaris how to stand in water that nearly reaches his head, patient when his motions grow wild. Then he teaches his son how to tread water, something Antaris picks up instinctively. They progress from there to floating. Again, Antaris flails at first, but Hiram says, "I've got you. Trust me."

He repeats it twice before Antaris shows signs of belief. Then once more when Hiram lets him float on his own.

"I won't let you sink."

And he doesn't.

Midnight finds Veda at peace. Breathing salty air, listening to the waves break against the shore, and timing the flashing light from a nearby lighthouse all occupy her time until Veda decides to wander inside for a glass of water before bed. She's almost finished when Hiram wanders into the kitchen.

Blessedly, he's wearing a shirt.

"How was the rest of the day with Antaris?" She hasn't seen him since he and Antaris left for the island's library.

"Good. We ate sandwiches by the pier and shocked the librarian. They didn't have any kids' books, so he donated his. I tried to stop him." Hiram's expression is fond, amused. "He can't be stopped when he's determined, it seems."

"Like father, like son."

"Exactly." Hiram's smirk grows as he edges closer. "He crashed from the long walk, so I carried him to bed." He steals her glass, finishes it, and sets it down on the counter beside her. "I was dozing when I heard you, and here I am."

"Here you are."

Resting his hands on her waist like they belong, he draws her to him as he has each night. No conversation is needed, only his presence and the quickened breaths between languid kisses. Veda rises on her tiptoes as he coaxes her lips and knees to part. Hiram wastes no time filling the space, kisses burning down her neck, craned in permission. The occasional hint of teeth makes her squirm.

"Can I see you?" His question is murmured against her skin, smooth and reverent. Warm like the fingertips that toy with the drawstrings of her sleep pants.

A small "Why?" escapes. Veda knows what he'll see and looks away to avoid the swelling in her throat that comes with thinking about the condition of her body. There are the scars and marks and bruises she can see. And then there are the wounds she cannot.

"Because you shouldn't hide anything about yourself. Not from me." He slips his finger under the collar of her shirt, sliding it off her shoulder, exposing a hint of the full story. Hiram pauses, and a slight inhale clues her in to what he's seeing.

Veda starts to turn, but his grip tightens and his lips brush the jagged skin on her shoulder.

"You're tense," he murmurs against her neck. "Let me help you relax."

"Why?" she asks again, voice stronger.

"Because you don't ask for what you want."

Veda remembers when she did, when she demanded what she deserved. Now she's reserved, restrained, weighed down by trauma, avoidant of anything that makes her uncomfortable and aware. But each day exposes more cracks in her fortress, waking parts of her that she thought were long dormant. Veda wants his touch, craves the hands of someone who has proven to know her. Her hesitant mind only falls in line when Hiram once again breathes on the edges of her cursed scars.

"You can . . . touch me," she whispers.

Hiram moves with careful precision. Before she can question it, her pants are at the middle of her thighs, his fingers teasing the elastic of her panties, then slipping inside. Veda doesn't realize she's tense against the counter until Hiram kisses her, gently urging her to relax.

"Don't tell me how you like to be touched. I'll figure it out." He moves beside her, teasing her earlobe as he runs two fingers through her lips, brushing her clit, and enjoying Veda's gasp when he sinks one finger inside her slowly.

"Fuck." Hiram muffles his own moan. "How are you this wet? I'm only touching you."

Heat explodes as a thick finger moves inside her, stroking, caressing. His breath dances across her neck, kisses and murmured words blending into white noise. Veda keeps swallowing moans and half-formed cries, her stomach tight, wanting to make it last but knowing it won't. Hiram turns to kiss her, his free hand resting on her lower back, confident. Just when her knees go weak, he stops.

"Wait—no."

He withdraws his hand and licks his fingers clean. "Just a second."

Veda's ready to protest until Hiram picks her up like he's done it a hundred times and carries her down the hall, closing his door behind them with a flick of his wrist. He deposits her on the edge of his bed, pants and panties abandoned, before sinking to his knees. They both moan in unison as his fingers return, then his tongue, lapping her clit. His mouth worships through touch; the low timbre of his moan is an ode of praise. Veda is quaking embarrassingly quickly, back arched, hand fisting his hair, right back on the edge she was pulled from. With an eager tongue and urgent fingers, he's pulling noises out of her she didn't know she could make.

She breathes his name, nails digging into anything within reach, tensing around his fingers and shaking at each flick of his tongue. Eyes watering, breathy, high-pitched sounds escape as she tries to keep herself together, while Hiram seems determined to make her fall apart.

"Just a little more," he murmurs, kissing the inside of her thigh, his finger finding exactly what she needs. "You feel so—"

Veda drowns in the rush of sensation, pleasure holding her under until Hiram pulls her free. He holds her as she shakes.

Whispering as they lie together, they share kisses laced with her taste as she slowly comes down from the finest high. He rubs her back as they drift in silent reflection.

Side by side. Face-to-face. Veda's thoughts and worries threaten to take flight, but one word grounds her to the earth. To him.

"Stay."

She closes her eyes, holds on tight, and doesn't let go.

Twenty-Six

Dense trees surround the house. Protected by layered canopies that allow only streaks of sunlight through, ferns and shrubs grow wild. Moss covers everything.

Hiram follows Veda on a morning hike with Antaris, watching her excitement when she notices something new. They find the path by following the shifts in the forest, catch the breeze by noting changes in elevation, discover the lake by following the stream. The trees touched by magic draw wildlife in with their energy. Hiram sits on a rock at the lake's edge, his back to the picturesque view, fully in awe of her.

Veda kneels beside Antaris, pointing out birds and letting him feel the moss. When something catches her eye, Hiram follows as she leads his son to a different tree. Veda touches the base of the tree, and the space between the bark glows.

"So many trees in this forest are touched by magic," Hiram remarks.

"Proof that nature is fine without human interference, but we can't survive without nature to give us what we need." Veda peers around the tree, her smile fading into something curious. "Like foxgloves."

Standing tall in a bed of ivy at the edge of a clearing beside the lake are dozens of lavender foxgloves in bloom. Hiram knows little about plants outside of herbs, but they are beautiful. "What about them?"

"They're poisonous, likely more potent due to their proximity to this tree. I don't typically forage poisonous plants, but foxglove poisoning is treatable if you're quick." When his eyes widen in awareness, Veda nods.

"I can dry the leaves to create a powder. Half a gram is enough to stop a heart. It'll work slower than a potion, but it's less prone to human error."

"Do you have what you need to pick it?"

Veda pats her bag and smiles at Antaris. "A trusty foraging bag is key. We'll have to get you one when we get back."

His eyes brighten as he nods, excited. They watch Veda work, precisely cutting the leaves and flowers and sealing them into bags with a spell she pays for with a small chill. They decide to turn back. Just as he did on their ascent, Hiram keeps glancing in her direction. Aside from kissing her forehead before starting breakfast, he hasn't acknowledged last night. Neither has she. A planner whose backup plans have backup plans, Hiram is determining when he can broach the subject when Veda falls into step with him, presses a hand against his back, and whispers, "Tonight?"

Then she's walking ahead to Antaris, helping him over a large log blocking the path.

Hiram's smile grows. Tonight, it is.

Back at the house, Antaris takes his snack on the balcony, giving Hiram a moment to nudge Veda against the wall, ignoring her sarcasm to angle for the kiss that will break their nightcap ritual. But his phone starts vibrating with calls and messages. Then hers does the same. The messages are from different people, but they say the same thing.

Your dad was attacked by Ariadne. He's in the hospital.

Hiram calls the pilot. Veda starts packing.

In the waiting room, Simran stands out, not for how she's dressed but because she isn't. His mother is in a long silk nightgown and tennis shoes Hiram never knew she owned. She looks years older, her eyes puffy from crying, her forehead in need of rebandaging. Simran notices him first, but instead of speaking, she returns to staring at the door, lip quivering, on the edge of tears. He spots Khadijah on the other side of the waiting room, white hair crinkled from unbraiding. Peter hops up from his spot across from Simran and walks to him.

"What happened?" Hiram asks.

"Apparently Ariadne is looking for her father. She walked into your parents' house at around six this morning. Their talisman let her in—"

"Because she's blood related. I changed mine."

"Good." Peter glances over at Simran, lowering his voice. "She took her time breaking all the bones in your dad's legs because he refused to give up his brother's location. Your mom woke up to him screaming, hit Ariadne with a vase, and was shoved into a wall, which is why she ended up with a concussion. Ariadne ran off, hurt but not obviously bleeding, and your mom managed to call me. Then I called Gabriel. By the time Khadijah and I got there, he was in shock. The medics weren't there yet, so Khadijah healed him. He has some internal bleeding they're working on now, but they believe he'll pull through. Where are Veda and Antaris?"

"At home . . . my home."

"Okay." Peter gestures to the door, which prompts Khadijah to approach. "We're going to go. I'd like to stop by tomorrow and have Khadijah do those tests I mentioned. I know the timing isn't great, but I think it'll help you and Antaris. Is that okay?"

"Yeah."

"Great. We'll bring everything. I've asked Gabriel to join with August. He's dying to see Antaris."

"That's fine. Is eleven okay?"

"Yes."

Hiram stops Khadijah on her way out. "Thank you for what you did."

Hiram watches her leave while bracing for the onslaught that doesn't come. Simran continues staring at the door for so long, he lets his guard down, which is precisely when she says, "I thought you blocked my number."

"I didn't."

"But you did not answer."

"I was away with Antaris."

Dark-brown eyes cut to him before returning to the door. "And Miss Thorne, too, so I have heard."

"We're not discussing this now," Hiram says. He knows she may sound cool and calm, but her broken nails and shaking hands betray her. "Are you okay?"

"No." She touches her temple. "I did not know about your uncle Phillip's daughter until recently. Have they found her yet?"

"No."

"She nearly killed him." Simran's voice is low, short of a whisper. "Now do you see why we did not want you involved in everything? This is dangerous business."

"We're involved whether we want to be or not. Turning a blind eye is what got us here. We're on the same fucked-up family tree, whether you acknowledge it or not. Uncle Phillip wanted to steal Sight from his own daughter, and no, it doesn't absolve her for what she's done, but it explains it. She's like the rest of us Ellises. No regard for anything beyond herself."

Simran turns toward her son, eyes wide. "Why would he want her Sight?"

"Why do you hate Seers?"

"I do not hate them, but they put us all in danger. They could overpower Mages in the blink of an eye. Their magic can cause more widespread devastation than anything a Mage is capable of. Vanishings. Curses. I just do not believe one group of people should have unlimited magic."

"Who are *you* to challenge the Cosmos?"

"I . . ." Simran falters. "Seers know too much, and their history is riddled with people who—"

"Want to be treated equally."

"They are *not* the same. They keep their secrets. They know things we cannot conceive of. Even the full extent of their magic is a secret.

History is riddled with Seers who have wreaked havoc on the world in the name of freedom—"

"And *our* history of terrorizing their communities and shackling their existence is just as destructive," Hiram argues. "Yes, there are Seers who break rules, but more who don't. We're all capable of cruelty, which shows every day in how society treats them. The expectation that they're supposed to take that mistreatment without complaint is absurd. All over a group of genes that activate when they're teenagers—" He stops short upon noticing Khadijah frozen behind his mother. How long has she been there, Hiram doesn't know, but she picks up the hat she left behind and leaves again.

Simran primly sits back in her chair. "I do not wish to argue with you."

"Because it makes you uncomfortable," Hiram replies. "I used to not bother myself with this, but that made me as complicit as you are. Uncle Phillip's bigotry isn't out of fear of losing power and control like yours; it's born of resentment. He wanted Sight. Her Sight. Ariadne wants it back, even if she has to steal it and kill anyone who gets in her way."

The doors open, and a familiar-looking healer emerges. Hiram remembers him from Veda's attack. Healer Michaels.

"Barrett Ellis's next of kin?"

When Simran nods, the healer approaches, offering his hand. She notes his name tag and the symbol on it designating him as a Seer.

Hiram shakes his hand when she doesn't move. "I'm his son, Hiram Ellis. This is my mother, Simran Ellis."

"He'll need to stay a few days to make sure that the bones don't rebreak, but the counterspell done before he arrived was brilliantly executed. He should be out of the woods by morning. He'll need time to recover, and therapy to regain his strength, but we will discuss that in the morning."

"Thank you," Simran manages to say, relief softening her prejudice. Finally, she shakes his hand. "May I see him?"

"Of course. He's sleeping right now."

He leads the way, and Simran follows but Hiram stays. He's not ready yet.

While Peter and Khadijah set up, Hiram opens the door, heaving an internal sigh at the grinning child before him. August is missing another tooth, his hair is an absolute mess, and he's wearing rain boots despite the clear skies.

The always cheery boy waves with both hands. "Hi, Mr. Hiram."

"Hello, havoc."

"I'm August!"

Behind him, Gabriel approaches holding a container of juice. Hiram leads them out back, where a table laden with food is in the middle of his yard. At the sound of August's footsteps, Antaris turns and grins. Undeterred by Gabriel's request to walk, August charges down the steps and stops short of throwing himself at Antaris to ask, "Is today an okay hug day?"

Hiram doesn't understand what he means until Antaris nods, and August proceeds to hug him tightly.

"Okay hug day?" Veda asks curiously, tousling August's already messy hair.

"Ant doesn't always wanna hug or play. His head gets fuzzy sometimes, so I ask, 'cause it's polite," August replies proudly while every adult realizes what Hiram already knows. "I'm . . . Dad, what's that word again?"

"Thoughtful," Gabriel supplies.

"Yeah, that one!"

After August all but drags Antaris to the rocky shoreline, a moment of silence passes, then Khadijah says, "So are we just going to ignore that Antaris has already figured out how to communicate with August?"

They erupt with chatter and laughter, dissolving into theories about when it started. Veda and Peter debate while Gabriel spectates. Hiram watches Antaris and August play, struck by how naturally in tune they are with each other.

He doesn't notice Khadijah step up beside him. "He's a good kid."

"I had little to do with that, but I intend to do what I need to do going forward to keep him good."

"Here." She offers him a box. "It's the trickster pendant. The Council wanted it, but Clinton said it needed to be here. We'll know why soon enough." At Hiram's arched brow, she rolls her eyes. "I have no idea. You know how cryptic my uncle is. I wasn't sure what you wanted to do with it."

Hiram isn't sure, either, but he pockets it. "I'll decide later."

"Fair enough." She glances over her shoulder. "And where does Veda fit in all this?"

"Wherever she wants to."

"She's been through a lot, and with that comes pride."

"So I've seen." His own pride has been battered by Veda a time or two. "I'm more concerned with keeping her alive than figuring out where she fits. Until then, I'm patient."

Khadijah looks as if she's seeing him for the first time. They return to the table, where Peter and Gabriel are now seated, and Veda calls over the boys. Hiram is placing the plates when Veda says, "Antaris?"

Hiram looks up. Antaris is rigid and terror-stricken, struggling to breathe as he tightly holds a bewildered August's wrist. It's hard to say who moves first, but Veda reaches him steps before Hiram. August warily calls for his dad, and he's there in an instant. The moment Veda touches Antaris's arm, he breaks into inconsolable sobs. He lets go of August and begins signing frantically, incoherently, before giving up and dragging both August and Veda toward the water.

Without hesitation, Hiram follows. He's never seen Antaris like this—cold to the touch yet sweating. For a second, he wonders if it's over, but his son races past them toward Peter and Khadijah, who are still at the table, exchanging looks before glancing up.

Dark clouds roll over the trees. It looks like rain, but it's the trees that are crying. The lake water begins to crystallize as azaleas bloom along the banks.

Hiram instantly recognizes the scent of ozone.

Magic thickens in the air. It's Antaris's nightmares come to life. Peter sweeps Antaris into his arms and bolts toward them, with Khadijah hot on his heels.

There's a sharp crack, followed by a moan like thunder. Everyone jolts when the top half of a tree crashes onto the table they all were standing beside moments earlier.

It's silent in the aftermath until a mystified Gabriel breaks it. "Well, *shit.*"

"That's a bad word, Dad!"

August lies on his stomach, racing toy cars across the floor, making chaotic crashing noises when they collide. Each time he asks Antaris to watch, it earns him a fleeting moment of attention. Antaris is too interested in the conversation happening in the kitchen. He's the subject, and *he knows*.

"Sight?" Hiram deadpans. "You think he has Sight."

"It's why I wanted Khadijah to test him," Peter admits. "I suspected there was a chance he'd develop Sight as a teenager because of his mother. It's easy to tell when Sight is manifesting at that age. Their hormones are out of control. However, with children, it's quiet. Subtle. Woven into his personality. Even then, the signs can be attributed to the fact that wild magic is normal for children as there is no cost. I considered it when I found out about his nightmares, but kids sometimes display wild magic because they don't pay for it. My suspicions deepened when he couldn't brew."

"He's *six*. He's far too young."

"The youngest recorded Sight manifestation was a four-year-old girl in Paris. My uncle was five," Khadijah says. "It's not impossible."

"Then we should talk *to* him instead of about him." Veda calls Antaris over, and he doesn't hesitate until they're all sitting in a circle. He's between Hiram and Veda, leaning against her while peering at him. "Can we ask you a few questions?"

He signs *yes*.

"Do you remember when you found the cat?" At his nod, she continues. "Did you know it was out in the rain?"

Antaris looks at Hiram, hesitant.

"You can tell the truth," Hiram says.

Slowly, he nods.

"Did you know about its mom?" Veda keeps her voice even, gentle.

Antaris nods again.

She looks at Peter. "He brings me umbrellas before I even know it's going to rain. I assumed it was attentiveness. He doesn't like strangers but quickly warmed up to August. To me." Then her expression softens with understanding. "You'd Seen me before you met me in Peter's office."

Antaris nods slowly, lip quivering.

"Did you See the furniture in the house?" Hiram keeps his voice as calm as possible despite his heart racing. "The paint? The drawings?" When the lights flicker, Antaris's breathing quickens, tears threaten. "It's okay."

"Thank you for sharing." Khadijah shifts so she's sitting in front of Antaris.

"So much for that zero percent," Peter mutters. "Can't have *potential* for something you already *have*."

"May I?" Khadijah glances at Hiram before adding, "It's not painful, but as a Sensitive, it might make you uncomfortable."

Hiram has heard stories about Seers struggling during Sight manifestation. Anxiety. Nightmares. Heightened emotions and sensitivity. Every clue was staring him in the face. Guilt whispers that he's a bad parent, but Antaris reaching for him makes his inner turmoil fade into the background.

"I can handle it." Hiram takes his son's hand.

Khadijah nods, focusing on Antaris as she offers her hand. He takes it, eyes fluttering shut. "My uncle told me that he remembers the quiet space he went to when everything was overwhelming. Sometimes he still goes. I know you peek out to talk to August but retreat back inside. Are you scared to lose your safe space?"

Antaris nods shyly.

"It's okay. It's yours. We just need to open the door and give you a key."

From here, her mouth moves, forming words Hiram can't hear but can *feel*. The air in the room explodes with colors and fragrances. It's too much, too intense. He can't focus on anything except Antaris, whose eyes are squeezed shut, hands clutching both him and Veda. Khadijah's expression shifts. A wave of pure ozone hits Hiram, but he doesn't buckle. A second wave sparks nausea that'll only end one way. Antaris's eyes fly open, irises glowing gold, and he gasps for air.

"I See his beginning. It was her end." Khadijah's eyes open, silver and fading, but her expression is troubled. Tears roll down her cheeks. "The hole in you is healing. Slowly but surely. It's okay to never be whole."

Antaris lets out a rough breath and grits his teeth, his head tilted back as if he's fighting something trying to hold him down. He releases Hiram's hand as if burned, then grabs him again as if he's the balm to soothe the flames.

"I See." Khadijah's voice is melodic. *"Every step is too much, too hard, too intense. Even touch."*

Hiram remembers all the flinches. The hesitation. The way Antaris curled into himself, shielding his body as if bracing for impact. He blamed grief. The fear of the unknown. Now he sees it was more; his son was at war with himself. A whimper breaks free from deep inside Antaris. His cheeks flush red, eyes blazing like the setting sun, but the unspoken anguish rips Hiram apart.

"You're too young to know the weight of grief, but you've been carrying it in your heart. It's too heavy. Too much." Khadijah cups his cheek, her own eyes flashing briefly. *"It's okay to let it go. Just for now."*

When the dam cracks, it sounds like a cough. Then it crashes. Grief rushes in as tears flow out. No one is ready for the onslaught. A torrent of magic erupts, and Hiram clenches his jaw. The lights flicker. The hands of clocks spin out of control. August's toy cars rise off the floor. It's potent, visceral, and burns as hot as the sun. Droplets rain from the ceiling. They taste like tears and evaporate the instant they touch skin. The floorboards creak and bend. Hiram can barely see through the shimmering, searing heat rolling from Antaris, heat that threatens to burn everything.

It fades like the glow in his eyes.

Timing has been Hiram's struggle, but it doesn't fail him now. He catches his son as he crumples, pulling him close, letting him sob against his chest and fist his shirt. Hiram has spent hours, *days*, agonizing over what to do, what not to do, what might help, what might hurt. But in the end, it's instinct, the need to provide refuge, that guides him. He picks Antaris up and carries him outside.

Hiram closes his eyes and lets his son feel it all. Every emotion that's been trapped beneath weeks, *months*, of silence. Hiram can't bring Grace back, but he can endure the fallout. Allow nature to run its course, all while reassuring Antaris that he won't be swept away.

I won't let go.

A mantra. A truth.

Only when the deluge has passed, only when his son's sobs turn into sighs, does Hiram open his eyes. The world is so different from even this morning.

Antaris is asleep in his arms, face tucked into the crook of his neck, grip still tight. His breathing is deep and even. Hiram collects his broken, waterlogged thoughts until Veda drops to her knees before him. She says nothing, only swiping a thumb beneath one eye. Then the other. They're wet. He never noticed.

"I need a few minutes," he murmurs, trying to recenter himself in a world that's shifted beneath his feet. "I know there's a lot to discuss..."

"Take your time."

He'll never be able to explain the relief he feels when Veda doesn't leave.

❦

Knowledge is a painful, double-edged sword.

August keeps throwing worried looks at the still sleeping Antaris, who is stretched out on the couch wrapped in one of his blankets. August sits close, keeping watch over his friend while sneaking peeks at the cartoons playing quietly. Veda seems to be on guard as well, though some of her vigilance is directed at Hiram, if the cursory glances and the grounding weight of her leg pressed against his are anything to go by.

"All I did was open the door to that safe space," Khadijah tells him, calm and steady. "He has to choose to come out. So now we wait."

"How long?" Hiram wonders.

"Until he's ready, continue as you are. Be his father. Steady. Patient. Present. Nothing different from now," she replies, expression turning serious. "I know what you're thinking. It's easy to mistake the manifestation of Sight in children for a trauma response. Don't blame yourself."

He does anyway.

"I think..." Veda hesitates, glancing at the couch. "I think he's the reason the herbs at school and Hiram's house have been growing like crazy. The olive tree... I think it's been him, too, however unconscious." She looks stricken. "I taught him a little protection symbol he does over everything. I didn't know..."

"Neither did he," Peter says. "He's an untrained child. He'll be taught to control his magic and the laws of Sight. What he's done so far is minor. Granted, what happened today was not, but he'll learn that he can't react so viscerally to every vision he has."

"Thanks." Hiram takes it all in until his best friend claps a hand on his shoulder in support.

"I'll take it from here. Talk to his teachers when the term starts. Get him enrolled in Clinton's classes for new Seers. Introduce him to other child Seers his age at the community center. We'll bring August in, too, to help him understand. *I'll* work with him on control, too."

"Okay."

"You need to make a decision about the Tree of Knowledge."

Hiram recoils at Khadijah's statement.

"I know, but it's a choice you *have* to make as his parent. You can elect for him to eat fruit from the Tree and become Unseen or not. The Ellises have used that option in the past when a child manifested Sight at a young age . . . or even as a teenager. Sometimes, even without the child's consent."

Hiram isn't surprised. They will do anything to maintain the illusion of purity.

"As far as the Registration is concerned, children are redacted until they turn sixteen," Peter tells him. "If you're worried about the rest of your family coming after him—"

"I'm not worried," Hiram replies, resolute. "I'm not taking away his Sight, and if anyone finds out and comes here to endanger him, *they'll* need protection. *From me.*"

The floating lantern hovers at the foot of Antaris's bed. Hiram sits on the edge.

Antaris has been like Velcro since everyone left, which is typically an indicator that Hiram will be spending the night on the floor in his room.

Sorry, Antaris signs.

"You think you've done something wrong?" Hiram asks.

He looks at his hands, meekly nodding.

"Look at me." Hiram gently shifts closer as Antaris meets his eyes. "I'm upset, yes, but at myself. It hurts to see you hurting. I should have figured it out, but I won't blame myself if you don't."

Hiram offers his hand. Antaris takes it. They shake on it.

"*Never* apologize for who you are." At this, Antaris's mouth forms a little O of surprise. "Your mom was a Seer, which means you have a little more of her in you." Hiram stops as Antaris looks at him once, his eyes searching. Resting a hand on the boy's damp curls, he adds quietly, "I'm not ashamed. I'm proud to be your dad."

Antaris surges up to hug him. Because he can, Hiram holds him a little tighter, a little longer, until Antaris lies back down and signs *good night*.

Good night, Hiram signs back.

He waits until Antaris is sound asleep before slipping out and heading to bed himself. Climbing under the sheets, he knows he won't sleep for hours—until Veda emerges from the bathroom, smelling like his soap. The bed dips as she joins him under the covers.

"You okay?" she asks. "Today was a lot."

"Better now that we talked."

"Good." Veda's voice is barely a whisper as she shifts closer, eyes finding his even in the near darkness. Hiram doesn't expect her to move, but then her lips brush his, slow and deep, soothing away the long day. Hiram leans into it, his hand trailing up her side. He knows Veda won't admit she likes his touch; she'll make excuses even as she shivers, because while her lips might lie, her body never does. When she pulls away, Hiram can admit it's not enough. Not even close.

"Thank you," he murmurs.

Veda rolls her eyes. "Must you do that? Soon we'll be fully civil with each other, and that sounds terrible."

He laughs because their fight at the school feels like a lifetime ago. "It does. Just awful."

"I'm glad we agree on something." Her gaze drops to his arm, not for the first time, lingering on his tattoos, fingers tracing her amulet's eye. When she catches him watching, Hiram draws her closer, dipping his head to kiss her covered shoulder, his hand tracing her shape.

"I'm not having sex with you."

"Not tonight," Hiram murmurs. "We'll get there." He grins at her sharp inhale. "You brought it up, which means you're already thinking about it." Brown eyes widen, lips part in protest, but he gently brings a finger against them before she can speak. "I thought I liked sleeping alone, but maybe I don't. See? I can admit that. Unlike you, who won't even admit that you like these . . . nightcaps. Or that you sleep better in my bed."

"Only thing I'll admit is I hate being cuddled."

She rolls onto her side, her back to him, but doesn't protest when he tangles their legs and wraps an arm around her.

"You lie," he murmurs near her ear. *"Terribly."*

"You're warm," she mumbles between yawns.

"And your feet are ice."

Veda doesn't respond. She's already asleep, breathing deeply. Hiram chuckles softly, pressing another kiss to her shoulder. Before he knows it, he's asleep, too.

Twenty-Seven

Dawn brings overcast skies and gray light breaking through the clouds. The lake is calm, the air warm and humid, and a gentle fog lazily rolls in. Hiram is already on the dock, looking on at Peter and Antaris, who sit with their legs crossed, eyes closed. Peter's palms glow white while Antaris's slide through an array of colors.

"It's a lesson in control." Khadijah joins Veda at the window. "Something we do with the little ones. He has to match Peter's color, over and over, until it becomes a smooth transition. They've been at it for about ten minutes. The first match usually takes fifteen and—"

Antaris's light flickers a bit before turning white.

Khadijah makes a pleased noise. "Excellent."

Veda smiles. "Hey, while they're outside, I wanted to talk to you about something."

She squints. "Is it about the fact that you haven't been home in *days*?"

"A week and three days," Veda deadpans. "But no, something else."

She excuses herself to Hiram's room and returns with her rucksack, pulling out what she found in the forest.

"Foxgloves." Thanks to magic, despite being picked days ago, they're perfectly preserved. "The island's forest was bursting with undisturbed magic. These are likely more potent. I know you and Peter have been looking for a safe alternative that'll slow my heart to the point of stopping."

"And you want to try *foxgloves*?" Khadijah asks, aghast. "I found a few options that are better on your system. A dream elixir, a pulse-pause potion, or Heartbeat Hollow's essence can work and won't poison you at the same time."

"None of these will stop my heart completely."

"Yeah, that's the point. They're not intended to *kill* you."

"The research said death will lead it out. The healer at the hospital when Ariadne-as-Everett attacked me said something similar. We have to mimic death, and if this curse was easily fooled, it would have left me after I was attacked."

Khadijah considers what she's saying before sighing heavily. "Prepare it, but I think we should be careful and use a potion we know how to control with magic from the outside that has minimal side effects. We can't manipulate foxgloves. Nature will take its course, and we'll be forced to use other methods to heal you. We only take the foxglove route if it's the last option."

"Okay. Want to help?"

Khadijah does. They find everything they need and put on gloves. Veda carefully places the foxgloves on parchment paper. The desiccation charm works instantly, drying the leaves and flowers before her eyes. Veda picks up the paper and deposits the foxgloves into the mortar and pestle, grinding them by hand until they're powder. Khadijah keeps the particles from flying away with a stasis charm.

Hiram comes in as she finishes. Hesitant, he asks, "Should I be concerned?"

"We're processing the foxgloves."

"My question remains unanswered."

Khadijah cuts her eyes. "We need something to put it in."

"I have something." Hiram is gone for so long, Khadijah sheds her protective gear to check on Peter and Antaris. He returns with a modest silver ring with striations and a navy opal stone. Ignoring her wide-eyed stare, Hiram flips it open, revealing a small pillbox.

"There's probably a story with this."

Hiram chuckles. "No story. It was my aunt's. My uncle wore it, and her wedding ring, around his neck after she died."

"And you're giving it to me?" Veda asks skeptically.

"You need a place to store your crushed foxgloves, and this will do."

Veda hesitantly accepts, carefully fills the pillbox and closes it. "If you want it back—"

"I already told you." Hiram slips it on the right ring finger. It fits. She looks at it, tests taking it off and putting it back on, while Hiram watches with an unrivaled intensity that's hard to ignore, even when he takes her hand once more.

"Worst-case scenario, it'll put me out of my misery."

"Don't talk like that," Hiram says. "I know it's a reality, but—"

"I know. I'm sorry." Anxiety breaks through like the persistent weed it is. "Let me clean up."

Taking extra precautions with the pieces they used, Hiram cleans the counters twice, stores everything in another room, and starts figuring out breakfast, his mood quiet and somber.

"Everything okay?" Veda asks.

"Yeah." Hiram abandons cracked eggs to tilt her chin and kisses her in a way that unravels the tightness inside her. A conversation without words. At the feel of his lips, time stills, their breaths syncing. Freeing and frightening. Veda thinks back to what she once told herself: He's a temporary insanity. Unfortunately, bursting their island bubble and returning to real life hasn't cured her one bit.

The talisman alerts them to a new arrival. "Expecting anyone?"

Hiram shakes his head. "I was planning a quiet day with you and Antaris after Peter's lesson."

Those plans crumble when Veda answers the door.

"Is there a place we can talk?"

Ruth looks frail. It makes it harder for Veda to hold on to her anger, especially after learning about the oath. When Veda lets her inside, Ruth drifts to the great room and stands at the glass door, watching Peter and

Antaris work on control. Khadijah returns, takes one look at Ruth, and mumbles something about needing to run an errand.

Hiram boils water. Veda sits at the table. Minutes pass as they sit in tense silence, trading increasingly skeptical glances. The clink of Hiram placing a cup of hot tea on the glass table startles Ruth, who draws a hand to her chest, closes her eyes, and takes a few settling breaths.

Hiram sits beside Veda.

"How are you?" Ruth asks at last, joining them at the table. "I know we didn't part on the best of terms."

"Moving forward, as I always do. But I'll admit you're making me nervous."

"I see Antaris is catching on nicely," Ruth smiles sadly. "The littles do struggle the most when Sight manifests earlier than intended."

Hiram tilts his head. "You knew?"

"No, but one of the volunteers suspected. Indica."

Don't stress, little one. You'll speak again in time.

"Child Seers are—"

"Nicknamed *littles*, yes. It's meant to be ironic, because they unconsciously do so much little magic that's overlooked. They need the most care. A father's love, a mother's strength." Ruth sips her tea, brow rising at Veda's expression. "You may not be his mother in blood, but you don't have to be to love like one."

Veda awkwardly studies her hands.

"Look out for Marlene and Everly."

The request lands oddly. "What's going on?" Veda asks.

Ruth reaches across the table and covers Veda's hand with her own. "Remember what I once told you, Veda. What you think is loneliness is actually *hunger*. Don't starve it, or it will die. Don't be afraid to indulge. To live. To want and to care. That hunger is what makes you human, and you will need your humanity to face the road ahead." Her hands shake, but she doesn't let go. "Remember the bad times, even when it physically hurts to do so. But remember the good times, even if it hurts more to know they're gone. Grieve. Let forgiveness come in its own time, when you're ready to move forward."

"What are you—"

"Giving you life lessons. There's more, but there is something more important we need to discuss." Veda starts to speak again, but Ruth hushes her. "Ariadne will come for you. I have Seen it."

Veda's eyes bug, alarmed. "You can't tell me your vision—"

"It will not matter," Ruth says, brushing her off. "Ariadne will be desperate. She will try Sight Unseen, as she has done before, and will again."

Veda is confused. "I'm not a Seer. I don't have Sight for her to steal."

"No, but because of your parents, you carry the potential for Sight, whether it ever manifests or not. And you two share blood. Meaning your potential for Sight now lives in her, too. Ariadne doesn't want to just kill you, Veda. She wants to *consume* you."

Knowing this leaves Veda strangely calm. "And the curse?"

"I don't know how she plans to extract it, but it's a problem she'll deal with once she has what she wants. Ariadne is brilliant, but her hunt for Sight has blinded her in other ways."

"Do you think she knew this would happen the night she cursed me?"

"No. This is a twist only the Cosmos could have created. I don't know how she figured it out, but if she is anything like her father, she wanted to take you so she could experiment on you until she found an answer. She is dangerous. You need to protect yourself."

An idea forms. "I'll do that by giving her a taste of her own medicine."

"How?" Hiram asks.

Veda turns to him. "The Liquid Curse."

Hiram's nod draws Ruth's attention. "You surprised me, Hiram Ellis. The world is wrong about you. I was, too. Continue to be the man we never thought you were."

Reflective and humbled, Hiram replies, "I will."

"Your father is home from the hospital." Ruth gives a knowing look before rising to her feet. The back door opens, and Antaris walks in. His hand slips from Peter's as he drifts forward, standing before the elderly woman as if waiting for his own message. "Hello, little one."

Antaris signs *hello*.

"You're closer now than ever." She rests both hands on his shoulders. "You're the soul of the Scorpion. You have your mother's heart and your father's will."

The boy steps closer, face full of questions.

"Did you know Grace?" Hiram asks.

"No, but I've heard much about her fighting spirit. I can only hope to show her fortitude when the time comes."

Veda's feelings for Ruth are complicated. A deep sadness fills her, an inexplicable ache. She can't pinpoint the origin, but the weight of it presses on her stomach, growing heavier as Antaris hugs Ruth around the waist. They walk her to the door, but before she leaves, she tells them, "Lead him to the still water."

They stand in the doorway until Ruth drives away. Veda lingers long after she's gone, unable to name the feeling that grips her. It's after breakfast when realization strikes.

"Why did it sound like she was saying goodbye?"

"I'm having dinner with my parents."

It's Hiram's calm decisiveness that makes Veda look up from the potions book. She's been poring over every scrap she can find about the Liquid Curse. He's dressed in gray slacks and a short-sleeved button-down. His hair, which has been relaxed for the last couple of weeks, is now parted severely. He's even shaved. Veda doesn't hide the once-over she gives him before placing her pen in the book.

"How long ago did you decide this?"

"Eight minutes ago."

Veda makes a small noise and stands, ignoring the strange looks he's giving her. "I should change."

"You don't have to come."

"I know," Veda replies, then asks, "How do you know they're having dinner now?"

"They have dinner at the same time every day, regardless of what's going on. My mother always makes it a production."

"How much time do I have?"

"Forty-five minutes."

Fifteen minutes later, Veda is dressed in a floral jumpsuit Khadijah bought her ages ago, paired with sandals. Her hair is slicked back into a low braided bun. Hiram and Antaris wait for her in the foyer. She does a double take at the sight of Antaris. Instead of the usual black, his knitted bow tie is . . .

"Green?"

Olive green, to be precise.

"That's what he chose." Hiram ruffles the curls his son has worn free only a few times. It earns him a funny look that makes Veda laugh.

Antaris leads the way to the car. Hiram stops Veda briefly with a hand on her stomach and a compliment that warms her.

The ride is as quiet as the finely dressed Simran when she notices their joined hands at the front door. She leads the way into an ornate dining room with soft light, where a pale Barrett sits in a wheelchair at the head of the table.

"How are you, Father?" Hiram asks, tone edged.

"I'm fine. My bones have been healed. The wheelchair is a precaution until I am strong enough to walk on my own," Barrett replies, his eyes dropping to Antaris, then sliding to her. "You have only joined us for dinner twice since your return. Why is today number three?"

"I wanted to see that you were okay, but if you want us to leave—"

"No," he says quickly. "Please sit."

Veda looks at Hiram when he pulls out her chair, but sits without a sarcastic response. He takes the seat on the other side of Antaris.

Dinner is served on beautifully decorated silver thalis: an assortment of vegetables, curries, naan, dal, chicken, and lamb. Antaris looks confused, so Hiram patiently explains each dish and how to eat them. Simran interjects occasionally, offering the cultural context Hiram doesn't know. Veda enjoys her meal while sneaking glances around the room.

After dinner, they move to the sitting room and watch Antaris wander the sunroom, visiting the plants. When Simran attempts to join him, he stiffens. Children aren't subtle. Antaris is no exception. He keeps a wide berth with Simran until she gives up and returns. Hiram replaces her, and the lights switch on. Antaris warms in his father's presence, smiling, eager to show him the plants. Barrett excuses himself to take his nightly healing elixirs.

Simran wastes no time. "I am surprised to see you here, Miss Thorne."

Me too doesn't seem appropriate, so Veda says nothing. The air between them is heavy, unchanged since their last interaction.

"I believe we are at a point where I can speak to you freely," Simran starts.

"You've never been one to mince words with me."

"Touché, Miss Thorne, but I believe the time has come for me to intervene. I would like my son back."

"I haven't taken him." Veda wants to say more—criticism burns within her—but she reins it in. A full confrontation would only devolve into unproductivity. "Hiram is a man who says *exactly* what he means. Instead of focusing only on what *you* feel is right, listen to him. Oh, and rip up the guardianship petition you're planning to file."

"I had no intentions of following through with that threat. I believed he would be more amenable to conversation than the inconvenience of a legal fight."

Veda nearly laughs in her face. "That version of Hiram doesn't exist anymore."

"I was not aware that you and Hiram were familiar enough for you to have such an opinion about his character."

"A recent development," Veda clips. "But you're lying. If you truly didn't know, you wouldn't have started this conversation with me. If you think I'm controlling him, you're mistaken. He controls himself."

Simran says nothing, smoothing a hand over her gold-embroidered burnt-orange saree.

"You're wasting your time testing me when you should be thinking about why Antaris prefers literally anyone else to you." Simran is momentarily taken aback, whether from Veda's tone or message, Veda isn't sure. "He needs as much family as possible, and it doesn't need to be blood. They just need to have his best interest at heart and give more of a damn about him than their own selfish wants. They need to encourage instead of discourage, breathe life into him instead of stealing it away. Instead of trying to bend everyone to your will, you need to protect them."

"You have strong opinions about a child who is not yours."

"I wasn't only talking about Antaris." Veda stands firm in the face of Simran's surprise. "There are no guarantees in life. I know this more than most. My parents . . ." Her voice catches. "I've *never* needed them more than I do now."

Simran is rendered speechless.

"No matter how old he gets, how angry or frustrated you make him, how much you push—he will never stop wanting a normal relationship with you. But that doesn't mean he has to tolerate your shitty behavior simply because you gave him life." Veda shakes her head. "I don't understand how you get a second chance and squander it out of a stubborn need to be right."

"No matter what you think, I do love my son. So much that I refuse to let him make mistakes."

"It's through mistakes that we learn."

"I left my family just as he left us. They did not approve of the choices I made in life, of the man I fell in love with. They told me I would fail, and I refused to prove them right. I married Barrett, fit into his family, his world, and became more than they ever believed I could be. Hiram—" Simran places a hand over her heart.

"Did the same as you, and you don't see you've become what you once ran from."

Simran looks away. "I push and I meddle because I want better for him. I want Hiram to be more than me. I do not want him to lose the Ellis name. It is what is owed to him, what is rightfully his."

"And if he doesn't want it?" Veda asks softly. "*Better* is subjective. It's an opinion, and opinions can be misguided. The highest duty he has isn't to fulfill your wishes, but rather his own. Respect the decisions he makes. Let him raise Antaris as he wishes. If you love him like you say you do, let him *breathe*, Simran. You've strangled him long enough."

Simran turns, but her gaze moves past Veda, mouth forming a taut line. "How long have you been there?"

Veda turns to find Barrett in his wheelchair, parked in the doorway.

"Long enough." His expression is impossible to read. "Simran, I'm tired. Aren't you?"

"We can discuss this—"

"Now. Not later," he cuts her off. "You weren't like this when I fell in love with you. My family . . . they've made monsters of us all, but I won't let them get to Hiram *or* Antaris. We lost *fourteen years*, and I'll be damned if we lose any more. I have lost so much because I have idly stood by and did nothing. I'm sick of losing. I nearly *died* for my silence. That ends today. Veda, please excuse us."

She doesn't hesitate, making her way to the sunroom. It's warm and pleasant. The plants are lush. Veda sidesteps a palm and pauses. Hiram holds Antaris, his back to her, pointing out the glass window, telling a story about how he climbed that fence, got lost in the forest, and found a cave. Antaris isn't looking outside in wonder, but at him . . . then her. Losing his attention makes Hiram glance over his shoulder. His smile at Veda fades as he seems to notice the muted argument behind her. "What's happening out there?"

"A conversation that's long overdue."

Twenty-Eight

Silence breaks with sniffles and soft sobbing. Bleary-eyed and barely awake, Hiram gets out of bed and approaches Veda from behind. She's clutching her phone in shaking hands.

"What's wrong?"

Veda turns into his embrace. "That was Gabriel. Ruth . . ." She chokes. "She's gone. Ariadne . . . There was a fire. It *was* goodbye."

Hiram feels a pang at her loss. Ruth's memory is complicated by everything that's come to light, so he can only imagine how Veda must be feeling. When she tries to pull away, he holds on. He's gotten better at fighting her instincts, at not reacting to her resistance, just holding and giving her shelter. Even when *she's* the storm.

"Let me take care of you," he murmurs.

"I need to go. Everly—"

"Is in Portland with Marlene at rehab."

"I—"

"You need to take care of yourself. It's . . ." He glances at the glowing clock. "It's three in the morning. There's nothing you can do now."

The last flicker of her resistance melts away. She doesn't want food, but eats the apple he slices for her. She isn't thirsty, but drinks the water he places in her hands. Veda showers and he gives her space to grieve. When she emerges in a towel, Hiram waits outside while she changes, returning only when she opens the door. Her damp hair is already frizzing, but she lets him sit her down in front of the mirror in his room.

After she moisturizes her hair, Hiram quietly brushes and fashions it into a single French braid to keep it from tangling. He's so focused, he doesn't notice her watching.

"You're not real," she murmurs.

"Remember that next time I piss you off."

Her smile is little more than a weak smirk. Nonetheless, it's a feat. She accepts a clean shirt and shorts that don't quite fit, then climbs into his bed. Beneath the covers, she initiates the tangling of legs and hands.

"You're afraid," Hiram whispers.

"Deathly." Veda's confession is barely a whisper. "Of things within my control and beyond."

"I am, too." Hiram lifts onto his elbow to look at her. "The only way out is through."

"I know." The corners of her lips dip into a frown. "I hate that I can't stay upset around you. I wanted to wallow. I never got to forgive her, but now I feel this fragile sense of peace. How did you know I needed to sit with everything?"

"Because I know you. Just as you know me well enough to call out my shit from the beginning."

Veda rolls onto her back, staring at the ceiling. "I'm trying to figure out how we got here so quickly."

"The sequence of events doesn't matter, we're here now." Hiram kisses her temple. "This is the last thing we should be thinking about. There's too much happening."

"You're right."

"And you hate it."

Veda scowls at him. "You're too smug about this."

"Am I?" Hiram makes a small noise. "And here I thought everyone wanted to be seen and understood by at least one person?"

"Not everyone. Not me." Veda's voice lowers. "To be seen is to be known, to have your problems laid out and weighed. You set yourself up for judgment, acknowledge your imperfections, and expose them."

"Because you'll be vulnerable, right?" Hiram shifts closer. "Too late. You already are."

"It's horrible. I don't recommend it."

He smirks. "I'm sure you don't. You'd rather suffer in silence. I know. I'm the same. But you yelled it out of me, so I think it's only fair I pay it forward."

Veda sighs. "Today is going to suck."

"It is."

Instead of sleeping, Veda melts into him, her hand resting on his chest until she is as steady as the pull of gravity. In the mooring silence, his heart anchors itself. Calm acceptance keeps him steady, equally as tethered to her.

He's known since the first wave, but there hasn't been time to dissect the feelings that have lurked longer than his practical heart cares to admit. Hiram doesn't shy away. He makes every choice that comes with loving her, and waits for Veda to accept him when she's ready. He isn't sure when that will be, if they'll have time or space to think beyond the imminent, but he'll be ready when the time comes. For now, he lives for these fragile moments, holding Veda until her breathing deepens. He wants to stay like this forever but closes his eyes until it's time to face the day.

Just after noon, Veda returns with a bouquet of Ruth's favorite flowers. Instead of attending the Seer's memorial, she holds her own, sitting on the dock and setting the flowers adrift.

The sun begins its descent, slowly sliding down to kiss the horizon, but Veda doesn't move. Antaris joins her for a spell, offering silent comfort. Then Hiram does, too. The dock slowly gets more crowded as Gabriel comes with August. Khadijah and Peter stop by on their way home from Ruth's memorial, Khadijah carrying a familiar floppy hat.

The couple sits on either side of Veda, talking. Only when they succeed in making her laugh does Hiram leave to finish dinner.

Everyone stays for an unusually quiet meal, but afterward, while Veda watches cartoons with the boys and Khadijah, Hiram walks outside. When Gabriel spots him, he ends what appears to be an intense call in a hurry and gives him a look that reminds him of August.

"I need another favor," Gabriel says.

"I *specifically* said to not need me anymore." Hiram then asks, "What is it?"

"Francisco is on a leave of absence, so I'm currently without a partner and technically on desk duty, which I hate because everyone is here for this manhunt and fucking things up. Anyway, I went canvassing alone by the Dalneau Bridge—"

"Terrible idea."

"I know." Gabriel rolls his eyes. "But I think I found what Everett meant when he said we'd find the rest of the truth there. I know they searched the area with a fine-tooth comb and found nothing, but I went out a few days ago while August was with his mom. At some point after a few hours, I realized I was walking in circles and touched a tree that turned to ash. Then, with every step I took toward a certain point, everything died. Eventually, I couldn't walk forward anymore."

"Omnipotent magic and concealment."

Gabriel nods. "I tried every revealing spell I could think of, but nothing worked. Now that this case is top priority, I'm supposed to alert my commander if I find anything, but I don't want a hundred people trampling over the scene and destroying evidence. Without Francisco, I don't trust anyone there, but I still want to go back. Since I need backup, and the kids are watching the movie right now . . ."

"I'm an attorney."

"I've seen you fight. Illegal amulet notwithstanding, I'd trust you to have my back just like I trust Francisco."

"How is he, by the way?"

"Mostly recovered. He's off mainly because he's gone to Portland with Marlene for rehabilitation. He has a lot of family in the area who are banding together to help. I'm glad they weren't here . . ."

Hiram is, too.

"How about you?" Gabriel waggles his brows. "Is Veda a permanent houseguest?"

Ignoring him is easy. "I have hiking boots in the trunk. Let me tell Antaris I'll be back, and then we can go."

"Wait, you didn't answer my question!"

Hiram closes the door in his face.

Fifteen minutes later, Hiram parks on the side of the road before the Dalneau Bridge and lets Gabriel lead the way into the forest on foot. Their destination is deeper off the road. He sees the pile of ashes first, then catches fragments of the barrier refracting the sunlight. Gabriel is watching him expectantly, which makes him realize his second purpose of being here. "You want me to try and tear it down."

"I thought you knew that."

Hiram laughs. "What was the strongest spell you used?"

"A shattering spell approved for investigators. *Concutere*." That spell is strong enough to take down a building if it lands in the right place.

"My amulet is designed to serve my best interests, but sometimes it won't absorb consequences from certain spells. I can *enhance* that spell, if you'd like."

Gabriel thinks about it. "A bit of an archaic way to cast, but worth a try."

Working together is useful when Mages aren't strong enough to withstand the consequences of some spells. The amulet will shield him from most of the blowback, but not all.

Gabriel raises his hand. *"Concutere."* Without direction or focus, an orange orb appears in the palm of his hand and hovers.

Hiram opens his hands around the orb, the heat of its magic warming his palms. *"Potentia."*

The orb grows hotter, turning from orange to ice blue. Hiram steps back, letting Gabriel guide it. Silently, it races toward the barrier with conscious precision, which shatters like glass, the fragments scattering across the forest floor. It sounds like someone screaming, high-pitched and terrifying. But it vanishes immediately, revealing what's been hidden all along.

It's closer to a shack than a cottage, though it's well maintained. Gabriel is instantly on high alert. He's the first to the wooden door. A talisman chimes in warning, but Gabriel puts it to sleep with a spell Hiram doesn't hear. Gabriel steps inside and quickly returns, looking shocked.

"You need to see this."

When Hiram enters, his first instinct is to pack Antaris and Veda up and return to the island. The shack is a mess, covered in nothing but pictures and frantic scribblings, trash littering the floor along with balled-up sheets of paper with numbers and incoherent words written in jagged penmanship. This is the prison cell of a man going insane but fighting it every step of the way. Hiram has chills. One wall is covered entirely with pictures of Veda. How long has Everett been watching? He estimates the time from her attire in each picture and guesses at least since February. It tracks from what Veda recalled about the shift in his behavior. There are a few photos of Khadijah and Peter, one of Antaris with Veda at the school holding pots of lavender, and several of Hiram marked with the word *cousin*. Everett had worked out the link between him and Ariadne.

But it doesn't stop there. Everett made more connections. Pictures of Marlene and Seren, with the word *trickster* scrawled across their faces. He knew. Pictures of all Ariadne's victims, including Grace, are marked with the same thing: *Sight Unseen*. How did he know she had performed the spell on each of them? Hiram's musings are interrupted by a photo of a familiar section of trees.

Did Everett find Veda's house?

"Look at this," Gabriel says from behind him.

In the corner, a small television flickers to life, already showing Everett on-screen.

"The remote was buried under a pile of garbage," Gabriel explains, holding it up. "When I stepped on it, this started." He waves the remote and unpauses the video.

"If you're watching this, I'm dead, and she hasn't found this place."

Hiram steels himself for more.

"I gave as many clues to as many people as I could, but it's not enough. I thought I—" Everett's eyes flicker red. He covers them, clearly pained. *"I Saw her real face in a vision, and now this is my fate . . ."*

"Has Veda been home since you got back?" Gabriel asks.

"No," Hiram replies, distracted by Everett. Veda's paranoia wasn't enough. Seeing this will send her into a tailspin he isn't sure he'll be able to stop.

"You need to do what I couldn't and burn this place down with everything in it."

The video cuts off. Gabriel grabs everything he can carry while Hiram walks out. Eyeing the nearby trees, he wants to make sure none are too close for this. By the time Gabriel emerges, his arms are full.

"We need to—"

"Burn it down."

Gabriel looks unsettled. "If *anyone* finds out I destroyed evidence, I could lose my job and compromise this investigation."

"Who says *you're* destroying anything?" Hiram raises his hand, amulet glowing fire red. *"Ardeat."*

Sparks land on the wooden roof. They catch, then spread. Hiram watches it burn, flames engulfing the structure until it is nothing more than a skeletal silhouette.

He doesn't move until only ashes are left.

The next morning, Veda wakes with a clear, determined mind. Hiram is barely out of the shower when she sets on him with a list.

"I'm scared."

"You should be. We're going into the woods to find the last four ingredients for the Liquid Curse, and you're coming. Gabriel says I need a bodyguard and *you* have an amulet." She goes into the closet and throws suitable clothes for hiking on the bed. Before she leaves, she says, "Antaris is already getting dressed."

The door closes and Hiram curses.

He'll take her determination over sadness any day. When Hiram emerges from his bedroom, Antaris and Veda are waiting for him. The former is wearing boots that clash magnificently with his T-shirt and bow tie, but when he looks at Hiram for approval, he says, "Perfect."

"One more thing." Veda vanishes in the direction of his office, returning with a small box. Curiously, Antaris opens it, excitement blooming when he realizes what's inside. His own rucksack. He quickly puts it on, draping it over his shoulder like she does. It looks good on him. Inside, Veda has packed a magnifying glass, a few small bags, one plastic vial, tweezers, and a pair of binoculars.

"He'll be able to add to it, the older he gets, the more his interests grow." Veda smiles, but it doesn't reach her eyes. "I ordered it and had it mailed to Khadijah. I wanted it to be a surprise."

Antaris signs *thank you*. His appreciation seems to warm Veda's spirits.

They drive to the edge of town and enter the forest after Hiram casts a spell on his car to conceal it from view. Not long into their trek, Veda tells him he walks too loudly, too confidently, *arrogantly*. On the island, it didn't matter, but here, wildlife scatters long before they get close. Antaris, by contrast, is quiet. Hiram sees Veda lose track of him, only to realize he's right beside her. When she pauses beside a tree, pressing a hand to its bark, Hiram is grateful for the break.

"Remember on the island when I showed you how to tell what direction you're going?"

Antaris nods.

"Show me which way is north."

His son circles the tree four times, gaze traveling up and down. Hiram, watching intently, mutters that the question is too difficult for him. Veda hushes him, clearly believing Antaris is up for the task. That belief is rewarded when he points north with certainty. Veda beams.

"How did he know that?" Hiram asks, surprised.

"I taught him that branches growing south spread south toward the sun, while the north side of the tree grows straight up."

From that moment on, Hiram pays close attention as Veda identifies the ingredients she finds, demonstrates how to properly harvest, and when they happen upon bushes of fruit, she explains which fungi and berries are safe to eat. Pokeweed is easy to find. Veda needs it for its root. Absinth wormwood needs to be as fresh as possible. The valerian and ivy are the last things she finds, but once they're secured, they keep going deeper into the forest. Antaris finds a particularly rare needlegrass that he wants permission to pick as his first ingredient for his storage room. Veda looks around, then kneels next to him.

"We can't pick this."

"Why not?" Hiram asks. Antaris looks to her for an explanation, too.

"There aren't enough. So with these, we look but don't pick," Veda explains. "We need to let them grow and spread. That way, there will be more when you come back. It's important to respect that there is a balance. Everything in nature is made of magic and connected to the Cosmos. If we don't respect it, the Cosmos will bite back."

As if on cue, a clap of thunder comes out of nowhere. A high-pitched squeak escapes Antaris as a spark slips from his fingers. The small ball of fire lands like melted glass in the leaf bed beneath their feet, spreading quickly. Hiram wastes no time pulling Antaris away and extinguishing the flames with a spell. The boy is shaken and devastated, but Hiram is quick to steady him by seating him on a nearby rock and tightening his boots.

"It was an accident," Hiram says calmly. "Accidents happen. They help you learn."

"He's right," Veda chimes in.

The birth of an idea makes Hiram look around. "Do you think we can find Nénuphar?"

Veda considers it. "Do you think he'll be able to see it?"

Antaris looks between them, blinking in confusion.

"There's only one way to find out."

They leave the path and go where the old forest steers them. It never matters the direction; magic is the reason the cave has always found them exactly when it's meant to be found. This is what Veda tells a fascinated Antaris. The trees thin and sunlight peeks through the canopy.

Veda's eyes brighten as she points to something ahead. "There it is."

When the cave's magic doesn't warp his son's world, a safeguard for those who do not need its power, Hiram knows he made the right choice in bringing him here. Antaris is the first to reach the cave's mouth, his trepidation clear. Together, they lead him to the water's edge, his eyes sweeping the amethyst walls and limestone ceiling, searching for the cave's pulse. Signs of overwhelm start to show.

"Do you remember what to do when you feel overwhelmed?" Hiram asks gently.

Antaris nods, closing his eyes and taking one deep breath after another.

"It's okay," Hiram reassures him. "I used to come here as a kid. I didn't know then, but each time I swam in the water, I felt a little better. The magic here only shows itself to those who need it."

Antaris points to himself.

Veda kneels next to him. "Even adults need healing. Do you want to try?"

He nods slowly.

"What you see will be a memory," she explains.

They only bother kicking off their shoes and socks. Veda waits at the water's edge while Antaris takes a tentative step. Realizing the water is warm, he seems to relax, growing more confident as he goes all the way in. He floats on his back, staring up at the shimmering rocks that drop from the ceiling. Hiram sees the moment Antaris slips into a memory. Hiram follows, and slips into one himself.

"Grace is gone. She's gone..." John's voice breaks. "You deserve to know."
"Know what?"
"Your son."
The world narrows to a single moment, then broadens so widely it feels indeterminate and terrifying. But his decision is made in an instant. "Send me your address. I'll be there in the morning."

Hiram inhales his way out of the memory. Seconds later, Antaris does the same. His eyes glisten. When Hiram gathers him into an embrace, Antaris signs a single word, repeatedly.

Mother.

"Did you see her in your memory?"

Antaris nods, smiling even as tears stream down his cheeks. No sadness, only peace.

❧

The drying spell leaves Antaris's hair in soft curls, Hiram's standing at odd angles, and Veda's as wild and voluminous as ever. Antaris bursts into giggles every time she tries in vain to pat it down. They emerge from the cave as the first streaks of sunset stretch across the sky. A pasture of blooming flowers greets them beyond the entrance, and Antaris rushes ahead, eager to explore. They keep watch as he wanders.

"Most of them are weeds," Veda says when Antaris plucks one. "But some weeds are useful. Like the dandelion in your hand." Hiram notices her body moving with more ease now, her energy lighter, back to her usual cautious calm.

"How was your swim?" he asks.

Veda starts walking, and he falls into step beside her, keeping enough distance from Antaris to give him a sense of independence without letting him feel alone. She says nothing at first, fussing again with her poofy hair. "My vision was from the night of Peter's graduation party. I saw you."

Hiram's lip twitches. "I'm disappointed it took you swimming to remember me."

"Had I seen your arrogance on display that night, I might have remembered you sooner. I know an asshole when I see one."

"Touché. I asked Peter about you, but he told me you were with someone."

"Ah, Tobias."

"Terrible name."

"Terrible partner."

They look at each other and dissolve into laughter, sobering only when Antaris returns with a handful of dandelions for Veda. She accepts them and tucks them into her bag.

"I'll show your dad how to make dandelion tea," she promises.

Encouraged, Antaris runs off again, eager to collect more. Hiram spots a white flower nearby and offers it to Veda when she looks his way. She raises an eyebrow. "You *do* know that's poisonous, right?"

Startled, Hiram drops it, trying to appear calm until he hears Veda snickering.

He scowls. "You're lying."

Her grin fades in a flash, head turning, alert. Hiram does the same. He hears it, too. *A voice.*

Antaris is still immersed in his flower hunt, touching one with careful fingers before picking it and doing the same to the next. He handles them reverently, as if he's greeting them or thanking him, an ode of respect.

They freeze when they hear it again.

Barely audible, hoarse from disuse, but definitely Antaris. A rush of realization leaves Hiram torn between approaching and retreating. Veda, however, focuses intently on Antaris, who is lost in his own world. He veers off, pausing to examine moss at the base of a tree before something more colorful catches his eye. Veda approaches from behind, placing a hand on his shoulder. Antaris startles, then relaxes when he realizes it's her. His gaze shifts to Hiram, who doesn't know how many steps it takes to reach his son. He kneels when he's there, with Antaris placing another bundle of dandelions in his hands.

"Are you thanking the dandelions before picking them?" Veda asks gently.

He looks from her to Hiram, hazel eyes bright as he nods. Shyness gives way to quiet determination. Careful as ever, Antaris steps closer.

A single whispered word changes everything.

"Hi."

Twenty-Nine

Failure is both mentally demoralizing and physically painful.

It's a waste to bleed and suffer lingering aches from the consequences of magic that leads nowhere, but that's the nature of risk versus reward. Veda holds the vial of the Liquid Curse to the light, reluctantly accepting the truth. She failed.

"I thought the potion was supposed to be clear *before* the two-day incubation period," Peter says from the doorway of the brewing room at Weston. Veda's been here all morning, taking each step carefully, paying the quiet price of the magic it takes to brew. The first sign of trouble came quickly after she started, when some of the vials in the storage closet began to vibrate, clearly affected by the pull of magic.

"Yeah, it is."

"Ah. Where are Hiram and Antaris?"

"Home," Veda replies absently, skimming the potions book. "We didn't think it was a good idea for Antaris to watch in case something went wrong."

"Home? We?"

She rolls her eyes. "Here you go."

Peter smiles. "I'm happy for you three."

Veda struggles with happiness. Like swimming in murky water, she can't see what lurks beneath the surface and has to tread with care. "I'm trying to enjoy these moments, but it's hard not knowing the outcome."

"It's harder when you do." They sit with the weight of what's to come until Peter picks up the vial. "What do we need to do to try again?"

"Change the environment. It's easily influenced by what's around it, so this potion needs to be brewed in virtual solitude, and I need a smaller cauldron."

"That's easy," Peter says smugly. "The cottage. Before you moved in, our brewing instructor used it for complex potions with the older Mages. If something goes wrong, the cottage won't explode or implode. That's why I gave it to you. Why don't you take a break and—"

"There's no time. I need to brew this correctly as soon as possible." Veda touches her nose, scowling at the blood, and grabs a nearby towel. "I wonder how Ariadne got her hands on the Liquid Curse for Marlene; it's damn near impossible to buy, and she can't brew as a Seer."

"I assume she convinced someone to make it. A few drops goes a long way. I called around, no one's selling it. Either they don't have all the ingredients in usable states, or the brewing and transport time make it impractical. If we pack the ingredients now, we can grab a new cauldron and stirring rod from the potions store on the way to the cottage. I'll sanitize the room and air with a spell. It'll need to sit for a bit, but that'll work well for what I'm leading to."

"Which is . . . ?"

"Khadijah found help for our ninth curse-extraction attempt."

Lucky number nine. "When?"

"Gabriel agreed to take Antaris for a sleepover. He said he'd call Hiram once we got off the phone. I figured we could start when they leave."

"Okay." Veda packs the ingredient vials carefully into the transport bag Peter offers, and they leave in his car. Purchasing the cauldron and clearing out the back room of her cottage takes time, but once they're finished, she steps outside while Peter casts a sanitizing charm. Blue mist spreads through the room as he shuts the door behind him.

"Ready?"

Even if she isn't, she has to be.

When they arrive at Hiram's house around noon, he's packing a sleepover bag. An excited Antaris hands her the unfortunate stuffed rabbit, entrusting his most prized possession to her while he's gone. She covers his hands when he gives her the black bow tie that's been absent since he decided to wear other colors. "I'll protect everything, okay?"

"Thank you," Antaris whispers, leaning against her leg. She rubs his back, still in awe at hearing his little voice. Hiram appears in the doorway with the cat carrier. Inside, the cat looks like he's pleading for freedom.

"He's going?" Veda asks.

"Yeah. Gabriel's thinking about getting a pet. This is a trial run."

"Oh my Cosmos." All she can think about is the exponential potential for chaos.

"Exactly."

Antaris doesn't bat an eye when Veda hugs him extra tight before loading him and the cat carrier into the car. Wearing soccer cleats, August is impatiently waiting in his seat.

"I didn't know he had a game today."

"He does." Gabriel looks back. "We'll do pizza with the group, maybe paintball."

Antaris glances down at his white shirt and fiddles with his orange knitted bow tie, eyes widening in horror. Hiram's reaction is, to her amusement, similar.

"There will be covers for your clothes," Veda says.

Antaris's relief is loud. Gabriel stifles a chuckle.

August says absently, "I don't like the covers."

"Of course you don't," Hiram grumbles.

Veda clasps her hands. "Okay, we'll see you later."

Stepping back as Gabriel pulls away, Hiram glances at Veda. "Peter filled me in on what happened with the Liquid Curse. I have an idea, depending on how this goes."

A last-minute decision leads to Veda sitting on a large blanket by the lake. The afternoon is overcast but breezy; the sun sneaks through the clouds. They're by the edge when Hiram checks on her for a third time. Veda nods at Khadijah and Healer Michaels, deep in conversation out of earshot.

Veda nods over at the two. "What's happening there?"

"They're debating which potion to use . . . *and* it looks like Khadijah is backing down."

"Impressive. We need to learn his secrets."

Expecting Hiram to joke, instead she finds him scooting closer to her. Hovering. He presses his lips to her forehead, toying with the end of her braid.

"Don't get maudlin now." She notices something in his hand. "What's that?"

"Antidote for foxglove poisoning."

"I could have—"

"Made one? There's no time." He glances back at the healers, then pockets the vial. "If this doesn't work, then . . ."

"We try the foxgloves. Alone."

"Khadijah is—"

"Going to be pissed. But we don't have much to lose."

"Only your life."

"Ariadne is coming for that anyway." At Hiram's wince, Veda adds, "You don't have to stay for this."

"Thanks for the out, but I'm not taking it." The double meaning is not lost on her.

Hiram stays with her when they wade into the lake. Water is the best conduit of magic, according to Healer Michaels, who casts spells to shield them from view and monitor her vitals. He hands Veda the vial of Heartbeat Hollow's essence. "Drink and count back from ten. You may be aware, you may hear things, but you shouldn't feel anything."

Hesitation lingers, even with the vial in hand, uncorked and ready for consumption. Veda has a hundred things she wants to say to Hiram, but drinks before she can speak her mind. Counting down from ten, she floats on her back and watches the sky. The breeze is warm, the air is crisp. The gentle lap of waves on the shore is so quiet, she can hear the occasional splash of jumping fish.

A hand in hers is the last thing she feels before darkness overtakes her.

Time loses shape and meaning, passing through Veda's fingers like smoke. She falls deeper and deeper into the contradiction of tumultuous peace.

"Hiram, hold her."

"It's working . . ."

"Oh my Cosmos . . ."

"No . . ."

Veda does not know when the darkness loosens its grip, but her eyes flutter open.

Blue is the first thing she registers—eyes so familiar, yet the man behind them looks like he's aged five years in seconds.

She doesn't need to ask. She can still feel it.

"It . . . it failed."

Strike two for the day, and unlucky nine overall.

Veda wakes late that afternoon, reflecting on the day's failures until Hiram drags her outside for tea on the dock. They watch the sun sink below the waterline and have a quiet dinner. It's peaceful despite the looming heaviness. Veda hardly thinks about the fact that they're truly alone for the first time, and by the time she does, Hiram says, "I think I should brew this with you."

"Aren't you—"

"It's not my best skill, but brewing involves more preparation than actual work. You're not alone, remember?"

She stares at him for a long moment. "Ready when you are."

The silent ride to her cottage is tense, but his hand on her knee stops her mind from flying everywhere. Veda stands in the middle of the living room, rocking back on her heels.

Hiram takes the lead. "What do you want me to do first?"

"Wash your hands. We both should."

Afterward, Hiram dries his hands and rolls up his sleeves one at a time. Veda watches with interest she doesn't have to deny. His brow lifts, smirk sharpening like glass when he catches her. She turns away too fast, bumps into the table, and curses under her breath. "I should finish preparing."

His chuckle follows her.

For the next fifteen minutes, Hiram observes her every moment like *he's* the meticulous brewer, but she ignores it, slipping into routine as easily as putting one foot before the other. Veda checks whether Peter's sterilizing spell worked. The small cauldron is dry, the cutting boards clean. She rebalances the scale, wipes the knives, and ensures the mortar and pestle are spotless. The vents are open and the windows are properly cracked. Nothing escapes her scrutiny. Not even him. Veda gives Hiram a brewing apron and puts on the other one.

"To avoid contamination," she murmurs as he lets her tie his.

Hiram doesn't let her go without tying hers in return, securing it snugly. Gloves on, they approach the table. Together, they move like cogs in a well-oiled clock. Veda only has to give instructions once. He starts mincing the moss first while she brings distilled river water to a boil.

"Do you know why Seers can't brew?" she asks, hushed. "Their power is like using a blowtorch to light a candle. They put out too much magic when potions only take a light touch. Costs nothing but a twitch."

She realizes Hiram's Sensitivity should make it easier to feel magic's slow ascent, to smell the precise moment she needs to begin. Maybe that's why she needs him. More than a sous-chef, he's a partner.

"Do you want to take the lead?"

He pauses while cutting the fresh ivy, a stabilizing agent. "What do you mean?"

"I'll walk you through it, but I need you to cast while I add the ingredients."

"You trust me?"

Veda hesitates only because the truth is so willing to break free. "I do."

When he casts the first spell, his amulet ring flashes blue. In perfect tune, the cauldron hums. They follow the potion book step-by-step. He casts as she adds each ingredient, maintaining the rhythm while watching him for any sign of strain.

"What's it like to smell magic?" Veda asks after watching his reaction to the ingredients blending.

"Hard to say. I don't know anything else."

She hums quietly, then it's time to brew in earnest. No stops. No pauses. Hiram's ring glows with each turning point as he recites the incantation. Everything flows. The work is almost silent, broken only by his recitation and bits of quiet conversation that dwindle as their concentration deepens. By the time they finish, it's nearly four in the morning. Veda uses a dropper to sample the clear liquid, smiling before sealing it into the vial.

"Is that good?" Hiram asks.

"Tentatively, yes. But the next two days will confirm."

He leaves first while Veda stays to stir the potion until it cools. When she joins him in the solarium, only dim solar lights glow in the room. The sun will be rising soon, but the world is still cloaked in darkness. He hands her the glass of water on the table.

"How did you know I'd want water?"

"I pay attention." Hiram looks at her. The softness provided by the dim light shifts, casting part of his face in shadow. "I'm observant of everything in my line of sight." He says it so easily, and it should ease the tension, but it does the opposite.

"Is that so?"

"I'm not complicated. I'm just particular about where I invest my time and energy. I prefer quality over quantity, and I won't entertain anything that isn't real."

Tonight, his words hold more depth. Fascinated, Veda rises to her feet. Her voice is soft but pointed. "You think this is real."

"I know it is." His eyes don't leave hers. "I told you before. I've figured out what you don't think you can say, which is why I'm patient. You'll come to me in your own time."

"Like some obedient animal—"

"*No.* Like someone who knows what they want, which you do." Hiram steps back. "But I'm not going to chase you or trick you. As if I even could. I said I'd show you who I am, and I have. Everything else is up to you."

She stares at him, voice low. "Why bother? I'm cursed and difficult, and—"

"I haven't changed my mind." There's no sarcasm, only sincerity. "I won't. We're walking through hell, remember?"

Veda forces herself to look away. That certain feeling rises again. She feels it most of the time, but nothing like right now. It's the space between close and too close. Never enough. "You're free to walk away at any point if this gets too hard."

"I'll remember that." He sounds playful, but his voice is much too low. Personal. "And you're free to tell me what's got you feeling like this tonight."

"Nothing."

"Lies. You've been in survival mode since I met you. Possibly longer. It sounds exhausting."

He's too close to the truth. It feels like dragging a boulder through a marathon she didn't choose, constantly pushing herself to a finish line she'll never reach. Veda folds her arms across her chest. Hiram isn't a threat to her, only the life she's grown used to. She wants to give in. It's hard to ignore what he's offering, harder not to want the sanctuary he's been building for her.

"The cracks are there. Something is bound to get through." The truth slips out with her next breath. "Like you did."

Hiram's steady eyes are an invitation. He's waiting for her. He's *been* waiting.

Veda looks him up and down before lowering her guard a fraction, moving into his space. There are a thousand reasons not to do this, and only a few reasons why she should.

"Take off your shirt." She leans in.

Hiram's brow rises. "Now?"

"Yeah." Veda's lips brush against his. "I'm tired of only allowing myself the bare minimum when I want so much more."

"We can start there." He steals a kiss. Then another. "We'll figure out the rest."

When his mouth meets hers fully, the thrill shocks Veda to life before it sinks into her skin, invades her bones, and bleeds into every nerve. Hiram is right there chasing her lips, drawing her closer, framing her face. The pressure of his kiss expresses everything he's been saying. He fills her awareness to the brim with him—only him.

When he pulls away, she's momentarily adrift until Hiram takes her hand and leads her toward her bedroom. The short walk is torture, air thick with unspoken desire, brushing hands, tension cresting in a thunderclap of motion as soon as they pass through the doorway. Frenetic kisses and moans, whispered directions and touches, untucked and unbuttoned clothes. They speed along until a lone discussion point stops Hiram.

"I didn't bring anything."

"I'm cursed. I can't—"

Hiram swallows the rest of her words with a kiss, only breaking to murmur directions as he takes his time undressing her.

Veda remembers what lies beneath too late. "I—"

"I know."

He kisses the black streaks on her shoulder. Each reverent press leaves currents of heat that shift as he moves. His lips skim every scar. He mouths every ugly vein and whispers homage to every wound.

Murmured words slide against her skin like a promise Veda lets him keep with a sigh as she closes her eyes, letting go.

"I don't see anything wrong," he murmurs, lifting her gently onto the bed. Veda is intoxicated, high on him, a greedy, shaking mess as his hands worship her while his mouth pours praise across her skin like water. She wants more. Molten heat pools between her legs as Hiram spreads her thighs and kneels between them.

It's instinct, the way Veda opens for him. There's purpose in the tilt of her hips. Her sharp inhale is loud in the silence as Hiram slips a finger inside her wet cunt, his kisses closing in on her core. Nerves spike, then flee in an instant, as sure fingers spread her lips and his tongue slides against her aching sex. A gasping breath escapes as she tangles her fingers in his hair.

Hiram takes his time, familiarizing himself with her body. The low timbre of his moan vibrates against her, sending a shock of arousal straight to her core. When she begins to quake, he slips a second finger inside, stretching and curling them in all the right ways to make her clench.

"Hiram."

He freezes for the span of a breath before doubling his efforts, his eyes on her—watching, learning, feeling. Arching against his mouth, she is frantic as he holds her shaking legs apart and urges, demands, *commands* her to—

She falls apart. Both trembling in the aftermath, they come together in quiet reverence.

Her bed is smaller than his, but that makes little difference when Hiram slips into it facing her. He kisses her deeply, draws her leg over his hip, and finds the right angle to slowly sink into her with a shaky gasp. He stretches her open until it almost hurts, overwhelming yet still not enough.

Sex isn't new to Veda, not even like this: lying on their sides with nothing to stop the sighs slipping between them. But Hiram is silent now that he's inside her. He touches her like she's something precious, reverently breathing her in, basking in the moment.

Then he shifts, cradling her as he rolls onto his back and brings her on top.

"Use me," he says.

Hands pressed to his chest, she begins to move, rising and falling on him. It's deeper like this, toe curling.

"Take what you need," he whispers.

She doesn't need to be told twice. Her control incinerates with a single roll of her hips.

Long suppressed, her desire ignites, movements becoming a self-fulfilling prophecy that make Veda want more. Desire consumes them. Hiram's body, lean and strong, matches her rhythm stroke for stroke. Everything burns in the best way. Broken moans and bitten-off words mark Hiram's command in each dip of her hips.

Frantic. Desperate. Messy. Neither is quiet. Pain and pleasure blur the edges of her vision. She leans forward, flush against him, sliding her hands in his hair, burying her face in his neck. She lets him take over. Lets him hold her too tightly. Lets him give her exactly what she's never asked for but always needed.

Hiram is right there with her, coming with her name on his lips. Their hearts pound wildly, out of sync, until stillness finds them—side by side, face-to-face. He rubs slow circles on her back.

"How do you feel?" The whispered question is followed by a kiss on her shoulder.

Veda falls asleep to the first fingers of light crawling across the sky before she can answer.

Thirty

Hiram wakes late in the morning to the sound of the shower running. The space beside him is empty.

Five minutes pass. Then ten. By fifteen, he is curious enough to test the waters after what happened last night. He abandons the warmth of the bed and walks into the bathroom, greeted by a wave of steam. Veda's bathroom is modest, the shower's curtain drawn but clear. She stands under the showerhead, eyes closed, looking lost in thought. They snap open when Hiram pulls back the curtain and joins her.

"Good morning."

"Hey."

Awkwardness tries to creep in, but Hiram doesn't let it. Hot water cascades over their bodies as he kisses her, his hand caressing the side of her neck while one of hers rests on his chest.

"Everything okay?"

"You interrupted my mental breakdown."

"How rude of me."

"Exactly." Veda runs fingers down his tattooed arm.

"Any regrets?" Hiram asks, fear in his throat.

"I tried to find a few, but couldn't."

"What a shame." He pulls her flush against him, catching her interested brow raise when she feels him hardening against her. "Are you staying?"

"Yeah."

They shower together, occasionally stopping for kisses or quips. Veda navigates his body in the light, and he does the same, watching black veins retreat from his touch. She yelps when he massages between her shoulder blades.

"Sorry."

"No, it's—I don't think anyone has touched me there in years. I didn't realize how sore it was."

That's how he ends up behind her, hands working across her back. She squirms beneath his touch, breathing hard, pained but relieved. The air thickens with steam and the scent of her lavender soap. Despite his best intentions, his thoughts turn.

The plan is to dry off and fall back into bed after such a late night. Instead, they don't make it past the bathroom counter. Unlike the night before, it's a race of wet skin and hair, digging fingers and deep strokes. Veda's legs are spread wide, head thrown back and lips bitten as she grinds against him, chasing her release. In no time, she's clawing at him, gasping for breath.

One sharp rake of her nails down his back is all it takes for him to catch up. He shudders, the edge of pain tipping him over. Pressing his mouth to her shoulder, he muffles a groan as release crashes through him. Even in the aftermath, all he can think about is how much he wants her again. And again.

For now, they kiss until the fog of desire lifts. After a quick rinse, Hiram dries off and dresses while Veda tackles her hair. When she winces while brushing through it, he takes over, eventually braiding it into the single French braid she likes after she moisturizes it.

"Where's your salve?"

She meets his eyes in the mirror, then hands him the container. The scent is less than pleasant, but as he applies it, the dark veins fade and the redness settles. He kisses her temple and leaves her to get dressed.

Hiram makes pancakes, the quickest option, and by the time she appears in her usual long-sleeved, fitted shirt and jeans, the last one is nearly done.

"Breakfast, too? You're setting impossibly high standards," she teases. "You've got to go soon, don't you?"

He does, but checks his phone only to find a message from Gabriel. "Oh, Gabriel is taking Antaris to August's T-ball game. He said he'll bring him home after. They had a good night. No nightmares." He glances at Veda. "Looks like we'll have a little more time after all. Not that I was planning on leaving you alone to spiral about last night."

"Is that so?"

Hiram steps closer, boxing her in against the counter. "I miss your cold feet."

Veda cracks a smile that turns into a chuckle. "Just for the weekend."

What's left of the morning passes in a haze.

Veda's cottage is devoid of food, and pancakes for lunch aren't nearly as appealing, so they return to Hiram's house for leftovers. She waits until he finishes eating, then straddles him.

"Haven't had enough?" he teases.

"No."

They make use of the quiet house, taking their time to learn each other's preferences. Veda's is simple: *him*.

It's hard to slip from her side as she dozes, but he manages, catching sight of the dead amulet she's been holding on to more and more these past few days. Hiram puts on shorts and wanders into the living room, making the most impulsive call of his life.

Clinton answers on the first ring, smug as ever. "Ah, Mr. Ellis. You're finally ready."

He rolls his eyes. "I guess I am."

"Veda's pride would never allow her to ask for help with the amulet, but your love for her will," he says, matter-of-fact. "Death is not the end. Nothing that dies is ever truly gone. It returns to the Cosmos that bore it, waiting to be called back. Then the endless cycle begins anew. Do you know how amulets are made?"

"You shape each gemstone and pour magic into it until it activates."

"A simplistic explanation for a complicated task, but essentially correct," Clinton replies. "You can do it, too."

Hiram remembers Veda saying something similar once, in the library. It feels like a lifetime ago. "I don't—"

"Stonemakers do, indeed, pour magic into each gemstone. It's an act of love, for both the craft and the person who will receive it. Born out of love, stonemakers create something that benefits the world. I've heard you like to create, too. Here's your chance to create something for her."

Hiram stares down at the amulet resting heavy in his palm. "How?"

"It'll never be what it was, but that's okay. This will be from you, reborn through your power and shaped anew. All it takes is a bit of determination. Call to the Cosmos: the moon, the stars, the earth, the planets, the sun. If an element does not answer, try another. Do this each day until it comes to life. It will require more than patience, more than strength and power. But you are ready."

Hiram keeps his eyes on the softly glowing amulet. "I am."

Clinton pauses, then continues, voice lower now. "But you can't wear your amulet while crafting this. You *cannot* hide. You must show your true face."

※

Hiram sits down for his monthly call with John, though it's earlier than usual. For the first time, he's not alone. After the usual greetings and check-ins, Hiram puts the call on speaker and passes the phone to Antaris, who stares at it for a long moment. Then, with a nervous tremor, he leans close to the mouthpiece and whispers, "Hi."

John's gasp is audible. "H-hi, Antaris. It's . . . it's so nice to hear your voice again."

Antaris buries his face in Hiram's shirt, and he gently strokes the back of his son's head. "You did well," he murmurs.

"You did," John echoes. To Hiram, he asks, "When?"

"It's been a few days." Hiram adjusts as Antaris leans heavily against him, staring at the phone. "He has Sight. He's had it since Grace . . . They think the stress of it manifesting early is why he stopped speaking."

"I should have known."

"I thought the same thing," Hiram admits. "I missed a lot of signs, but that's okay. We're working with him now."

"Oh, you're not—"

"Going to take it from him? Never."

"Good, good." John pauses and asks, "Is he still there?"

"Yes."

"Antaris . . . your mom is so proud of you."

The boy clutches Hiram a little tighter, a little longer, even after the call ends. He wanders off to find Veda outside watering the herb garden.

Their tender little bubble of happiness bursts when Hiram's phone rings again.

"Hiram, there's been an incident . . ."

The hotel is on the edge of town. FCD investigators swarm the grounds, reporters are on-site, and the only reason Hiram isn't turned away by a spell-happy enforcer, who looks fresh out of the academy, is Francisco calling him through.

"I thought you were in Portland," Hiram says.

"I was, but Marlene said I needed to come back and get that bitch, so here I am."

Hiram feels the same way.

Investigators part for them like the sea, granting them a narrow path to the shit show. Reporters close in at once, flinging questions he doesn't hear, though the sheer volume of them confirms it's bad.

Hiram starts mentally preparing—for what, he's not sure. It doesn't matter. Nothing could have prepared him for the scene.

For one harsh second, Hiram thinks his father is splayed across the driveway like a ritual sacrifice. But the details—the clothes, the shoes, the lack of a watch—hold his grief at bay. That, and the spider lilies pushing through the cracks in the concrete. He hasn't seen his uncle Phillip since childhood, but his mother used to say how much he resembled Barrett.

"Ariadne got to her father," Francisco explains.

"Why is he *here*?"

"From what I've gathered, in my absence and with Gabriel on desk duty, our superiors found your uncle and brought him in to put him under protection. Somehow, she found him. They're interviewing everyone who knew his location—"

"And the magic," Hiram murmurs, staring. "I've never smelled anything like it."

"The scene analysts believe she performed Sight Unseen again. But this time she didn't bother to cover it up with a wasting curse or conceal her Imprint." One grim thought ricochets in Hiram's mind as the medics carefully cover the body in preservation sheets.

Ariadne has only one option left to get her Sight back. And she's waiting at Hiram's house.

"We need to call Gabriel."

They get back in Hiram's car to make the call, filling Gabriel in on what's going on. Dread settles in the depths of Hiram's stomach. There's no telling if Ariadne learned something while she posed as Marlene, Seren, Everett, or even Veda and held on to it for the right moment. "We need a way to get ahead of her."

"Let's meet at your house. I have an idea."

Francisco groans. "The last time you had an idea, I ended up waist-deep in shit searching for smuggled deactivated amulets."

"I was right, though! They were there, just somewhere else on the farm," Gabriel says.

"I smelled like cow shit for days."

"But did you die?"

Hiram is beginning to understand where August gets his chaotic streak. He sighs as deeply as Francisco, who's now pinching the bridge of his nose. Still, Hiram bites. "What's the idea?"

"We set a trap with what we already have," Gabriel says simply. "We use Veda as bait."

"Absolutely not," Hiram snaps.

"Not the *real* Veda. Let's take a page from Ariadne's book and use her arrogance against her. She gave us the trickster pendant. Let's use it. Someone can pose as Veda and ride her bike through town. Ariadne's watching, waiting. If she takes the bait—and I think she will, because she's desperate and time is running out—she'll make a move on the fake Veda, and we'll be waiting for her."

Hiram and Francisco exchange looks. "This is a wildly chaotic idea."

Gabriel chuckles. "We've been steps behind her. Let's try getting ahead for once. What do we have to lose?"

When they return to Hiram's house, they begin preparations and decide to keep the plan secret—limited only to the core group already involved. After filling Veda in, they call Peter and Khadijah, who drop everything and come over. Once everyone is present, they plan in earnest.

There are more than a few steps involved in the final idea, but it's surprisingly simple. Veda will lower her security measures at home. Hiram will have them safely in the air and out of reach while this all happens. Peter will watch his house. Khadijah will use the pendant to impersonate Veda. August will stay with Francisco's family as a precaution. Gabriel will tell the enforcers Veda is aiding the operation and station teams, hidden, in the surrounding forest. He and Francisco will be positioned inside.

After giving Khadijah the pendant box and adjusting Veda's bike with her Imprint, everyone leaves. Within minutes, Hiram puts the pilot on notice.

Once they're alone, Veda starts wincing. "Might've been a little too enthusiastic earlier," she mutters.

"Probably." Hiram chuckles. "How about I run you a bath when we get back from your house?"

"Sounds like a plan."

That's when he first notices something amiss. Black veins creep above her collar. Not wanting to alarm Veda, Hiram waits to call until she's wrangling the cat.

"To what do I owe this surprise, Ellis?" Khadijah asks in lieu of hello.

"Veda has veins above her collar. Can you—"

"Come back and take a look? Sure. I'll turn around and meet you at Veda's so I can bully her into it."

"Thanks. We'll leave in twenty."

Hiram returns to find Veda finishing up with the cat's food and toys for the trip. "Ready?"

"Yeah." A sharp pain makes her clutch her side. "I'm a little more sore than I thought."

Hiram keeps an eye on Veda during the drive to her house. Antaris is in the back, looking out the window pensively. Khadijah is waiting when they arrive. Veda looks over at Hiram, who promises to explain shortly, before she heads inside. Khadijah approaches the passenger window as Hiram rolls it down.

"I didn't see any veins on her collar."

"They were there . . . unless they moved."

Khadijah frowns in the direction of the cottage. "They shouldn't be."

Hiram's phone buzzes, stops, then buzzes again. He ignores it. "What do you mean?"

"If her veins are moving, the curse is waking up."

"*What?*" Hiram snaps. "It's been moving like that for a few days now."

Khadijah swears under her breath and bolts in the house. Hiram scrambles out of the car with Antaris in tow. His phone buzzes in his pocket again. By the time he gets inside, Khadijah is examining Veda's collar. At first, he sees nothing, exhaling in relief. Then the black, fractured veins appear, crawling toward Khadijah's fingers like they're drawn to her touch.

"Oh shit," she breathes, pressing her hand to Veda's shoulder. The veins ripple beneath her skin. "Your curse is waking up."

Veda's face falls, and with it, Hiram's heart takes a dive.

"How long before the block breaks?" she asks, voice shaky.

"I don't know."

Hiram's phone rings again. Irritated, he pulls it out and sees Gabriel's name. "What the hell is it?"

"Are you home?"

"No."

"Good. We heard a call on the radio about an incident at your address. Your neighbor reported an issue with your talisman. Someone tried to neutralize it, but it backfired and is now sending out shock waves. This is exactly what Everett did at Lucinda's. Francisco and I are en route to check it out, but there's a . . ."

Whatever else he says becomes background noise.

Veda's eyes roll back, and she collapses into Khadijah. In sync, she and Gabriel say the same thing.

"We have a problem."

Thirty-One

Time slips through Veda's fingers like sand in an hourglass. Fear burns her chest, but when she looks at Antaris, she steadies herself.

The inevitable is here.

"I'm fine," Veda insists when Hiram hesitates, torn between staying and going. "Let's keep moving forward with the plan." Her voice falters. "W-we have time."

Not much.

Hiram knows it. Veda sees it in his eyes, feels it in the way he kisses her goodbye. For the first time, he makes her the same promise he always makes Antaris. "I'll be right back."

Khadijah is still staring when the door closes behind Hiram. Veda's eyes slide to Antaris, then back. "Keep it normal."

Khadijah nods and walks away, returning with a glass of water. "You should sit down, you probably passed out from the fever. It's high."

"I didn't realize I was that warm." Veda sinks into the sofa. Mere seconds is all it takes for Antaris to sit next to her, anxiously wringing his hands. She drinks slowly; the water burns like acid. Still, she pulls him close and holds him tight. Whatever happens, she knows this is going to be hard on him.

Khadijah checks her temperature again. "You're still too warm."

"I just need to rest."

And that's when they all hear it.

Glass splitting.

A crack bisects the protective cloak of magic around her cottage. A single point of impact that shouldn't exist. It spiderwebs out in all directions, the pitch equivalent to nails on a chalkboard, making them grit their teeth and cover their ears.

Too late, Veda realizes what's happening. She pulls Antaris and Khadijah away as the cloak implodes. Fractured magic rains down like shrapnel, smashing through the glass ceiling of the solarium.

"We can't stay here!"

An explosion rocks the foundation of the cottage. Instead of falling, Veda instinctively grabs the startled Antaris and drops to the floor, shielding him from debris. The floor shakes in the aftermath, sending vibrations through the room. Khadijah scrambles toward the refrigerator for support, while Veda hurriedly scoots her and Antaris to the couch. Her ears are ringing.

A cheery, girlish giggle cuts through the space. "Oh my, look what I've done," the voice lilts, saccharine and sweet. "Knock, knock. Is anyone home?"

Freezing, Veda locks eyes with Khadijah. She would recognize Ariadne's accent anywhere.

"It was *so hard* to get here," Ariadne says, rot curling beneath the honey. "Then, lucky me, a few weeks ago, when I was looking for this place, I got lost, took a few wrong turns, and oh my Cosmos, I happened to see a familiar bike pull onto the street from outta nowhere. It was kismet. I just knew this *had* to be the place."

Veda locks eyes with Khadijah again and points to the solarium. It's a terrible idea, but they're out of options and there's no time.

"I know you're here, Veda," Ariadne coos, exposing more of that rot. "Don't be shy, I only want to *talk*."

The last word crashes through the house with a spell. The walls quake from the force. Veda clutches Antaris to her chest. Adrenaline racing, she cradles his head tightly as the floor trembles so violently, she feels the tremors deep in her bones.

Khadijah holds up three fingers.

Lights flicker as approaching footsteps echo on the floor.

She drops one.

Veda blinks through the pain, vision swimming.

Two more fingers drop.

Khadijah rises from her hiding spot, cold eyes glowing silver. She snaps her fingers, and there's a crash.

"Nice of you to throw me into a wall," Ariadne greets coolly.

"It's the least I could do."

A click of a tongue. Ariadne's spell barely misses Khadijah, whose defense holds strong. With no time to look, Veda grabs Antaris's hand and runs, catching glimpses of the two women locked in battle. A spell whizzes past Veda's head as they dart through the broken window, leaping out onto shattered glass.

Into the forest, they run until the cottage fades from view. The sounds of war are swallowed by trees. A wave of exhaustion crashes over Veda, forcing her to stumble, then push through. Antaris looks stricken with worry. She wipes sweat from her brow, turns her head, and coughs. Her body tenses when she sees specks of blood in her palm, but she quickly wipes it on her jeans and keeps going.

"It's fine," she reassures Antaris. It's the first lie she's told him.

She pushes on, deeper into the forest, searching for sanctuary. She knows every hiding place, the closest being hollowed-out trees, all dead from rot. Veda finds one and tells Antaris to crawl into it. He's safely tucked away before another explosion cracks the air, its echo finding them in the trees. It came from her house. Antaris leans out, distracted and breathing harshly. Cupping his cheeks, Veda makes him look at her.

"Antaris." Somehow she keeps her voice calm, even. "I need you to hide here. Don't move. Don't come out. Not even if someone calls your name."

He shakes his head, and the sob that escapes him is too big for his small body.

"It's okay, it's going to be okay." Veda takes his hands. "I need to keep you safe."

Tears keep falling.

"Mom."

The word knocks the breath out of her.

She pulls him into a hug. "You're the soul of the scorpion, remember?"

Antaris nods, face pressed to her neck. Veda pulls back, meeting his tear-filled eyes as he keeps sobbing.

"Where are your dad's notes?"

He pulls a few out of his pocket. She tucks one into hers with the vials of the Liquid Curse while putting the other two into his hands. "Close your eyes and be very quiet. Think about your dad, and he will find you."

Antaris nods numbly.

Veda presses her lips to his forehead in a moment of comfort for them both and closes her eyes. She doesn't know if she'll ever see him again. There's no easy way to say goodbye, and she doesn't want to, but she forces herself to pull back.

Antaris obediently sinks into the tree trunk, and only then does she run.

Veda heads away from him, toward the school. Adrenaline stops being enough to shield her from the ache in her ribs, the blood in her cough, the dizziness and nausea that come in increasing waves. Her run devolves into a staggered walk.

What once was loud is now eerily quiet.

A twig snaps. Her blood runs cold.

Veda whirls around to see Ariadne stomping through the forest, heading in the direction where Antaris is hiding. For Veda, the decision is easy. She starts running, sending a flare into the sky. Bursting over the trees, the flare alerts Ariadne to her presence. Veda runs harder than she ever has in her life, but it's not enough. Her lungs burn for air, and her body slows despite her brain screaming for it to keep moving. She slumps against a tree, panting, knowing it's over. There's nowhere left to run.

"Well, well, well." Ariadne's voice drips with delight from behind her. "It's a pleasure to see you again. Had I known *you* were the answer, I would've taken you that night in the apartment."

Veda turns to face her. "Where's Khadijah?"

"Alive." Her sickly smile twists. "Barely. I was running low, and she gave me *exactly* what I needed."

Veda's stomach turns.

"Oh my." Ariadne covers her mouth, eyes on Veda's neck. "Thank the Cosmos I got you alone just in time; I can finally get back what I deserve."

Veda dodges a blue orb that embeds itself in the tree behind her. Cornered, she charges toward Ariadne, barely avoiding a bolt of magic that glows like the sun. Her fist connects. The force sends Ariadne stumbling back, but she gets back up with a smile, as though the pain is a pleasure.

"Nice." She spits out red, running her tongue over the blood smearing her mouth. "My turn."

Like fighting an unstoppable force, the more Veda dodges, the faster Ariadnes comes at her. Curses fly. Veda ducks behind trees and stone, breathing harshly before countering the best she can with what repercussions she can afford. Chills. Cuts form on her skin. A splitting headache. Her lungs tighten when she diverts a glowing red spell, forcing it into a nearby tree. The bark blackens, cracking and falling in a harsh crash, before it ignites. Flames frame the leaves as smoke billows around them.

Veda uses the distraction to levitate the burning tree, hurling it in Ariadne's direction. The impact sends Ariadne flying backward, slamming her into the base of another tree.

Veda coughs up blood, and her vision blurs. She doesn't know what hurts more, the waking Sanguis curse or each consequence she pays for the magic she uses. The strain from her effort reaches the marrow of her bones. Sweat drenches her forehead, and blood streams steadily from her nose. Holding her ground, Veda pours her remaining strength into casting spell after spell to keep Ariadne at bay.

Still, it's no use.

A gray orb hits her square in the chest, robbing her of breath. She can't move. Can't see. Breathing in the smoke, there's no air left for her to exhale.

Ariadne forces Veda to her knees, stepping closer with a chilling smile. "I've been waiting for this."

White-hot pain explodes through Veda's body. Black veins paint her skin, threaded with red. Ariadne's essence flows through her bloodstream.

"Visus." At first, Ariadne's spell doesn't hurt. Then it burns. Veda's eyes throb. The forest thickens with youth, thins with age, burns with death. Past. Present. Future. Then it fades into Ariadne's delighted eyes. "There it is. *Potential.* What lives in you belongs to *me.*"

Veda feels like she's been split open. Cracked into two halves of what once was whole.

Everything stops.

"Wait, no. No. *No!* Not now," Ariadne screams.

What's been in hibernation is now fully awake.

Still trapped behind the block, Sanguis roars to life in her cells, tearing through muscles and sinew. Veda's head swims. Blood thunders in her ears. She grips her chest, struggling to breathe, every muscle locking tight as she curls into a fetal position.

Ariadne drops to her knees beside her, hands moving like she's trying to capture it. But she can't.

"It's . . . coming for you," Veda gets out.

Ariadne's panic turns into fury as she grabs Veda by the neck, squeezing until her airway closes. Veda struggles, her body writhing, but her hand finds exactly what she's looking for. One vial slips from her grasp. The other she clutches tightly, even as the edges of her vision darken.

"When I'm done here, I'm going to find that sweet little boy of Grace's and—"

Veda surges up and headbutts her.

Ariadne stumbles back, momentarily stunned. What follows feels like being electrocuted repeatedly. Veda hears screaming and realizes too late that it's her own.

Ariadne releases her. Veda drops to the ground, coughing so violently, she vomits. There's no mistaking the blood. Or the cracked vial next to it. The potion spills, clear and bright, beading like mercury instead of sinking into the soil. A sudden kick to her ribs sends her sprawling on her back. Then a hand grips her hair, yanking her upright as Ariadne begins to chant. With her last burst of strength, Veda slams her hand down onto the broken vial and reaches up, slapping Ariadne across the face, cutting her words off.

They both scream from the pain.

Ariadne recoils, looking furious, ready to end it all.

But she doesn't. She *can't*.

She shakes her hands but nothing happens. No magic.

"What did you do to me?" she shrieks.

"I killed us both," Veda rasps. "Liquid Curse."

Ariadne pales, shock stealing her breath. Then the anger comes roaring back as she punches Veda in the face. Welcoming the blow, Veda laughs, broken and breathless.

Ariadne staggers away, clawing at her arms as if she can scrape the curse off. She won't get far. Rolling onto her stomach, Veda tries to crawl, gasping for breath and finally feeling what she's been ignoring: agony. Bone deep, the torment is ripping at the seams of her soul. She coughs, and red tar escapes her mouth, thick, putrid, and alive. It lands on the ground with a wet plop, then slithers away into the underbrush.

Veda's finally free of Ariadne's blood . . . if only for a few minutes.

She tears off her ring, flips it open, and takes the crushed foxgloves. It'll be quicker this way. She forces herself to roll onto her back and stare at the sky.

Sight Unseen

Only the Cosmos bear witness to her screams and sobs. The trees stand silent, listening long after her cries dissolve into choked, gasping breaths as she surrenders to her fate. Blood seeps into the earth, spreading until she no longer feels pain. Only peace remains when the smoke and fire close in.

The last thing she remembers is squeezing the note in her pocket, Hiram's name on her lips.

Thirty-Two

Hiram's house is crawling with investigators and enforcers, most of whom are lying on the ground, dazed. He spots Francisco first, who taps Gabriel, and they break away from the group of enforcers, approaching him with urgency.

"We quieted the talisman by putting it to sleep," Gabriel says. "But, as you can see, this took effort."

Hiram stops dead at the realization.

"It's blood-tied to me," he says slowly. "You can't do anything with my talisman without me."

"But you didn't register it as a blood-tied—"

"Of course I didn't," Hiram interrupts, scoffing. "This was a decoy."

He's already fishing his phone from his pocket, dialing Veda first. No answer. As Francisco begins giving orders, telling everyone to pack up and leave those on the ground for the healers and medics, Hiram tries Khadijah. No answer.

Worry sets in.

"No one is picking up." Hiram opens his car door. "Veda's sick from her block unraveling, but Khadijah wouldn't ignore my call—not with Antaris there, too. We need as many people as possible over there *right now*."

Gabriel rushes over to Francisco, and Hiram can tell the moment he delivers the news. Shouts ring out as a mad scramble for their vehicles begins.

"We'll follow you," Francisco says, climbing into the passenger seat of the car parked next to him. Gabriel takes the driver's seat, starting the car with his Imprint. Hiram wastes no time. He starts his own car and pulls away quickly, dialing Peter as he speeds toward Veda's house.

"Where are you?" Peter sounds frantic.

"I'm on my way back to Veda's. The alarm at my house was a diversion. Where are you?"

"Khadijah called me. It sounded like a war zone over there. I'm ten minutes away."

"I'm bringing everyone with me," Hiram says, forcing down the rising dread. He presses harder on the accelerator, refusing to let the fear take hold.

❧

The sense of wrongness is as jarring as the felled trees scattered like matchsticks across the road—as obvious as the path that's meant to be invisible.

Hiram doesn't wait for permission. His ring glows white when he whispers a spell, moving the trunks out of the way. He turns onto Veda's path, a knot of nerves twisting his stomach tighter with every car that follows, all heading down a trail they were never meant to see.

There's no time to brace for the sight of Veda's cottage.

Peter is already there, trying to claw through the rubble that used to be the front porch. The roof is partially gone, bricks and debris scattered in all directions. Smoke coils from the scorched trees, and the earth is marked with blast damage. Veda's bike is untouched, but Khadijah's car is destroyed.

Hiram steps out, his legs nearly buckling beneath him. Crippling dread tells him that no one could've survived this. Before he can help Peter clear the debris, Gabriel intercepts with a grim expression. "Let us go first."

So he doesn't have to see what's left, Hiram finishes in his head.

"Do it."

It takes three investigators to clear the doorway. One of them tries to block access after Gabriel and Francisco enter. In an uncharacteristic outburst, Peter snaps, "Move out of my way or I'll make you."

"You and what amulet?" the investigator sneers.

"His."

Before Hiram can step in to back up Peter's threat, Francisco bursts out of the building, panic written all over his face. "Call a healer—*now!*"

While orders fly, Hiram and Peter rush past the threshold. Magic burns each of Hiram's senses, watering his eyes and choking his lungs. It's hard to wade through the potent waves, but he forces himself.

Gabriel is on his knees, performing chest compressions in a desperate effort to keep Khadijah alive. Her leg lies twisted at an unnatural angle, her arms and hands marred by cuts and bruises. Once white, her hair is matted with blood and ash. Peter moves Gabriel out the way and takes over.

Hiram pushes past them, searching the wreckage for any sign of Veda and Antaris, calling their names, panic mounting with each unanswered shout. Then Francisco calls for Hiram, and he runs over to them again.

Khadijah is conscious, trying to catch her breath. "They . . . they ran," she rasps. "I held Ariadne back . . . as long as I . . ." Her words dissolve in a coughing fit. "My Sight . . . she—she took it."

The horror that rises in Hiram is snapped by the sight of a red flare exploding in the sky.

"Veda," he breathes. It *must* be her. Then it hits him—Antaris's notes. Thank the Cosmos he thought to enchant them. Without hesitation, he points toward the rear of the house, speaking the incantation to trigger the tracking spell. *"Invenire aliquem."*

His ring glows green, confirming the direction. Francisco and Gabriel follow him out the broken pane of the solarium and into the forest. Each wrong turn makes the amulet in his ring glow red.

Sight Unseen

Terror claws up his spine, driving him to run faster, shouting for Antaris and Veda. He's met with silence. The green glow is his only comfort, his only guide, until he sees a clearing littered with dead trees. Gabriel and Francisco shout for Veda. Still no answer.

"Antaris!"

A rustling sound comes from one of the fallen trees. Hiram sprints forward as his son crawls out into view.

"Dad!" Antaris sobs, throwing himself into Hiram's arms. Shaking and terrified, his son refuses to let go. It's only when Hiram sees his trembling hand rise, pointing toward the smoke, that he understands what Veda did. *She hid him.* She's still out there. Something else draws his attention—the green light of his ring flaring anew.

He stoops in front of Antaris, wiping his tears. "Did Veda take a note?"

His son nods frantically.

Hiram turns to the others. Gabriel is already calling for backup.

"Francisco, I need you to take Antaris out of here."

"Of course."

But Antaris clings to Hiram, refusing to let go. The smoke in the distance is thickening when he kneels again. "I need to find—"

"Mom. Find Mom."

Smoke blankets the sky and rises from the ground, thickening the deeper they go. Somehow, it feels familiar to Hiram, though he's never been here before. The scent of magic grows stronger with each step. His amulet is still glowing, guiding their way. He doesn't see the source through the wall of smoke until it's right in front of them: a blazing ring of fire.

Gabriel extinguishes it with a charm. Hiram steps over the smoldering brush and nearly trips over something solid.

A body.

He recognizes the shoes.

Veda.

Blood. There's *so* much blood.

The curse is leaving her body, tearing her apart from the inside. Black veins have already spread across her exposed arms and legs, slowly creeping across her face like a shadow. Hiram freezes. It's only the burn of Gabriel's location spell that jars him out of his shock.

Antaris's note is clutched in her hand. Hiram's ring lies beside her, pillbox empty.

He drops to his knees, hesitating before touching her hand, her arms, her face. He doesn't know where the blood is coming from, why there's so much of it, or how to stop it. Something dark rises in him, but he forces it down. Her fingers tighten around the note, and her eyes flutter open.

"She's breathing," Gabriel says.

Not for long, Hiram amends silently, but the thought can't dim his relief.

Veda is a void. She smells of nothing. No magic. No energy.

"Don't move," he murmurs to her as he searches his pocket for the vial of antidote, tipping it into her partially opened mouth. She swallows, and he's relieved until he realizes they need time for it to work into her system.

It may be too late.

"Ant . . ." she croaks.

"We got him."

When Veda relaxes fully, her other hand opens. Blood pools in her palm and spills onto the ground. "The curse . . . I—I did it."

Gabriel hears and glances around, peering through the smoke. "Ariadne couldn't have made it far." He doesn't wait before running off to find her.

"Tell him . . . I'm sorry." Veda's eyes close, her breathing growing more labored. "I knew . . . it would end like this."

Sight Unseen

Hiram ignores her words, he *has* to, or he'll lose the last shreds of composure holding him together.

"I don't . . . regret you."

The final shred is eviscerated. His resolve crumbles, and so does he. Hiram pulls her into his arms, closes his eyes, and forces himself to ignore the wetness on her back, the black threads thickening and consuming her skin, the rattle in her chest.

Determination strikes him like a bolt. He picks her up and steadies himself, knowing exactly where he needs to go. Nénuphar. The cave isn't a cure, but it might keep her alive long enough for the antidote to start working. Hiram wanders the forest, directionless, thoughts of giving up flickering at the edges of his mind—

Finally, *finally*, he sees a western hemlock. He's close. By the time Hiram reaches the mouth of the cave, Veda is limp and motionless in his arms, her breath faint.

He doesn't stop to remove his clothes, walking straight in and carefully lowering her into the healing waters. Cradling her head above the surface, he begs for time. Pleads to the Cosmos for it.

But nothing happens.

Holding his breath, he waits, and waits, and waits, hope slowly dimming until he sees something dark slink away beneath the surface. Then another. Smoke escapes her lips. Dark liquid spills from her veins, retreating from her skin. Her face begins to clear. The shadows writhe and scream as they're dragged from her, consumed by light.

Hiram holds her until the last of the Sanguis Curse flees her body.

Nénuphar closes her wounds. Still water slips into her mouth.

Veda breathes, albeit shallowly, but it's a sign that the antidote is working.

Still, she does not wake.

Thirty-Three

Reality jolts Veda with a surge of adrenaline that should have forced her into an upright position, but she can't feel her arms or legs, let alone move. She can only blink and breathe.

Needing to calm the rising panic, Veda focuses on the simple act of wiggling her toes. The relief that accompanies the sensation is palpable. Opening her mouth, she tries to call for someone, anyone, but nothing comes out.

Her memories are a blur. The forest and blood and fire and water, and opal. Nothing makes sense. A knock on the door startles her before a doctor enters, visibly shocked to find her awake. He raises her bed and checks her reflexes. The doctor mentions that Veda will always carry the scars; some were too deep for even the cave waters to heal.

"Everything looks good. Your voice should come back. It's likely strained from the tubes. Rest will help you regain some strength."

Once he departs, Veda takes in her surroundings properly for the first time. Her room is a forest of potted plants—pothos and monsteras, bamboo and palms, orchids and peace lilies, roses and English ivy. Plants cover every surface, line the windows, and stand in the corner, elaborate and beautiful. It reminds her of the greenhouse. Her safe place. But her gaze is drawn to something smaller, near the head of her bed. Insignificant to some, but it means the world to her.

A lantern.

Clinton is led in by Peter, and he sits in the chair beside her, his walking stick in hand. Peter hovers close by.

Peter looks frayed, like he hasn't slept. Still, he smiles. "I told you . . ."

He never finishes the statement, but she understands. He told her she would survive the impossible—and, more importantly, that she would live.

"Fuck . . . off," Veda croaks, her throat burning.

Peter laughs. "Of course that's your first sentence after three weeks."

Three weeks? Time has moved on without her. As petty as it seems, it's all she can think about, and she obsesses over until it leaves her weary. She has to let it go; she's not strong enough to hold on. Blinking at the ceiling, she takes several deep breaths to release it, swallowing the growing lump in her throat.

Her second attempt at speaking is one word: "Khadijah?"

Peter's expression turns solemn, and Clinton's does the same. "What matters is that she's alive," he says gently. "But she . . . she no longer has Sight."

The news knocks the breath from Veda's lungs. She tries to sit up, but Peter stops her.

"She's okay—well, she's acclimating. She's in a therapy session right now. We'll come by when you're discharged."

"After your magical testing," Clinton adds before she can ask. "There's been considerable attention on Ariadne—"

"She . . ."

"Survived? Yes. Do you want to know? Hiram didn't want any updates on anything except you."

Her heart races at the mention of his name, but she needs to know. "Tell me."

"Gabriel found her not far from where he and Hiram found you."

Flashes of him flutter through her mind, too quickly to grasp. The way he broke down. The way he held her. Carried her. And something else . . .

A dream, maybe, where she floated, but . . .

"Ariadne is awaiting trial," Peter says. "She's in a high-security prison hospital in Montana, denied bail. She'll never be free ever again. The public knows everything—about the Great Vanishing, what she did to the Council, Everett, Grace, Khadijah, Marlene . . . and you."

"Is Ariadne—"

"Cursed? Yes," Peter confirms. "They're maintaining a block to keep her alive and will let nature take its course when it fades."

Death, it seems, would have been too merciful. Veda settles back on her pillow, drained but not quite ready to sleep. A knock at the door draws her attention, and when she sees who it is, whatever weariness she feels dissipates.

Hiram stands in the doorway, holding a thermos. Peter and Clinton offer quick excuses before slipping out. Clinton squeezes Hiram's shoulder on the way, and Peter exchanges a look of quiet understanding with him. They're alone and Veda can't look away from him. Hiram is impeccably dressed but visibly exhausted. Frayed at the seams, his face shadowed with stubble, quiet even as he settles into Clinton's empty chair. Silence rolls on, but all is not still, least of all when Hiram picks up her scarred hand, the one that bears faint scars from the shattered vial. His palm engulfs hers.

"Antaris?" she asks.

"With August and Gabriel. He's anxious to see you, but—"

"I don't . . ."

"Want him to see you like this? I know." Hiram dips his head, not to kiss her knuckles but to rest her hand gently against his cheek. As he leans into her touch, weariness seems to pour off him like fog descending in a darkened hall. It spreads through his demeanor, settling his slouched shoulders and half-lowered lids over crystal-blue eyes. Hiram looks like he might fall asleep like this. It won't hurt to let him.

"They want you to rest before your magical test," he says quietly, just for her.

"Then we rest." She raises the cover in invitation. Hiram is careful when he joins her. The breaths that follow are measured by the beat of their hearts. Foreheads touching, eyes drinking each other in, Veda moves first, brushing her lips against his, then seeking more. He gently cups her nape and deepens the kiss, the scratch of his hair against her skin sending sparks down her spine. Hiram tastes like survival, revival, and something purely him that carefully unravels the tightness in her chest. After she kisses the piece of his hand she can reach, they touch only for the desire of contact.

Movement catches her eye.

"Did *you* bring my lantern here?"

Hiram offers a weary smile. "Antaris didn't want you to have bad dreams."

✽

The last visitor Veda expects is the one sitting next to her when she wakes.

Simran's saree is burnt orange and trimmed with ornate gold designs. Beautiful and sharp, like her. Deep in concentration, she crochets something sock shaped. It's not perfect, Veda can see the flaws, but her expression offers no place for commentary.

"I thought you would sleep until I finished." Simran's eyes cut to Veda. "Unfortunately, I am not quite as dexterous as I once was."

"That's not for me, is it?"

Veda earns a look cold enough to freeze magic. "And if it is?"

"I'll be surprised by the latest development in . . . whatever this is. Why are you here?"

"Three weeks ago, my son told me to be his mother for once in my life in this very room, and I'm doing just that." Simran sets her project on her lap, resting the hook and sock atop the ball of yarn. "I have never cared for you, Miss Thorne. I believe the feeling is mutual."

"It is."

"But it seems we are, for better or worse, entwined." She rises, moves to the windows, and opens them one by one, letting light flood the room. When she returns to Veda's bedside, she reaches out and gently touches the end of her braid. "I have always believed that hair is an extension of the self. There is a certain intimacy in caring for it."

Veda says nothing.

"When I taught my son to braid, I will admit, I did so because I had no daughters, and I did not care for anyone touching my hair. Braiding is an act of love, care, and creativity. Hiram has not braided my hair since he was a boy begging for my attention, but I still recognize his work, even in a simple French braid."

Suddenly self-aware, Veda pulls back from her touch. "He must've braided it again while I was unconscious."

Simran tilts her head. "Again? How many times?"

Veda is too tired to lie. "This makes three."

Observation turns into an assessment. "I have underestimated you. I believed your sole role was to encourage Antaris to speak. You fought like he was *yours*. I did not realize that would extend to my son. Let it be known, I do not approve of you—"

"Well, it's a good thing your opinion doesn't matter." Veda stops herself. "Not that I'm in any position to be seeking approval."

A frustrated breath escapes. "You did not allow me to finish. As I was saying, I do not approve, *however*, I am willing to try. The socks were meant as a gift."

"Perhaps you should focus that effort on Hiram and Antaris. Not me."

"I intend to. I was told to be his mother, for once in my life, and this is why I am here. I need to step outside of my own expectations of him and begin to see what he values. And that is you. He has coordinated everything, paid for the best care for you, and insisted not only that you have the room with the best light but also that no one brings cut flowers because potted plants—"

"Are more sustainable, can improve the air quality, and reduce stress." Realization of how deeply he not only listens to her but knows her disarms Veda. "I—"

"Hiram is a creature of habit. He faces a decision and makes his choice. He waits, yes, but he rarely changes his mind."

The patient man.

"I am proof of this," Simran says grimly.

"And where does that leave you?" Veda asks quietly.

"Fighting to change his mind about me."

Veda sinks into her pillow. "Okay, then you need to protect him and Antaris. I doubt what's happened hasn't reached the rest of your family."

"It seems Phillip, even in death, has stirred things up—conversations about the forgotten branches of the family tree. They have distanced themselves from him publicly, made statements. Some of the castoffs have begun to speak. Children he fathered out of wedlock with Seer women, discarded when they did not manifest Sight. I imagine there will be quiet deals made, money paid, and silence secured. I will continue to ensure Antaris and his . . . *Sight* do not become part of that."

"Antaris is a Seer. He's your grandson. His value isn't in his abilities—it's in who he is as a person. The same goes for Khadijah. She saved your husband's life and sacrificed so much so Antaris and I could get to safety. Clinton, too. Any Seer."

Simran is quiet for a moment. "I wish to change," she says finally. "I do not know where to start. Your friend Khadijah will not speak to me."

"Hold yourself accountable. Hold your friends accountable for their actions and words. Educate yourself. Books and articles can start helping you see the world through a lens other than your own. We live in a world where Mages make the rules and Seers are expected to follow them. It's not Khadijah's or any Seer's responsibility to convince you or change your mind and see them as worthy of existing alongside you. There's more I could say, more I can tell you to do, but ultimately, it's on you. You aren't going to change overnight. I don't expect that. What I do expect is for you to mess up along the way, but I hope you don't quit."

Simran walks back to her chair and picks up her knitting before sitting once more. "I do not intend to quit. I do not know how to do such a thing."

"Good."

It isn't a guarantee, but it is a start. A new beginning.

It goes unspoken, but it's understood, after it's determined that Veda's magic is returning normally, she goes back to Hiram's house. He walks with her, each step slow, but steady. The moment Antaris sees her, he freezes, apprehension clouding his face, anxiety stopping him in his tracks.

"Hi," Veda says gently.

The single word snaps him out of stasis. Hiram quietly encourages him, and Veda doesn't wait. She opens her arms wide and hugs him tight. Her body aches, muscles sore and protesting, but she ignores it, her focus entirely on him.

"It's okay," she says softly as he tentatively pulls back. "I know you were scared, but you did so well. You were so brave." She wraps her arms around him again, this time even tighter and without a care about the pain.

He needs this. *She* needs this.

His tears come fast, soaking into her shoulder as she squats to his level. Her knees throb, but she doesn't move. Antaris sobs harder, burying his face in her neck, and Veda whispers quiet reassurances to let him know she's here. Real. *Alive*. Veda takes a moment to remind herself, too. She doesn't let go until his sobs fade into soft sniffles, and he leans against her, damp-cheeked and exhausted.

Later, Peter comes by with Khadijah, as promised. Veda joins her on the back porch while Antaris sleeps, the two of them staring out across the water. It's strange to see her again. There's much to say, given everything they lost, yet neither speaks for a long time.

Veda breaks the silence. "How are you?"

Khadijah turns slightly. "Me? What about *you*? Tell the truth."

"Recovering from foxglove poisoning isn't for the weak, but I'm here. Grateful for it, even." Veda rolls her shoulders, wincing slightly. "You? Peter told me what happened."

"I'm Unseen," she says bluntly. "I'm coping. One day at a time. Peter's been helping me adjust, but I'm more shocked by everyone's reaction. The Unseen are usually left to drift, but people keep bringing food to our house, keep checking in on us . . . I know it's because—"

"They care." Veda fidgets. "I'll never be able to thank you for what you did."

"Then don't," Khadijah tells her earnestly. "I would have made the same decision again knowing the outcome."

Veda rests her head on her friend's shoulder and wraps an arm around her, grateful not only for her sacrifice but also her friendship. Khadijah rests her head on hers, and they settle into a comfortable silence, watching as sunlight dances across the surface of the lake—still, yet endlessly moving.

Walking through the wreckage of her cottage, Veda assesses the debris. She's not alone.

Hiram holds her hand as they move from room to room. She tells him stories about what the place was like when she first moved in, her voice soft as her fingers trail over battered furniture. She looks at the scorched remnants and shares memories, though she doesn't need to take any with her. Not even her ruined talisman. Instead, she thanks the scorched walls for what they once held. Hiram senses her sadness in yet another thing she has lost, but also her contentment. In the charred remains of the solarium, she stands still.

"This is no longer mine, but that's okay. Let's go," she says.

"How far?"

They return to their island sanctuary. It's as they left it, but they are not.

Hiram is the first to fall asleep. Antaris and August doze in the hammock, swaying gently, while Peter and Khadijah nod off in the breeze on the balcony overlooking the Sound. Veda stays awake and watches the sunset in grateful reverence. It's dusk when she's interrupted.

"You're supposed to be resting," Hiram murmurs, his sleepy voice loud in the quiet surrounding them.

"I will."

He tugs her back to their room before Veda eases into the bed with him. A careful arm wraps around her as she turns on her side to face him. Hiram's gaze holds something she can't articulate, while her own feelings and sentiments sit on the tip of her tongue, ready to be expressed. Yet she doesn't voice them.

"Did you sleep at all?" Hiram asks.

"Not yet."

"I think today was the first time I've been able to sleep since . . ." He trails off, the storm in his eyes encroaching.

Startled by the painful undercurrent of his answer, and lost in the swell between them, Veda reaches out as much as her body allows. She's still sore, but she twines their hands together, sweeping a thumb over his knuckles repeatedly. The rest of her energy is devoted to brushing her lips against Hiram's, letting them linger. There's nothing more vital in the world than this single kiss. This fragile moment is firm but tender. Hiram doesn't pull away until his heavy eyes flutter shut and his body begins to relax beside hers.

"What keeps you awake?" he asks.

Veda shifts closer, too tired to lie. "Thoughts. Memories. *You*."

Hiram tenses, his eyes as blue as the sky stretched over a treacherous sea. Tumultuous and untamable. Indifferent to mankind's whims. Veda does nothing except wait him out, but that doesn't stop her from trying to navigate the storm.

"Have you processed everything yet? Talked to anyone about finding me? I—"

"I have." Hiram touches her face, looking at her as if she can't be real. "But I don't want to talk about that tonight."

Instead, he tangles their legs together and draws her closer. Veda's fingers slowly, tentatively caress his face. She's on the cliffside of affection, nervous that she's going to fall.

But maybe you should, an errant thought whispers.

"I don't have plans," she murmurs. "I didn't expect to survive, but now . . . I-I'm overwhelmed with options."

"Are you leaving?"

Veda considers him for a long moment. "Not unless you are."

Hiram is fully awake, nerves ghosting his features. "I'm not."

"I want to figure out what I want, what works for us, and I'd like to do it together."

"Why?"

"Because I have time, and I no longer want to waste it."

The corners of his lips twitch. "And why else?"

Her glare sharpens. "You're going to make me say it, aren't you?"

"Of course I am," he says smugly. "I think I've earned it."

She rolls her eyes. "You're aggravating."

"I know," Hiram says.

"And an arrogant shit."

"I know."

It's madness. It's irrational. It's terrifying. But it's time.

Veda settles her head on his chest, his hand running the length of her back. She closes her eyes. There is grace in surrender. Peace in the free fall.

No more excuses, no more running. It's time to stop denying herself happiness.

Veda relents. "You're lucky I love you."

"I know." His smile softens, words earnest, only for her. "I love you, too."

Epilogue

Winter has never been Veda's favorite time of year, but now that it's here, she realizes its purpose isn't only frigid dormancy. It's a season for growth and evolution. Veda has picked through the rubble of her old life and made a new one that's all her own.

Under the cold winter sun, in her freshly constructed greenhouse, she stands in a new safe space as Hiram wraps his arms around her. There aren't any plants yet, and the fruit trees won't arrive until next month, but soon enough this place will be teeming with life. Veda winces through each movement thanks to soreness—from an exhaustive afternoon not of pleasure, but of hard work. Thickening by the hour, a blanket of white stretches beyond the windows. In the warmth of the greenhouse, Hiram has a picnic set up. It's a Vietnamese spread, and more than enough for them. They eat until they're stuffed while Hiram listens to Veda's plans for the space with a small smile on his face. The food is incredible, but watching the snowfall on the other side of the glass is better.

"I have something for you," Hiram says after a while. He reaches into the basket, pulling out a slender box.

Veda's brow rises as she accepts the gift. "Christmas isn't for another two weeks."

"It's something I've been working on since July. Took longer than I planned, but . . . it's yours."

She doesn't understand until she opens the box and sees it. She's utterly shocked. Mouth parted, her hands tremble as she lifts it from its velvet cradle. The chain has been replaced, and though the twisted stones still bear the same cracks, there's something different about it. It hums in her palm when she touches it. Beneath the sapphire, a soft white light glows, reminding her of a moonlit night. There is no doubt in her mind what it is. And whom it belongs to.

"My amulet . . ." Her voice breaks as she looks at him, tears in her eyes. Hiram helps her clasp it around her neck, the feeling both new and familiar. Changed, but undeniably hers.

"Where did you—"

"I brought it back myself."

"With your magic? That must have taken *months*."

"Yeah, a few drops of magic every day paid for with temporary but blinding headaches."

"You couldn't use your amulet."

"No." Hiram touches the gemstone. "You're worth it." He cups her face, pressing a kiss to her forehead, then her lips.

Reborn. For her. *Because* of her. Love was his driving point. His purpose.

"You're making Christmas gifts hard for me to top."

Hiram laughs, but his smile slowly sobers. "I'm happy you're here."

Veda's heart melts. "Me too."

The moment is broken by the buzz of Hiram's phone. It's Antaris, calling from Gabriel's place, where he's staying with August. At first, he doesn't say much, but August's enthusiastic chatter hypes him up enough to get him talking about learning to ice-skate. When the call ends, Hiram sets the phone down, a thoughtful look on his face.

"I didn't have to tell him that I'm coming back."

Veda leans in, pressing a kiss to his cheek. "Because he knows."

The celebration of Hiram's law firm opening takes place a few days later, surrounded by everyone who helped bring it to life.

Peter, who has been newly elected to the Oracle Council, is there with Khadijah, Clinton, and the rest of the new appointees, all of whom are now clients. Everly and Marlene are here, too. Francisco comes late, followed by Gabriel and August. John will be in town for the grand opening the week after New Year's. A surprising number of Seers turn up to show their support. When Hiram's parents arrive, late and unannounced, Veda watches Hiram quietly excuse himself from his conversation with Moab's oldest son and Francisco. He crosses the room to greet them. Simran hands him a gift bag while Antaris tentatively approaches Barrett with the cat he's introduced to every adult in the room.

Much to Veda and Hiram's surprise, his father scratches the growing cat behind his ears. His deep voice carries when he asks, "What's his name?"

"Mint," Antaris says bashfully, then flees to her side.

Veda hugs him close until he settles.

"Thanks, Mom."

And he's off to the next person. She can't help but smile.

Peter sits next to her. "Five minutes."

"What?"

"It'll be five minutes before Simran approaches you."

Veda pouts. "I rue the day I challenged her to change."

Peter laughs. "No, you don't."

"No, I don't."

They sit in companionable silence, watching the crowd until Peter speaks again. "I know you have your own greenhouse, but you're always welcome at Weston's. My storage is still yours."

She bumps him with her shoulder. "I know, and trust me, I'll take you up on that. How's the new person working out?" Veda left Weston in September to start at Khadijah's clinic, where she's been knocking the dust off her skills in preparation for restarting her internship in March.

"Well enough, I think. She's got big shoes to fill . . . Right on time. Incoming."

With that, he has the nerve to leave her alone to face Simran. For a fleeting moment, Veda considers locking herself inside Hiram's office to avoid the encounter, but for the past few months, things have been somewhat amiable.

"A pleasure to see you as always, Miss Thorne," Simran says with impeccable poise.

"Likewise, for the most part," Veda replies with the barest hint of a smile. "You can call me Veda."

Simran raises a brow. "Duly noted, Miss Thorne. I will see you three for our quarterly dinner tomorrow."

It's the first of its kind, and Hiram's idea. A trial run of reconciliation, so to speak.

"You will," Veda confirms.

"Thank you for helping us get to this point with him."

"I did nothing. It was all Hiram. He'll try as long as you do."

"I have been."

Veda knows. Simran's been donating to the Seer clinic. The donations are returned each time, just as Khadijah continues to decline Simran's invitations for tea. But in both respects, Simran remains persistent, continuing to unlearn her bias. Perhaps one day things will change, but she isn't waiting. She's doing what Veda once told Hiram: showing them who she is . . . or rather, who she wants to become. Watching Simran walk around, greeting everyone the same, is still strange to see, but it's another step toward progress.

After the party ends, they clean up, activate the talisman, and head home. It's near sunset when the urge to walk the forest strikes. The decision to search for Nénuphar today is unconscious, but Hiram drifts in the direction he remembers as Veda and Antaris follow. The sun slips lower while they search the forest. North to south. East to west. They don't find it.

Dusk marks the end of their search, when they finally accept that the healing waters won't appear this time. They gather around Antaris, each one hugging him gently as his shoulders dip.

"Nénuphar is only for those who *need* healing," Veda explains. "I don't think we need it anymore."

Still a little fractured individually, together they are whole.

Veda takes both their hands, and they all walk home in the soft dark, moonlight gently rising behind them. Home greets them with open arms, but there's something else.

A familiar, healing olive tree.

Veda turns to Hiram, who smiles. "Figured it was only fitting that it would be the first resident. Peter had a few of the staff deliver it while we were at the party."

She stares at the tree for so long that she doesn't realize Hiram and Antaris left and the former returns with hot chocolate—spiked for the two of them, sweet and simple for Antaris. They're armed with blankets when they step outside to savor the crisp night. Antaris will join them again shortly. The sky is clear, the moon is new, and the stars, unhindered, blaze across the sky, shining in full splendor. They settle on the dormant grass. Veda leans against Hiram as she catches him gazing skyward.

"I thought you didn't care much for the stars."

"I've been told I should look at them more often to gain perspective."

Veda smiles in the face of his smirk. "Now, who told you to do such a thing?"

"Someone extremely aggravating, and bossy, and—"

"Such romantic adjectives."

Hiram rolls his eyes but smiles.

"So . . ." Veda sips her drink. "How does it feel to have your own practice?"

"Surreal," he answers quietly. "But no more surreal than watching you and my mother today. You know why she keeps cornering you, right?"

"No."

"She's checking your hand—not for the pillbox ring, but for a new one."

Veda recoils. "Absolutely the *hell* not. We've been together for five minutes."

"Six months."

"You're making that up."

"It's a generous estimate." He laughs when she sulks, but soon sobers. "Is that a permanent no . . . or a no for now?"

"For now. I want peace with you and Antaris before we change anything. What do you think?"

"I agree," he says. "I love you, and I'm in no rush. I've waited about a decade, what's a few more years?"

"A *decade*?" Veda bursts out laughing. "The graduation party where you never even talked to me? You're insane."

"When you know, you know." He leans closer. "We took the long way around."

The back door swings open, and Antaris comes out carrying two lanterns. One his, one hers. Curious, Veda sheds her blanket and follows him to the water's edge.

Hiram joins them. "What is it?"

Antaris offers Veda her lantern, then concentrates on his finger until there is a tiny flame hovering over it. Veda's smile grows. She can't contain how proud she is of him doing magic without fear.

"Well done." Hiram kneels beside him.

Antaris grins, then tries to guide the flame toward the lantern.

"You want to light it?" Veda asks, confused.

"I've caught them all," Antaris whispers.

Nightmares, sadness, grief, and everything that left him struggling at night.

"Me too." Veda holds her own lantern, struck by a profound feeling of knowing it's time to let it go. "Let's do it."

Antaris's eyes brighten when he lights his lantern with Hiram's help, and Veda lights hers with both their support.

Three. Two. One.

They let go.

Beneath the crescent moon, the breeze carries their lanterns skyward until they are mere specks on their way to join the stars.

Acknowledgments

My patient family, who fled at the sight of my laptop. My supportive husband, who smiles and nods. All my friends who dragged me to each finish line—you know who you are. K, the yin to my yang. Casey, who counts all my *but*s and is quick with a spreadsheet. Krampus. Listeners of my unhinged tinfoil-hat ramblings. Thao, who has read eight hundred versions of this novel. Sunny's legendary sixteen-minute voice note defending a character. My editors, who whipped this book into shape. Anyone who has ever yelled at me to charge my phone, drink water, or sleep. Just know, you're all the real MVPs.

Do you love fiction with a supernatural twist?

Want the chance to hear news about your favourite authors (and the chance to win free books)?

Christine Feehan
J.R. Ward
Sherrilyn Kenyon
Charlaine Harris
Jayne Ann Krentz and Jayne Castle
P.C. Cast
Maria Lewis
Darynda Jones
Hayley Edwards
Kristen Callihan
Keri Arthur
Amanda Bouchet
Jacquelyn Frank
Larissa Ione

Then visit the *With Love* website and
sign up to our romance newsletter:
www.yourswithlove.co.uk

And follow us on Facebook for book giveaways,
exclusive romance news and more:
www.facebook.com/yourswithlovex

PIATKUS

RAISING READERS
Books Build Bright Futures

Dear Reader,

We'd love your attention for one more page to tell you about the crisis in children's reading, and what we can all do.

Studies have shown that reading for fun is the **single biggest predictor of a child's future life chances** – more than family circumstance, parents' educational background or income. It improves academic results, mental health, wealth, communication skills, ambition and happiness.[1]

The number of children reading for fun is in rapid decline. Young people have a lot of competition for their time. In 2024, 1 in 10 children and young people in the UK aged 5 to 18 did not own a single book at home.[2]

Hachette works extensively with schools, libraries and literacy charities, but here are some ways we can all raise more readers:

- Reading to children for just 10 minutes a day makes a difference
- Don't give up if children aren't regular readers – there will be books for them!
- Visit bookshops and libraries to get recommendations
- Encourage them to listen to audiobooks
- Support school libraries
- Give books as gifts

There's a lot more information about how to encourage children to read on our website: **www.RaisingReaders.co.uk**

Thank you for reading.

hachette UK

---

[1] OECD, '21st-Century Readers: Developing Literacy Skills in a Digital World', 2021, https://www.oecd.org/en/publications/21st-century-readers_a83d84cb-en.html

[2] National Literacy Trust, 'Book Ownership in 2024', November 2024, https://literacytrust.org.uk/research-services/research-reports/book-ownership-in-2024